Death, On Ice

Madcap Adventures

Rene Vecka

RV A&E LLC

To Mike—who got me hooked on D&D—without whom these books would not have been possible.

Mid Dreki Realm Map

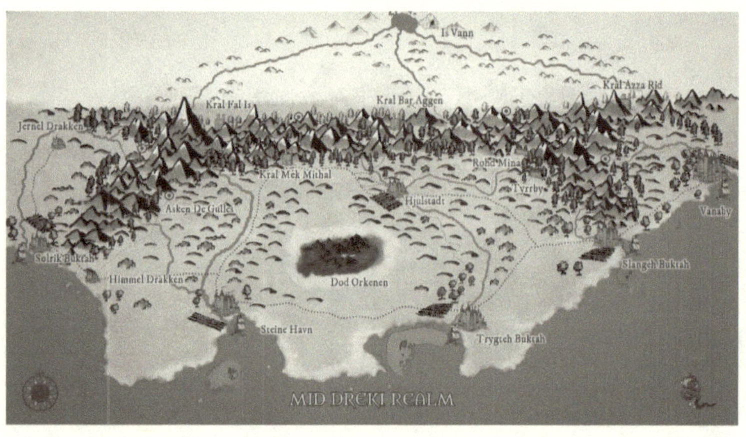

Contents

Chapter One

AN OLD FRIEND

RORY

My leather cap slipped off my head as I ducked another of Manic Mick's wild strikes. I straightened, my muscles tightened like a coiled spring, and I waited for a less obvious spot to counterattack. I'd already smacked Mick's sword arm a half-dozen times, and his right thigh twice.

Each move between us was a wordless dialogue, punctuated by the clunking of wood and the rhythm of our boots crunching on the earth.

Well, *my* rhythm. His movements sounded more like the slide and stomp of a troll with one short leg.

Mick stabbed, his body leaning precariously forward, too much weight on his front foot. He was getting better. But after exchanging a score of blows—his arms and legs weary—he'd regressed to his old form.

He and Serafina, the half-alvae healer—who watched us along with my wife, Ingefær—had been training in the martial arts for the last three moons, developing their melee skills to help Injustices Righted become a formidable foe on all fronts: magic, blade work, healing, and stealth.

Swish. Clack.

I deflected his thrust. "Too predictable, and you left yourself exposed. Again." I pirouetted past him and slapped the young man on his backside with the flat of my wood blade. I could have gashed Mick across the back of the neck, taken an arm, or pierced the thigh of his forward foot.

Patience, I said to myself. *He's still a novice.*

It had taken me years—and a vile spirit possessing me—to gain the skills I now took for granted.

Mick squeaked at the sting of wood on his rear and spun about with a backhanded slash. "Predict this!"

The young thief, now on the side of good, slashed right to left, knee high. His dull wooden practice sword whistled through the air.

Using my magicked feet abilities—*thanks, vile spirit*—I shuffled back in time. Mick's sword passed mere inches from my knee. That would have hurt.

"Hmph," I said. "Good one. You're learning."

Be balanced, be unpredictable. And, most of all, be patient. I struggled with the last one.

Serafina and Ingefær clapped.

I raised my hands. "That's enough for today."

Mick bent over at the waist, huffing. "Thank the gods. I've been needing to go for so long, I'm about to start a river down my pant leg."

"Don't be gross," Ingefær said, but her eyes twinkled.

Rivulets of sweat ran down the good thief's forehead, and he brushed them away with a sleeve. His tawny hair stuck out in all directions—like it had been struck by lightning and then used by crows for a nest.

Mick wiped at his brow again. He pointed a finger at me. "You cheated."

Nodding, I grinned. I had used my fleet feet, something no other opponent in the Realm had. Well, as far as I knew. "Aye. Don't want you to get overconfident. Against a good opponent, you wouldn't have been alive to deliver the blow." I raised my hands. "But it was a well-placed strike, and quick. You don't have to sever an artery in the neck or plunge steel into a gut. Having a foe lose a leg or a sword arm leads to victory as well."

Mick nodded.

Ingefær hefted her wooden blade and hoisted a shield—something she seldom used. "You ready for your turn, Serafina?"

The golden-haired, half-alvae pulled her mace from her belt loop. "Today is the day I get past the shield."

"Just remember," I said, "no headshots. The helmet isn't reinforced."

Training in a way that ensured we didn't kill each other required a few adjustments, like extra padding and bulky armor, wooden blades, and similar. Except for headshots, all blows from a mace rarely killed outright. And with Serafina being a healer, everything else could be rectified with one of her spells.

Mick laughed. "Ah, but the rest of Miss Ingefær looks like a plump plum ready for plucking."

Ingefær pointed a sword at him. "Tomorrow, you and I dance. You'll see this plump plum kick your rump."

Mick stuck out his tongue. Three days ago, my wife had used the shield to break his nose and bloody his lips.

The ladies checked themselves over, and I reiterated the lesson for Serafina. "Work on your footwork. Everything starts there. And you're telegraphing your blows, too. You don't have to swing backward. The weight of the mace will do the work for you. Disorient or disarm first, then deliver the killing blow."

From beyond the corral and barn, Hiram shouted at us as he ran. His arms swung like they swatted at miniature drekis—the flying, fire-breathing lizards. "Master Belkin! Master Belkin!"

We all turned and waited for the farm hand supervisor to reach us.

When he arrived, he blew air out in gusts. "There's a d-d-d'oglemann by the well."

Well, spit. That wasn't good news.

Ingefær and I exchanged glances.

"A d'oglemann!" Mick drew his dirk. "I've never seen one of those before."

"Put that away," my wife demanded.

I nodded. "Aye. That's a friend."

"You're frying my eggs," Mick said.

Vidarr Allefar or I'm a bugbear. I shook my head.

What did Vidarr need from us? Delicate spy work his organization could deny? Or was there someone in need of rescuing, but because of politics, his organization couldn't be overtly involved?

With his scale-covered body and long lizard-like snout, Vidarr stood out in any crowd. His manner of arrival—sudden and unannounced—portended bad news. *Yeah, bad news trailed Vidarr like the stench of troll dung clamped to a boot heel. But maybe, Injustices Righted could earn some dreki coins.*

"How can you be so sure it's a friend?" The lines around Serafina's emerald eyes scrunched. Her once deathly grayish-green skin had livened up to a radiant silver-green, a benefit of fresh farm air, daily workouts with weapons, and healing incantations.

"Because visitors come by the main road and up the path past the house." I pointed in the other direction and set off, waving for the others to follow. "If there's a d'oglemann by the well, it means that Vidarr Allefar has come to visit."

Ingefær explained. "He's arrived via a teleportation spell." She touched Hiram on the sleeve. "Was anyone else with him?"

"Oh, aye." Hiram blushed. "I guess there was. A man. Dark hair."

We walked past the newly constructed barn, the smell of hay and horses pleasing my nose. Past the corner of the structure, I spotted Vidarr and Ilmarien, both Havís, or High Ones, in the Tyrrby Order—the equivalent of the Realm's arbiter of truth and justice, hashing things out between city-states, the jarls, and other elites.

Vidarr's magical prowess specialized in the Aether, and Ilmarien's the air. Both were accomplished mages, much more so than Ingefær. But they'd been at it for far longer. Vidarr was doubly powerful because he wielded the Rod of the Dreki, a magical artifact that granted him endless stamina and quintupled the amount of power he could draw from the five magical planes.

We walked past the tilled but unplanted rows of potatoes and peas. *I love the smell of loam.* Hiram and the lads needed to get the planting done before the first freeze...now less than a moon away. The farm had belonged to my now-deceased parents, and Ingefær and I had rebuilt the home with a plan to use farming to supplement our genuine passion: Injustices Righted.

We operated our bounty hunting service to capture criminals, to find lost or stolen items, and to solve mysteries. Which, ever since the return of magic over a year ago, seemed to have multiplied like mutated bunnies, though our adventures were always the opposite of cute and cuddly.

The five of us arrived at the well to find Vidarr slurping water from a ladle he'd dipped into a bucket attached via rope to the well. Ilmarien yawned, his long black hair tied in a ponytail. If the teleport spell bothered him, he wasn't showing it.

Vidarr stood half a foot shorter than me. Though it was smaller, he had the elongated, dreki-shaped snout, which was covered in copper-hued scales. He was a wingless miniature of a dreki. And while he couldn't breathe fire, he could cast fireballs at will. He wore an orange tunic and brown breeches with a blue stripe down the sides—the uniform of the Tyrrby Order. Ilmarien wore the same outfit.

I made introductions.

Serafina's eyes were wide. "I've not met a d'oglemann before. How are your scales...." She trailed off with her hand hung half-outstretched in the air.

"How are my scales...what?" Vidarr asked.

"Compared to a dreki?" She laughed. "Sorry. Stupid question. No one has touched a dreki and lived."

Drekis were enormous: twenty strides long from snout to tail, and the same length from wing tip to wing tip. D'oglemenn and drekis shared the same blood, said to aid them in channeling the arcana roiling all around us on the material plane. Something my wife and Serafina could see when they focused. Alas, Mick and I were magically color blind.

"Eh," Vidarr shrugged. "Not entirely true."

I studied my feet. Icy prickles danced up and down my spine. I had seen a dreki. Once. A golden-scaled beast who hadn't even looked at me, but left me quaking in my boots. They have an aura about them, the drekis. It stopped my brain from thinking. Not once did I weigh a thought of attacking or running or...anything. I stood there, trembling, and soiling myself.

Mick's eyes bulged, and he shouted his question. "You've met a dreki?"

Vidarr grinned, causing Serafina to step back. His mouth full of teeth gave the Haví a feral look. "My scales are about a tenth as thick and as large compared to Toryl's scales."

Mick's jaw dropped. His hand wavered, but he reached out. "C-can I touch you?"

Vidarr closed his eyes. I was sure he hid his eye roll. "I suppose. But make it quick. There's business at hand."

Both Mick and Serafina stepped forward to feel the inch-wide scales that covered Vidarr from head to foot. Except around the eyes and mouth, where the scales grew quite small.

Vidarr smiled, this time thin-lipped. "A proper d'oglemann greeting is to shake hands, gripping each other's forearms."

When they finished shaking Vidarr's hand and arm, the d'oglemann stepped around and approached me and my wife. His coal-black pupils were pinpoints in the golden vertical slits of his species. "Rory, Ingefær, the Tyrrby Order needs your help."

His tunic no longer had the visage of Tyrrell, the dreki God of Justice. Instead, a silver sword and a gold sword dangled beneath the business ends of a double-headed war hammer. Up close, the colors defined the shapes, making it look like a scale for weighing goods. Almost. But from a distance, it appeared as a three-legged clump. It was a new design, and, in my opinion, needed work.

"With what?" I asked.

"The d'oglemann mining enclave of Nikkel Bakken has been destroyed."

"The gods!" Serafina exclaimed.

Mick guffawed. "Nothing like a bit of enchanting news to brighten the day."

His timing was awful. Yet my earlier guess of Vidarr bringing bad news was confirmed.

Ingefær and I exchanged glances.

Great. Just great. The news was worse than I had feared. Death was already in the air.

"How?" Ingefær asked. "By whom?"

"Details are scarce." Vidarr's lips pressed thin. "I received Hombir's messenger bird late yesterday."

Hombir Tramanek. The d'oglemann chieftain, or All-Watcher, of Kobber Unter Smuss, and Vidarr's second in charge of all d'oglemann enclaves.

"Where is Nikkel Bakken?" Serafina asked.

I sighed, my tone weary. "The Ice Plains." I placed my hands on my hips, knowing the answer to my question. "So, why come here?"

Vidarr licked his lips. "I need you to go investigate."

A squawk escaped Mick's lips as a hand tugged at a tuft of his ruffled hair.

Vidarr and Ilmarien exchanged looks. Ilmarien's brows crimped. "Does he always do that?"

Serafina chuckled. "Eh. Almost always. Sometimes he crows like a rooster."

"Surely you know something?" Ingefær asked.

"Very little." Vidarr waved the Rod of the Dreki in a sweeping arc. "Hombir reports the entire enclave destroyed. His note said that since Gods' Day, he's lost two trade caravans. He reports the dvaergs of Kral Bar Aggen have also lost one, a half day east of the enclave."

"So, why us?" I asked. "Have the dvaergs investigate."

I'd rather have a tooth pulled than go back to the Ice Plains. Over the course of my life, I'd almost died on many occasions. Never more so than on the trip across the Ice Plains. Two teeth pulled. Both molars.

"Nikkel Bakken isn't their concern. And outside of Hombir, there is no d'oglemenn with the requisite skill set. You're a woodsman and tracker, and Ingefær is a battle mage."

I replayed his request in my mind. He had asked us to go, not for us to join him. "Why don't you go?"

Vidarr ladled more water. "I'm off to Vanaby for negotiations. They've taken too long to set up for me to reschedule them now."

"What sort of negotiations?" Serafina asked. Vanaby had once been her home.

"Oversight of justice." Vidarr took a drink, his tongue lapping much like a dog. "They've dispensed with the military command structure and have elected a governor."

Progress. Of that I was sure, having been subject to a wayward lieutenant's prejudice.

Serafina grinned. "Good. About time."

She, too, had suffered from alvae martial law injustice. My wife and I had helped the half-alvae healer with the fallout from her unfair imprisonment and subsequent escape. It had required lots of messenger birds and the aid of Tyrrby with a truth spell before Captain Alvertos himself had been needed to vacate her sentence and clear her name. And to get the persistent alvae bounty hunter Melinda to pursue other outlaws.

Ingefær said, "I don't know, Vidarr. We've got the fall planting."

"And you're talking about the Ice Plains." I eyed Vidarr. "Winter is coming."

Vidarr dipped his snout and bypassed both concerns by not addressing them. "Tyrrby will pay. A thousand dreki to identify who did the deed. And five thousand—"

"Five thousand?" Mick shouted. He looked wide-eyed at me. "I get a fourth of that, right?"

At the end of our last assignment, we had agreed to split the spoils four ways. I nodded and put a finger to my lips.

Vidarr's mouth pulsed, and he shot me a glance. He hated to be interrupted. "Five thousand silver dreki coins to eliminate the threat. Pirate Recovery laws also apply."

Any recovered bounty not traceable to an owner within two moons of loss, or any items not regained after two months, belongs to the finders. Most often, the owners of such plunder were dead. So...much loot could be had for the taking. As long as we lived to take it.

Vidarr set the ladle down. "The nickel in the mines is critical to the Realm. There's something in it that prevents steel from rusting. The effects are far-reaching."

He left Tyrrby's aid of Serafina unstated. I suspected it was his trump card if we said no.

"You're such an optimist," I said, winking.

Vidarr ignored my joke. "I need the enclave to thrive. Repopulating it has been a monumental task. And, in a year's time, I had wanted to start operations at Hule de Jern. Once the others hear of the news, I expect no d'oglemann will want to go to either enclave."

He leaned in. "The iron at Hule de Jern is magical as well. Keep it to yourselves. I don't want anyone to move into the mines before I can convince my brothers and sisters to do so."

"What sort of magical properties does it have?" Ingefær asked.

Vidarr licked his lips. "Fire retardation. Quite handy in almost all applications."

Mick pawed the air. "You's frying our eggs. How can the iron be smelted then?"

Once more, Vidarr closed his eyes, then opened them. "I don't have time to explain it all. I'll tell you this: I want my kin to repopulate Hule de Jern."

I didn't think he had to worry. Hule de Jern was on the southeast side of the Dreki Mountains, two weeks north of the alvae city of Vanaby. It was doubtful dvaergs would move in—it was too close to their eon-old adversaries. And while humans had the capacity for the task, finding enough willing miners to trek so far from a human city seemed unlikely.

Some two years ago, the d'oglemenn at Hule de Jern had been annihilated by Sandarin, a vile alvae. A moon later, Nikkel Bakken had been almost destroyed by stygg skapps operating out of Is Vann. I cleared my throat. "You don't think it's a bunch of albino stygg skapps exacting revenge?"

He shook his head. "No. The wounds on the bodies point elsewhere. At something...that doesn't exist."

Mick shrieked.

Vidarr's storytelling could be so melodramatic. I turned to Mick. "Don't let your imagination get ahead of you, young man. Control those outbursts. Vidarr is exaggerating for effect."

Mick hiccupped. "W-well, it-it worked."

Serafina asked. "It's not dark magic, necromancy?"

Vidarr shook his head. "Implausible, but I can't rule it out. The damage appears to be physical. Well. Most of it. There's another oddity. Hombir will clue you in...if you go." His eyes locked with mine.

I got his message. *I helped you, now it's your turn to help me.* Ah, the barbs of loyalty.

Vidarr pointed at Ilmarien. "My comrade must take me to Vanaby now. He'll return for you in the morning." A smile revealed his teeth. "Which gives you time to pack. There's a moon of fall left. Then winter arrives. You know how it is on the north side of the Dreki Mountains."

Great. Just great. I knew. And I disliked having very little choice.

There wasn't a worse place in the entire Realm as Gods' Day approached...the day winter's breath took a hold of the Ice Plains and clamped down its icy maw.

"Let us confer," I said.

Our conversation didn't take long. We were bounty hunters because Foremost Aerica, Vidarr's superior, had signed a decree granting us broad powers of policing. And since Tyrrby had helped to clear Serafina's name, we were indebted.

Mick wanted to go because of the lure of silver. And Serafina because she knew to whom she owed her freedom.

Ingefær lifted her chin at me. "Fall planting?"

I shrugged. "Hiram can handle it. Can you think of a reason to say no?"

She twirled the pearl snowflake she wore as a choker around her neck. "No."

I nodded. "Me neither." I smiled at her. "We're here to help those in need. And I feel a sense of duty to help Hombir. And Tyrrby."

Serafina smiled, crinkling the green skin around her eyes. "I've never been to the Ice Plains."

There were several other things I could say. Like, 'Be careful what you wish for.' Or, 'There's a good reason sane humans and alvaes don't live there.' Instead, I eked out, "Soon, you'll see that your smile is misplaced."

Ingefær turned to Vidarr. "We'll go pack."

Chapter Two

NAUSEATING TRAVEL

INGEFÆR

The following morning, we packed our rucksacks. Serafina distributed vials of healing to everyone and kept an extra one on her person. She stashed her Rod of Animal Summoning down her trousers along her left hip.

Mick tucked his scroll of invisibility and a magical light stick into his blue vest, where I knew he kept his door- and trap-bypassing implements, along with a slingshot with peach-pit sized stones. He also tucked away three different daggers in various hidden spots on his person.

Rory possessed nothing magical to carry around. His magic was innate. He could outrun a horse for some five minutes before he grew tired. And when his life was threatened, Roskva, a dazzling pinkish-orange fylgjæ—as Rory had described her on several occasions—showed up. When she was around, Rory could run four times as fast as any human...and never tire. Per my husband, the sparkling spirit was maybe a foot tall and reed thin. She had fronds for arms and legs, and a block-shaped head with no eyes, ears, or nose. She communicated with gestures.

As for me, I wore a mage belt underneath my chainmail armor. It contained pouches of various ingredients I used to invoke spells using the air and fire planes of magic, as well as a few utility incantations from the Aether plane. I saw all the colors of magic when I focused on them.

But I excelled at drawing whites and reds—air and fire, respectively. The yellow of the Aether took more concentration and effort. The browns and greens of earth and the blue of water resisted my pulls. *Maybe one day.*

I placed a fireball scroll behind my back, wedging it into my leather pants, right above my butt cheeks. The scroll didn't require me to draw on the colors of the plane of fire like a manual fireball incantation. An added benefit was not needing material or hand gestures.

I also wore a choker around my neck; it had a pearl-like stone with flecks of fiery red in it. Last year, I'd learned that it guarded against frost-based spells. I wore it because it dazzled in the sunlight and because it was a wedding gift, reminding me of the day I married Rory.

With our rucksacks packed and equipment ready, we waited for Ilmarien's return. I advised Mick and Serafina not to eat, and to drink sparingly. Rory spent his time outside, going over the remaining tasks with Hiram, plotting out the next moon of toil.

Ilmarien arrived closer to noon, Rory walking him up from the well. The Haví looked pale.

At my invitation to take a break, he shook his head, grimacing. "No. I must get to Himmel Drakken tomorrow to retrieve Foremost Aerica."

"You travel a lot, then?" Serafina asked.

"It's been a busy moon." Ilmarien sipped at his skin of water. "But it does wonders for keeping the weight off. I eat at night. The rest of the time, it does me no good. What goes down comes back up."

"Uh-oh," Mick said.

I turned to the tawny-haired lad. "You didn't?"

A sheepish look. "I-just a couple of radishes, and eggs, and a slice of buttered bread...with honey. I thought you were joking."

With a shake of his head, Rory slung a backpack onto his shoulder while holding his crossbow in the other hand. His sword hung on his hip. The rest of us geared up, and we walked to the well.

I patted my pocket, making sure I had the ruby signet ring bearing an 'R' etched in gold. The ring aided a mage with stamina, but I had yet to learn its command word and couldn't activate its powers. Perhaps Hombir, when he had a spare half day, could analyze it for me.

Outside, near the well, Ilmarien walked us through the routine. Teleporting wasn't instantaneous. A three-week trek by horse could be spanned by a six-hour ordeal through the miasma. "It's disorienting. You twist, turn, and tumble, all at once...and for quite a long time. Which is why it's recommended not to consume food...and for first-time travelers, drink."

Mick paled.

"Do you know where we'll arrive?" I asked.

"A spot five minutes outside of Kral Bar Aggen. Away from trees and walls and other objects." Ilmarien offered his version of a reassuring smile, which was the equivalent of someone eating three-day-old undercooked fish and trying to convince the master cook they liked it. "Have your winter cloaks within easy reach."

Rory slapped Mick on the back. "Let's hope your teleporting aim is better than Mick's sense of humor."

Ilmarien chuckled. "Yes, let's."

We gathered around in a circle, with everyone placing a hand on their neighbor's shoulders.

Mick hiccupped. "Nervous-*hic*-is all."

"Did I ever tell you the story of the talking sheep?" Four shakes of the head. Ilmarien dropped his gaze to the ground. "Let's see. How does it begin?" His boot drew a line in the dirt.

Was he serious? Lifting my head, I glanced around.

Ilmarien made motions with his right hand above Mick's head, and I felt his left rustle my red hair. His foot scratched a second line, splitting the first in half. "Hmm. I'm forgetting how it starts." As he drew a third line, bisecting the first two to make a sort of star or a child's snowflake, he blew five quick bursts of air out and said, *"flaer herfra til der Kral Bar Aggen."*

Spinning about is one thing. What we did was more tumultuous. Not only did I go sideways around but also head over heels, with many leaping twists thrown in. I lost what was left of my breakfast tea and saw stars. Yellow ones, then green ones, then purple ones. Time and the miasma stretched. At least that's the way it felt to me, because my innards wrapped themselves around my outer being. Then, the longest eye-blink later, they snapped back.

I was sure I threw up again. I had no control of my limbs as I flailed through the grayish murk.

Darkness creeped in from around the edge of my vision, full of grays, blues, and purples. The colors oscillated like they were being whacked and sliced by a demented warrior's blade.

More vomit, this time bitter bile.

After hours of mind-jarring and gut-wrenching falling ass over head, the Realm stopped tumbling, and we landed as soft as a feather. I took a deep breath, then another. I spat the bile out of my mouth and wiped a sleeve across my lips.

My vision returned, the multi-colored grays morphing into a pale yellow. The ground beneath my feet was covered in grass going into hibernation. Peering at the moon and stars, I guessed we had traveled for nigh on eight hours. Which matched my prior calculations. By horse, Kral Bar Aggen was a four-week trip from Slangeh Buktah, a city to the south of our homestead.

I struggled to lift my still-spinning head. Blinking my vision clear, I saw that everyone else, save Ilmarien, had their heads down. "That was...discombobulating."

"What a, *urp*, word." Holding his stomach, Manic Mick fell to his knees and spat out bits of egg. "I'll never, *urp*, eat again."

Ilmarien reached down and patted the young thief's head of rumpled, tawny hair. "You get used to it after a while."

Before I could offer a snarky reply, a chill wind blew in from the north, ruffled my hair, and slid down the back of my bright red cloak. I shivered. Grabbing my wulv overcoat, I glanced around at the tottering landscape. The sight of the moonlit Dreki Mountains to the south, reflecting snow-covered peaks that stabbed at the dark sky, steadied my legs. I tied the wulv pelt tight.

"The gods!" Mick screamed. "Leave me be." His body spasmed as he dry heaved.

Serafina shuddered as she drew her wulv mantle around her shoulders. Her silver-green skin had lost a shade, but her emerald-like eyes appeared pinpoint, focused.

Rory's hand shifted to the hilt of his sword, a reflex from too many years of trouble finding him. "The Ice Plains," he grumbled. "Last time, I nearly froze my cods off out here."

"Language," I chided. "Though I must confess, having arrived chills my enthusiasm. A lot."

"Can't say I fancy the idea of trudging through blizzards while watching for lindwyrms and albino stygg skapps," Rory said, sighing.

Albino skapps were as ugly as ordinary skapps, except bigger and shaded in a mottled white and light gray to blend in with the snow. Otherwise, they had the same disfigured eyes, ears, and nose, and different lengths to their arms and legs, causing them to shamble off-kilter.

Rory tugged at Mick's arm, trying to gather the kid to his feet. "Not to mention wærgs and bears and...oh my."

He stopped hoisting Mick up and pointed with his blade.

A foursome of dvaergs clad in woolen brown shirts hiked our way. The late fall of the Ice Plains was like a full-on winter for us down south. Though it was impossible to tell by looking at the approaching foursome, as the mountain dwellers had yet to garb themselves in furs.

Dvaergs preferred to stay indoors, mining, crafting gems, and brewing ale. Other than to hunt or trade, they rarely came outside during the day, not caring for the brightness of the sun. Still, they had sturdy hides, thicker than the stoutest of humans.

"We're expected," Ilmarien said. "Vidarr sent a bird before we left Tyrrby."

Serafina's lips curled into a look of distaste. "Dvaergs."

"Great friends of ours," I said. "Let's meet them halfway."

Rory yanked Mick to his feet. "Walk it off, lad."

Mick spat at the grass. "Easy, *urp*, for you to say."

I waved at the approaching party.

My husband attempted to divert Mick's attention from his stomach pains with talk of fancy meads and ales. However, I wasn't ready for it yet, and a fresh round of pain seized my guts.

Mick's color brightened to a shade above almost-dead. "I don't know, Master Belkin. I'm in no mood for drinking."

Serafina said, "I've heard dvaerg ale is worthy of a couple of sips. Please, dear gods, let it be as folklore tells it."

We had had a discussion about the gods several moons back. They were locked away in Asagard and not at all nice and friendly to anyone living in the Mid Dreki Realm. I don't think she believed me and Rory, but she agreed to keep an open mind...and an eye out for any gods on Gods' Day.

The dvaergs neared, raising meaty paws in greeting. Tugg Dowadugg, his salt and pepper beard fluttering in the breeze, stepped forward. "Oi. We be warned of yer arrival." His narrowed brown eyes swung from person to person. His gaze arrested on Serafina. He dipped his head. "Me lady."

A better welcome than I had anticipated.

Serafina's eyes widened, but she recovered and bowed her head. "Good sir."

Tugg flashed a bearded grin. "Welcome. Been waiting for hours."

I glanced above the dvaerg foursome. Behind them, some three hundred strides, stood a massive forty-foot wall like a sentinel over the plains. The black wall of finely hewed rock, well-polished by arms and eon-old magic, reflected the moonlight. Towers jutted up at intervals where the walls shifted angles. Having been here before, I knew the outer keep was half of an octagon. The back half was the sheer mountain itself, reaching for the sky at least five hundred strides above us all. Dvaergs lived inside the mountain.

I surveyed the Ice Plains to the north. While I didn't care much for this place, no way could we quit the job before we started. Vidarr was a good friend. Even if he hadn't helped us get our bounty hunting charter and led the team to clear Serafina's name, I would have come. Knowing my husband would go where I went...as I would go where he went.

I exchanged looks with my husband. His smile and kind eyes warmed me. The gods, how I loved that man.

He waggled his head toward the dvaergs. One by one, we shook hands with them all.

Tugg's voice rumbled like distant thunder. "Glad ye arrived at night. The blasted sun stings me eyes. Be ye ready to get out of this infernal wind?"

Serafina shuddered inside her cloak.

Tugg's beard shifted, revealing teeth. "Then let's get inside Kral Bar Aggen."

Tugg led us over the brittle grass. Soon we reached the open, massive gates, with the portcullis in the up position. A dozen guards manned parapets above us. Two more sentries stood at each corner section of the half octagon. A standard watch out here in the northern wilds, if memory served.

I followed Tugg through the colossal wooden doors set in the outer wall and into the outer keep proper. Half of it was dedicated to farming.

This late in the year, what crops there were had been picked. Cows, pigs, and horses were corralled in their own sections. Several sheds anchored various pastures.

We walked to a massive panel of shiny metal ensconced in the mountainside. Serafina's and Mick's jaws dragged the ground, their heads spinning one way, then another. The walls were impressive, but the inside of the mountain was where the true dvaerg engineering feats were on display.

Tugg pounded on the great sheet of wrought metal and provided the password. One half of the door opened, revealing hinges. If I hadn't seen it with my own eyes, I would have never guessed the polished metal plate was indeed two halves of an immense door.

Chapter Three

MYSTERIOUS TROUBLES

RORY

We stepped through the oversized metal doors into a shaft six feet wide and eight feet tall, the floor as smooth and clean as a just-changed baby's butt.

Tugg rubbed at his eyes. "Good to be back in natural light."

Natural? He meant tunnels lit by magic cascading through the shaft in a soft, whitish-blue hue.

"Our escapade to Is Vann be less than two years ago and I be not looking forward to another long trip onto the Ice Plains. The cold be miserable, the sun like an assassin with twin daggers stabbing at me eyes. Ach." He waved a meaty arm. "Don't listen to me grumbling. We'll get by with woolen scarves and brimmed hats."

And warmth spells. A wonderful adaptation of the healing spell, castable by both healers and mages. It lasted an hour, but if a fire wasn't available, it made all the difference in survival.

On our trip to Is Vann two years ago, Ingefær had learned to cast magic. It was also where she and I—after working together as friends for several years—had first made moon eyes at each other. A wonderful trip...if I edited out the hordes of stygg skapps, the Jotunn attack, a pack of wærgs, a squirm of lindwyrms, and the score of dead friends succumbing to the elements.

Why ruin otherwise pleasant memories?

We continued down the shaft, ever descending and slightly turning. Compared to the outside, the air grew warmer, and the scent of stone and earth mingled with the faint aroma of hops and barley, or brewing ale. The latter grew stronger as we entered the visitors' hall.

"Remarkable design and quality of workmanship," I murmured to Mick and Serafina, pointing at the carved out hall with its perfect circular shape and walls, floor, and ceiling with nary a pit, crevice, or bump.

I peered at the ceiling—I hadn't quite gotten used to having all that rock above me. But it was the same as it was two years ago. The visitors' room was perhaps forty strides in diameter. A lot of folks could drink, dance, and roll dice in here. Off to the left stood the bar, behind which several ales were stored in tapped barrels. That I knew from my last visit.

In the center stood a pair of oversized bat-wing doors, which led into the kitchen. The aromas of ham and cabbage reached my nose and woke my stomach. Off to the right were three statues of the dreki gods: Reagun, Baladuhr, and Allefar, the Gods of Craftsmanship, Peace, and the Father of All.

I shouldn't have been surprised, but my jaw dropped nonetheless. During the Serafina affair, Vidarr had warned me the dvaergs remained steeped in dreki God culture. Asserting the gods could no longer be seen on Gods' Day was bad enough. But reporting them as nothing better than brigands and adulterers was too much for them to hear. It would take them time. Maybe a generation of no one seeing a dreki god on Gods' Day.

Between the god statues and the bat-wing doors was an oversized hearth, flames crackling and radiating warmth. We stripped off our wulv overcoats.

The visitors' hall contained a few dvaergs and a pair of d'oglemenn, the latter two sitting at the center round table. Hombir and his healer wife, Jonuku. The gods! That brought back more memories.

A baby d'oglemann, Vidarr's son, racing across the floor to reach the arms of his mother, Danika. Then an old nightmare flooded in, unbidden. I had given Ingefær the cold shoulder when we had met here after three moons of being apart. Not that I blamed myself for that, as I had been possessed by a dark spirit at the time: Laehvateinn. Evicting her out of my head had almost killed me.

A ghost's stroke raked down my spine. I shivered.

Laehvateinn was stored somewhere in this keep. Warded to keep folks away and to keep her mind-numbing magic from entrapping another.

Breaking my divergent thoughts was a threesome of dvaergs who shuffled in, each unpacking a carrying case. A small kettle drum was pulled out. The second dvaerg got his fiddle out and strummed strings to tune it. The third blew a ditty into his flute.

I reached over and shook Hombir's arm, then his wife's. "Well met. I'm thrilled to see you. Though I wish the circumstances weren't so dire."

Hombir waved at us to sit, while Tugg issued orders to the three dvaergs that had come in with us. They left for the kitchen.

Tugg sat next to Hombir. "Dinner meal be coming. I know ye be hungry."

Mick shuffled over, stopping out of reach of Hombir. "I saw one of you's before, now there's two."

Hombir raised his bony brows at the lad. "Yes?"

Mick cleared his throat. "Sorry. Before yesterday, I never seen a d-d'oglemann."

Jonuku smirked. "Well, you'll soon find out we're not much different from you. Same wants, same fears."

Ingefær put an arm around Mick and guided him to the other side. "Sit."

The trio started up with the violin and fiddle playing a soft, yet plucky tune. The dvaerg with the kettle drum also had a pan on his knee, which he tapped with some sort of wire brush. All around, a pleasant sound.

We made ourselves comfortable, nodding in thanks as a dvaerg, who had come out of the kitchen, placed mugs of water before us and bowls of the same in front of Hombir and Jonuku.

Tugg sat opposite Serafina, his eyes staying on the golden-haired alvae. "We have some ham and potatoes coming. And a sweet and juicy vegetable, kohlrabi. Picked within the last moon."

Serafina sniffed at the air. "It's interesting." Faces turned to her. "The room smells...nice. After the cooked meat and vegetables, I get a hint of sweet earth and switchgrass and the tang of stone."

"The sweet earth and tang of stone is the room itself." I grinned. "The switchgrass is the smell of dvaergs."

"What?" Mick asked.

"Dvaergs don't sweat," I said. "Vanaby, by comparison, is a stinky place. No offense, Serafina."

"True. A cat urine-like stench hovers when the wind doesn't blow off the ocean." She looked up at the ceiling. Her silver-green skin lightened.

"Everything alright?" I asked.

"Just getting used to the idea of the sheer weight of rock above my head."

I grunted. "You get used to it. Though it might take a while." I wasn't sure I was there yet myself.

"Not bothered by the dvaergs bustling about?" Ingefær asked.

"No. Everyone seems nice." Serafina looked up at the ceiling again. "How does it all stay in place?"

I didn't know how to explain it. And I wasn't the one to issue comforting words. I disliked the idea of sleeping underground. But I didn't want my first night here to be outside. Not when I had several weeks ahead of me. I had yet to acclimate to the change in temperature.

Hombir said, "The dvaergs use magic to keep the rock from shifting. Don't you worry none. A more secure abode outside of this dvaerg keep doesn't exist. Well, maybe a dreki cavern." His smile faltered and his snout dropped to the table. "But then you would have a different problem."

Something about the look on Hombir's face caused the chuckle in my throat to die off. The thought of being in the same room as a giant scaled beast that breathed fire and flew faster than a ballista bolt would indeed be the last problem most of us would ever have. But I sensed that wasn't what bothered the All Watcher.

As if on queue, the trio switched to a melancholy song. The violin cried while the kettle drum echoed throughout the room.

I glanced at Jonuku. She gnawed on a lip, her eyes cloudy, like she was close to tears.

Aye. We were here to deal with a serious issue. "Sorry. We're still sorting ourselves out after our travels." I chinned at Hombir. "Tell us about the situation at Nikkel Bakken."

He closed his eyes; his jowls tightened. Then he nodded. "I arrived here from Nikkel Bakken two days ago. Fifty couples of my kin are dead or missing. Out on the plains, we found thirty bodies. Each was stripped and gnawed down to the bone. Their blood had soaked the ground. Grisly. Something ate them. Of that, I'm sure. Not even entrails were left behind. Just...stains and bones."

Mick hiccupped, then asked, "How do you-*hic*-know there were thirty-*hic*- then?"

News of death and violence unsettled the young man. As did promised violence. He'd been on but one gnarly expedition prior to this one.

"I counted skulls." Hombir eyed the lad, who gulped, then hiccupped.

I shuddered. The idea of anything eating d'oglemenn soured my stomach. More so than teleport travel.

"Inside the den holes, we found fifty-six more bodies. All intact. Dead with nary a mark on them."

Jonuku sobbed, putting her snout in her hands.

"Nothing unusual?" Ingefær asked.

Fifty-six dead with no mark sounded unusual to me. The violin player behind us squealed out a plaintive set of notes. The flutist moved in with a peal of his own.

"Well, no." Hombir sniffed. "I mean, yes. There were a few we found lying there in wet clothes. One pair we found sitting in a puddle in the middle of their den. But what killed them? I don't know."

Wet clothes?

Hombir continued. "Fourteen of my kin are unaccounted for. Maybe they're dead, maybe not. But they're not anywhere in or near the enclave. We searched the mining caverns and the surrounding area."

Had the missing been killed by now? If not, they knew their prospects.

Hombir wet his lips. "The dead need avenging. That's the first thing. The second is the Ice Plains needs to be secured. Trade must flow unimpeded. Well, as much as it can out here. Last, I need more volunteers to resettle and mine the nickel. But once the report of the dead and missing gets out, I won't get any. Not until the problem is dealt with."

Jonuku said, "And it's only right to tell them before we ask anyone else to move to the enclave."

Hombir's eyes—black pupils in an ellipse of gold—locked on me. "I cannot do it alone. Even if I had a hundred warriors with me, I fear we'd end up just as dead." He sniffed. "I was hoping Vidarr would come."

His moist eyes pleaded for our aid.

Ingefær nodded. "Me, too. Something that kills over four score sounds powerful and evil."

Mick kept up with his hiccups.

My wife asked, "No sign of the attackers? Like errant odd-looking blood stains? A footprint? Did your kin hurt or kill even one of these mysterious murderers?"

Mick tugged at his tawny hair as he gritted his teeth. A prelude to an outburst. I put a finger to my lips to warn him off.

Hombir sighed. "No. Not a single clue. The ground is hard this time of year. Whatever killed them, and took the others hostage, left no trace."

Hombir was hoping the fourteen were alive. I didn't have good thoughts about that.

A pair of dvaergs served dinner: eggs, ham, potatoes, and a sliced white vegetable. Tugg informed us it was his vaunted kohlrabi. Ale was ladled into mugs, but me and Tugg were the lone ones drinking.

The trio moved on to a song we could dance to...if we were in the mood. The kettle drum alternated with the large pan, this time being struck with a pair of spoons.

I sipped the tastiest brew in the Realm, a hint of cinnamon and honey in a base of wheat and hops. I growled my appreciation as I found Hombir's eyes. "Vidarr said you had a trade wagon wiped out?"

Hombir nodded and stabbed a potato. "Two. One, almost a year ago, sent from Kobber. It never made it to Nikkel Bakken. We figured it was lindwyrms, stygg skapps, or wærgs. A second caravan disappeared two moons ago after stopping at Kral Bar Aggen. The third wasn't ours. A half day northeast of Nikkel Bakken, as we searched for our missing kin, we found a dvaerg caravan that had been plundered and pillaged. Dvaerg and horse bones littered all over, lying in dried pools of blood. Strewn clothes, broken planks, shattered wheels, and ripped canvas from the wagons were the only things left of the caravan."

He looked at Tugg. "Since I arrived here, I've learned Tugg's folks have had several more supply wagons destroyed. Tugg says they've lost three, and Kral Fal Is reports two wagon trains lost. Kral Azza Rid hasn't reported any losses, but a bird was sent upon my arrival to ask. I suspect they haven't experienced problems because they send but three convoys a year, according to Premier Mina."

Premier Mina was the leader of the Kral Bar Aggen dvaergs. She was smart and kind, and never one to back down from helping others.

"Seven times trade wagons have been plundered," Hombir's deep baritone cracked. "And this last time, so was the enclave of Nikkel Bakken."

Tugg nodded along. He seemed focused on Serafina. But his gaze didn't appear threatening, just...interested.

"The raids on the transports sounds like a dvaerg problem," I said, attempting to shift the burden off Injustices Righted.

Ingefær pointed a fork at me. "I have to agree with Rory. Why isn't Kral Bar Aggen dealing with this?"

Tugg tipped his mug, draining the last of his ale. Finished, he placed it on the table with a solid thump. "After the second missing caravan, we increased the size of our escort. Whatever be marauding the wagons, it killed off twenty Avarkæsir in the last raid. It be our wagons that be plundered east of Nikkel Bakken."

That was a sizable military patrol. And they were experienced soldiers, knowing how to deal with the elements and the critters that called the frozen plains home.

Even with Hombir's magic, the problem seemed bigger than the four of us could handle. What killed eighty plus could kill the six of us. And while I liked to help others—especially those less fortunate—I didn't like to risk our lives more than necessary.

Hombir dabbed at his elongated snout with a cloth. "The Kral Bar Aggen wagon train left here two weeks ago. It's a week's ride and a day to Nikkel Bakken, except during winter."

With heavy snow underfoot, it would add a couple of days. With snow flying and frigid blasts of air blowing, three or four. The beasts out here were bad. The weather, worse.

Hombir took his wife's hand in his. "We missed the attack by a day or two."

"Less," I said. "If their clothes were still damp, you missed the attack by six to twelve hours."

A dead body put off heat for quite a while. The Ice Plains had a dry climate. Except for winter, when the moisture came down as snow. Lots and lots of snow.

Tugg sighed, his fat fingers twiddling with his salt and pepper beard. "Getting back to yer query, Miss Ingefær, we be dealing with the problem the best way us dvaergs can—sheer numbers. Not knowing the real danger, Premier Mina hasn't authorized a full military deployment. She wants to keep the bulk of the Avarkæsir here to defend. Until we know who, or what, be behind it all. Aye, it sounds like beasties. But maybe it be *made* to look as such."

I struggled with the idea of someone faking the gnawing of flesh off bones. But the part confusing me most was Hombir's description of the dead bodies inside their dens—untouched, but with sodden clothes. That sounded like magic.

Tugg toyed with his empty mug. "Kral Azza Rid needs produce and protein. Oh, they won't starve, but they might get a tad thin at the waist. Premier Mina has ordered another caravan. We'll send a proper guard this time. Two hundred forty of me best fighters."

An entire company? That sounded like a good-sized military deployment to me. Ever since time began, dvaergs had a fifth of their population who trained as Avarkæsir, or Honor Warriors. They were supported by taxes on the rest of the keep's citizens. Their military might was always on the strong side. Even those who didn't take on the soldiering vocation trained in the martial arts of shield and axe, spear, and crossbow.

"If the marauders attack again, I want to be there." Hombir jabbed another potato. "I want to know who or what killed my kin. And kill them."

I never knew him to be the first in a fray. Mages were best operating from the rear. I swallowed ham. "Any mages go along with any of these supply wagons?"

Hombir shook his head. "Not ours. While the return of magic nigh on twenty moons ago has increased our numbers, all new mages are whelps when it comes to the arcane ways."

Tugg nodded. "Not ours, either. We have a few new mages. Hombir be kind enough to spend a week on their training every time he passes through. Most of ours be trained in mining, not fighting. Right now, they be apt to hurt themselves more than any foe."

Which was why Vidarr came teleporting to find me and Ingefær. There were other talented mages in the Realm, but none that owed him a favor. I knew what the answer would be from the others, too. No human would go so far north to help a dvaerg. Let alone a d'oglemann. And most alvae would cheer the destruction of dvaergs and shrug at news of dead d'oglemenn. Yeah, south of the Dreki Mountains, the races, while not warring, weren't friendly.

Which made Tugg's cordialness toward Serafina stand out all the more.

Shoving the last forkful of ham and potatoes into my mouth, I asked, "So, what's the plan?" I looked up to see Ingefær frowning at me. I closed my mouth, finished chewing, and swallowed.

"Don't have one yet," Tugg said.

Mick offered the cavernous room a screech that echoed off the wall. The trio behind us stopped playing for a few breaths.

"Really?" I asked.

He gripped a side of his hair and tugged. "It sounds like an enormous monster is terrorizing out there."

"Might be more than one," I said.

Mick put a hand over his mouth.

"Worse," Tugg said. "Winter be coming." He pointed at Ingefær and me. "Ye two know what it be like after Gods' Day."

I sighed. We were some five weeks away from the harshest season.

Serafina cleared her throat, the ham on her plate untouched. "No offense, but couldn't this wait till spring?"

"It could," Hombir said. "Except there's fourteen missing."

My shoulders pinched. "After a week plus? I don't know, Hombir, that may be a fool's hope."

Hombir nodded. "True. But I think we should try. Besides, the sooner we figure this out, the sooner I can repopulate the mining enclave. The dvaergs need the nickel."

Tugg scratched at his beard. "And I'd like to go ahead of the trade wagons to Kral Azza Rid. To check things out. So, whether or not ye come, I be taking a squad and joining Hombir."

We had come here to help a friend. But at Hombir's description of events, my resolve had waned. I leaned in over the table. "Well, team? What are we going to do?"

Mick shook his head. "I see little need for my skills."

I didn't see much use for Mick's twitchy fingers, either.

Serafina chewed on her lower lip. "I see the need for a healer. But if I'm honest, I'd rather go home and find another job for us to do. It's cold and—no offense, but is the addition of the four of us enough to deal with whatever is out there?"

I glanced at Ingefær.

She twirled the pearl-white snowflake with the fiery center that adorned her throat. Ever since we'd shaved our heads over a year ago, she'd transferred her worry signal from twisting her hair to spinning the magical wedding gift. Even though her hair had grown back past her ears now, her twirling habit stayed with the snowflake pendant.

I grunted. The protection it provided against frost could be helpful out here, though the one mage I knew with the talent of hurling magical blasts of ice was Vidarr.

Ingefær said, "What you say is true, Mick. Serafina. But our word is important. As is our relationship with Tyrrby."

I was on the edge. The safety of the team was being put to the test versus the value of our word and Tyrrby's support. I looked into Hombir's eyes and then at Jonuku's tears. They were friends. Friends who needed help.

I said, "Ingefær and I will go with you."

Serafina huffed. "Well, we're not splitting up the team. So, if you go, I'll come."

Mick grumbled. "I still ain't all that good with a blade. And it sounds like the stones I hurl won't do much against any of the beasts out here. That, and it's blasted cold outside and Master Tugg says it will get worse."

I peered at him. "If you truly don't want to go, you can stay behind. But I think you'll find a way to contribute."

Mick harrumphed. "Just cause you say it, don't make it so." But he nodded. "I'm coming."

"May your resolve bring light to these dark times," Jonuku said, her voice as squeaky as a mouse. "For in darkness, even the smallest spark can herald the dawn."

"Let's hope it's a spark of light," Mick blurted. "And not a fireball or someone ready to ignite a disaster."

I was about to chastise him when a cacophonous noise came from the entryway, interrupting the three musicians' work. They, like us, gawped at the newcomers.

Chapter Four

OPPOSING VIEWS

INGEFÆR

I turned toward the noise of clanging metal. A foursome of dvaergs had come in and dropped their shields, helms, and swords into a loose pile. The largest dvaerg, a brown beard dangling to his waist, scowled at us as he marched over, the other three trailing in his wake.

Without rising, Tugg said, "Meet Sett, captain and second in command of the Avarkæsir."

I stood and offered my hand, looking almost eye to eye to Sett. The dvaerg was huge. Rory climbed to his feet, wiping grease off his palms.

Sett looked at my hand with beady brown eyes, then turned and shifted his gaze to the d'oglemenn, before resting his gaze on Serafina. A corner of his bearded lip turned up, along with a nostril. "I see deliberations started without me."

Tugg's brows narrowed. "As I didn't know when ye would return, it seemed pointless to waste everyone else's time." He raised his head to look up at the standing dvaerg. "And as I be in charge of the Avarkæsir, it be my decision."

A chill came over the room as Sett and Tugg glared at each other. The musicians began packing their instruments away.

I had been to Kral Bar Aggen before, but never met Sett. Why were he and Tugg so disagreeable with one another?

I placed my hand on my hip and shifted my feet to get in front of Sett. "We just agreed to head out in the morning. Will you be joining us?"

Sett's scowl turned to me. "No. I be commanded to stay behind. But me preference has been to seek the raiders. With a company of *dvaergs*. We should have left yesterday."

The emphasis on his kind further cooled the room. As did the musicians filtering out of the dining room without seeking payment for services. Usually, a mug was passed around for tips of silver. But they preferred to be gone than to receive payment.

Rory smirked. "You don't want our help?"

Sett's head swiveled in slow motion. "Nah. A bunch of pasty humans from down south will slow us down."

Dvaergs were hardy and could march in three feet of snow much faster than humans. But they also didn't fare well in sunlight and preferred traveling by night, which invited predators more so than by day. The latter was but a change in scope of a couple of degrees. Daytime travel on the Ice Plains wasn't safe either.

Rory stepped closer, his smile broadening. "This pasty human will run circles around your lard butt."

"Enough!" Tugg climbed to his feet. "We be on the same side. No point in hurling insults."

Sett shifted focus. "Commander, I request *again* to lead a group of volunteers and search for what killed our kin...what killed me younger brother."

That helped explain Sett's animosity. Though I hadn't figured out why he took his anguish out on us. Maybe the brute was naturally grumpy.

Tugg moved around the table to stand before Sett, dwarfed by half a head. "Yer request to lead a team be denied. If ye don't like me decision, ye can always appeal to Premier Mina."

Sett grinned. Then his eyes raked over the rest of us, once more landing on Serafina. “Good luck with a half-alvae in yer midst. Their kind be nothing but trouble.”

“You dare?” I exclaimed, my hand going to the handle of my blade. I expected that kind of behavior from children and alvaes—who held a high opinion of themselves—not dvaergs. Sett’s aggression was out of control.

Rory put a hand on Sett’s shoulder. “Careful there, Sett. Would hate for you to have to see a healer.”

Sett’s grin widened, his teeth showing through his brown beard. “If ye wish to spar, I’d be happy to teach ye a thing or two.”

A part of me wanted my husband to educate Sett. Hel, a part of me wanted to do it myself. But that was a lousy way to start the mission. I shouldered my way between them. “That’s enough out of both of you.”

Tugg pointed at the entryway. “Aye. Sett! Go.”

My heart ached for Sett’s predicament. In a way, he was like Rory, ready to avenge a loved one’s passing. An idea stormed over me. Was it a good one? Maybe it would repair whatever rift Sett saw between us. “Wait. I have a suggestion.” I turned to Tugg. “With your permission, of course.”

I looked into Sett’s beady brown eyes. “What if Sett leads the caravan and we join up at Nikkel Bakken? It will give us time to investigate, and then, assuming we find clues, we can decide on where he goes from there.”

Tugg’s beard dipped at the corners, his meaty hand going to his chin.

Sett turned to look at his commander. “I’d be happy to lead the caravan to Kral Azza Rid. Maybe we’ll get lucky and whatever killed me younger brother will attack us.”

That didn’t sound like luck to me.

Tugg's mouth pinched under his beard. "The reason I don't want ye to lead an expedition be because ye be hot headed. Ye cannot lead if yer emotions lead ye. Understand?"

Sett snarled. "Aye. I understand. I be beyond vexed at ye because ye won't let me do anything."

"And I don't want ye racing our clan folks to their deaths because yer heart be full of vengeance. Vengeance clouds yer thinking."

At that, Sett took a deep breath. "Aye. Me heart be heavy with it."

Tugg pulled at his beard. "The caravan has a leader already. But I'll order the changes. Sett, ye be hereby ordered to escort a company of Avarkæsir to Kral Azza Rid. May the gods speed ye on yer journey."

Sett dipped his bearded chin. "Thank ye, commander."

Sett waved at his companions. "Let's find a place to eat that doesn't stink."

The brute liked to get the last insult in. I thought it childish and unnecessary, but elected to give him some grace, yanking on Rory's arm so he wouldn't respond with a retort.

When they had gathered their gear and shuffled down the shaft, Mick whispered, "That was rude."

I sat back down. "I'm sorry he lost a brother, but it seems there's more to it than not being allowed to lead a search party. His insults aren't from vengeance alone."

Tugg sighed. "Aye. He disagrees with me approach in finding the murderers."

I pursed my lips. "Meaning?"

"I advised Premier Mina to join with Hombir and ye, rather than a solo dvaerg endeavor."

She was the democratically elected leader of Kral Bar Aggen. I'd met her twice before. She was ever fair, and always helpful, with a keen eye on long-term consequences.

Rory asked, "He doesn't care for half-alvaes. Or us. He got anything against d'oglemenn?"

Tugg shrugged. "Maybe. We don't talk much. Not even before he lost his brother. He petitions Premier Mina monthly to become commander. Has done so since spring."

Mick hiccupped. "You's can't fire him for insubordination?"

Tugg sighed. "I could recommend it before a tribunal. He be an officer and an excellent warrior." He cleared his throat. "Before this disaster, before he lost his sibling, he be not insubordinate. It be but two days since he developed a rotten potato attitude toward me and me cautious approach. With a death in the family, I have to be patient, knowing he be grieving. But after tonight, my patience be worn out. If it be the same when we return, I will take action."

Serafina said, "His eyes wanted to cleave me in two."

Tugg nodded. "Aye. There be many dvaergs who don't cotton to having a half-alvae inside our keep." He scoffed. "Bah. It be two thousand years since the dvaerg-alvae wars."

"The Forgotten War," I said.

At a puzzled look from Mick, I added, "A war fought that the history books can't ascribe a reason to."

Except Rory and I knew. Vidarr had told us. The war had been fought over fylgjæ, the stick-figures from the elemental planes. As Rory had one, it was best not to mention it in mixed company, though Tugg already knew.

Tugg got down on one knee before Serafina. "Me lady, I apologize for my kin's actions. Though many might not like ye being here, if ye be a help to Rory and Ingefær, then ye be alright in me book."

Tugg's words were appropriate, but the bending of a knee seemed overwrought.

Serafina blushed, her green face darkening. "Ah, thank you."

Mick said, "So, about me going with you? Since Sett is leading a horde of soldiers, can I stay here?"

I cocked my head at him. "I thought you agreed to go with us."

Rory slapped Mick on the back. "You're among the best. Don't fret. Tugg and his Avarkæsir will provide the brute strength while Hombir and my wife will handle the sorcery. You and I will do our best to contribute."

"But, y-y-you don't need thieving skills." Mick pointed at Tugg. "An entire company is marching."

Rory shook his head. "Nonsense. We don't know what we're going to need. And you've proved yourself crafty."

I came around the table and hugged Mick. "You saved our lives in that deadly dungeon. You're clever with traps and things. And I value the different perspectives you offer."

Mick blushed. "Aw."

Rory sat down and drank from his mug. "Besides, if you don't go, you don't earn your share of the reward."

Mick grumbled and threw his knife and fork at the plate before him. He'd eaten everything, including the kohlrabi, which I had found to be crunchy, juicy, and sweet. "I'm going."

Serafina said. "Look on the bright side. At least we don't have to teleport there."

Rory winked at Mick. "But in your case, I think we'll make an exception."

"Ha, ha," Mick said. "None of you know the spell."

Hombir said, "I'll send a bird to Kobber Unter Smuss and let them know I'll be gone for a while."

At the mention of an extended stay out on the Ice Plains, a foul sense came over me. Maybe it was Mick's reluctance. "Remind me, how long to Kral Azza Rid?"

Tugg waggled his head. "Before the snow flies? Not quite three weeks. After that? A moon, easy. Probably that long for the return trip."

The corners of my lips dipped. "Sounds like we're going to spend more than a moon on the Ice Plains."

I thought I had left the memories of my last time here well buried, but they came back, torturing my belly and mixing with the grease of the potatoes and ham. I forced a smile and uttered words to convince myself as well as Mick. "Don't worry. Jonuku, Hombir, and I know how to cast warmth spells. And I can teach Serafina. We'll be fine."

Tugg said, "We'll bring our own healers. A few know the incantation from our prior escapade."

"Horses?" Rory asked.

Since Winter Solstice was less than five weeks away, I said, "For the four of us. In case speed is needed, or when the snow flies. They can also carry goods."

Or the dead. I shook my head. *Stay positive!*

Rory said, "Worse, come to worst, horses are a superb source of protein."

And I thought I was the one with a sour mood.

Serafina said, "Gross. Horse meat?"

Mick guffawed. "There's no fish up here."

Serafina, Rory, and I had a thing for fish. Meaning that we cared little for them, as we'd eaten more than our share in a short time.

Tugg said, "Oi, there be fishes, lad. Until the rivers freeze. Good eating, too."

Rory and I grunted in unison. I would have to be mighty hungry.

Mick said, "I'll season mine with shaved radish."

The three of us with Injustices Righted groaned. Mick loved the spicy vegetable. But it didn't like him all that much, giving him gas. I'd made sure he had brought none for this trip. We would be in the close confines of a tent.

"Let's pack up," Hombir said. "We leave at first light."

The meeting broke up. Tugg led us to our rooms, deeper into the mountain. Serafina's neck craned as we walked down one shaft after another, ever deeper.

I couldn't help but notice the extra words and offers of services Tugg presented to Serafina. If she wanted, he said, he would get her hot towels and a tub to soak in.

A hot soak sounded great to me, as did getting cleaned up and a good night's rest.

But sleep proved hard in coming. At first, Rory wanted to check on the treasure room where his onetime spirit was locked away. I convinced him to forget about Laehvateinn by kissing him. Which led to other pleasures.

Later, after we'd gone to sleep, I kept waking up from my nightmares.

Jotunn hurled frozen balls of death, followed by albino stygg skapps chasing after me and Rory. The ugly brutes were the largest humanoid species next to trolls. They were misshapen and, according to Vidarr, had but five distinct thoughts: eat, sleep, procreate, plunder, and kill. As they ran in groups of twenty or more, pillaging was ever at the top of their minds.

Chapter Five

WYRMS

RORY

Before the sun rose, we gathered outside the keep proper, arranging our gear and getting the mounts ready. As the sun peeked over the eastern horizon, a chill wind sprang up from the north. We rode through the gates with the sun shining. It offered little warmth, though its rays helped to soothe my spirits.

I wore a woolen undershirt and a black outer gambeson underneath my black tunic. Over the top of it all, I had on a dark leather hauberk and a woolen cloak with a fur-trimmed hood. My sword and scabbard were cinched at my hip. I tied my crossbow to the back of the dapple mare, one of four horses Tugg's folks used for tilling the earth that they loaned to us. While not plow horses, they were stout, built for cold weather. I stuffed my wulv pelt overcoat into one of two saddlebags and mounted my horse.

Ingefær had on a similar outfit, except she wore a chainmail hauberk and had a red woolen cape, hat, and matching gloves. She had her blade on her hip, and her pouches of magic ingredients stored in a belt under her chainmail.

Mick had an assortment of his specialized goods stored in his leather vest. He and Serafina elected to start the journey with their wulv capes draped around their shoulders but not cinched closed. With the extra gear, the two of them looked like they'd put on a dozen pounds.

Both of them had ridden some on the farm, but as we rolled along, I spent a few minutes on the necessities of winter-weather equine care: don't overwork the horse and cause it to sweat. And be liberal with the water.

"For that matter," I said, looking left at Mick and right at Serafina, "make sure you drink plenty yourself. You wouldn't think it, but the cold dries you out as much as a blistering sun."

Once out of sight of the keep's black walls, Hombir's dozen d'oglemann guards took the point as we shifted eastward, followed by Hombir and Jonuku. The d'oglemenn traveled on foot. Their hardy taloned feet never needed a boot, not even in the snow. Each warrior carried a rucksack, a sword at the waist, and hefted a short spear that they used as a walking pole. Hombir had two rucksacks, one of which I knew to be laden with sorcerous and historical lore. He never left his home village without them.

Mick, Serafina, Ingefær, and I clopped along behind them. In the rear, Tugg and four soldiers also went on foot, leading a pair of donkeys laden with firewood, torches, tents, food, and water.

South of the Dreki Mountains, we'd be a threat to any brigand party of the human or alvae variety, especially if they didn't have mages. But on the north side, we'd be on equal footing with a pack of wærgs or a squirm of wyrms.

Did we have the strength to fight off whatever had marauded the caravans and destroyed the d'oglemann enclave? Were two mages enough?

I shook off my dark doubts and kicked my dapple mare into a half-trot.

Whatever had destroyed the d'oglemann village at Nikkel Bakken, and seven caravans over the past year, sounded as powerful as the mighty Jotunn.

But we made peace with them. Hadn't we?

I expressed my concerns to Ingefær, who rode her mare beside me.

Her shoulders heaved. "I've been wondering the same thing. I guess it could be the giant blue beasts. But I didn't know them to eat the flesh of dvaergs and d'oglemenn. Let's keep our minds open."

"Well," I said, "we didn't stop to chat while we were running away from their ice balls of death."

The six-stride tall brutes could throw a two-foot round ball of ice full of rocks a quarter of a mile—with lethal accuracy. Ingefær's fireball incantation was good for a quarter of that distance. And crossbows? Forty strides to kill a hjort. Unless we were within twenty, I didn't think a crossbow bolt or a bow arrow would pierce the blue giant's hide. It was unlikely anyone would ever get that close.

***

For three days we rode east by northeast, keeping the Dreki Mountains to our right. During the day, the temperature never got above chilly. At night, every growing thing froze. At least the clouds stayed away. That couldn't be said for the wind, which increased in ferocity each day, ruffling—then flattening—the blanched grasses on the hills and in the bowls.

On the fourth day, an hour before our mid-day feast of pemmican and water, we reached a sort of basin. It was an elongated depression between two ridges set a league apart. We walked down a rocky ridge and into the flat of the valley.

Hombir and his warriors led us through the frosted grass. Not two minutes into the valley, the ground exploded in a shower of dirt, rocks, and dead grass. D'oglemenn were scattered and thrown to the ground.

My mare reared, and I struggled to hang on.

A dozen strides in front of me, a lindwyrm of gigantic proportions reared high into the air, its cavernous orifice rising two strides above the horse I rode on. It swooped down and snapped up a fallen d'oglemann as it plunged into the earth, dragging the warrior with it. The d'oglemann's screams died quickly.

The other d'oglemenn lay there, their jaws hung open in horror.

"Get out of there!" I hollered at Hombir and his troops. Where there's one lindwyrm, there would be more. "Back to the ridge!"

But I may as well have been shouting at naked mole rats—one of the rare deaf animals that eked out a living in the harsh wilds.

Only Hombir got up. He helped Jonuku to her feet, and they ran toward me. The other d'oglemenn swiveled their heads, looking around, their butts frozen to the ground.

"They're beneath you!" I waved an arm at them to retreat.

A quick glance over my shoulder showed Tugg and his dvaergs scrambling to higher ground...where there were sheets of bedrock beneath their feet.

I growled. Help or run?

I heeled my horse forward, but she refused the command. My Muffin would have gone. So would Ingefær's Thunder. But we rode horses unfamiliar to us and ones not trained for combat.

I jumped off and drew my sword before landing. Using my fleet feet, I charged toward the fallen and still stunned d'oglemenn, passing Hombir and his wife along the way.

An eye blink before I arrived, the earth erupted in a second geyser of dirt and debris. The gaping cavity of a second lindwyrm stared down at me and the remaining d'oglemenn warriors.

"Rory!" Ingefær screamed.

I braced myself, ready to race in the opposite direction.

The lindwyrm snatched at the legs of a d'oglemann, who was scrabbling away on his scaled butt. But not fast enough. The giant wyrm drew the soldier deeper into its round, toothy maw. The d'oglemann's cry was cut short as the lindwyrm closed its sphincter-like mouth full of jagged teeth.

Blood stained the white beast's outer husk and dripped to the ground; the d'oglemann's legs dangled on what may be passed for the creature's chin. The lindwyrm submerged rearward, taking its meal with it.

A third lindwyrm surfaced four strides to my left and snapped at a third d'oglemann. I charged and slashed at its exposed underbelly, or possibly its upper torso. Hard to tell, and it didn't make a bit of difference. Lindwyrms' exoskeletons were as hard as rock, and my blade clanked off its hide. Like an opponent wearing thick-linked chainmail armor, stabbing was the sole way of hurting the thing.

A salvo of fiery darts lanced the underside of the lindwyrm. It didn't disgorge its prize as it slithered back under the earth.

"We need fire," I yelled, recalling how sensitive these beasts were to flame.

"Run back!" Tugg shouted, waving his arm at us from atop the knoll. "There be hard rock here."

The group splintered.

Serafina and Mick turned their mounts around, joining Hombir and Jonuku in their mad scramble for hard ground.

Me and the remaining d'oglemenn, now count of nine, formed a loose circle, with Ingefær splitting the difference between the two groups.

"Get out of there!" My wife urged us on with a wave of her arm.

I nodded and motioned for Hombir's soldiers to get moving.

I searched the area. Where was my mare?

I spotted her fifty strides to the north. She must have spooked when the second or third lindwyrm erupted out of the ground. But in the wrong direction.

Great. Just great.

"Cover me!" I raced to the mare.

Ingefær hollered at me. "Wait!"

I skidded to a stop and turned to yell...'for what?'

But before I could—two strides before me—the ground exploded and a fourth lindwyrm flailed through the air, snapping its round mouth full of serrated teeth. Her shout had saved my life.

Ingefær sent a flaming bead towards it. And me!

Uncharacteristically, I froze.

The fiery bead flew past me, then the lindwyrm.

She missed?

An explosion of fire ripped through the air. I covered my face against the flash of heat.

The fireball blast had been well placed. Her shot had missed the mare and me, but engulfed the lindwyrm.

The lindwyrm didn't scream or roar. It flopped over with a hair-raising thud, bounced once and lay still, not a stride from my feet. A good chunk of its body remained exposed above the ground.

At the explosion, my mare raced even further north. I shouted at it to stop. After a long moment, it did. The dapple mare looked left, then right, then grazed on frozen grasses.

Wow! What a witless horse.

Tugg and another dvaerg raced toward me, lit torches in hand. They passed Ingefær, who stood there with her hands on her hips.

Tugg stopped before the dead wyrm. "That be good eating. Watch me back."

With more dvaergs and more torches—lindwyrms feared fire and had an uncanny ability to sense flame from beneath the ground—the dvaergs extricated the rest of the giant wyrm's body.

While Tugg and his crew struggled, I made my way north, this time with a torch in my hand. I tiptoed to my mare and gathered her reins. We walked back slowly, trying to be as quiet as possible. I kept watch for any signs of vibrating dirt and trembling grasses.

Ingefær shook her head at me. Though I knew I had been lucky, I smiled into her scowl.

Tugg's crew worked in harmony and cut the creature's exterior hide with a crosscut saw designed to fell timber. Then they carved out the flesh, cutting it into long strips. When there was enough for an armload, a dvaerg took the bounty back to the rocky ridge.

With a load of fresh meat that overloaded the donkeys, we moved closer to the Dreki Mountains and crossed to the next ridge. Maneuvering through and over the rocks and trees near the steep slopes took twice as long to traverse than if we'd crossed the valley. But we didn't need to burn torches. Out here, wood was a premium commodity.

When we reached the craggy foothills on the other side of the valley, relief flooded through me and, I suspected, everyone else. We set up camp and started a fire.

"Could've done without dancing with wyrms," Ingefær grumbled.

Serafina asked, "How can such big things move under the ground...and so fast?"

Mick hiccupped.

Tugg said, "We be standing on rocky ground. The valleys be fertile soil. Ye can't tell by looking at the near-dead grass. But beneath it be some of the richest soil in the Realm. It be well aerated. It be the lack of warmth and steady rains in the summer preventing anything from growing too big. The deep freeze in winter kills off anything that be pretty."

The last part, Tugg said while he gazed into Serafina's green eyes. And the timbre of his voice had shifted.

Mick cleared his throat. "Why are you looking at her like that?"

Tugg smiled. "She be attractive." Without waiting to see the effect of his words, he turned around and ordered his dvaerg companions to pass out spits.

On the spits, we all skewered hunks of lindwyrm meat. "Their outer hull be as hard as a rock. But the insides...hmm." He rubbed his belly for effect.

"What we don't cook, we can cure and salt," I said.

Tugg said, "No point in salting. The spice melts the meat. We eat what we have at every meal. In four or five days, what be left be thrown out."

Serafina walked to my side. She lowered her voice. "Ugh. Nasty looking, and Tugg wants us to eat it."

Mick warmed his hands against the fire, standing on my other side. "I think a couple of radishes would have enhanced the flavor."

"The gods!" Serafina said, a grin spreading across her face.

I chuckled.

Mick frowned. "But Miss Ingefær took the ones I'd stashed in my rucksack."

With the spits leaning against rock, we left the meat to cook and gathered in a circle to mourn the dead d'oglemenn. Hombir offered words of sorrow. With no bodies to bury and a desire to be far from this place, the ritual didn't take long.

The wyrm feast wasn't a joyful one, but the strips of meat were tasty: juicy, with a hint of garlic and sage. Not at all stringy, nor chewy, like I had expected.

I teased Serafina until she tried a bite. "Oh! That's like akkar from the ocean."

I asked, so she described an underwater boneless lump of pinkish-tan flesh with six tentacles. Most weighed around three hundred pounds. She asked for a second strip of wyrm. Tugg had a convert on his hands.

After eating an excellent lunch, I snuffed the fire out.

A couple of hours past high noon, we rode atop a plateau. The clop of horse hooves told me we were traversing a rock bed.

Without the fear of lindwyrms, tonight we would sleep soundly.

I hoped.

Chapter Six

A WÆRG

INGEFÆR

Approaching the evening of the seventh day since heading out from Kral Bar Aggen—about a day out from Nikkel Bakken—we made camp near a mountain spur covered thick in pines and spruces. Clouds appeared to the north, and the wind took on a shrillness it hadn't reached before on this trip. With it came a damp cold.

As we pitched tents, Tugg opined it would snow in a day or two. "Expect a hard frost tonight or tomorrow." He grumbled some more. "Be good if we had more firewood. We used up more than we should have to eat the wyrm."

I noticed he had set his tent up next to Serafina's and Mick's. After he left to talk to a clanmate, I waggled my brows at the healer. Speaking low, I asked if she was alright with the extra attention Tugg was showing her.

Her grin was slow in coming, but it grew wide. She nodded.

We had a fledgling romance.

With the tents set, and with the sun still shining, I corralled Mick, Serafina, and Rory, and we worked in pairs as we ranged up the hillside and into the forest for firewood.

Before we had our first armload, Serafina called out. "Over here!"

Dragging a stunted dead tree behind me, I made my way over. "What's the problem?"

She pointed with her mace.

What lay five strides from her feet was a wærg—once formidable, but now lifeless and torn to shreds. Its gray fur was matted with black blood, and maggots crawled all over the body. The stink of the rotten flesh took my breath away.

Rory showed up on the other side, with Mick in tow. "Wærgs bleed red, so the black means it's been dead for more than a day. There're a lot of maggots. I think it's been dead four or five days, maybe more."

He scanned the skies. "Tree cover is thick above. That explains why no scavenger has had itself a meal."

That, and there weren't many birds on the north side of the Dreki Mountains. Perhaps in the summer months, a few species made the trip. But this close to winter, they'd already headed south. In a day or two, the maggots would freeze over and take up where they left off with the spring thaw.

Rory broke off a branch from a log he had dragged over and poked at the fur.

"Careful," Mick said.

Rory replied. "That's my middle name."

I stifled a chuckle. He had no middle name, and if he did, it would be 'stumble-tongue,' or 'leaps-before-looking,' or some other such epithet. I toed the dead beast while looking at Rory. "You want help to roll it over?"

"Oh, gross," Serafina said. "Why?"

"To see if there are more wounds on the other side," I replied.

Serafina gave me a full body shiver and made a face while pointing at the maggots.

"Whatever did this is not something I want to meet," Rory said, scanning the surroundings.

Mick let out a yowl as he spun about, his head jerking left and right.

I said, "If you make too much noise, you'll attract what killed the wærg."

That shut him up.

I joined Rory at the backside of the wærg. The thing weighed more than me and half of Rory combined. When alive, it stood half the height of a horse. In a pack, they were deadly, taking down humans and horses unless outnumbered. And their packs usually had at least eight. More often than not, I thought of myself as wærg food.

Rory said, "You know, where there's one wærg, there're more."

Mick whimpered.

Serafina patted him on the shoulder. "That's not what worries me."

Mick and I looked at her.

She offered a thin-lipped smile. "What if there's more of what killed this one?"

Mick crowed like a rooster.

Rory hauled off and slapped him...none too gently. "Ingefær told you to be quiet."

Mick had the dungeon of Jarl Retzlaff for expedition experience. It had taken a while, but he'd learned to keep his outbursts to himself. Most of the time. Being in a new environment, at least for him, I understood why he struggled to stay in control.

That said, Rory was right. Too loud of a noise out here was asking for a mighty big heap of trouble.

Rory pointed at the two of them. "Keep watch."

I told Serafina, "Get your befriend spell ready. Out here, you never know."

What luck she would have in friending a wærg, I didn't know. But the four of us would be hard pressed to kill more than one without extra help.

Rory and I heaved and rolled the wærg over. The wounds on the first side had done damage. But what killed it was a massive wound running from its front shoulder to its rear haunch. By the odd position of the foreleg, the strike had broken it and took a good chunk of flesh and fur, cracking ribs along the way.

A nasty stench struck my nose. I gagged. There were thrice as many maggots at the underside wound as the topside one...now reversed.

Rory pointed with his boot. "If you're ever starving, those maggots will save your life."

Serafina fell to her knees and puked. That caused a burp to sneak up my throat, bitter bile flavoring my tongue.

I exchanged looks with my husband, my eyes shifting left, then right. *Do we want to search for more wærgs?*

Rory's lips twitched. He nodded.

I said, "Mick, you take Serafina and the wood back to camp. Rory and I will scout some more. Tell everyone to monitor this ridge."

It may have been foolish to send them off. But I had sorcerous powers, and Rory could run like the wind. Besides, we each had a vial of healing. The two of us could fend off a wærg or two and fight a retreating battle. But with Mick and Serafina to fret about, our ability to protect them would be stretched. I hoped not beyond the breaking point.

After they left, we explored around. "I don't see any tracks of what killed it. There's the trail of blood left by the wærg as it dragged itself here."

"Aye." Rory followed the crimson trail leading away from the slain creature up and over the ridge. "It crawled away to die."

"How come whatever killed it didn't come for the spoils?"

Rory shrugged. "Don't know. Maybe the beast got distracted or had something else on its mind."

I found that unhelpful and swallowed the remnants of bile. "Shall we?" I wagged my head in the direction of where the wærg had come from.

Adventures come at odd times. Searching for the cause of death of a wærg wasn't what I had signed up for. But there was a puzzle to solve, and I needed to know what killed it. *Needed* might be too strong of a word. But *desperately wanted* was a close second. By searching, I hoped to find a clue about the beast's nature. Something that would give us an edge. I feared we would run into our mysterious monster. But I tucked that emotion away. We had a job to do.

"Hope whatever did this isn't looking to add 'human' to its menu," Rory said. "Cause I'm tough and stringy and would make a terrible roast."

I shook my head. The situation was all wrong for jokes. But then, I couldn't resist. "I agree with you. You are an acquired taste."

"Ah, but you, my dear, are a feast for the eyes."

The corner of my mouth twitched up despite the gravity of our situation. "How sure are you it's been dead for several days?"

"Positive," he said.

It hadn't snowed or rained since the start of our trip, so it seemed plausible. I scanned south to a spot where I thought our camp might be. But the tracks went west, cleaving through the dry pine needles as it disappeared into the forest.

"Are you sure we're tracking the wærg?"

"What else?" Rory replied.

"Well, perhaps that way leads us to the sanctuary for something that shuns the day's embrace and cloaks itself within night's fell grasp."

"You could have said the 'monster's hideout,' without all that flowery jibber-jabber." Rory grabbed the hilt of his sword and drew his blade. "But no, I'm not sure. So, stay sharp."

He crept forward, and I followed. It's a funny thing. He was the fastest of us. Not even close. But I knew he wouldn't run off and leave me. Like I would never leave him. That's the thing about loyalty; it cuts both ways. We either lived together or we died together.

I took a deep breath to cleanse the dark thoughts out of my mind. The sun had said its farewell as we scampered up the slope, leaving a sliver of a moon to light the way.

The deep shadows cast by the pines hid the blackened trail of blood from time to time. The air grew colder, if that was possible, biting my skin with its invisible fangs. I strained to hear any sound beyond my own movements: a scuffle, a breath, even the faintest whisper of fur against a branch or a footpad on rock.

"Watch where you put your boots," Rory warned, his eyes flicking down.

My gaze followed his to ensure my feet weren't about to stumble upon anything loose or crunchy. Sound carried at night farther than by day. A skittering stone would reveal our presence...if anything was out there. Like the rest of the pack. Or what had killed the wærg.

I said, "A misstep here could be rather consequential."

"Nothing like a bit of understatement to keep spirits high." Rory offered a half-smile and pointed. "This way."

I said, "That wærg was killed by something much, much bigger. That massive claw swipe was three of my hands in width. The maggots were arranged in three deep furrows, each at least two inches deep."

Rory nodded, sidestepping a spruce. "That means the talons on this beast are at least that long. Probably twice that." He stopped to hold up a flat hand next to his face. "Now imagine a skull thrice, nay, four times, as big as my head. Not just in height, but also in width."

"Lokke's spawn. What could be so big?"

"Kjottspisers might vie for the size, but their claws aren't that wide. Besides, they would track the wærg to finish it, and for sure eat its or their fill. And, I think, a pack of wærgs would kill a kjottspiser, who hunts alone."

I shuddered. It would be a bloody battle. Wærgs would sacrifice themselves to give their pack mates an opening. Had the pack gotten our mystery monster and lost a mate in the process?

On Thunder, my gelding—who I missed more and more each day—I once outraced a kjottspiser, a twelve-foot-long beast with a three-foot elongated maw. Kjottspisers had a black fur coat and lived in higher, more desolate places. Like this place. Except they didn't like it too cold, and stayed to the south side of the Dreki Mountains.

Rory walked over the spine of the ridge we'd been hiking up.

"Hey," I said, "what are the odds that we'll run into the rest of the wærg pack?" Maybe we should have had Serafina stick around.

Rory shook his head. "If my suspicions are correct, there're more dead wærgs."

I blinked at that. Holy horrors. Could one of the mysterious monsters kill an entire wærg pack? "And if you're wrong?"

Rory chuckled. "I'm not. I'm a hunter and know a few things."

He could be so insufferable.

"Go on."

Rory flashed me a grin and a wink. "Wærgs eat their dead. The fact there's an uneaten body doesn't bode well for the pack."

"They wouldn't run off if outmatched?"

"For a while," Rory replied. "But they would come back."

I had thought the wærg had been out hunting with its pack when it got caught. *Ah.* That's why he was eager to come searching with me.

I stopped him by tugging his arm sleeve. "Are we unnecessarily risking our lives?"

"You're a mage, and I can outrun a beast." A full-on smile, his brown eyes sparkling. "Don't worry. I won't let it eat you."

"I will save my last breath and spell to crisp your cute tush."

Rory teased me. He wouldn't endanger our lives so cavalierly. He was certain the wærgs were dead. But what made him certain whatever killed them had left the area?

I asked.

"Yeah, it's gone. Otherwise, the maggot infested wærg wouldn't have been left behind."

I sighed in relief.

Focusing on the purpose of why we were here, I went over what we knew. So far, all we had was Hombir's odd clues of stripped-clean bones and dead d'oglemenn in their dens. We needed more information.

"Are you sure we can best whatever killed this wærg?"

Rory's nose scrunched. "You and I are the best suited for it. Brawn and speed for me and smarts and magic from you. Hombir is a close second, if Tugg is at his side." He took a breath. "We need more clues."

I cleared my throat as I fondled a fresh pinch of sawdust from inside a pouch of my mage belt. "I'm ready. Fireball first, then ask questions."

Any sorcery flying about the ridge would warn the others down the hill of our distress. They would, in all likelihood, be too slow in coming. But we had a clue in the deep claw wound, and it made sense to find another.

Rory continued on, now angling down the hillside, scrambling over a series of decaying logs. "This way." He pointed with his sword as a vale appeared through the thinning trees and foliage-less brush, lit by dim moonlight.

The yellow grass-covered clearing was shaped in an oblong bowl, widening as it moved away from the rocky hillside that shot up at ridiculous angles. Rory stopped and pointed.

I gazed past the tip of his sword. A small, dark shape broke up the outline of more rocks and boulders.

We walked toward it, side by side, my head swinging around, checking our rear.

Once close enough to the dark shape, it resolved into a hole. It was a cave. Some two feet high and three feet wide.

"I suppose you want to go in?" I asked.

He grinned like a kjottspiser.

My hands went to my hips. "I doubt there are any clues in there."

"You don't know that," Rory said. "The opening is small enough that I can guarantee the beast isn't inside. So, it won't hurt to look. If there were any wærgs left alive, we wouldn't have made it this far without being challenged."

Chapter Seven

DEATH IN A CAVE

RORY

The stench wafting out of the cave hit me hard as I kneeled at the entrance; a pungent mixture of blood, guts, and decay clawed at my nostrils. I pulled the hood from my head and stretched it around and over my mouth and nose. But it did little to ward off the odor. Peering in, the cave's mouth swallowed the dim moonlight like a svartkatt gulped its kill.

"Lokke's spawn," I muttered under my breath. "It smells like a troll's armpit."

Ingefær grimaced and scraped her tongue over her teeth. "You're right. There are dead wærgs inside. More than one. And their deaths in such close confines have amplified the assault on my nostrils."

"Or, in plain speech, it reeks something fierce and I can taste it." I flashed a grin, though my brows had furrowed. Something had indeed killed the wærgs. That something would make a quick goulash out of us. Though I was certain it wasn't in the cavern.

I chinned at Ingefær. "Keep a watch out and holler if something comes. Don't worry about me." I locked my eyes on hers. "I repeat: we would never have got this close without a challenge if a wærg remained alive."

She reached up and touched her snowflake pendant. "Be careful."

"I love you, too."

We looked at each other. I had the better view.

After a moment, Ingefær said, "What?"

"We don't have torches, and I need a light."

She half-sighed, half-growled. "Mick has the light stick." She huffed. "I'll cast the incantation, but all I can do with it is hold my hand to the opening. I haven't figured out a way to attach the spell to an object."

Back home, Ingefær studied and worked hard. In addition to the light spell, she and Serafina had worked on making potions of healing. So far, they'd made bitters, suitable for poisoning pigs. Ingefær had also been trying to divine the keyword for the magical ring with the 'R' emblazoned on the ruby stone. That vexed her more than the failed potions.

Ingefær cast her light spell, and I poked my sword into the hole. I then dragged it left and right, metal scraping on stone.

No resistance. No sound warning me off.

Promising. I poked my head into the hole. The opening was narrow, big enough for a wærg, some two feet high and three feet wide. The entry tunnel kept the dimension, but turned to my left.

I crawled on my hands and knees, grimacing at the small stones jabbing into my flesh.

After another half-turn of the tunnel, the pungent aroma of decay wrapped around my head like a wet blanket. I gagged, trying not to breathe. Then I willed myself to keep my dinner to stay put.

Blech. Blurch. Aggh.

I lost the battle, and gnarled chunks of lindwyrm floated up into my mouth, along with some stomach fluid. I wiped my mouth with an arm sleeve.

"You alright in there?"

"Yah. Just decided to lose some weight is all."

By the dim cast of Ingefær's light, I shuffled past my puke into a wider and taller shaft. Reaching up, I confirmed the rock confines hadn't grown enough to permit me to stand. A couple of knee-hand shuffles later, I found a dead wærg. It, too, was covered in maggots. The powerful stench couldn't come from just one body. I suspected I would find more.

I checked the wærg for injuries under a murky light. The body was that of a female, and her gut was covered with teats. The underside of her belly had bits of her entrails peeking out. That added to the stink.

I shouted out of the hole, my voice reverberating. "Another dead wærg. Maggot covered, like the first one."

Five strides later—thirty knee-jabbing shuffles—the tunnel turned again. This time, it opened into something six humans could lie down in. They just couldn't stand without bending their heads.

Another body lay before me. Shadows flickered, revealing little in the darkness. There had been too many turns for Ingefær's spell to be of help this deep.

I shoved the wærg to the side using my shoulder. That maneuver caused maggots to jigger loose and onto my head and neck.

I growled as I brushed at my ears and my kinky black hair.

A sound! From in front of me.

What the Hel is that?

I kneeled there, listening. There it was again. Real soft, real faint.

A whimper.

No way!

I crawled a couple of strides, my gaze sweeping the dark shadows. It was too damn dark, so I searched with my free hand. By touch, before me lay a bed of straw. I reached in.

A cold body, no bigger than my hand. Then another. Then a third.

The softest whine.

I pushed more lifeless whelps aside and reached in.

My fingers brushed against the softest fur in the Realm. It was warm.

And it let out a contented groan at my touch.

The gods!

How does a pup survive for nigh on a week without food and water?

"You're a tough one."

For a moment, I considered. Do I leave the whelp here? Yeah, no. That wasn't me.

I got into position and scooped the whelp into my hand. Then I edged around until I faced the way I had come in.

"I'm coming out."

I sheathed my sword real slow. No point in gashing my leg...or more important bits.

I crawled out, but not before planting a knee in my own vomit. Outside, I extended myself to full height and stretched my back as I held aloft my prize.

"What in gods is that?" Ingefær demanded.

"A pup. It's alive." I smiled. Big.

"I can see that." Ingefær doused her magic light. "What are you doing with it?"

The whelp whined.

"Shh, it's alright," I said. "No monster is going to get you. Not while I'm around."

Ingefær stared, maybe glared, at me. There was a long silence between us. I corralled the pup to my chest, giving it some of my body heat.

"No way are you keeping it."

I lowered my gaze at her. "Them's fighting words. No way am I leaving it to die a horrible death."

Ingefær rolled her eyes. I think she mouthed 'men,' but I wasn't sure as she spun on a heel. "You ready to go?"

I looked down at my prize. The pup's eyes were closed. Whether from the light of the moon, something it wasn't used to, or because it was near death, I didn't know.

"Yeah. I need to get it some water or milk." I took off at a fast pace. My eyes roved the countryside as I went over my brash decision. I spoke in whispers, using what I thought was a soothing tone. "I'm a hunter by training, so I hate to see the young mistreated so. Not that it's your parents' fault."

Before us lay a trail that meandered through the thick pines as it wound its way over the ridge. A quarter of a mile into the forest we had ambled through earlier, but from another direction, we crossed the dead bodies of four more wærgs. That made seven adults in total. These had been stripped of their fur and meat. Just bones and four skulls.

"Shit." I feared wærgs, and if one attacked me, I'd do my best to kill it. But I hated to see them so...so defiled.

Ingefær said, "You were right—the pack has been wiped out."

I gnawed on a lip. "Why eat these, but not the one on the trail along the base of the mountain?"

"Something must have interrupted it. Or them." Ingefær shuddered. "Wærgs scare me. One could take out two or three unwary travelers. An entire pack would doom a party of ten."

I nodded.

She spun about with her hands outstretched. "We're stuck with *one* clue as to the beast's nature. It—or they—took out a pack of wærgs. We know it has a big-ass claw. But that's it."

She rarely swore. Ingefær must be agitated. Maybe more minds could fathom something out of it, but I had my doubts. "Come on. We've been gone too long."

For a part of our return journey, we trekked beside a brook, its waters burbling. Once we reached the undulating valley, I turned right, toward where our camp should be, while the brook went left.

I stroked the pup in my arms. "Its brothers and sisters, five of them, died of hunger and thirst. This one is the biggest, a male. He's tough, Ingefær. He held out on his own for at least five days, maybe a week."

Tears welled in my eyes. "Maybe I'm in denial, but something about that whine of his...and then when I poked him, he sighed in satisfaction. It broke my heart, Ingefær."

She squeezed my hand. "I know. You love animals. I get it. But what are you going to do with it when it grows up?"

"That's thinking too far ahead. Right now, I'm going to nurse it back to health."

I spoke true; I didn't know what I would do later. There were considerations, like controlling a beast whose nature said humans were good eating. But for now, my heart wept at the pup's predicament.

Back at camp, we got yelled at for worrying the group.

Tugg put his hands on his hips. "Ye two have been gone for quite some time."

Hombir shook his head. "And you didn't bring back any firewood."

Serafina and Mick smiled sheepishly. The half-alvae shrugged. "We heard a noise and ran for it."

"Sorry," Ingefær said. "We got distracted."

I showed off my prize, beaming like a proud father. "Look what I found."

We sat around the fire while several d'oglemenn were sent out to retrieve firewood. Me and Ingefær told our tale. Which begged the question: what had killed the wærgs?

Hombir snuffled his snout. "The same beast or beasties that wiped out Nikkel Bakken."

"And our trade wagons," Tugg threw in.

"Aye," I said. "We have a new clue."

Ingefær said, "Your description of the dead bones of the d'oglemenn pointed at some sort of beast. But then the description of your clanmates killed inside their burrows threw us off. How did they die?"

I fussed with my newfound treasure, dribbling water into its eager mouth. "We still don't know that. But we know that they have a foot-wide hand—well, a claw—with maybe four-inch talons. At least three, but I'm guessing four." I caught Tugg's gaze. "Do you have any milk?"

Tugg scowled. "No. But I have cheese."

"Great. I'll take it."

Serafina said, "I can heal it, if you want?"

I stroked the mottled-white fur of my prize. "Yes. Thank you. I don't think anything is wrong with him, other than he needs food and water."

"Then I'll do a stamina restoration spell, like I do with Ingefær when she's tired from spellcasting."

After the whelp had been healed and while I fed it chunks of cheese, finely crumbled for its teeth had yet to come in, we discussed our next steps.

Hombir said, "I don't think it changes our direction. We go on to the enclave."

Ingefær nodded. "I agree."

Tugg eyed the half-alvae and stroked his beard. "Aye."

Serafina flashed a smile at Tugg. "Yes. I'd like to get someplace warm."

D'oglemann dens were warm when the fires were lit. They weren't all that big, though.

Mick tugged at his tawny hair. "Well, I can't go back on my own. So, I guess I will go with you."

Ingefær said, "All the dead wærgs beg a question. They marauded the d'oglemann village over two weeks ago. But the deaths here are at most a week old."

Hombir's snout jerked left, then right. "We didn't run into anything foul besides lindwyrms."

I shifted back to feeding the whelp water. "There are no tracks in the grass that I could see. A week is a long time, especially if there's no rain or snow to memorialize the beast's passing. Either *it* or *they* went up into the mountains, or they moved off to the east."

Jonuku scowled. "You think they're ahead of us."

"Good odds." I shrugged. "It, or they, may have gone north onto the Ice Plains. But my gut says no."

Ingefær asked, "Did you make a *Bal Bronne* when you were out here, Hombir?"

D'oglemenn used a *Bal Bronne* as a celebratory fire. It was huge and only built on special occasions.

Hombir's snout dipped. "Aye. A commemoration of life for the dead. And also as a beacon, in case there were any survivors. We left the next day."

I said nothing, but it was possible the *Bal Bronne* had been seen...and the mystery monster came back to investigate. "Whatever it is, it's east of us. I'm guessing a week. Though they may be waiting for us in Nikkel Bakken."

The d'oglemenn Hombir had sent out returned. Their haul of firewood wasn't great. Then again, it was dark, and there had been brutish beasties about. I suspected they had stayed within sight of the moonlit camp.

Tugg scowled at the meager haul. "We head out in the morning...after we gather more firewood."

CHAPTER EIGHT

NIKKEL BAKKEN

RORY

Three hours past the noon meal of the following day, Mick, Serafina, Ingefær, and I rode out front, spread out in a line thirty paces across. My mare's hooves crunched on dead grass as we came up on Two Hunchback Pass.

This place, and Nikkel Bakken, scarred me two years ago. Last time I was here, I killed dozens of alvae soldiers. I had a good reason: they were trying to kill the d'oglemenn of Nikkel Bakken. I learned later the alvaes had been magicked with a vile potion, one that made them see the blood of d'oglemenn as essential to their survival.

What bothered me most about that day was I had enjoyed spilling alvae blood. That had been Laehvateinn's doing, the vile spirit that somehow lived in my sword, then in me. But the truth of it was, I had given her control over my mind and body. And my bloodlust had led to the death of my friend, Daran.

As I glanced up the trail, a part of me hungered for Laehva's knowledge and skill and the aura of power that came with her.

Ingefær touched my arm. I hadn't heard her approach. She smiled wanly, her blue eyes searching mine.

I sat straighter in the saddle. "I'm alright."

"The promise of something better is a lie."

Her gaze dared me to argue. I flashed a smile. "I know." And I did. Though I couldn't say my hand didn't itch to hold that magic blade.

She nodded to the east. "Keep your eyes open for any signs of our mysterious beast."

I pointed at Serafina. "It's why I volunteered us to ride in front. Her eyes are our best chance of spotting the enemy before they see us."

An hour later, the quartet of Injustices Righted rode over the last ridge and looked upon the enclave of Nikkel Bakken. We had seen no sign of any other creature. How could something so big not leave a footprint?

The enclave was as I remembered it. A league-wide bowl between two ridges. Three enormous caves were to the south, on my right. A hundred holes in the ground, d'oglemenn dens, each had a stone totem next to them, though some had been knocked over.

I sniffed the air. Clean. Maybe a hint of dead grass. My nostrils froze, for the moisture in the air had ticked up ever since we found the wærgs. I looked at the sky. Clouds, thick and as black as iron, hung over our heads. It would snow today.

This place had never been charming, even when it was full of live bodies. Now it was decidedly worse, as an ominous foreboding welled out of the empty burrows.

Hombir stepped beside my steed. "We buried the bones and the bodies in one mass grave." He pointed. "Past the eastern cave."

I spotted the mound of earth. "You still using the center cave as a meeting site?"

"Yes." He looked over his shoulder and wagged his head at someone. "Makes sense for everyone to gather inside. There's firewood and coal ready for use. Or was when we left."

I rubbed my chilled shoulders. "A fire sounds grand."

Ingefær said, "I'm so sorry for your loss, Hombir."

Jonuku joined her husband, her gaze fixed on the dens. "This place troubles me."

She was being kind.

"Chin up, dear," Hombir said. "There's work to be done. This enclave must be restarted."

"Sometimes I wish you didn't care so much."

Trouble in the Tramanek household?

I sympathized with Jonuku. Repopulating the enclave was Vidarr's doing. He was a persistent cuss. Possibly the lone one more hardheaded person in the Realm than my wife...and me. I grunted. He was, too often, right. Right about direction and strategy, tactics, and even righteousness.

Mick broke the tense silence. "Cheerful place. Looks like the kind of spot where hope goes to freeze to death."

I cleared my throat.

Ingefær said, "Must you?"

"What?" Mick raised his arms in question.

Serafina said, "Oh, go eat a radish."

Tugg and his crew, along with the donkeys, stopped atop the ridge. "I have never been this far east."

Hombir pointed. "To the central cave. We'll make our home there until your caravan arrives." He stepped down the slope. "It will give us time to re-inspect the dens and see if there is a clue we missed."

We tied off our mounts near the opening. Once inside the giant cavern, d'oglemenn sprung into action, starting two fires and showing me and my crew our spots, where we laid our gear.

Mick turned around in a circle. "The gods! I need a raise."

Serafina said, "Cold, desolate, and now dark. I'm inside a cave...again. You two rub elbows with the strangest of beings."

I grinned at her. Her eyes followed Tugg more and more each day. But I said, "I don't know. Having been imprisoned by an alvae, falsely I must add, and having spent a dozen nights under tons of rock, and too many moons on the Ice Plains...well, in the latter, you just might be right."

Ingefær pointed at the cavern opening. "It's snowing."

"Great. Just great." Serafina stole my line.

I pulled the wærg pup out of my coat pocket, still wrapped in my undershirt, and fetched the last of the group's cheese. "I'm going to need something else to feed him. Ow!" I jerked my hand free, shaking it. "Bastard bit me."

"He getting his teeth?" Ingefær asked.

I raised my finger high; no blood dribbled down it. "Uh, not yet. He's got a powerful jaw, is all."

"And just think," my wife teased, "soon he'll have big teeth, too."

"Wærgs are smart. I'll teach him not to bite me."

Mick said, "Oi! What about the rest of us?"

I smiled but didn't say anything.

Ingefær punched my shoulder. "He'll make sure the whelp doesn't harm anyone...or I'll take matters into my own hands."

I rubbed my sore shoulder. That woman knew how to throw a punch. Ignoring her, I chinned at Hombir. "What's Varanusian for survivor?"

"O'erlevendeh," he replied.

"That's his name." I stroked his mottled gray cheeks. "O'erlevendeh, you're a mighty tough son of a bitch."

"Rory!" Ingefær raised her voice.

"What? He's born of a female wærg, which is a bitch. He's her son."

The others chuckled, but Ingefær's lips turned taut and thin.

I shrugged. She would not win the fight...not this time. Not when it was the truth. O'erlevendeh had survived up to a week without nursing. I'd never heard of something like that happening.

I asked, "Does anybody have any food? For the pup? The lindwyrm is too chewy for him."

Serafina said, "There may be some leftover stores here."

"Ooh, moldy cheese." Mick made a face. "I wish I had my radishes."

"The gods, no." I grimaced at the thought. O'erlevendeh's teeth wouldn't come in by tomorrow, when we would have to throw the wyrm meat away. It might be another week or two before the pup could chew on anything that we had, like pemmican. Milk was the best option. But we didn't have any.

I ended up feeding O'erlevendeh pieces of bread, softened in water.

At dinner time, we gathered around one fire, deep in the center cavern. The snow kept coming, though we were a day shy of a moon away from Gods' Day. There was a chance we could get off the gods' forsaken Ice Plains before the worst of winter hit. But my gut said it was a fool's hope.

Chapter Nine

A CONCLAVE

INGEFÆR

Folks finished eating the last of the lindwyrm, washed down by mugs of hot tea. Rory fussed with his new pet, letting the thing gum his fingers. I smiled whenever my husband yelped.

Hombir cleared his throat. "Thank you for coming out here." His gaze stopped on me and he held my eyes. "I worry two mages aren't enough for what lies ahead. We may need Vidarr and the Rod of the Dreki to rid us of whatever is befouling these plains."

Vidarr was sorely missed. With the Rod, he could blast the entire enclave into ant-sized chunks. I nodded, acknowledging the need. "There is the matter of my signet ring. The one with the gold 'R.'" I thought about digging for it, but now wasn't the right time. "It is said to grant the wearer additional stamina...I want to say unlimited, but I don't know if it's true."

"What's the problem?" Hombir asked.

I whirled the snowflake-shaped pearl around my neck. "The command word to activate its powers has eluded me."

"I might find some time to scry while we're waiting," Hombir said.

Grimacing, I nodded.

Rory picked his head up. "Are the dens cleaned out?"

Hombir nodded. “Yes. Equipment, blankets, and tools are stored here.”

“But no food stock? Like cheese or something soft for the whelp?”

A shake of his head. “All the perishables we found were brought back with us to Kral Bar Aggen. Everything else was burned in the *Bal Bronne.*”

Rory scowled as he stroked the pup lying in his lap. The baby wærg must have tired. My husband’s lips moved, murmuring to his new love interest. A pang of jealousy strummed through me. But I pushed it away. This was a phase.

Diverting my thoughts, I surveyed our group. Hombir had turned to speak with Jonuku, while seven of the d’oglemenn warriors stared into the fire, not speaking to one another. A pair stood outside on watch.

Tugg’s dvaergs sat farther away, their faces hidden in shadow. Tugg sat beside Serafina, their heads close. The half-alvae giggled ever so softly.

I turned to Hombir. “Why don’t you go over what you found here...one more time.”

“Because we love to hear tales of woe,” Mick said.

“Hush!” Rory said, his voice firm. “It’s a good idea to remind everyone of what’s at stake.”

“There were fifty couples living here,” Hombir said. “Fourteen individuals are missing based on my counting of skulls and bodies. We found the bones of thirty, presumably the warrior males, near the ridge east of here. And the dvaerg caravan a half day east of that.”

Serafina sighed. “And I thought we’d be safer once we got past this place.”

“Ain’t no sunshine to be found,” Mick said. “We’ll freeze our asses off.”

I put a finger to my lips. The turd rolled his eyes at me. Rory would have a few choice words with him later. If he ever stopped cooing at that pup.

Hombir sniffed and wiped his snout with a taloned hand. "Fifty-six bodies were found inside their burrows. Everyone was dead. Their bodies limp. I couldn't tell how they died."

"No visible wounds?" I asked, though I knew the answer.

Hombir shook his head. "Their bones weren't broken, nor were they torn apart like the others."

I spotted the look on Rory's face. "What's troubling you?"

"Whatever attacked the wærgs didn't go inside their den. It, or they, fought with their massive claws against the wærg's tooth-filled maws. Here, the d'oglemenn were broken—crushed perhaps, before they were eaten—outside the burrow. And here, the beast or beasts also killed the ones that hid in their dens."

Hombir narrowed his bony brows. "Say that again?"

I explained. "Rory found several grown wærgs inside their den. Their wounds were fatal. But because the pups were untouched, we suspect the wærgs had gone out of the cave to fight, and then crawled inside when they were dying. Here, the d'oglemenn knew better and hoped to survive by hiding. But it did no good."

Rory nodded. "The attacker is too big to fit inside the dens."

Jonuku's voice pitched high. "But they killed them anyway."

I bowed my head. "I know. The one clue Hombir mentioned earlier was that a few of them had wet clothes, and there was a den or two with puddles of water. Is that right?"

Hombir nodded.

I said, "There's something we're missing. Something we don't yet know about these beasts."

Jonuku burst into tears.

Hombir stroked his wife's backside.

Mick screeched. "The gods! I don't know why I signed up with you all."

I eyed him. "Make yourself useful. Get some firewood."

Rory stared Mick down. "Get a grip, young man. Believe it or not, once we answer these questions, the task before us will get easier, for then we can plan on how to deal with...whatever is killing out here."

In response, Mick pulled out a tablet and stylus. He mumbled, "Book of grudges."

Rory chuckled. "I thought I was already listed."

Mick's nose twitched. "Well, you're moving up."

The pair of d'oglemenn came inside to end their shift on watch. Hombir spoke to them in their Varanusian. Words I understood, unless they spoke too fast.

Hombir sent out two other warriors and turned to the rest of us. "The snow is steady now, about an inch an hour."

Tugg disengaged from Serafina. "The air tastes mighty damp to me. We might have a foot by morning."

Rory scratched at the pup's belly. It sighed, its eyes closed.

Tugg said, "It be a tough road to Kral Azza Rid now."

I swept my gaze beyond the fire. "There's more at stake than just wagons and goods."

Tugg grunted, his shoulder leaning into Serafina's.

Rory stood and paced with the pup cradled in the crook of his arm. "Let's take this one step at a time. Hombir, you told us about seven attacks. Are we certain there aren't any more?"

"Certain?" Hombir said. "No. But no one else has claimed any missing wagons."

"Alright." I took Rory's cue. "Give us the rundown of each caravan to be attacked. Take it one keep at a time, but start with the first known attack."

Tugg pulled away from the half-alvae. "The first be a caravan from Kral Fal Is, which reached Hombir's clan at Kobber Unter Smuss in the thirteenth month of last year. It then went on to me keep, stayed over

Gods' Day, then made for Kral Azza Rid, leaving in the first moon of this year. But it never made it."

Each year comprised thirteen months of twenty-eight days, with Gods' Day coming right after Winter Solstice. The Realm's year consisted of three hundred sixty-five days.

The thing about Gods' Day was that the plane of Asagard and the material plane of the Realm meshed. Sort of. One couldn't go over to the other, but sometimes, one could see and hear. And before the gods were banished to their plane, a select few could spot one. It was deemed beneficial, marking maybe one out of ten viewers as special.

The other thing was that it messed with the weather. In most places, it created a fog. For a cold environment like here, it would raise the temperature; in a hot one, it would lower it.

I said, "So, somewhere between Kral Bar Aggen and Kral Azza Rid, the caravan met with calamity?"

Tugg said, "Aye."

I turned to Hombir. "Do you know if it made it past this enclave?"

Hombir looked at the cavern wall, his eyes narrowing. "I can't be certain, but I think so. I was here that moon, helping the others get settled. In fact, there was an All Watcher election that month, and scouts reported seeing dvaergs, but I don't recall wagons being mentioned."

"Alright," I said. "Say it happened east of here. Let's say it was destroyed between here and Kral Azza Rid." I chinned at Tugg. "When did the second wagon train from Kral Fal Is get wiped out?"

"That would be the sixth moon of this year," the dvaerg replied. "It left Kral Fal Is but never made it to Kobber Unter Smuss. Lindwyrms were blamed."

My eyes squinted at that. Five moons had passed, and more than half the Ice Plains had been traversed. The distance didn't trouble me, but the direction seemed odd. Maybe lindwyrms were to blame.

"Go through Kral Bar Aggen's destroyed convoys," Rory said.

Tugg said their first destroyed caravan had been sent in the fourth moon of this year. "It never made it to Kobber Unter Smuss."

"Go on," I said.

"The next one be four moons ago—well, five now—in the eighth moon of this year." Tugg heaved his muscular shoulders. "It too didn't make it to Hombir's enclave."

I scratched my head. Confusion seeped in. The marauders had traveled westward, but now they stayed in place?

Tugg went on. "The third wagon train was hit east of here. Almost three weeks ago now."

Hombir nodded. "Yes. As Rory said, I likely arrived the day after the attack. It took us a couple of days of gathering bodies and searching for kin. That's when we found what was left of the wagons. After the funeral pyre, I sent a bird to Vidarr, and we made for Kral Bar Aggen."

"The attack three weeks ago occurred in the twelfth month," Serafina said. "We're in the thirteenth as of yesterday."

Four weeks, less a day, until Winter Solstice. I shuddered, for I knew the depths of cold that came after Gods' Day.

Rory said, "The attacks came back east. I don't see the pattern. There are too many gaps."

I swung my gaze toward Hombir. "What about the two d'oglemann wagon outings?"

Hombir's long snout pinched. "The first occurred in the third moon of this year. We don't send caravans out until well after Spring Equinox. But the enclave needed additional supplies to get the mining going. I know it passed through Kral Bar Aggen, for they traded for more goods there, but it never arrived here."

He continued, "In the tenth month, we sent this year's winter supplies. It, too, arrived at Kral Barr Aggen, but never made it here. Which is why I came out to investigate. A moon too late."

My mind spun. I took each member into my gaze. "Any ideas? Anyone?"

Quiet filled the air.

I heard scratching and turned to Mick. "What are you writing?"

Mick's stylus hovered over his wax tablet. He cleared his throat. "I made a chart. All the attacks occurred east of the places where I marked an X." He held it up for me to see.

		Attacks	KFI	KUS	KBA	NB
KFI	Dvaerg	Moon 1 East of				X
KUS	D'oggle	Moon 3 East of			X	
KBA	Dvaerg	Moon 4 East of		X		
KFI	Dvaerg	Moon 6 East of	X			
KBA	Dvaerg	Moon 8 East of		X		
KUS	D'oggle	Moon 10 East of			X	
KBA	Dvaerg	Moon 12 East of				X

"Well, I'll be." I tousled his hair. "There's a pattern. They traveled west and then back again."

"What?" Rory said, coming over to us, the pup snuggling in his arm.

"Pass it around, please," I said.

When everyone had looked and gasped, I moved to stand beside Rory. "The attackers—I think we have to assume there's more than one—completed a loop in a little less than a year's time. They spent the harshness of winter traveling west from somewhere east of here to somewhere west of Kobber Unter Smuss."

Jonuku gasped.

Hombir shook his snout. "We never saw anything. Nor were we attacked."

Rory asked Mick to hold up the tablet for him. "They first attacked—I agree with Ingefær that there's more than one culprit—the first moon of the year. Maybe they came from the north."

"From Is Vann?" Hombir asked.

My gut recoiled at the idea. "No. At least I don't think so." I asked Tugg, "Isn't that Jotunn territory by agreement?"

Tugg's head waggled. "That be the dividing line. Can't say it belongs to anybody. A sort of demilitarized area."

"Great. Just Great."

I had to agree with Rory. If they came from beyond Is Vann.... "Are we dealing with the Jotunn?"

Rory said, "No. I mean, not directly. The beasts have massive claws. The Jotunn, giant hands."

A clanging sounded in my head. Jotunn ran around with ice grizzlies. "What if the wærgs were killed by the Jotunns' companions, the ice grizzlies?"

Sharp inhalations were drowned out by Mick's sudden rooster crow.

I shushed him.

Rory said, "I think a pack of wærgs would down at least one ice grizzly. We didn't see any bear bones."

I scratched at my chin. "How did the Jotunn, if it's them, kill the d'oglemenn hiding in their burrows?"

Tugg said, "Not the Jotunn, then. Some other beastie."

I said, "I won't go to Is Vann, or points north of there. Not when the heart of winter is coming."

Vidarr would have to come out here and deal with the Jotunn himself. Would the Rod of Dreki give him the edge he needed?

Rory paced. "Maybe they didn't come from the far north. Look at the grid. They're maybe a week north of this area, or east of here. That's not even close to Is Vann."

The unfrozen lake, or Is Vann, was a two-week trek due north of Kral Bar Aggen. We were a two-week hike from it as well. Three now, since the snow started flying. "I agree with Rory. But where did they come from?"

Rory blew out a gust of air. "You would think something so deadly would have been seen before. Large swaths of missing individuals would have sounded the alarm a long time ago. Where have they been all this time? Why have the attacks started this year?"

Mick screeched again.

This time, I joined him.

Chapter Ten

CLUELESS

RORY

When the hubbub inside the cavern died down, I said, "We're not traveling to Is Vann. Not without Vidarr and his Rod. Hombir and Ingefær could keep us warm with their spells, but then they'd be too exhausted to fight."

We had a handful of healing potions, but against Jotunn, it wouldn't matter. A boulder crashing into a group killed all on impact.

I swept the group as I cuddled O'erlevendeh tight. "We search around here. When Tugg's folks' caravan arrives, we have a decision to make. Do we join them on their way to Kral Azza Rid, or do we return to Kral Bar Aggen?"

Ingefær stood. "I agree with Rory. If it's the Jotunn and their grizzlies behind all this, then we need Vidarr."

Hombir said, "I'll send a bird to Tyrrby tomorrow morning. But right now, all you have is speculation."

Tugg scratched at his salt and pepper beard. "Aye. If I knew for certain the attackers be at Is Vann, I would muster me entire host of Avarkæsir. We'd give the beasties a good thumping. But as we don't yet know for sure, Premier Mina would override me orders." He stared into the fire, then nodded. "I say we go to Kral Azza Rid. Ye coming with us increases the odds of the wagonload making it to me kin."

Hombir's snout snuffled. Having seen the look before, I knew he was agitated.

"What's on your mind, Hombir?" I asked.

"We're getting ahead of ourselves. We need to search the area here. Again. And then we can decide in which direction to go."

Tugg nodded. "Aye. Sorry if me words implied otherwise. Of course we'll help ye here."

Mick raised a hand. "Do I get a vote?"

Ingefær and I spoke in unison. "No."

Mick made a face, and I was pretty sure he pretended to write in his book of grudges.

I moved to stand by him. "That was some mighty fine deducing you did with your tablet and stylus. We all had the same information, but until you laid it out, it was a jumbled mess."

Ingefær ruffled his hair. "And you thought you wouldn't be of much use."

Mick sat taller. "Thank you. It was a tangled web for me, too. That's why I wrote it down."

Serafina heaved her shoulders in a deep sigh. "Well, I can't say I like this place." She glanced out into the darkness. "Snow. I had never seen it before."

"And now?" Tugg asked.

"I'm sorry that I have." She smiled, dimples dotting her cheeks.

I teased her. "And what about dvaergs?"

She blushed as Tugg nudged her with a shoulder. "I was told they stink. But you know what? Dvaergs smell less than humans and alvaes. Almost as much as d'oglemenn."

"Switchgrass and cucumbers," I said. "Respectively."

Her green jaw dropped. "I knew the first. I've been trying to put a name to the second. But that's right."

Jonuku said, "You don't want to hear what we think you smell like."

I put up my free hand, the other holding my whelp. "No, we don't. Let's leave this on a pleasant note."

"Too late," Mick said.

Ingefær said, "We'll decide on direction, not Is Vann, when Tugg's folks arrive."

With that, the gathering broke up. We headed to our respective bedrolls and put in for the night. Tugg's dvaergs and Hombir's d'oglemenn rotated guard duty and fire watch.

In the morning, we woke to an inch less than a foot of snow. I spent my first hour feeding O'erlevendeh water-soaked bread and then giving him a bowl of water to drink.

What I was doing was the bare minimum to keep him alive. What he needed was milk, and in a week or two—when his teeth started to come in—raw meat. The former would be difficult out here on the Ice Plains. The latter could be achieved by hunting. I knew what I would do later today.

But first, Hombir organized den searches in teams of three. One dvaerg, one d'oglemann, and one human—with Serafina included in the last group. "Different perspectives to see if there is anything me and mine have missed."

I was paired up with Jonuku and a dvaerg by name of Nikk. Hombir assigned each of the four groups their share of burrows. Jonuku led us to our first den. I was surprised at the lack of stink, especially since d'oglemenn had died inside. But other than a musty staleness, it was no worse than an unused bedroom in my parents' home. It was as cold inside as it was out. Three weeks of no fires had seen to that.

The burrows were small, big enough for four grownups. I hunkered down, avoiding the low ceilings, which hung less than a foot above my head.

Each den had a kitchen placed near the entrance to air out any smoke. Next to that was a sitting area, and beyond that, a bedroom. Past the bedroom was a cutout with a drape, which, from my prior visits inside a den, I knew to be a privy. Except for the privy, the three areas were open to the air...no walls. Instead, the three main rooms were divided by alcoves and shelving. The alcove between the kitchen and sitting area served as a joint pantry and storage area. All the shelves were bare. The den was a cave in all comparisons save for the manner of exit...through a heavy drape and up the stairs.

Our search of the first den revealed nothing of interest.

I stopped in the middle of the kitchen and asked, "Is this burrow one that had bodies?"

Jonuku nodded stiffly. "Yes."

I moved to the stairwell, shoved aside the woolen drape, and looked up at the thinning gray clouds. There were eight steps—rather tall and shallow compared to human ones. But d'oglemenn were spry and capable of leaping quite high.

We repeated our search in twenty more dens, by which time my eyes had glazed over.

Nikk grumbled. "This be a waste of time. There be no clues left behind."

Jonuku nodded. "I know. After we'd buried everyone, Hombir rushed us, and we emptied everything into the cavern that we couldn't carry in our wagon."

"Alright," I said. "Let's finish our allotment and head back to the cave."

Finishing with the last den, we emerged to almost clear skies, the sun pushing through the remaining thin layer of mist. It had stopped snowing. But with a foot of snow, it was hard work to trudge back to the cavern.

"Take us to the stuff you pulled out of the dens," I said to Jonuku. I had ulterior motives regarding O'erlevendeh.

But that, too, proved unhelpful...as far as providing clues to our mystery and providing any sustenance for the whelp. Blankets, clothes, pots, mugs, utensils, books, pictures, keepsakes, and all manner of detritus.

I asked for permission to take some clothes. "For O'erlevendeh. I need to make him a better bed. And he has my spare undershirt, which I need to wash."

One by one, the teams returned.

Last was Ingefær, who led her dvaerg and d'oglemann to the fire, where lunch was being prepared. She hoisted high a piece of a purple vase, maybe three inches high and two inches wide at the bottom. It came to a sharp point. A shard.

"This is it. I've never seen dens so clean."

I stood. "We had no luck either."

She raised her finger. "Well, this piece is lucky." She had everyone's attention. "I cast a find magic on it."

Mick exclaimed. "It's magical?"

"No," she replied. "It was magicked. Is anyone an expert with pottery?"

Shakes of heads all around.

"Wait," Serafina said. "How can you tell it was magicked?"

Ingefær reached into a pouch of her mage belt and waved both hands in the air, even the one holding the vase shard. Her lips moved. When she was done, the purple piece glowed the dimmest orange. Had we been outside, I might not have spotted it.

She nodded as if she followed my thoughts. "In the darkness of the dens and this cave, you can see it. It's faint, but it's there."

Hombir examined the vase. "Cast magic fades. I mean, a fireball flashes and is gone. I've never studied how long it takes before any sign of its presence disappears."

Ingefær grinned. "Me neither. But I know the effects of my find magic spell take about a minute to dissipate. So. We'll conduct a test. I'll cast a fiery dart on an intact piece of pottery, if there is something like that here in the cavern."

Mick reached the conclusion I was muddling over. "What you're saying is, if you can tell that furniture and other goods were magicked, then the bodies found inside the dens...were killed with magic."

"That makes sense," I said. "There's no other way I can think of killing someone without leaving a mark. Well, poisonous gas is a possibility. But I think Hombir would spot it on his clanmates' faces."

Poison hurts, twists guts, and can cause muscles and limbs to spasm.

"Magic," Hombir said. "Come on." He led us back to the stored goods where he cast a find magic of his own.

And the wall and floor with the detritus glowed the dullest orange. Well, about half of it did.

Ingefær said, "This adds a clue to the marks on the dead wærgs. These beings are massive, they have claws, and now we know they're magical."

Great. Just great.

A magical beast with razor-sharp claws on hands thrice as big as mine.

Serafina said, "Could it be Jotunn?"

My mouth pinched for a moment. "Eh, they are magical. Though Vidarr described it as mind magic."

Ingefær said, "While Vidarr and Hombir cast fireballs at the Jotunn we ran into, they hurled giant snowballs at us. They didn't cast any incantations."

"No, they didn't," I said. "But Vidarr couldn't get them to stop throwing their giant snowballs using his mind magic."

Serafina said, "Now who's frying whose eggs?"

Hombir said, "No one."

Tugg added, "I be there, lass. They be telling the truth."

Serafina shivered.

Mick tugged at his tawny hair, but didn't scream. "But mind magic wouldn't affect the vase. It's not sentient. Would that type of magic leave a trace?"

Hmm. The lad might be onto something. "You may have a point. But honestly, I don't know."

Ingefær agreed. "We don't know enough about the Jotunn. So, I guess it doesn't rule them out, or conclude they are the culprits behind the attacks."

Serafina said, "We're no further along than before."

"In some respects, that's true." I scratched the back of my head. "But I think we've solved how the d'oglemenn here were killed."

With results both enlightening and disappointing, I confirmed for myself the need to get out and hunt. Food for O'erlevendeh, and field experience for Mick and Serafina. I mentioned my idea to Ingefær. "You want to come along?"

"No. Hombir has agreed to look at my ring."

"You alright if I take the young ones out for a stroll?"

She laughed. "Tugg said earlier it would snow again later today. So, be careful."

"Ah, my middle name."

Chapter Eleven

WHO'S HUNTING WHO?

RORY

After eating a light lunch, I got Tugg to watch my pup. We emerged from the cavern to a steady but frigid breeze. While we'd eaten, the once light cloud cover had darkened again. By the extra bite on my cheeks, I was certain the humidity had ticked up too.

I led Mick and Serafina eastward, breaking the trail in the foot of snow. Serafina had marveled at it at first, but now, not five minutes since leaving the comforts of the cavern, she stomped and kicked at the mounds of white stuff. Mick trudged beside me, but kept glancing over his shoulder like he'd left his one true love behind.

Out here, once it started snowing, it didn't stop for nigh on five moons. Oh, the nasty weather took three- or four-day breaks. The pattern was a function of Is Vann, or Ice Lake—which never froze—and the cold air that flowed from the north, at least during winter. We were wrapped up in cloaks, and though neither of my companions complained aloud, I saw them shivering. They would warm up once we hiked for a bit.

I counseled patience for myself. There were things I wanted to teach them. After a fresh snowstorm, hunting success increased. Though midday was the worst time for it. The wind helped for the moment by remaining breezy, but I couldn't rely on that for long. I wanted to train the two newest members of the team, and to find food that wouldn't spoil as fast as the lindwyrm had—for O'erlevendeh's sake.

I pulled my hood over my head as a sort of shield. We hiked, following the undulations of the earth. "Get your crossbows ready."

A quarter of an hour later, Mick said, "This is troll shit. I don't need to learn how to hunt this bad."

"You do," I replied. "If you are ever caught out in the wilds, you need to know how to survive. Hunting is but one thing I'm going to teach you in the next three hours."

"Three hours!?" Serafina's wide mouth and wide green eyes said it all.

"Stop bellyaching." I narrowed my brows at them. "The good news is that it snowed. It reveals tracks. The bad news is...out here, the wind can pick up at any time and erase those tracks—including your own. Getting lost is easy."

I waved a hand southward. "The mountains are your guides. We're going east. So, if we get separated and sight lines become poor, find the mountains and head west."

"Easy enough," Mick said.

I glared at him. "Back at the farm, I've had you practicing with the crossbow. I hope you get the chance to show you've learned something."

I pointed at Serafina. "Which way is the wind blowing?"

She rolled her eyes. "It's slight from the north."

"Right." I spun around and faced east. "So, which way will whatever animal is out there be able to tell if we're coming?"

A heavy sigh. She said, "One to the south."

I looked at them. "So, if we want to have a chance of seeing something worth eating, which way should we hike, Mick?"

"Uh, north?"

"Good guess." I waved an arm in that direction. "But there's not much game on the Ice Plains, except maybe lindwyrms and ice grizzlies. So, I'm going to show you a hunting maneuver my father taught me."

We hiked for a half an hour southward, gaining elevation as we scrambled up the steep slope. Soon enough, cloaks opened up as body heat became a problem.

We reached the top of the hill, the two of them breathing hard, their faces glistening with sweat. Fresh flurries fell on our heads, nice and steady.

Serafina giggled and opened her mouth, catching the flakes on her tongue.

I let them rest for a moment, then got them ready. We hiked down the backside of the hill into a long, narrow valley covered in rocks, naked bushes, and pines, all frosted and powdered in snow.

I pointed. "We go east for a half an hour, then back up the slope."

"You're having us go in a circle," Mick's tone whined.

I smiled. "Yes, that's right. Change the attitude and maybe you'll learn something."

A dozen minutes later, I spotted tracks and stopped. "What do you think made those?"

They were fresh, maybe ten minutes old, as the falling snow hadn't filled them in yet. I surveyed left and right, trying to see if there were more is-hjort tracks. They were herd animals, so a lone is-hjort was odd. It had gone downwind of us, which, if we pursued it, made our hunt more difficult.

Mick ambled over to a set of tracks. He bent low. "Don't know."

Serafina said, "A hjort."

"Close. It's their smaller cousin, the is-hjort. Both are good eating, and both have cute faces, big ears, and a white-tailed behind. This time of year, in these environs, they've lost any hint of brown and have gone all white. Did it go north or south?"

Serafina's turn. "No idea."

Mick looked left to right, following the tracks of where it came from and where it was going. "The front hooves go together and point in the direction it went." He chinned southward.

"That's right," I said. They were learning an important survival skill. "Each species has its own telltale marks. Learn them...and live. An is-hjort's front hooves are slender and rounded. When they plant them, they come together, and it points in their direction of travel."

I looked into Mick's brown eyes. "Did you know, or did you guess?"

"Guessed." Mick grinned, then hefted his crossbow. "Fifty-fifty chance. Do we go after it?"

I shook my head. "No. It's downwind and most likely went over the next ridge. I don't know these mountains, so I'm wary of getting lost. One ridge over, no problem. But if you go over another and get turned around—when you can't see more than a hundred strides and everything around is big and tall—you're asking for trouble. In a snowstorm, it will literally all look the same."

We continued east. When I thought we had gone for fifteen minutes, I shifted us northward, back up the ridge. We spread out in a line. "Keep an eye out now. We're downwind of anything ahead of us. We have the advantage."

By the time we reached the top of the hill, the wind picked up, shoving the wet flakes into our faces and obscuring vision beyond a hundred strides.

Serafina pulled her hood back up over her golden locks.

Mick yanked at his hair.

"Where's your cap?" I asked.

"Back at camp."

I shook my head and gazed at our surroundings. The kid liked to learn the hard way.

Suddenly, the wind howled, and the flurries tripled in volume. Visibility dropped to fifty paces.

Our hunt had become a game of chance. We'd be lucky to see anything now.

I pointed north. "Spread out, but stay within sight of me and walk slow. Hurrying is never your friend when hunting."

Stride by stride, we ambled down the ridge, heading toward the Ice Plains proper. The wind decided it would make up for its earlier slack and shrieked with a fresh force, driving the snow sideways. If I saw thirty strides ahead, I'd be lying.

I sighed. "Our hunt is over. When we hit the Ice Plains, we'll make for the cavern."

At the bottom of the hill, we turned left, westward. We hadn't gone for more than a minute when Serafina, ten strides to my right, waved a hand at me. "Psst!" She pointed northward with her other hand.

Being half-alvae, her eyesight was better than mine. I signaled Mick until he nodded and shifted toward us, then I moved to Serafina.

In a low voice, I asked, "What?"

"Something moved over there." Again, she pointed northward.

"How big?" I asked.

Her green eyes widened. "Huge. Enormous."

"Compare it to something I know." I cautioned Mick not to yell.

"As tall as your home," Serafina said, her voice hoarse though she whispered.

My head snapped northward, and I peered into the blowing snow. I didn't see a thing.

"Do-do-do we go after it?" she asked.

"No," I replied. "I know nothing that big that lives out here." Well, a lindwyrm, but we were on rocks, and it only came up when it had a meal to snatch. I peered into her face. Was she playing a prank? "Are you sure?"

Her green face had whitened, and her eyes remained wide and round. Her head twisted in jerks as she searched the area. Fear. I recognized the look.

"Come on," I said, pulling at their arms. "Stay as quiet as if you were creeping down Jarl Retzlaff's tunnels."

We moved fast, westward, keeping the rugged slopes of the mountains to our left. The flying snow obscured them outright, but by watching the shifting shadows, I knew we were close. Maybe a minute's walk to reach the base of the ridge.

Moments later, an eerie feeling came over me, and a tingle ran up my spine. I'd had those feelings before—when I was being watched.

I said, "Run!"

Being the fastest and most experienced, I stayed behind them. I urged them to sprint. "You can walk in a couple of minutes."

I wasn't sure what caused my senses to tingle like that, but I trusted them. Glancing over my shoulder at intervals, I didn't see any shadows moving. My sparkling spirit, Roskva, hadn't appeared either. She would, if real trouble presented itself. The knowledge eased the tension between my shoulder blades.

Running in a foot of snow takes it out of anyone, and after a five-minute dash, Serafina slowed, her breath harsh. Mick slackened his pace to stay next to her and gulped air.

I caught up.

"How come...you're not...out of...breath?" Serafina asked.

"Magic feet," I replied, my eyes glued to the northeast.

The wind screamed, and the snow curled around, making pockets as thick as any fog I'd ever seen. Our tracks were being obliterated. That was a good thing.

"Walk," I said. "When you can, run, run to the cavern."

"What are you going to do?" Mick asked.

I had a choice to make. If I went with them and there was something on our trail, then I might lead that something to our base camp. Yeah, I didn't like that one bit.

"I'm going to distract whatever's following us." I pointed a finger at them. "Go. Now!"

They jogged west. Before I turned around, they were sprinting, which in a foot of snow was like a fast walk.

Good.

I took a deep breath. Was I crazy?

No. I was saving my charges' lives. What I had to do was lead whatever trailed us away. Not just from Mick and Serafina, but from the folks inside the cavern, too.

Chapter Twelve

SEEKING ANSWERS

INGEFÆR

We sat on fir logs in our makeshift quarters inside the cavern, as the fire cast dancing shadows across the walls. D'oglemenn and dvaergs took turns keeping the fire going, throwing in coal now and then. Tugg sat off to one side, his beard dipping often as he glanced at the cave opening. He watched the whelp by keeping it wrapped up in a blanket by his feet.

To my right sat Hombir, and to his, Jonuku. I traced a finger over the familiar contours of the signet ring I had kept in my pocket. The gold band and inlaid 'R' in a deep red stone reflected the firelight.

Hombir's toothy smile flashed as he eyed the oversized ruby stone inset in gold. "What sort of magic have you tried?"

I went over the detect magic incantations and the number of activation words I had mumbled through. "I varied the amounts of elemental magic from the Aether, fire, and air. Nothing seems to work. There's not much on Jarl Retzlaff the First in the Slangeh Buktah library."

He nodded. "I doubt the command word to activate the ring is known publicly. Not anything like 'Retzlaff.'"

I chuckled. "That was the first word I tried." I told him about the history of Hexerei Mansion and the jarl's interest in necromancy. I also described our encounter with Jarl Retzlaff the Fifth.

I explained the surprising twist to our adventures in Retzlaff's deadly dungeon. "When we had recovered the ring, which belonged to one of his forbearers, we plundered through his journals and desk. We found nothing about the ring written down. Nothing to point us in a direction."

Hombir's lips curled as he turned to face the fire, his hand propping up his elongated snout. "Presumably, the jarl who created the ring was married and had offspring. The command word could be the name of his wife or one of his children, or perhaps his father or mother. Those kinds of records should be available."

I nodded. "With the proper application of silver coins." And a tremendous investment of time. But as I'd already spent innumerable hours trying to divine it, I suspected it to be the right course of action.

"I presume you don't want to wait until your return home?" Hombir grinned outright.

"That's right. Is there a way to activate the ring without knowing the command word?"

"In theory, yes, but in reality, that is incredibly difficult." Hombir shifted his seat, straddling the pine log. "Let me see it."

I handed it to him.

The d'oglemann mage fiddled with the ring, turning it in every way possible, and fingering the gold engraved *R*. "There is a variant of the find magic spell. Seldom used, because it doesn't reveal wards."

As far as I knew, that was the primary reason to invoke the find magic incantation.

He smiled at me with his lips closed, keeping those sharp teeth hidden.

I waited. "And that variant would be?"

"Show magic instead of find magic." Hombir fumbled with his mage pouch. "Watch the colors. They won't be orange."

With his left hand, Hombir pinched some sort of fine gray dust from his mage belt while he held the ring in his right. Three times in a row, he moved both hands as if he were grabbing shutters and swinging them outward. "*Avslore magika.*"

The ring glowed. But not orange. Wisps of white, brown, gold, and black—black!?—floated off the gold-coated *R*.

Hombir's golden slits narrowed, and his lips twitched. "He used those four planes of magic to create the ring. Air, earth, the Aether—you know those. The black comes from the plane of Hel."

"Hel?" I damn near shouted. "I thought there were but five planes. You're saying there's six?"

"Yes. The source of power for necromancers."

I shuddered at the thought of summoning black magic. I hadn't known that. My mind raced. "Why haven't I been told this before?"

He returned the ring to my palm. "The sixth one is not taught or talked about for obvious reasons. There's little written, too. I have a tome, back in Kobber Unter Smuss, that speaks of the dangers of that plane."

"But there's a lady I know who tried to raise her dead sister."

"Did she succeed?" Hombir asked.

"No. She went around and married mages, each specializing in a type of magic. She never got that far."

Tugg picked up the pup and stretched. "The snow be coming soon. I be going for a short walk."

"Don't stray too far," I said as he passed.

Tugg ran fingers through his beard and his gaze searched the cavern opening. He wasn't worried about the weather. I called to his back. "She's been gone for but an hour."

Tugg nodded without turning around. His fist plunged into his overcoat and he stepped outside.

I turned my attention to Hombir, who said, "Did any of the husbands summon magic from the plane of Hel?"

I shook my head. "No. At least, I don't think so. Each was a specialist of the five *normal* planes."

Hombir's snout dipped. "Good."

"So, now that we know the colors used, you have any ideas? Because I don't."

He nodded. "One or two." He questioned me about the ring's providence.

Hombir cast one detect magic after another in combination with various keywords while I held the ring before him. The invocations varied with him using words such as *finne, sohke, forestilling*, and *avslohre.* Find, seek, show, and reveal were but a few of the many he tried, in combination with necromancer, Retzlaff the First, or the number one, Hexerei, and other tidbits describing what I knew of the man. When he tired, Jonuku healed him, and he started on another combination.

Midway through the process, Tugg returned. "Snowing again. Wind be nasty."

There was an undertone to his words, and his fingers twisted the ends of his beard.

I nodded at him. "Aye. Rory is a hunter. He won't get lost." I grinned at him. "Don't fret, he'll bring back Serafina."

Tugg grunted. "Ye think it be folly, the two of us talking?"

I smiled wider. "No. She seems to enjoy your company."

Another grunt. "Aye. But dvaergs...and alvaes?"

Jonuku said, "Let the Realm talk all they want. What do you care?"

His beard flinched, which, I think, meant he'd smiled for a moment. Tugg moved back to his former sitting spot, pulled the pup out from his overcoat, and warmed his hands and the whelp before the fire.

Hombir kept at the ring, trying unique phrasings, like 'Jarl Retzlaff,' or 'Retzlaff the Fifth,' in combination with the different command words. He even tried different hand motions. An hour later, he'd exhausted his wife, who went to a corner to lie down.

After yet another six failures, Hombir said, "Sorry. It's beyond my ken."

I sighed. "It was a long shot. I have vials of healing to keep you going, but I think those should be saved for urgent situations." My shoulders drooped. "Conjurer Elise in Slangeh Buktah told me to seek a mage in Jernel Drakken. She says she's the most powerful one she knows—well, for this type of invocation."

Hombir harrumphed, then smiled. "Since I can't figure it out, she might be right. But you should study Jarl Retzlaff anew. That may help in finding the keyword or words. Like I mentioned before, names of loved ones could do the trick."

Maybe the year the mansion was built. I now had a host of ideas to try. But here and now wasn't the time. I twirled my pearl-white snowflake dangling from my choker. "I see a trip to Jernel Drakken in my future."

We took to staring and poking at the fire.

A short while later, Mick and Serafina stumbled into the cavern, their faces flushed, and both huffing air. Snow clung to their clothes, and ice had formed around their mouths and eyes.

"What happened?" I felt my heart shift, suddenly pounding. "Where's Rory?"

Mick swallowed hard. "Rory stayed-*pant*-behind to face the beast." His voice cracked. "He made us-*pant*-run here."

"What kind of beast?" I asked as I rushed to them.

Serafina took a deep breath. "We didn't get a good look. The wind blew too hard, and the snow was too thick."

"You saw something!"

"It was big," Serafina said. "But all I saw was a shifting shadow."

"How big? Be specific!"

"As tall as your house," Serafina said.

Lokke's spawn!

Tugg arrived with a pair of blankets. He handed Mick one and wrapped Serafina in the other.

My arms flew to cross across my chest. "That dunderhead husband of mine."

Serafina pulled the woolen blanket tight. "He said he could outrun it and he didn't want it to follow us."

Tugg nodded. "Smart. He didn't want the beastie coming here."

That was Rory.

The damn fool.

I kicked at a pile of firewood. Out on the Ice Plains, one mistake led to a series of others. That's how folks died.

Think positive. Rory is a grand hunter.

But could he outmaneuver a giant? Jotunn knew mind magic. And they could hurl a ball of icy death a quarter of a mile.

Only a mage could duel a Jotunn. Two would be better. But they had to get close enough.

"How long did it take you to reach the cavern after you separated from Rory?" I asked.

Mick's shoulders scrunched. "Not sure. Maybe half an hour?"

"Sounds about right," Serafina said, her chin bobbing.

That wasn't that far. But a beast, maybe a Jotunn, had come quite close to Nikkel Bakken. That didn't bode well.

My stomach lurched. Pain filled my heart. I closed my eyes and breathed deep. This trip had turned to troll shit. A tear rolled down my cheek.

I hate the Ice Plains.

I took a deep breath, trying to calm my nerves. Should we wait? Or should we try to find my husband? There were problems with both approaches.

I hated waiting. A trait I'd picked up from Rory. And I knew, if the situation were reversed, Rory would come searching for me. The lunkhead.

"All right. Let's form a search party." I spun on my heel. "Everyone up. Get dressed!"

I tugged at my snowflake. "We have to find my husband."

Tugg said, "Now lass, yer husband made his choice to keep us safe. If we go out there, we be defeating his objective."

I nodded. "Aye. But with Hombir and me, we have two mages. And I can't leave my husband out there alone. Not in this weather."

I waved an arm at the cave's occupants. "I want your help. But you don't have to come, if you don't want to."

Hombir said, "My wife and I are spent."

I glanced at Serafina. "How are you?"

She shrugged. "Tired. Cold. But I have all my spells."

"Alright then." I locked gazes with Hombir, pleading with my eyes. "Serafina will restore your stamina. We have vials of healing if we need them."

Hombir nodded. "Aye. We'll help."

Tugg said, "If ye insist on going, me folks will go with ye." Then, "Someone has to stay with the whelp, I think."

Chapter Thirteen

THE HUNTED

RORY

I squinted into the onrushing sheet of white, trying to glimpse the form that had tracked us. When my sixth sense had quivered between my shoulder blades, I was certain we were being followed.

With my two charges lost in the storm to the east, I move due north, away from the Dreki Mountains. Other than the persistent wind, it was the lone anchor point to determine direction out on the Ice Plains. My aim was to keep the beast away from Nikkel Bakken, which lay maybe a half hour hike away.

All around me was white. Snow crunched beneath my boots; flurries filled the air all the way to the horizon. I couldn't discern any of the various knolls by sight, but I felt the ground undulating under my feet as I went over one mound after another.

There!

Off to my right, eastward, the snow struck a tall object, creating a void—a space of silvery-gray shadows. With a fresh gust—and possibly movement—it was lost in the thick, wind-driven snow.

Lokke's spawn. The thing was almost as tall as a Jotunn. Maybe it was a young one.

"Over here!"

I didn't wait for it to spot me and jogged north, leaving tracks. Well, for a couple of minutes. The wind whipped, strafing fresh flakes more numerous than sands on a beach. I knew that because I tried to count them as they stung my face and blinded my eyes.

A low growl penetrated through the whirling white muck.

Not sure if it had turned to follow me, or if the beast had moved eastward, I stopped and cocked my crossbow. "Come on! You big...galoot!"

Galoot didn't sound all that insulting. Would it understand my words? For effect, I fired in an arc, hoping the wind would drive the bolt farther than its normal range.

"Yaargh!" came a guttural howl from downwind.

I got its attention. Great. Just great.

I reloaded, my eyes on the southern horizon, which, in this gale of flurries, was all of thirty steps away.

The gods. I was crazy.

I hunkered low to the ground, trying to get lost in the snow.

A massive, shadowy figure loomed ahead. Blurry gray gave way to an outline in white, visible only because the white moved. The giant came closer.

Its face was as white as its arms and body. Except for one charcoal-hued round orb, which, by the motion of an enormous head, swept its gaze through the storm.

What the Hel was that?

Its gaze alighted on me, sending a shiver down my spine and filling me with dread.

Roskva appeared. My creamy pinkish-orange sparkling fylgjæ.

The beast raised its arm, a taloned-hand pointing at me.

Roskva's frond for an arm jabbed through the air.

I got the message. *Run!*

I dashed east.

For a man with legs not too long, but not short, I was fast. Using my magicked feet, I could outrun all but a falcon, and would give the svartkatt a good workout. For about five minutes. But with Roskva around, I would outrun even the falcon, and the bird and any other beast would tire long before I ever did.

The deep snow slowed me some and caused me to work a little harder. But I gauged the impact as negligible. Maybe a lightning bolt spell could catch me.

After several hundred strides, I skidded to a stop. I couldn't outrun my pursuer. Not yet.

"Hey. Fluffy stuff. Over here!"

I need to work on my insults.

Crouching, I aimed the crossbow off to the left of the path I'd taken, and adjusted for the shrieking winds.

Hmm. Is ten degrees sufficient?

Roskva shook her block-shaped head at me. I usually complained about our inability to communicate, other than through gestures. But, at the moment, I was content she couldn't tell me how stupid I was.

I peered into the storm, the snow pelting the side of my head. I had a hood, but hoods obstructed peripheral vision. And I needed all of it in this blizzard. The wind froze the icy pellets to the scruff of my week-old beard.

My one glimpse of the beast told me it wasn't a Jotunn. Those giants have blue skin, and while they wear wulv and bear pelts, they were clean shaven. This beast was white-furred from its feet to its head.

And the Jotunn have two eyes. This one had...a huge orb so dark it sucked in the light.

I shuddered.

Motion. To the left of my aim after adjusting for the gale. The beast spotted me, its mouth opened to reveal a maw almost as big as I was around, with gnarly-looking teeth the size of my fingers.

I fired.

Not needing encouragement from Roskva, I used my elemental augmented speed and sped eastward to stay away from Nikkel Bakken.

A ray of silver energy strafed the ground to my right, billowing snow and dirt into the air, and leaving a foot wide and a foot high trail of ice, all crackled and jagged.

"What the—?"

I wended left, northward.

Keep your wits about you, I said to myself.

Direction was a problem without sightlines to the Dreki Mountains. But for now, I had to rely on the wind. If it shifted...or stopped...I was doomed.

After running at half Roskva's speed for over a minute, I slid to a stop. My fylgjæ stood before me, her hands on her squarish hips. The block for a head shook from side to side. She jabbed a frond arm over her shoulder.

"No," I said. "I have to pull it away from Nikkel Bakken."

As an elemental from where the plane of air mixed with the plane of water—as Vidarr once explained it to me—Roskva didn't have eyes. But if she did, I would have seen an eye roll.

I cocked the crossbow and lay in the snow.

When the furry beast, standing maybe fourteen feet high, stomped into range, I aimed center mass. This time, the wind was behind me. The bolt hit right above where a belly button would be, if it had one.

"Gragh!" Its taloned hand came up.

I jumped left, eastward, and sped off.

Behind me, the silvery ray blew snow and dirt high into the air. In moments, I lost the beast to the snow. I had to hope the charcoal eye couldn't see any better than I could.

A half minute later, I jigged northward, slowed to my normal speed, and ran into the wind for a couple of minutes.

I came to a stop and turned around. Stepping into the cross brace, I cocked my weapon.

Roskva stood before me and turned both frond arms over, like she was saying, "What did you expect?"

I nodded.

"Alright. One more time." I couldn't have the beast give up. Not yet. I needed it to move farther away, to not connect me with Nikkel Bakken. As I looked nothing like a d'oglemann, I figured I had a good chance of that, as long as I didn't move west.

Roskva gave a slight shake of her glittering creamy pinkish-orange head.

I peered into the howling snow, made easier as I faced south, the same direction as the wind. I went over the beast's use of its ice ray.

The blast hits the ground, and the beast adjusts it toward its target.

I grinned. "It can't judge distances."

Before me, a shadow moved. I hollered. "Hey! One-eye!"

I jogged north, into the wind, hoping to confuse it.

Behind me, the ground shook to a pounding rhythm. Was this the first time it ran at me? Or had I been so panicked before that I hadn't noticed?

I increased my pace until I couldn't hear the pulsing stomp behind me.

After a while, I stopped to catch my breath. Well, it wasn't like I was panting. But, despite the cold, slogging through the deep snow at my rapid pace caused me to sweat.

As I took deep breaths to calm my nerves, a sensation of impending doom came over me. Darkness billowed about me, suffocating, squeezing. My eyes blurred.

Roskva jabbed east.

I willed myself to move and sped off like an osprey diving for its meal.

Two rays, one from the south and one from the north, strafed the ground.

The one from the north missed me by a foot.

This time, I didn't stop. As I ran east, I cleared my head of the cold death feeling. That was too close!

Where did the second beast come from? How did it know I was there? Maybe the beasts had a way of communicating I couldn't hear. Definitely mind stuff.

"Alright, Roskva. We're out of here."

I slowed to a normal sprint—which in the foot of snow was akin to a lazy man's jog. To the rhythm of my breathing, my boots clomped and stomped. A dozen minutes later, I turned to what I thought was south, the wind at my back.

If there were two beasts, were there more? How many more? And were any south of my position? I stopped long enough to load my crossbow.

Then, I jogged toward the Dreki Mountains.

I hoped.

Chapter Fourteen

SEARCH PARTY

INGEFÆR

From inside the cavern, I looked out into the fury of the storm. Pellet-sized flakes swirled about, thicker than fire ants whose mound had just been kicked. *Lokke's spawn*! It would take a miracle to find Rory.

As if reading my mind, Tugg slapped a meaty hand on my shoulder. "I have to tell ye...it be mighty difficult to find someone in this blizzard."

I contained a growling retort. He was telling me what I knew, but didn't want to acknowledge. The problem was that my heart wasn't listening to my head. Rory risked his life to save ours. Now I wanted to risk ours to save his. That's the thing about love and loyalty—they bind both ways.

Once Serafina had finished healing Jonuku, the d'oglemann healer said, "I'll restore my husband's stamina. Save your spells."

Folks were getting dressed. I quick-stepped to my gear and did the same.

Hombir said, "Two of mine will stay behind to keep the fire going."

"And to watch Rory's crazy fetish," I said, pointing at the wrapped-up pup.

Hombir grinned, showing his row of sharp teeth. "I wouldn't want your husband to be mad at me."

Serafina flipped up the hood of her cloak. "Master Belkin had us run off so he could distract...whatever it was I saw."

"A shape as tall as a giant, you said." I glared into her emerald eyes.

Her silver-green skin paled. "Yes."

I asked Tugg, "Am I crazy to search for him?"

"The right kind of crazy." Tugg winked. "Oi! Lads. Finish up."

I glanced outside the cave again. Dark would be upon us in two hours. The snow fell thick and fast, driven by the ferocious wind. Not once in all my days out here had it ever snowed just an inch or two. Not once had it snowed for but an hour. The graupel and snow fell for days and always in feet. After taking a couple hours' break earlier, the storm was now working on day two and its second foot.

Mick slipped a bright blue cap over his tawny hair. "I'll go with you. Don't stress, Miss Ingefær, Master Belkin knows what he's doing. If anyone can find their way in this storm, it's him."

"Aye." Tugg searched my face. "The lad has the right of it."

I frowned at him. He'd just said I was the right kind of crazy.

As if reading my mind, Tugg said, "Ye both be right."

Serafina pulled on gloves. "I'm ready."

"Me, too." Mick flashed a wavering smile.

No snark, no jokes. But his taut jaw lines revealed his worries.

Was I right to go search for Rory?

Hombir and Jonuku, and six of the nine remaining d'oglemann warriors, stepped into a loose formation, their wulv cloaks wrapped around their torsos, hoods flipped up.

The mage said, "Instead of gallivanting about, we should set beacons. A string of lights so he can find his way back."

"That makes more sense than what I had in mind." I had planned on running east until I found my husband...or collapsed. My hands clenched. Once again, Rory's actions had me all flustered, and all in the wrong way.

"How do the beacons work?" Serafina asked.

Hombir said, "It's a variation of the warmth spell. Hold on." He moved to his rucksack and pulled out a tome. After flipping through pages, he stopped to read. He looked up at me with a sheepish grin. "I haven't cast it since—well—ever. Haven't had to." His finger jabbed at the page. "You can cast it on a person or animal, and it moves around. Or you cast it on an object, say a spear, or a torch, that you plant into the ground."

My eyes widened. "So, it's like a light spell." I had wanted to do something like that with Rory and the wærg cave.

"Yes. Though not as bright, it has a hue that can be seen far away." Hombir put his book away. "And it uses different material. At least I do."

"That's not a bad idea." I motioned. "Let's do that. Tugg, you and your troops grab some spears or some planks of wood. I think there's a pile of shelving in the far corner."

"Aye. We could hack one end into a spear point and use a hammer to pound it into the ground." The dvaerg leader motioned and a duo of his soldiers ran off.

Hombir went over the spell motions and incantation. "For material, I think a bit of candle wax would work."

It proved simple in concept. "With the healers along to restore our stamina, we can string a line of beacons for quite a way?"

A ten-minute hike under normal conditions.

"Sure," Hombir replied.

Mick said, "But whatever you light, will draw the...the *thing* just as easily as Master Belkin."

"Gaah!" I raised my hand, palm out, threatening Mick—telling him I didn't want to hear that. Then I clenched my hand and dropped my arm. "Sorry. I'm not mad at you. It's the truth I'm furious with."

I paced. "But I can't just sit here. I have to look for him. I have to help him find his way back-even if we have to fight...whatever Serafina saw."

Tugg said, "Alright. We'll go out and set yer beacons. After ye and Hombir run out of spells, or perhaps even beforehand, if we get the idea it won't work, we can turn back. At that point, we'll have to decide if we keep the beacons lit. Or not. I be not fond of attracting this beast to the cave. Not until me Avarkæsir arrive in strength."

"We travel together as a group," I said. "No stragglers."

Tugg's dvaergs retrieved the shelving, and unlit torches were passed around for the group to carry—in case we stayed out longer than the plan called for and the sun dropped behind the horizon. We set off, stepping out of the comforts of the tepid cavern and into the frigid blast of an early winter storm.

Some thirty strides to the east and ten strides from the base of the ridge, Hombir cast the first beacon spell, and Nikk pounded the shaped shelf into the hard ground.

Hombir's muzzle scrunched. "Hmph. Will it do the job?"

It glowed a dull red and didn't burn the eyes to look at it. While not bright, it had a luminescence to it that filtered through the fluttering snow. "It's better than nothing. I mean, it works."

We set off east and marched for less than a minute.

Mick cried out. "I can barely see it."

Sixty paces in a thick blizzard. I should count myself, or rather Rory, lucky.

Hombir pointed at the ground. "Another beacon here."

This time, I cast the spell, two fingers of my left hand rubbing a chunk of wax between them. Thrice, my right hand mimicked a tiny, rippling explosion, like a stone dropped into a mug of water. "*Fyrtarn an haep.*"

Nikk pounded the next piece of shelving into the earth. My bluish light radiated a stride above the ground. It was brighter than Hombir's, and more pleasing. At least to my eye.

"Nice hue," Hombir said.

"Why does it shine more and in a different color?" Serafina asked.

I shrugged.

Hombir scratched his scale-covered head. "Don't know. Might be the planes we draw from to cast the spell. I relied on the plane of fire."

That made sense. "Air for me."

Mick said, "If Master Belkin runs into the hills fronting the Dreki Mountains, he won't need a light. We should be further to the north."

"That's...true." My husband's actions had me rattled. "Thanks, Mick." A new plan formed in my head. The initial idea of following along the Dreki Mountains was redundant. "We need to create a set of lines running north, each pointing back to the mountains." I blinked at the flitting snow. "We need to split up. Two teams. Say several hundred paces apart."

Tugg grumbled. "Splitting up be risky."

I grimaced. "I know. It will speed things up, though."

With Mick, Serafina, Tugg, Nikk, and three d'oglemenn, I trudged through more than a foot of snow for a tenth of a mile. We stopped at the burial mound filled with over eighty bodies.

I looked around. Nothing but swirling shades of white. No sign of Hombir and his team.

With my crew's help, we set the first beacon thirty feet from the eastern edge of the mound. Then we headed north along the start of the ridge.

"Let me know when the light gets too weak," I said.

Some seventy strides later, we set the second beacon. I'd cast three spells. Three to go, before I needed Serafina's healing powers.

After my sixth spell—four beacons—I had to blink to clear my mind, and I felt a weakness in my knees. I was getting stronger. This past summer, I had almost passed out when I'd cast the sixth spell. Serafina invoked a restoration spell, imbuing me with fresh stamina.

As I surveyed the white wilderness through frosted-over brows, an icy draft swept past my wulv cloak. I ignored the cold's bite. I had a man to save.

We were two hundred twenty strides from the base of the hillside. Just over a tenth of a mile. "It's not enough."

Tugg said, "True. But he may see a beacon further east. One along the ridge."

North or east? I went with the ridge for topography. It was a landmark Rory might recognize and follow in. I was spell limited, even with Serafina's help. There was too much area to do both.

I growled under my breath. "Come on. To the ridge."

We traced our way back to the first beacon and ran into Hombir. He'd gone fifty strides farther than I had and was on his way to set the next row.

I informed him of our revised plan. "I'm going to the ridge. You should go back to the first row and go out as far as your spells let you. You'll be the north anchor and I'll be the east."

Before we separated, Hombir said, "I have but one more set to light. I don't want me or Jonuku to become drained. Just in case. Like you said earlier, the vials of healing are for emergencies."

I wanted to argue that this was an emergency, but my head told my heart that he was right. Instead, I chastised myself for setting the beacons I had, acting before thinking it through.

My team moved on and hiked east to the ridge. Four hundred strides out from the far eastern cavern, I set the first beacon seventy paces from the hill slope, and we trudged across the ridgeline running north—the eastern end of the d'oglemann's valley. Together, we set six beacons across a short quarter of a mile.

I wobbled on my feet.

Serafina healed me.

I shook my head to clear the snow off my hood. It wasn't enough. I wanted to go farther to the north.

Tugg said, "Time to turn back. We've been out here for an hour."

My heart grew heavy. I, we, hadn't done enough. A tear dropped from my eye, freezing on my cheek.

"One more set," I said, pointing into the wind.

Tugg eyed me. "We be getting dangerous now."

I leveled my glare at him. "I'll go alone if I have to."

Serafina said, "Hombir may have returned to the cavern by now."

"If anybody wants to go back, that's fine. I can set the beacons myself." I held my hands out for the hammer and planks of wood.

Bundled in their arctic wulv cloaks, the three d'oglemenn moved off south, along the beacon-lit path, on their way to the cavern.

Tugg grumbled, and Nikk watched the departing d'oglemenn. Mick's jaw worked, but he didn't say anything.

Serafina sighed. "If you're so determined, I'll go on with you."

The five of us set another six-beacon picket, extending the string of beacons to almost half a mile. Between trudging through the snow and the steady use of my arcane talents, I felt woozy. The sun shirked its duty, and I knew it neared the western horizon. In this blizzard, the night would be damn dark. But maybe the beacons would be all the brighter for it.

Serafina looked at me. "I have one spell left in me. If I use it, you may have to help me walk back."

I gritted my teeth. "Heal me, Serafina. Tugg and Nikk will help you back."

Tugg's eyes sparkled. "With pleasure."

Mick said, "That sounds like you ain't coming back with us."

I mulled it over. "I'm thinking about it. Heal me. Please."

Serafina said, "I won't heal you until you promise you'll return with us."

I growled. "Shouldn't that be my choice?"

Mick said, "We're a team. If you use up all your spells, who's going to do battle? Me and my sling and stones?"

Gritting my teeth, I eyeballed him. But he was right. "The gods! When did you get smart?"

Mick and Serafina chuckled.

"Alright. I'm coming back with you. I promise."

After Serafina used her last spell, she put an arm around Tugg's neck. He helped her walk. Nikk trudged beside her, but left some space between them.

We slogged back to the base of the Dreki Mountains.

Mick said, "You've done plenty, Miss Ingefær."

"Aye. Rory's bound to run into a beacon," Tugg said.

"You promise?" I asked. Gnawing on my lip, I reconsidered breaking my word and heading east.

Tugg eyed me. "Rory be my friend. Trust in his skills, same as I do with me own kin."

"You are coming back with us, right?" Mick asked.

I sighed and paused to think. Rationally, not emotionally, though it pained me.

Trekking into the storm on my own was as daft as Rory's heroics. I had a few choice words for his decision. If only I had the gods to pray to…I would entreat them for the chance to speak my mind.

I blew a gust of air out that ruffled the flying snow. "Let's go back."

With head hung low, more from sadness than trying to keep my face shielded from the gale and graupel, we trudged west…back toward the central cavern. The last of the sunlight that had permeated through the clouds and snow winked out.

Chapter Fifteen

A MYTH

INGEFÆR

When Mick, Serafina, Nick, Tugg, and I reached the red beacon east of the central cavern, I called for a stop.

Cupping my hands around my frost-covered mouth, I shouted. "Rory! Rory!"

Serafina yanked at my cloak sleeve and Tugg took a hold of my arm.

Mick said, "You can't stay out here, Miss Ingefær."

The weather had turned uglier after the sun had set. The winds howled nonstop, and the snow slammed down. By morning, there would be two feet. Maybe more.

I dragged my feet as we made for the central cavern, searching for signs of footprints. But the wind and snow laughed at me. "Hombir should be back, right?"

"Only one way to find out," Serafina said.

"Come on, lass, it be dark," Tugg said.

The gods! Could Rory survive through the night?

I jerked my arms free. "Rory! Rory!"

Tugg got insistent, grabbing my arm in that meaty hand of his. "Inside, lass. Now."

We strode through the entrance, its wide maw letting snow pile up almost three steps in.

"Hey! You made it."

Rory's voice.

My mind spun as my eyes darted toward the fire.

My husband sat, his back leaning against a boulder and his feet up on a log. He chewed on pemmican with one hand and stroked O'erlevendeh with the other. He took a bite, the pup's gaze following the motion.

My heart exploded with joy. I jerked myself free from Tugg's grip and jounced over to him. He had just risen to his feet when I jumped into his arms. "You're alive."

"Well, duh," he said. His pemmican-holding hand drew me tight. "You miss me?"

I smacked him on the shoulder. "I was scared to death you were dead!"

He took another bite. "There were a few troubles, but nothing my fast feet couldn't handle."

"Roskva show up?" If she had, he'd been in real danger.

He nodded, chewing. "That's when I knew I was over-matched."

I glanced around. Hombir and Jonuku had removed their cloaks and were warming themselves by the fire. "How long ago did you return?"

"Maybe five minutes," Hombir said. "My warriors showed up and said you were extending your beacon string. We waited for you. But then the sun set, so I brought everyone in with me."

Mick threw his coat across a log and rubbed his hands near the flames. "Thanks for scaring the you-know-what right out of us, Master Belkin."

"You came back like I told you," Rory said. "That's what's important. I led the beast Serafina saw away from the trail leading..." he motioned with a sweep of his arm... "to this place."

Tugg asked, "Could the party take on whatever ye saw?"

Rory picked up a bowl and fished out a soggy piece of once-dried meat. He tore off the smallest bite and fed his whelp. He glanced from Hombir to me. "With two mages? Yes, I think so." He pointed the mushy stick of meat at himself. "But I couldn't kill one. Not by myself."

"What is it?" Serafina asked.

"Yes, tell us," Hombir said. "You've put me off, saying you wanted to tell it once."

Rory motioned with a hand, holding the bowl. O'erlevendeh growled as his food moved away. "Get yourself comfortable. I know what marauded the caravans and killed the d'oglemenn here. I know how the claw marks were made on the wærgs and how they killed the den occupants without leaving a mark."

Grabbing a hold of Rory's chin, I planted a firm kiss. "Showoff."

He grinned, his chocolate eyes glistening. He fed another tiny bite to the pup.

We sat around the fire. I nodded at him. "Tell us of your exploits, please." There was no reasoning with the man. He'd risked his life to gather intel. I was mad at him for it. But it would do no good to hold on to my anger. He was trying to solve the mystery, to save lives.

Rory told us of their failed hunt and of his attempt to teach Mick and Serafina a few tricks of the trade. Then he reported the half-alvae healer spotting a shadowy figure.

We all knew this. He was building up.

"It was a good thing, too. Another half a minute and it would have seen us, and the three of us would not be here to report or warn you."

"The beast?" Hombir prodded.

Rory described his maneuvers, running north and east and north and east before turning south. "Had to draw them away from Nikkel Bakken."

"Ye don't think they tracked ye here?" Tugg asked.

"It's why I went in the direction I did. With the wind wailing and driving the snow, I knew the combination would obliterate my tracks in a mere five minutes. My maneuvers shouldn't give them a reason to tie me to the d'oglemenn of Nikkel Bakken."

"Them?" I asked. "As in plural?" Rory rarely misspoke.

"Aye. There are two out there. Maybe more. Though I think this storm confounds them, limiting their vision. Maybe as much as us, well, not a half-alvae."

"The beast?" Hombir asked.

Rory chuckled as he set the whelp down and let it drink water from the bowl. "Aye. It's as tall as two and a half humans. Shorter than a Jotunn at least by a head. Doesn't have blue skin. Instead, it has white fur all over. So, it's not a giant." His mirth disappeared. "Big claws for hands, which they used to cast beams of ice. The magic threw the snow and dirt up into the air, leaving shards of rime a foot high and wide in its place."

"An ice ray?" Hombir asked.

Rory nodded.

Hombir's bony brows furrowed.

"What?" I asked.

"Something tickling my memory." Hombir waved a hand at Rory. "Go on."

"Yeah, that's not their weirdest feature. They have one eye. It's big and round and centered on its head."

Mick crowed like a rooster.

Serafina shushed him. "The gods! What is it?"

Hombir growled. "I need my rucksack. Give me a minute."

Rory went on. "I was playing with the first beast, learning what it could do, and shooting bolts at it when I could. They can run. Perhaps as fast as humans, or maybe as quick as d'oglemenn hopping. I think they don't like to do so, or can't for long."

I shook my head. "You are such a man."

"I love you, too," Rory said. "But that's where I got into a bit of trouble."

We waited for him to go on.

Rory picked up O'erlevendeh and cuddled him into the crook of his arm. "Oh, before I forget. I hit it with an arrow, but all that did was to render it wrathful. The bolt didn't slow it down. It howled at me. I may as well have offered it my bolts for a backscratcher. Anyway, I was waiting for the first one to come into view again, to give it a second spot to scratch, when I had this sense of foreboding. Roskva got real animated, which was my cue to skedaddle. I raced off a second before two rays of cold blew the ground up behind me. I think the first one communicated with the second one. Mentally."

"Mind magic?" I asked.

Rory shrugged. "Something innate to them, so not magic? But like the power Vidarr used to have."

"Lokke's spawn," I said.

Mick hiccupped. "Re-remind me, w-why w-we're out h-here a-again?"

"To help our friends," I said.

"To earn five thousand dreki," Rory said.

Shaking his head, Mick continued to hiccup.

Serafina said, "What's this power your friend Vidarr has, or had?"

"Mind magic is a common way of saying psionics." I swallowed with some difficulty. "It gave Vidarr the power to control thoughts and even emotions. He could make someone do something they didn't want to. He worked hard not to use it."

"But unless he was changing your thoughts," Rory said, "you couldn't feel him reading them. That he could do willy-nilly. Though again, he refrained from doing it with his friends. Enemies?" Rory shrugged. "No restraint."

"And can he do that now?" Serafina asked.

"No," I replied. "He lost that power almost two years ago."

"Now he's just a powerful mage," Rory said.

There was a lot more to it, but as it was in the past, they didn't need to know.

Hombir shouted from the other side of the fire. "Aha! I found it."

The portly mage came around with his finger stuck in the middle of his tome. "Jörmonruk. That's what that beast is."

Jonuku gasped. "But...that's a myth."

Hombir nodded. "From the first epoch."

Tugg growled, his hands waving in dismissal. "Fables. There be tall tales of battles by me ancestors, glorifying the dvaergs from Kral Bar Aggen." He scowled, his bushy brows forming a solid ridge. "It be said they be the reason there be three keeps anchoring the Mid Dreki Bergs. Kral Fal Is to the west and Kral Azza Rid to the east."

Hombir jumped in. "Says in this folklore tale that the Jörmonruks were wiped out."

"Aye, that aligns with our legends." Tugg scratched beneath his beard. "Giant battles and mighty mages, centuries before the Forgotten Wars, an eon before the Great Departure. Stories told to babes."

My eyes blurred. "The end of the Forgotten Wars marked the end of the first epoch. We're in the fourth one now—two years in since magic has returned."

"When did these Jörmonruks come back?" Serafina asked.

"About a year-*hic*-ago was when the first caravan-*hic*-*w*as attacked," Mick said.

I stood, swirling the snowflake pendant with a finger. "But how did they come back? Where have they been for the past two and a half thousand years?"

Something niggled at the back of my mind, but I couldn't grasp it.

Rory spoke with a warm resonance, the pup sleeping on his chest. "Folks. We've made a lot of progress. We now know what the enemy is. Send birds to Kral Bar Aggen and to Tyrrby, and anywhere else where they might know something about how to fight them."

"The wagons be here in a day or two." Tugg took to pacing. "If the blasted snow hasn't stalled them. Dare we go east to Azza Rid?"

Rory said, "Tell your correspondence partners to send reply birds here and to Kral Azza Rid. Who knows where we'll be?"

I said, "I think we go on after the wagons arrive. In the interim, we prepare defenses."

"Right." Rory chinned at me. "One mage on duty at all times. I don't mean to scare you, but you can't fight it in conventional ways. I think their cold beams can reach up to eighty strides. A crossbow is good for forty. And it's like sticking a pin into a cushion. They don't care. You'd have to be within ten strides to more than irritate it. The poor sight lines the storm created saved me."

Rory could evade one with his speed. But crossing paths with a ray of cold would undo him as quickly as the rest of us. "Magic is our way out."

Could two mages fight off two of the beasts? What if there were more?

I heaved a sigh. "Alright, folks. Get some rest. I need four crossbows by the cavern entrance. I'll take the first mage watch." Turning to Rory, I said, "No one goes out alone except you, my dear. And right now, I need you to run out and collect all those beacons we set. I don't want these Jörmonruks finding their way here."

"But I just got here." Rory winked at me.

I crossed my arms, not in the mood for his jokes.

Rory dipped his chin as he stood and stretched. "For you, my love, I'll do anything."

Chapter Sixteen

SIGNS

RORY

For three days we stayed busy gathering timber, making quick hunting forays—never to the east, always to the south by going up and over the ridge—and working out alternate battle plans. The latter was all guesswork, and if...when...it came time to engage the Jörmonruks, we would have to adapt fast.

Kral Azza Rid had been warned via bird. So far, none had returned to provide further information. We were relying on a tome Hombir said was over a thousand years old, and that was a book of tales to enthrall children, to make them mind and keep close while traveling in the wilderness.

The clouds had departed the day after my return to the cavern, leaving two and a half feet of the white stuff. By the third day of waiting—the caravan delayed—the sun, while not warm, did the job of a hundred dvaergs trampling all over the Ice Plains. The pile lessened to a six-inch deep patch of crunchy snow.

By midday of the fourth day since our encounter with the Jörmonruks, Tugg spotted the caravan's advance troops. Arm waves and hand gestures ensured no trouble was afoot. Our gear was packed, ready to keep going if the wagon train reported no big furry beasties. If they reported otherwise, then trouble was both behind us and ahead of us, muddling our choice of direction.

Six wagons rolled behind a hundred Avarkæsir. As they made their way down the western ridge, another hundred soldiers traipsed behind. Forty more walked way out north, acting as scouts. Like a cloud rolling over the land, the flanking guard bent their arc and swooped their way in. We stood in the middle of the village, near what had once been the All-Watcher's den. The ten-foot-tall stone totem now splayed out on the ground.

When the dvaergs neared, I spotted Sett in the lead. I glanced at Tugg. Was his jaw clenched?

Sett led his group to us. He stopped and surveyed what comprised Nikkel Bakken. "Hel might be more pleasant than this place."

I wanted to reprimand him for his insult, but he had the right of it. The Ice Plains in winter with a bunch of fifteen-foot-tall beasties running amok did not make for an enjoyable setting.

We swapped stories. Other than the snow, which had caused them to lose two days by their reckoning, they'd had no trouble.

Tugg nodded. "That cannot be said here. Ye already know about the d'oglemann massacre. Now we know what did it." He described the beasts.

Sett guffawed. "Now ye be telling children's tales."

I set my jaw and eyed him. When he stopped laughing, I said, "Not a tale. You'd do well to listen."

Sett's brows narrowed. "Ain't going to listen to the likes of ye."

Tugg's retort was sharp. "At ease, Sett. Rory has seen more beasties than ye and yer kin have for generations. His word be good and ye best be respectable to him."

Sett didn't like that by the look on his face. He stared Tugg down, but the Avarkæsir leader was having none of it.

Hombir broke the tension. "There's still fourteen missing d'oglemenn. I don't hold out hope that they're alive, but it would ease minds if we knew of their status."

I shifted the conversation further. "Are you up to keep going? Or do you wish to stay the night, to rest?"

Sett opened his mouth, but Tugg made the decision. "We go. The longer we stay here, the better the chance of another storm to stall us." He circled the group. "Unless there be objections. I be open-minded."

Sett looked down at his feet, then up at Tugg. "Aye. We keep going."

Ingefær nodded. "Aye. The sooner we go, the sooner we reach Kral Azza Rid."

We let the caravan group rest for an hour, feed their horses and the like. I directed our group to make final preparations. Hombir agreed we could take as much firewood from the cavern as we could carry.

I looked north. So far, the clouds looked thin and white and held off, leaving the sun to shine. When Sett's company was ready, I motioned to Mick and Serafina. "We have the horses. We're the advance scouts."

Mick groaned.

With about five hours of sunlight left, we struck out from Nikkel Bakken. Ingefær, Mick, Serafina, and I rode ahead.

I said, "Serafina, we're relying on you to spot the beasts before they see us."

She nodded. Her silver-green jaw was set firm, in recognition of the importance of her role.

That evening, I directed that no fires be made. Instead, the mages used their heat spells to warm up a dozen tents. The rest tried to stay warm by huddling under their wulv cloaks.

The following morning, we set out. With nothing but sunshine and slushy snow, we continued eastward until we stopped for the midday meal.

We were a day's hike from Nikkel Bakken. I searched the area and then my memories. I had ridden this way two years ago. Not that I remembered the ridges and trees and the shape of the land with any details. It was all a feeling. Somewhere around here, my friend Daran had been killed...because of my foolishness. Nay. My stubbornness.

I glanced north. The weather had shifted overnight, the wind gusting more often than not. Dark gray clouds portended copious amounts of snow. Whether a day or two, I couldn't say. What I knew was that the clouds soaked up the moisture thrown off by Is Vann—a lake heated by underground lava beds. The darker the clouds, the more snow would fall.

"Two days at most," Tugg said, as if he'd read my mind.

By that time, we would be some ten days out from Kral Azza Rid. Though the sun shone, the temperatures refused to rise, making what was left of the first snowstorm into a crunchy pile of snow by night and a sodden mess of slush by day.

I ate a quick meal of dried goods and water, and fed soggy bits to the wærg pup. It was coming up on a week since I'd taken the whelp out of his cave. I estimated that he'd survived another five days, possibly a week, on his own. Dogs got their baby teeth at three weeks. And because I didn't have any milk, I needed to get him on a diet of meat within the next week, or O'erlevendeh would tear everything he could to shreds.

Tucking the pup into my cloak, I gathered Mick and Serafina. "Let's hunt."

Mick whined. "Really? The last time we almost got eaten."

Ingefær overheard me. "I'm coming with you."

"I welcome your help." Finding Hombir, I informed him of our plans. "We're going over the ridge and then east. After an hour, we'll cut back over and should see you. Give us a half hour before heading out."

"We'll keep an eye out." Hombir looked south, then east. "I'll send a red beacon spell high in the air if we don't connect an hour before our planned stop." His dark eyes, set in a field of gold, darkened. "If I signal earlier and it sparkles yellow, come riding hard."

Serafina asked me, "You're not concerned about getting lost, or separated?"

I sensed a teachable moment. "If we cross back over the ridge before the wagons have gone past, what will we see?"

"Nothing. Melted snow," the half-alvae replied.

I nodded. "Which means we'll do what, Mick?"

The lad tugged at his tawny hair and scrunched his brows. Then his face cleared up. "Just kidding. We'll wait."

"Right, and if we see their trail, we'll ride a little faster than a walk and catch up."

"You make it sound so simple," Serafina said.

"That's because it is." Ingefær scanned the Ice Plains. "He's spent a fair bit of time in the woods."

Mick cleared his throat. "Ain't no woods out here."

Not quite true. The woods were over the ridge. We could see timber going up the slope to the ever-rising Dreki Mountains. But out on the Ice Plains, the lad had it right.

My wife winked at him. "You know what I mean."

I rode off, with the others following. As we crossed the southern ridge, the wind at our backs, I loaded my crossbow and told the others to do the same.

In the narrow valley running east to west, we turned left and walked the horses as we spread out. Trees made an appearance, as did scrub bushes. The latter were devoid of foliage, and the branches were gnarly and twisted.

We rode for an hour; the woods to our right thickened, which increased our chances of coming up on game. I looked at the sky. "Hold up." We had drifted southward. Well, the valley had, and we'd followed.

I worked in another teaching session. I pointed and moved my arm. "The sun is reliable as it moves east to west. Of course, it drifts a little depending on the season." Removing my glove, I wet my finger and told the others to do so. I asked, "Which way is the wind blowing?"

Mick shivered. "I ain't sticking my finger in my mouth."

Serafina said, "Cause you know where it's been."

Mick stuck his tongue at her. "That ain't it." Shamed into it, he pulled off his glove, wet his finger and held it high in the air.

"Which way is the wind blowing?" I asked again.

"Well, it blows from the north out here. Almost always." Serafina looked at me. "But if that's the case, then it's a little behind me, more at my shoulder."

"Correct." Ingefær said. "Which means?"

"We've turned southward a little," the once thief said.

I nodded. "Excellent. Let's leave the woods and head back over the ridge. I suspect we'll have to ride a little longer to get back to the Ice Plains."

Serafina scowled. "This place is gods' forsaken."

I jerked a thumb at her. "You got point, green eyes."

We followed her north, up the barren snow-covered slope.

As we reached the top of the ridge, she stopped, raising a fist high in the air like I had taught her.

I eased my horse beside hers. "What do you see?"

She pointed slightly to our right, where a copse of fir trees created a place to wait out a storm. "There is something about the ground over there that doesn't look right."

I peered, squinting. After a hundred strides, all that white just coalesced into a shapeless horizon, which the trees did a decent job of breaking up. I shifted my focus to the base of the trees.

And I saw it. Well, I saw sticks jutting out of the ground. White sticks. I growled low. "That's not natural."

Serafina paled. "No, it's not."

"What is it?" Ingefær asked.

I heaved a heavy sigh. "Something dead. But maybe not. Keep your crossbows handy. Be prepared to use swords. And magic."

I dismounted and gave Mick my reins. "Follow me in."

On the ground, I was faster than any horse, and if violence was needed, I planned to race in and administer death blows.

The snow sloshed and crunched under my feet. That, the horses' clopping, and the whistling of the wind, were the sole sounds to be heard. I raced ahead.

As I neared the white sticks, I knew what I saw. Hombir's missing d'oglemenn. I waited for the others to catch up. When they arrived, they dismounted.

I said, "The rest of Hombir's clan, I think."

We searched through the mound of bones. I kicked a pile aside, brushing crusty snow with my boot. The ground was stained red.

"Ugh," Serafina said. "I didn't need to see that."

Ingefær counted skulls. "There's thirteen skulls here."

Mick groaned. "An unlucky number."

Ingefær searched the area. "So where is the last d'oglemann?"

I glanced at the sky. Three hours of sunlight. We hadn't brought our camping gear, nor much food beyond a day's supply. We needed to reconnect with the wagons before it got dark. The whelp squirmed under my cloak. And O'erlevendeh needed to run a bit.

Before the Winter Solstice, surviving one snowless night was doable. Afterward, not so much. Not without a mage. I grinned at Ingefær, causing her to give me a puzzled look.

"A quick scout," I said, regathering my composure. We were at the northwest point of the copse of trees. "Serafina, move around the fir trees to the south. Ingefær, circle to the north. Mick, stay here and watch our butts."

"Which way are you going, Master Belkin?"

"Straight into the trees." I made eye contact, received confirmation, and nodded.

Stepping past the piles of bones, I hiked toward the trees. Maybe two dozen in total. It was an odd grouping in an odder place. The forest proper was half an hour to the south, over a ridge. I glanced about for Roskva. No sign of her.

Would there ever be a time when she failed to show up in time?

I shuddered. It was a bad time for dark thoughts. Like there ever was a good time.

Amongst the pines, in the snow, I found tracks. D'oglemann tracks. The snow had melted and refrozen since they were made. But the imprint of a d'oglemann's taloned foot was unmistakable. That meant it was less than four days old. Three since the storm abated, and one for our travel time.

I followed a few steps and spotted the track of a beast's taloned foot some four times as wide and long as my boot.

Great. Just great.

I trailed the tracks out of the copse and found Ingefær and Serafina. I pointed at the d'oglemann tracks, then at the giant beast's footprint. "He or she—well, *they*—went that way."

Instead of turning to look in the direction I pointed, both Ingefær and Serafina looked up at a tree behind me.

I turned around. "What the Hel is that?"

"Some sort of symbol," my wife replied. Which didn't tell me anything new.

On the tallest tree at the southeast end, about fifteen feet up on the south side of the tree, the bark had been cut or ripped off. Etched into the meat of the wood was what looked like a double *S*. Except at the top right and bottom left, there were clear head shapes carved out, like the design was meant to be snakes. I couldn't tell where the tails ended as they looped about the heads.

I frowned. Snakes. Not a typical critter to find out here. "What do you think it means?" I asked.

"Why are you asking me?" Ingefær replied. "I don't know. I've never seen anything like it."

"Mick!" I hollered. "Come around to the front of the trees. Bring my mare."

We waited until the lad showed up. When he arrived, I pointed. "Copy that in your wax tablet. Please."

Mick's gaze followed my arm. "Agh! Who would make something like that?"

"Duh," Serafina said. "The Jörmonruk."

Ingefær said, "It's something Hombir and Tugg need to see."

I circled, looking off into the distance. "I wonder if more of these signs are out there, and we've missed them."

"There are no trees on the Ice Plains," Serafina said.

I nodded. This place was an aberration. "Maybe there are signs inscribed in the dirt and rocks. But now they're covered with snow?"

"But why make them?" Mick asked as he worked his stylus.

I had but one answer. "They're marking their territory."

Wærgs did it. So did stygg skapps and humans. We all had our ways.

When Mick was done scribbling, I mounted my mare. "Now we follow the tracks of the d'oglemann." And the Jörmonruk.

"Do we have time?" Serafina asked.

"Maybe an hour, if the tracks continue southeastward." I dared to hope as we trotted. No blood meant the d'oglemann was uninjured—well, maybe he or she was, but the wound had been cauterized, or the blood had frozen over.

"Look!" Serafina pointed to the northeast.

A red flare burst in the midday sun.

"It's not yellow," Ingefær said. "No danger. They're going to stop in an hour."

Which was early. Why? I wanted more time to explore. I sighed. "Keep following the tracks. Come on."

Ingefær said, "We should ride northeast, not southeast."

"Trust me," I said. "We'll make up the time."

I turned my mare and trotted after the tracks. After a few minutes, the tracks turned east, which increased the time we could follow them. And after an hour of riding—Ingefær grumbling the entire time—the tracks kept going.

Why east? It made no sense. There were no d'oglemann enclaves within a hundred leagues. Hel, not within two hundred. Hule de Jern was to the south, a three-week hard ride. Kobber Unter Smuss was three weeks back west.

I waved an arm. "Since it's east, Hombir and Tugg have stopped maybe a half hour's ride north-northeast. At most. I say we keep going."

Ingefær sighed hard, her breath misting in the air. "It's going to get dark soon. I say we join up."

O'erlevendeh squirmed inside my cloak. "There's no emergency," I said, jabbing him with a finger. "We have almost two hours to spare. So we show up late for dinner. Let's ride."

My wife rolled her eyes at me. "Why are you so adamant?"

"That's Hombir's kin we're tracking." I raised myself tall in the saddle. "If he or she is alive, time is running out. It's going to be beyond freezing tonight. If the weather doesn't get them, the Jörmonruk trailing will."

Mick hiccupped.

Serafina warned him off. "No screaming out here. You'll attract the beast."

The other reason I want to go was, if there was a lone beast ahead of us—as the tracks indicated—the four of us could take it. At least, Ingefær could. I would be a distraction. The tricky part would be to keep Serafina and Mick safe. I raised my brows high and gave my wife my urgent eyes.

Another sigh. "Let's hurry, then," she said.

We rode off, interspersing a canter between trots. An hour later, I looked up at the setting sun.

"Time to meet up with the wagons?" Mick asked.

"Yeah." I growled. It bothered me to leave the d'oglemann behind. But I didn't trust our luck at night. Without a sun, and without flying snow, that round black eye might see better than both of Serafina's green ones.

Ingefær touched my arm. "At least we have information for Hombir."

I chewed on my tongue for a moment. "I know. But I wanted more. I wanted to find the d'oglemann alive." I stared into her eyes. "It's good to have hope. Somewhere out there, a d'oglemann's hope is waning."

Mick opened his mouth.

I raised my finger. "Don't say nothing."

Ingefær turned her mount north-westward. "Let's ride." She set off at a canter.

I glanced over my shoulder and hoped the escaped d'oglemann was alive. But if the trailing Jörmonruk hadn't gotten him, or her, then the Ice Plains had, or soon would.

With a rage-filled shout at the sky, I heeled my mare and raced after the group.

Chapter Seventeen

INAPROPRIATE CHATTER

INGEFÆR

We found the caravan just after nightfall. Thankfully, two hundred forty Avarkæsir left a deep, wide trail.

As we approached, we were challenged by a foursome of dvaerg guards. In the night's darkness, I couldn't blame them. Still, it unnerved me to have crossbows leveled at us as we rode the horses in.

Once we were close enough to be recognized, the dvaergs lowered their weapons. We headed for a campsite, in the center of which flames flashed and lit the area.

Rory groused. "I thought we agreed to not light a fire?"

I put a hand to my throat, ready to tinker with my pearl-white snowflake, but the wulv cape covered it. I wondered if its stated purpose would work out here. "Find out why first, before you get all riled up."

Rory grunted.

We dismounted, and I led Rory, Mick, and Serafina to the picket line someone had set up for the draft horses. There, we brushed, watered, and fed our mounts. "The horses got sweaty, so find a blanket and cover yours up."

Finished, we made for the campfire, which was dying.

Rory chinned at Tugg. "What's with the fire?"

Tugg wagged his head toward Sett. "He started it. The d'oglemenn scored an is-hjort. Fed half the troops with it. Sorry, none be left."

My stomach lurched at the thought of missing the tasty game.

Rory pulled O'erlevendeh from inside his cloak. "Got any bones left? Or the hide? Gristle and fat works, too."

Sett turned his head to eyeball us, then jumped to his feet. "What in the Realm ye be doing with that?"

"Looking to feed it," Rory said.

Sett stepped forward. His hands went to his hips. "A daft move. Ye should kill it."

Rory grinned. "Not a chance. And if you hurt him, you'll answer to me."

Sett scoffed. "Daft." Then, "Ye be risking the party with yer escapades. Running here and there. We sent the flare two hours ago."

While the oversized dvaerg made my earlier points with my husband, I defended Rory. "Wærgs serve a purpose in the animal cycle. And I won't see a young pup die from starvation. It's inhumane."

Tugg said. "Don't go starting things, Sett. They got here fine and there be no emergency. Why don't ye find out why our friends be delayed?"

Sett continued on, refuting Tugg's suggestion. "They're not me friends. They disappear for half a day. The d'oglemann mage wasted a spell, and if I hadn't made a fuss, he'd have wasted more."

Rory moved closer to Sett, exceeding the large dvaerg's height by several inches. "We were hunting game."

Sett made a point of looking behind us. "Not much of a hunter, then?"

I barreled between Rory and Sett. "You're looking for a thrashing with that kind of talk."

Tugg said, "Aye. If you don't ease up yer mouth, I'll help them."

Rory said, "Why do you—"

I interrupted. "We found signs of the fourteen missing d'oglemenn." I cupped my mouth. "Hombir! We have news of your kin."

Sett and Rory eyed one another. Based on my experience, they were seeing who would flinch first. With Rory's quick feet, if he flinched, he'd be burying the blade inside Sett's beefy torso.

Tugg said, "Stand down, Sett. Or I'll report ye to Premier Mina, and yer dreams of being Avarkæsir leader will be dashed right here, right now."

Sett's mouth twisted up at an angle. "Watch yerself, wanna-be woodsman. The Ice Plains don't tolerate errors."

I jabbed Rory in the ribs before he could retort. "Thanks for your concern," I said, and shoved Rory to the side.

Rory got my hint and took to scrounging the area until he found the is-hjort hide. Using a dirk's edge, he scraped sinew and fat into a small pile. The whelp dug in. Just a few of his pup's teeth had come in, so it was mostly gum-smacking and his saliva that broke down the leftovers.

Hombir approached with Jonuku in tow.

Standing before a loose circle of listeners, I reported our findings. "Two things. First is, we found the bones of thirteen d'oglemenn. Just like you reported earlier. Hombir, I'm sorry, they were stripped of their flesh and scales in the same manner."

Jonuku's taloned hand flew to her mouth. "That leaves one unaccounted for."

Rory nodded. "We tracked the d'oglemann—and a Jörmonruk—east, for nigh on two hours. We weren't lost, but once we found the bones, we didn't take time to hunt."

I said, "Other than tracks, we saw no sign of the survivor or the Jörmonruk."

"I think the tracks were at least three days old." Rory scooped the pup up before it ate too much. "But it could be four."

"We'll ride south to search tomorrow." I checked with Mick and Serafina and received nods. "The tracks parallel your route."

Hombir asked, "You sure about the number of days?"

Rory nodded, giving the whelp some water. "Four days ago is when the storm ended. There were signs of melting and refreezing. I don't know how your clan mate stayed alive for so long. Nor do I know if he, or she, is still alive."

Jonuku whimpered.

Hombir said, "He or she may have switched to cold-blood mode to survive the frigid nights. But then switched to warm-blood mode in order to move with speed by day."

I'd forgotten about that particular d'oglemann trait. It's how they survived the winters on this side of the mountains.

Sett said, "Bah. It be a waste of time. The d'oglemann be dead. Yer supposed to be our advance patrol." He chinned at Serafina. "At least the half-alvae be not entirely useless."

Tugg blindsided him with a haymaker.

Sett took the blow, staggered, but remained upright. Blinking his eyes, he turned to Tugg. "Ye want to have a row?"

"Don't talk about Serafina that way." Tugg stepped chest to chest and looked up at the brute of a dvaerg. "Ye mind yer tongue, or I'll do it for ye."

Sett's eyes flashed to the half-alvae. He snorted. "Ah. Ye be sweet on her." He turned away, laughing.

Tugg took a huge breath. "Sorry about all that."

I shook my head. "He's such a boor. How did he manage to rise in your ranks?"

Tugg growled. "Politics. His clan be growing in power. And, well, ye seen Sett. He be a monster. No other can fight him."

Serafina stood before Tugg and stroked his face with her slender fingers. "Thank you."

Mick grinned. “Weren’t you scared he would throw a punch of his own?”

Tugg shrugged. “Scared? No. Sett’s got a mouth on him. But he be pretty sharp up here.” Tugg tapped his head. “If he wrangled with me, the others—well, except for his direct clanmates—would be on me side. Also, I outrank him.”

Mick chuckled. “He’s like the turd in the washbasin.”

No one else laughed.

“Sett makes camp unappealing with his sharp words,” I said. Then, weary of that subject, I shifted focus. “The d’oglemann has survived for nigh on three weeks. Ever since the mauling of Nikkel Bakken. I say there’s hope.”

Mick said, “I think at least one furry beast had the fourteen d’oglemenn tied up somehow. And it, or they, used them as a food source.”

I gave Mick an evil eye. “No need to be so grim.”

Serafina added, “And disgusting.”

Rory said, “Sorry, Hombir.”

I said, “We’ll head out tomorrow and follow the tracks. But there’s another issue that we ran across.” I motioned at Mick. “Show them your drawing.”

Mick pulled the wax tablet out of his jerkin and passed it around.

Tugg said, “What we be looking at?”

Serafina said, “It’s a copy of an etching we found on the south side of a pine tree. Fifteen feet up.”

Rory said, “Had to be made by the beasts. Which means they’re smarter than a typical predator. I mean, we suspected it to be so, what with their silent communication. But this proves it.”

Hombir took the tablet and looked at it. “That could be a ward.” He glanced up at me. “Did you cast find magic at it?”

“No,” I said. I hadn’t considered it. “At the time, I didn’t think about it. You think it’s magical?”

Rory frowned. "I think it's just a boundary marker."

Hombir's scaled head waggled. "Might be. Might be something more. It's worth checking out."

Rory grumbled. "That's backtracking."

I said, "I'll ride out that way by myself."

"You will not." Rory's hands moved to his hips. He almost stepped on his whelp. "We all go, or no one does."

"But you need to search for the missing d'oglemann," I said.

"I won't have you go missing." Rory's eyes were hard. His normal warmth was gone. He scooped the pup up and cuddled with it.

Tugg asked, "How much time be lost by backtracking?"

Rory pursed his lips for a moment. "Two hours one way, after an hour's ride south."

We turned to Hombir. I asked, "Does the missing d'oglemann take precedence over the sigil?"

Hombir's jowls quivered. He shook his head. "No. That etching means something. Why else put it there? No other creature out here would see it, so it isn't much of a boundary marker. We need to know if it's magical." He tapped at Mick's tablet. "It looks like two snakes looping about each other."

"Yah, that's right," Mick said. "With two heads, one above and one below. What do you think it means?"

"No idea. But to put it so high in a tree makes my scales itch."

Mick chuckled. "Aye. My skin crawled walking about the pile of your kin's bones."

Jonuku burst into tears. Hombir hugged her and whispered to her.

I shook my head at Mick. He and I would have words when we were alone.

The group broke up, and we made for our own tent, one Tugg and his crew had erected on our behalf. I sighed, shifting my gaze from Rory to

Mick and back. My arms crossed my chest. "You two need to find some tact."

"Me?" Rory asked.

"Tack? Like a sharp pin?" Mick asked.

"No, she means like bridles, saddles, and such," Rory said, winking.

I narrowed my eyes at him. "That's not funny. And you darn well know what I said. Tact. With a 't' at the end. Be sensitive. You talk about the dead like it's nothing."

Mick hung his head, but I spotted his eyes eyeing me.

Rory said, "You're right. We got riled up with Sett's talk. At least I did."

Mick said, "It's not that I don't care, it's that there's nothing to be done about it. They're already dead."

"There're the feelings of the kin to consider," I said.

"Jonuku is struggling with this. That's plain to see," Serafina said.

"Just be more sensitive around her. Please?" I asked.

Mick nodded.

Rory showed off a dimple. "But not with Sett. He's earned my ire." He elbowed Mick. "Why, if I had a book of grudges, he'd be in it."

***

In the morning, we ate breakfast. O'erlevendeh whined at not getting more is-hjort gristle. We saddled up and rode off south. When we found our trail from the day before, we followed it back to the copse of trees.

"Do you think it's magicked?" Mick asked.

I shrugged.

At the circular stand of trees, we looped around, making sure the area was safe. I stopped us at the southeastern end and reached into my mage pouch, pulling out flax seed. Thrusting it into the air with my left arm, I made a circular, wiping motion with the other. "*Finne magicka.*"

"Well, I'll be," Serafina said.

Mick screeched, but kept the volume down. It reminded me of the sound I'd made when my da had pulled one of my baby teeth out.

The sigil glowed a subtle orange. My jaw dropped.

"Hombir was right to worry," Rory said.

I pointed. "Do the snakes look green to you?"

"Yes. They weren't green yesterday," Serafina said.

Mick let out a rooster crow.

"Come on," Rory said. "Let's get out of here."

"Wait a moment." I studied the carving. Had the snakes' heads shifted? The one on the top right had either moved down and to the left, and the bottom one to the right and up.

Lokke's spawn!

I pointed and told the others.

Mick pulled out his tablet and compared the two. "Aye. The snake heads have moved."

Serafina asked, "What does that mean?"

No one had a clue. Somehow, the magic sigil was alive. Or certainly operative.

"Come on." I jumped into my saddle and heeled my horse. "Let's ride."

We cantered to get some distance. My frequent glances over my shoulder revealed nothing. Two hours later, we picked up the trail of the d'oglemann, now a day older.

We cast prudence aside and rode faster than yesterday, trying to catch up to the track makers. We ate the midday meal standing up. The horses drank melted snow out of a frying pan I'd heated with a warmth spell, and ate grain from my hand. O'erlevendeh was less happy with the circumstances. The hard pemmican was too much for his nascent teeth, and we didn't have time to soak it. He ignored my offer of an apple piece and got by with water.

Remounting, we took off at a quick trot. Some two hours later, we crossed a ridge, running back to the Dreki Mountains on our right. All this time, I couldn't think why the d'oglemann kept going east.

Had he or she gone south, they would have reached the mountains by now. And there were places to hide. If nothing else, the timber provided cover.

Then again, there were better odds of crossing paths with a wulv or a bear or some other beast. To the north lay nothing but misery, and, in all likelihood, more Jörmonruks. Why hadn't the d'oglemann gone west?

As we stood at the top of the ridge looking east, past some craggy ground and onto a barren valley, Rory pointed at the ground. "The Jörmonruk stopped chasing after the d'oglemann. See its tracks? It turned north."

Had our caravan crossed paths with the beast?

"We need to return," I said.

Rory said, "Send up a flare."

"We didn't talk about what that might mean." I gnawed on a lip. "I don't want them to waste time and come this way. Sett will blow up."

Rory's mouth pinched, but his eyes twinkled. "Send up the flare. I want to see Sett agitated."

Serafina said, "A flare signal from us should stop the caravan. But I doubt they turn south. Maybe they'll send a search party."

She had a point. I worked with what I remembered and sent a beacon light flying. I didn't know how to make it sparkle the way Hombir did. After the blue light fell back to the earth, I said, "I don't know if it got high enough."

Rory nudged my horse with his. "We shouldn't delay. If they saw it, someone will come. If not, well, we need to hurry either way. The

Jörmonruk leaving the trail may mean the d'oglemann has found a place to hide."

Mick guffawed. "Now that's wishful thinking."

I scowled at the young man, and he shut up.

Down the ridge we went.

As we crossed a ravine, Rory gave a shout. "Over there!"

I brought my steed to a halt and scanned. A d'oglemann lay in the gulley. It wore a white winter cloak and umber trousers. But little else.

Rory dismounted and ran to it.

I got off my horse and made my way closer, waving at Mick and Serafina to follow.

Rory removed the white hood. He looked up at me. "It's Dartak."

"Is he—"

Rory lifted the snout and let it drop. "Yes. We're too late."

Dartak was, or had been, an elite guard from Asken de Gulles, the enclave where Vidarr had been born. What was he doing in Nikkel Bakken?

We rolled the d'oglemann over, and Serafina searched for wounds. He looked unharmed, but also scrawny and ragged.

"What killed him?" I asked.

Serafina shrugged. "I want to say the elements. But with the beasts casting ice rays, it could have been that."

I shook my head. "I don't think the beast got him. If it had killed Dartak, it would have eaten him. I think Dartak hid in the gulley, but was too weary to continue."

Mick stomped about, his head jerking back and forth.

"Knock it off." I jerked at his arm. "Get a hold of yourself."

Rory lifted Dartak up and over a shoulder. "We take him to Hombir and Jonuku."

I had Rory put him on the back of his horse. "Give the reins to Mick, so you're free to run. If needed."

Mick's nose twitched. "Um. Thanks?"

Serafina waved an arm. "Come on. Let's join up with the others."

As we rode, Rory asked, "I don't understand. Why was he going east?"

I didn't discern Dartak's reasoning either.

Mick tugged at his tawny hair. "Now we'll never know."

We rode in silence. Rory fussed with the whelp, who seemed tired of hiding inside a cloak. If nothing else, the wærg kept my husband occupied. Rory may well have gone off exploring otherwise.

Chapter Eighteen

ENEMY SIGHTING

RORY

After we caught up with the caravan, we handed Dartak's body to Hombir and Jonuku.

I said, "He was a fighter. He escape after weeks of captivity, and he hiked for four days with a beast behind him."

"I don't think the Jörmonruk got him. He probably died from exposure and lack of food and water." Ingefær bowed her head. "He was lying face down in a ravine."

Jonuku covered her eyes as she sobbed.

Hombir's lips turned down at the corners. "Thank you for finding him. We'd hoped, but it wasn't meant to be."

Sett came up. "Let's get a move on."

Serafina turned on him. "You are such a mean brute."

Sett's beady brown eyes narrowed. "Ye be holding up the caravan. Snow be coming, and the beasties ye folks think ye saw might come with it."

"Folks need time to grieve." I sauntered over, hands at my sides. "And I know what I saw. You're big and thick. Does the latter feature extend to your skull?"

"Careful, human. Rile me up and ye will find out."

"Hey." Ingefær tried to butt in between us, but I shifted using my special feet.

The double-speed motion caused Sett to blink.

"Yeah," I said. "You'd last all of ten seconds."

"Oi!" Tugg ambled over. "What be going on?"

"Sett's being rude," I said. "And we were discussing our next step."

Sett's eyes shifted left, then right. "Go on then, grieve. We roll in ten minutes. With or without ye."

He turned and left.

Serafina said, "I don't like him."

We informed Tugg of finding Dartak's body.

"Hoist him up into a wagon." Tugg's gaze floated over to Serafina. "We'll hold a proper burial tonight."

When that was done, we moved east and stopped for the night. We built a pyre downwind of our campsite and dedicated Dartak's body. Normally, songs would be sung in Varanusian, but none of the d'oglemenn were up to the task. A pair of dvaergs with some musical talent sang a dirge for the dead in Dvaervish.

I said a few words about him. "Dartak was a reliable friend. To me, my wife, and to Hombir and the clan. But also to Vidarr, whose visit to Asken de Gulles could have ended differently if not for Dartak's aid. He was a capable warrior and stout of heart. I miss him already."

Hombir spoke as well. "He'd been elected All-Watcher this past winter. And he'd found a bride this spring. His second, as his first, died in childbirth. I performed the ceremony. Under his leadership, the mines opened, and the fields were sowed. They'd brought in their first crop three moons ago."

He raised a hand. "To Dartak."

The d'oglemenn around the pyre shouted, "*Bra gort*!" which translated to 'well done.'

Jonuku lit the pyre.

Afterward, I fed the whelp pemmican soaked in water. His teeth were making a pronounced showing. In another day or two, I would feed it to him dry. What he needed most was a fresh kill.

In the morning, as we packed and readied ourselves for another day on the gods' forsaken Ice Plains, I scanned the horizon to the north. The clouds were a darker gray than the steel of my sword. And they were on the move. The high winds returned. The snow that hadn't melted and refrozen was lifted into the air, stinging my face. I was in no mood for another blizzard. But I had no choice but to endure.

To make things worse, O'erlevendeh tired of warming next to my armpit. He scratched and writhed and either tore at my flesh or created a seam for the cold air to seep through. I had enough of it. I swaddled him in a blanket and tucked him into a saddlebag. He wasn't too happy with that, either. But I made sure he couldn't squirm free.

The snake sigil we had found caused my guts to twist. Seeing the snakes' heads shifting filled my bones with an eerie sensation. None of us had heard of something like that happening before. We'd seen plenty of wards. But none of them had moved or changed. Ingefær had noticed that the glyph had taken on a green sheen. An inkling in the depths of my mind scratched at my memories. But I couldn't place it.

We had solved one mystery, but now had another. Where the Jörmonruks had come from remained unanswered. Why they marauded was a mystery, too, though why wulvs and svartkatts hunted and killed was no mystery—they were hungry. But these beasts were sentient, of that I was certain.

Out of nowhere, a new species had erupted on the Ice Plains. Well, not altogether new. Over two thousand years ago, they had once roamed the Ice Plains.

What the Hel is going on?

Birds had been sent to Tyrrby and Kral Bar Aggen with a hundred questions. So far, no reply. That wasn't unusual. There hadn't been enough time, and we were in between keeps, so a bird finding us—especially in a blizzard—was improbable.

Tugg hollered at me, and I stopped my horse, waiting for him to catch up. "This next ice blast will be as bad as the first, snow-wise. Except colder."

"We have two mages and four healers who can cast warmth spells," I said.

"Aye. But we don't have Vidarr's Rod of the Dreki."

"Ah. Wise counsel." The mages and healers would exhaust themselves trying to keep all the tents warm enough. Their spells were good for an hour. With over a hundred tents, we would wear them out.

Tugg said, "We be alright for now. But if we be out here in a moon—well, freezing to death will be on everyone's mind."

"Then let's not be out here in a moon." I winked at him.

"What I be saying be that once we reach Azza Rid, Sett and the others might not want to go back out. Not unless they have a good reason. Not until the spring months."

Oh! Well, troll shit.

"You can't order them?" I asked.

"No. The caravan be keep business. And until the Jörmonruks attack a keep proper, going in search of them be a voluntary campaign. That be how our system works."

I had counted on the dvaergs' strength in aggregate. "But we can ask for volunteers?"

"Oi, aye. Always. But coins or a split of the spoils will be expected." Tugg moved off to talk to a soldier.

So, when the truly frigid weather hit, there'd be maybe two dozen of us. That lessened the burden of keeping everyone warm, what with two mages and two healers. But would that be enough strength to fight the white-furred, one-eyed beasts?

I already knew the answer to the question. Nudging my horse, I shifted toward Ingefær and relayed Tugg's nugget of information. "You up for riding out in the heart of winter without a company of dvaergs?"

She frowned. "We could claim the thousand silver and report our findings to Vidarr. But it would leave a foul taste in my mouth to leave a job unfinished."

I flashed a smile. "We haven't traded blows in a proper fashion."

"You think we can take them?"

"One or two at a time?" I rolled my shoulders. "I think so. Their entire clan? No. Not at once."

Her bright blue eyes twinkled. "We need more information."

The sun went down that evening just as the clouds arrived. Tugg's crew passed out pitons—a nifty device for anchoring the tents in high winds. As we crawled into our tents, it was snowing hard, and—no surprise—the wind howled, making it a blizzard.

We snuggled in our tents, wrapped in our cloaks, even as we dug deep into our bedrolls. O'erlevendeh decided he wanted to sleep outside of mine, settling himself on the tarp covering the ground.

Mick nodded his head a dozen times.

"What are you doing?" I asked.

"I'm agreeing with myself."

"About?" Ingefær asked.

"You's all are crazy. You've been out here before, so you know what it's like. Yet you dragged us out here."

"You came of your own free will." I shifted my cloak to cover more of my legs, which were buried in the sleeping roll.

"Ah, the lure of coin." Serafina's emerald eyes shone. "Has led many to their deaths."

"Now don't start talking like that," Ingefær said. "No one is dying. We're unraveling the mystery. We know who—well, *what* it is."

"But not where they are." Mick screeched with his mouth closed. "Nor how to kill them."

"A couple of fireballs will change their prowling ways." Ingefær rolled over. "Now shut up and go to sleep."

I wondered about that. I hoped she was right. But the beasts had surprised me a couple of times, and something pinched between my shoulder blades, telling me more surprises were in store. The dual shifting snakes kept me from falling asleep for far too long.

***

We woke to half a foot of snow. As the white stuff continued to fall, we dressed, ate, and packed. After storing our tent in a wagon, I joined the others, who stood with the horses already saddled.

"Buck up, husband of mine," Ingefær said as she squeezed my hand. "We're going to need your unique skills."

"What? To run away?" I forced a laugh.

"No, to scout ahead." She smiled at me. "Tugg asked."

That made sense. I was the best tracker. "I'm going to need Serafina's eyes."

Serafina licked her dark green lips. "As long as I'm on horseback."

Ingefær said, "Keep your eyes on the horizon. Don't engage. Come and warn us, mister fast feet."

"You and Mick aren't coming with us?" I asked.

"No." Her brows wrinkled, and she bit her lower lip. "The more bodies up front, the bigger the chance someone will get spotted. And it's more bodies to fret about in retreat. We use our strengths to our advantage. That means Tugg's soldiers, and Hombir's and my magic."

"And the worst thing we can do is to lose a mage, cutting our power in half." I kissed my wife, savoring the sweet and salt of her lips.

Serafina and I rode out ahead, cantering to start. After a dozen minutes, I slowed my horse to a walk, and she followed suit. The wind had lessened, so the sight lines weren't horrible...maybe two hundred strides from atop a knoll.

Serafina asked, "What do we do if I spot them? Not just one, but say a dozen?"

Ingefær had already said what we should do. But I understood her question. I had a habit of improvising and reckless self-endangerment.

"We ride like the wind," I said, meaning it. "No heroics. Myself included."

After a half hour of walking the horses, I surveyed the horizon. It wasn't snowing as thick as it had in the first storm. But it would soon enough. I asked, "What do you think of all this snow?"

"I like it. It melts on the tongue and tastes like the cleanest water in the Realm." She swiveled her head to the right. "But the cold is another matter. Back in Vanaby, it rarely ever froze, and then for but a day or two. I didn't spend enough time in Slangeh Buktah, but I suspect it's the same."

I nodded. "The spine of the Dreki Mountains forces more of the cold to the human side, though the city seldom freezes. It snows north of the city two or three times a season. Maybe a couple of inches. But with each day's ride north, it seems to double."

The value of selecting me for my tracking skills disappeared in a blizzard. The snow wasn't too bad. But the wind had picked up again. I looked at a sea of white. And when I shifted my gaze to the north, I blinked as flakes struck me in the eyes and face.

The day ended with no sightings.

***

Our routine firmed up. Serafina and I rode point by day, leading the caravan ever east. By night, we huddled in our tent with Mick and Ingefær.

For four days, we rode over undulating ground covered in snow. I believed we were four or five days out from Kral Azza Rid. The second storm of the season had lasted three days. Then it took an unusual one-day break and started up again in the morning.

Tugg agreed the pattern was off. It either meant we'd see four days of the white stuff, or it would all clear off on the morrow. One thing remained consistent: the wind never quit. Well, two things. The temperature stayed below freezing the entire time, day and night.

After lunch, I was on horseback with my pup growing irritated with me as we waited for the others to reconnect. It didn't take long to report nothing, and soon enough, we were back out front. The wind stayed a persistent howl. The snow increased. Visibility dropped to a crossbow shot.

I'd always been of the opinion that when riding out in the wild, a boring day was a good one. It increased the odds of staying alive. We crested a ridge, and my gaze swept the horizon as that familiar eerie tingling ran up my spine.

A few seconds later, Serafina hissed low. "Stop!"

We were side by side, and I did as she said. I followed her gaze down the ridge we had just climbed. Putting a hand over my eyes to keep the flying snow out of them, I said, "I see nothing."

"Shadows moving. I'm sure of it."

Shadows. Plural.

I peered into the snowy haze. Nothing.

Maybe a flicker. Darker. There.

"It's coming this way." Serafina's voice notched higher.

I spun around. "Come on."

"It's big. Like what we ran into the first time." She had yet to turn her mount around.

I reached down to grab the reins of her horse and pulled her about. "Let's ride."

A mighty roar, as loud as a perturbed dreki, exploded to our rear. I heeled my steed and held on to her mount's reins, pulling it and Serafina with me.

We raced away from the sounds of erupting ground, and the air crackling as it froze.

A Jörmonruk had spotted us.

We galloped the horses down the ridge and raced for the caravan. As we reached the shadows of the advance scouts, I shouted. "Jörmonruks!"

Tugg's form emerged as the distance dwindled. "More than one?"

"Uh, I'm not sure," I said. "Serafina spotted one. And it saw us."

"It saw ye?"

I nodded. "Fired its ice blast."

"How far behind?" Tugg asked.

I shrugged. "Three minutes. Or not at all."

Tugg asked, "We run? Or fight?"

I smiled. I knew what he wanted. Me, too. But sometimes running was the best choice. I thought about it.

The dvaergs were hardy and could run far. But two hundred forty dvaergs and a half dozen wagons couldn't run fast. And if we ran, we'd be going the wrong way in a snowstorm. And if we ran, it would allow the beast to pick us off one by one.

Besides, we needed to test our mettle, if my suspicions about their numbers were right. Best to learn how to fight one or two at a time, rather than a couple of handfuls all at once.

If there were good gods, I'd have prayed that there weren't more than a couple of handfuls.

I said, "We fight. That's my counsel."

Tugg called for the crossbows and pointed, shouting more instructions in Dvaervish. Dvaergs assembled into three lines, seventy soldiers in each. Sett came up and asked what the hullabaloo was all about.

The caravan had stopped, and Ingefær and Mick rode up to join the impromptu council. Only Hombir was missing.

I said, "At least one Jörmonruk. It spotted us."

Sett scoffed. "Ye let it see ye?"

I smiled at him. "I did. On purpose. Just so he could chase us here and you could see one with your own damned eyes."

Tugg growled. "Both of ye. Knock it off. Sett, go anchor the far-right flank. We use the snow and poor sight lines to our advantage. Take two score, half with crossbows. If I give the signal, I want ye to flank them."

Sett's gaze bore down at me, but I smiled back. He grunted and jogged off.

Ingefær said, "You shouldn't let him rile you."

I smiled at my wife. "Oh, he didn't rile me any. I was riling him."

Tugg shook his head. "That's the last thing we need."

"Get Hombir up here." I motioned to Ingefær. "You two should be spread apart behind the dvaerg lines. But not too far from the center trail that Serafina and I left."

She told Mick to find the mage, dismounted, and handed her reins to a dvaerg standing by Tugg.

"Why aren't you deploying all of your troops?" I asked.

Tugg chewed on his lower lip. "To keep a reserve to either reinforce a flank or to lead the assault. And to guard the wagons."

Tugg turned and motioned another dvaerg over. He spoke in Realm's Tongue, so I knew what was going on. "Get the wagons ready to roll west. Ten soldiers to the north, south, and east of the caravan. Watch me signals."

"Serafina," I said, "you have scout duties."

Mick came running, with Hombir and Jonuku hopping behind him. D'oglemenn have surprising speed. They can jump a dozen feet from a standing position.

I waved with a hand westward. "We need to discuss our tactics. Follow me."

With Tugg and everyone else in tow, I led us to the center of the long dvaerg line, but stayed a dozen paces behind the third rank. The front two rows were filled with axe- and shield-wielding Avarkæsir, and the rear flank held the crossbowmen.

I said to the group, "With Sett anchoring the far-right flank, we'll use the center and left as our main engagement line. While crossbows are effective to forty strides, my bolt made it mad."

Tugg grumbled. "Ye be saying we let the beasties get closer than forty paces?"

"No." I blew a steaming gust of air out. "The problem is, at sixty paces, its ray blast will make mincemeat of your troops."

"What do ye suggest?" Tugg asked. "To stand there and take the brunt of the spell?"

I patted Ingefær on the shoulder, but spoke to Tugg. "Your troops are the bait. Ingefær and Hombir will be behind you, a bowshot apart. My wife stands in the middle and Hombir takes the left side. Upon a call of sighting the enemy, they'll raise magic shield walls."

The sergeant anchoring the rear line frowned. "That stops our bolts going the other way."

Ingefær's brows pinched. "Yes. But I can shape my wall of air and move it around, too. I'll place it five strides before the first rank and will holler when I've made it waist high. If the beast is within range, you should have the angle. As soon as it blasts its icy ray, I'll raise the wall again."

Tugg's mouth puckered. "Risky. Timing be tricky. But I like the idea of having sorcery on our side. Haven't had a mage in battle since Vidarr."

The wagons and thirty soldiers became our rear guard, reinforcements, and counterattack all in one. D'oglemenn formed a personal guard around Hombir and Jonuku, who agreed with the battle plan and moved to the left flank.

We waited. I estimated our quick roundup of troops and discussion had taken five minutes. Though we had galloped the horses, the beast or beasts should have reached us by now.

The wind wailed, and the snow slashed at us from the north.

After waiting ten minutes, and with no sign of the Jörmonruks, I suggested we advance.

Tugg agreed. At his command, we trudged forward. I tapped Mick on the shoulder. "You stay with my wife and Serafina, you hear?"

Wide eyes met mine. He nodded. "She's my best chance for surviving, isn't she?"

I nodded. "Your slingshot and stones won't be of much use. Not saying you shouldn't try...."

"And where will you be, husband of mine?" Ingefær asked.

"Scouting." I had to make sure we knew how many of them there were. My gut told me there was more than one out there. I took several steps to my left.

She hollered at my back. "Don't get into the line of fire."

Leaving my horse with Mick, I waved, acknowledging I heard her. As I sped north, flanking the dvaergs' left edge, I searched for my fylgjæ.

Roskva hadn't showed. Yet.

Chapter Nineteen

TRIAL AND ERROR

INGEFÆR

We marched east in a wide arc. The front line of dvaergs were elbow to elbow, with the shield of the warrior on the left covering the one on the right. Two steps behind was the second line, their shields above their heads and parallel to the ground, protecting from projectiles. The third line was five strides back, the Avarkæsir holding their crossbows across their chests in both hands.

In the center of the entire formation, Tugg hiked behind them, with Serafina beside him. Thirty paces off to my left, Hombir walked with Jonuku. Mick and I were ten paces to Tugg's right, slightly off center. Behind us rolled the wagons, with the rest of Tugg's company spread out in a loose formation.

Rory's prior escapades hung heavy on me. His tactic of spying out the enemy was sound. But I didn't like it.

After five minutes of hiking through the blizzard up a shallow slope, Serafina gave a shout, pointing left of center. Tugg gave a command, and the line stopped. Dvaergs hunkered behind their shields, the second rank moving to the first. Shields overlapped shields. The crossbowmen lined up behind them. By the strained necks and jerky head motions, they were peering into the wind-driven snow, trying to spot a target.

My gaze swung out, but I saw nothing. I flashed my eyes to my left. Hombir was motioning with his arms.

Better early than late, I raised a wall of air using goblin bone dust. It was wide but low, and I placed it about ten feet before the first line of dvaergs in order to provide maximum depth of coverage. My shield wall covered the width of some twenty dvaergs. There would be gaps, either height-wise or width-wise. But the beasts would have to find them, or get lucky.

Rory's suggestion of using a wall of air shield spell made the most sense. The hard wall of air was visible in direct light—not the overcast skies we had. In these conditions, spotting the reflected twinkles of light along the wall's edges would prove difficult.

I could have countered Rory's suggestion and used a fire shield wall. The problem was, the spell wasn't solid. It burned hot, which should counter the ray beam—maybe obliterate it by melting it. But maybe the blast of ice would punch through. Likewise, a crossbow bolt could fly through the fire shield, maybe catching flame as it went. The bolt wouldn't burn up before it reached its maximum range.

We couldn't know for sure which tactic was best. And I didn't want to find out. Ever.

Serafina pointed. I shifted my wall to the left.

I peered into the blowing snow. A smudge on the horizon moved. What was that?

A shadow shifted. Closer. I blinked snow out of my eyes.

A silver-white shimmering beam strafed the ground and raced toward my wall, throwing up dirt, rock, and snow, leaving behind a foot-tall ridge of ice.

I braced for the hit.

The ice ray bashed into my wall. I grunted as I pushed back.

The beam of silver-white climbed the wall and skirted the top. Ice formed above and beyond the wall and dropped, crashing onto the dvaerg formation. Fortunately, the shards of ice weren't huge, and they bounced off the shields, the crystals shattering in every direction. Not unlike a hailstorm, except with pumpkin-sized chunks. Dvaergs cried out. A quick scan showed me that none had fallen. Their shields, helmets, and armor had diffused most, if not all, of the falling particles.

The ice ray stopped.

I resized the air shield to a mere two strides. "Fire high!"

Tugg yelled. "Fire at its head."

Crossbows launched their arrows.

The Jörmonruk strode forward, stepping into the bolts, waving its arm like I would at a host of pesky flies.

I saw the beast clearly. Fifteen feet tall and covered in white fur. One giant eyeball, almost a perfect circle, as black as night.

It raised a hand. I shifted the wall back to original height.

The Jörmonruk fired at the ground, throwing rock and soil against my wall. The debris bounded off, but the pummeling jarred my shoulders.

The ice blast stopped for a second. The beast restarted its magical ray straight at my wall. Ice covered the front, sticking to the air shield, blocking visibility and adding weight.

My wall grew heavy. "I can't hold it."

"Fireball!" Hombir shouted.

I glanced over. Both of his hands gyrated. He must have dropped his wall of air. I could hold the wall of air up and cast a fireball at the same time. But it would take longer. The effort also drained more of my stamina than normal.

I strained to keep the wall of air upright. "Ugh. Hurry!"

If I dropped it, the front line would be dead. And a couple of seconds later, me, too.

Hombir's flaming pea sailed over the heads of the left flank, right at our assailant.

The ice ray must have stopped, as the weight ceased getting heavier. I could no longer see through my wall; it was so clouded over from ice.

But I held it, groaning as Hombir's fiery bead exploded. The flash of fire radiated red and orange in the white denseness. The Jörmonruk's fur flamed, and it dropped from view. Heat flashed and hit my wall, melting some of the ice, but not all.

Then the blizzard kicked up and obscured my sight lines.

Tugg motioned with an arm. "Forward."

Oh boy. I tried to shove the wall of air forward, but it was all I could do to keep it upright. Risking it, I dismissed the spell and followed the dvaergs.

Chapter Twenty

FIGHTING BLIND

RORY

I had moved around the left flank of Tugg's dvaerg line and, using my magic feet, I'd sped as fast as I could in the snow, angling north-eastward to the ridge's crest. After descending the short ridge, I slowed to a walk and moved south-eastward. Either I would run into a beast, or I would circle around the one Serafina had spotted. At least, that was my plan.

I scanned ahead of me, keeping the crest of the small hill to my right. Snow struck me from behind. It was my one advantage, besides my fast feet. If the beast looked my way, it would have wind-driven snow to peer through. Come to think of it, I didn't remember seeing the beast blink.

A fireball exploded off to my right, just at the range of my vision. The detonation illuminated a Jörmonruk standing atop the ridge. It blazed in reds and oranges as it fell to the ground.

I pumped my fist in the air. *They can be killed.*

Whoops. Spoke too soon.

The no-longer-white and no-longer-furry beast crawled on all fours for a dozen paces down the slope of the short hill, then climbed to its feet. Charred all over, the beast jogged east, passing my position at max crossbow range.

Alright. At least it could be harmed.

As I considered dashing in and hacking at its...knees?...soft thuds sounded to my left. Dropping to the ground, I pulled my crossbow off my back and cocked it.

Come closer. Closer.

The second Jörmonruk, pristine white, stopped twenty strides before me, looking toward where the fireball had come from. Either the snow thinned or the wind took a breath. For all at once, I could see the dvaergs and Hombir and Ingefær standing at the ridge.

They were looking the wrong way. The beast raised its massive paw, a talon extended.

I fired my crossbow at its exposed side.

A solid *thwack*.

I didn't wait. I jumped to my feet and raced east to its rear. Roskva joined, shaking her head. Unexpected tactics won fights. This unpredicted maneuver placed me in higher danger than most would consider sane.

I drew my sword and made a sharp turn, aiming right at the white-furred beast. It had ignored my gnat-like arrow and had its back to me as it walked its ice ray beam toward the front line of dvaergs.

The line of rime and dredged-up dirt crested the ridge, striking the right side of the formation. Ice sprouted up a dvaerg's shield, climbed up and over, and slammed into the dvaerg's face. Then, in a matter of an eye blink, ice began to encase the dvaerg.

The Jörmonruk strafed his frost weapon left, shattering shields and coating three dvaergs in crusty ice.

I sliced with my sword, aiming for the backside of the beast's knee joint—which was as high as I could slash with any power.

Blood spurted, and the Jörmonruk howled as it crashed onto its back. The ray ceased.

I pirouetted and slashed at the beast's neck as it rolled onto its knees. Blood gushed.

An arm swung and flung me ten feet sideways. The snow softened my landing. Who was I kidding? Hitting the ground took the air out of my lungs.

By the time I got to my feet, so had the Jörmonruk. It bled. A lot. If it didn't get healed soon, it would die.

It raised a hand, and I stepped closer, ready to dart between its legs. But the hand kept going to its maw. It bugled.

Was that a sound to attack...or a call for help?

I didn't wait to find out. I raced in, slashing at the good knee. This time I hit bone, and my sword jarred loose from my hand. I dashed left.

I turned around. The white beast staggered as it worked its way east.

"Come on, Roskva. Let's finish it."

I sprinted to the pool of blood and found my sword. The Jörmonruk was ten strides away. It didn't run, but each giant step covered three of mine. Its back was an inviting target.

Roskva shook her head at me.

Yeah. Tempting the fates isn't the smart move. So, I changed my mind.

I raced toward the dvaerg line, which was obscured by a fresh salvo of blowing snow.

When I could see the dvaerg formation, I slowed to a stop and waved an arm for them to come. They worked their way down the slope and stopped where the snow had melted, revealing the hard-packed dirt of the Ice Plains.

I nodded at a dvaerg who let me pass and met up with Tugg. Moments later, Hombir, Ingefær, Jonuku, Mick, and Serafina joined us. I told Serafina to keep watch on the eastern horizon.

Tugg asked, "Anything interesting to report?"

I wiped the blood off my sword using clumps of snow. "You wounded one with a fireball. It's as crispy as fried potatoes, and shambled out of here on unsteady feet. I cut one pretty good. It's bleeding from the neck and knees. So, it moved in slow lopes as well."

Sett showed up, out of breath.

"What was that sound?" Ingefær asked.

"It bugled, using its hand and mouth. I think it was a retreat order. Or maybe just a call to regroup."

Tugg cursed. "We be fighting blind out here. I've lost six outstanding soldiers, and all we did with our arrows be to lose a hundred."

Sett said, "Ye should have had me anchor the center." His dark brown eyes found mine. "Ye say ye wounded one?"

I nodded, waiting for something tart to come from his mouth.

"Good work," he said.

What had changed his mind? The unnatural noise? Or losing kinfolk?

Hombir said, "The way to fight these is with magic, not swords and axes."

"So, ye want to be taking the front line, then?" Sett asked. But his tone had changed, and he had a grin on his face.

D'oglemenn are hard to read. Humans blush and pale, as do dvaergs and alvaes. But the scaled ones' complexions almost never shift. Not that I'd seen. Sett's comment, however, showed everyone they paled.

Hombir shook his head.

We discussed the alternatives.

Mick suggested returning to Kral Bar Aggen. I think he joked.

"It be ten days easy, more like two weeks, to reach Kral Bar Aggen," Sett said, glaring at Mick.

Tugg shook his head. "No. We can't turn back. Not when we be so close."

I cleared my throat. "Azza Rid is east of us. And so are the Jörmonruks. How many days out are we?"

Tugg scratched under his beard. "Four days with the wagons."

Hombir looked back the way we had come. Then east. "Aye. We keep going."

I stood tall. "The Jörmonruks are between us and our destination."

Ingefær said, "They can be hurt. With teamwork."

I nodded. "Alright. Let's go."

Chapter Twenty-One

MAKING PLANS

INGEFÆR

I raised my hand to get everyone's attention. "Not just yet. There's something else to discuss."

Through the flying flakes, I felt all eyes on me.

"We need to evaluate our battle tactics. And decide if there should be any changes made."

The group grumbled; some looked at the ground. I chinned at Hombir. "Rate our success as mages."

Hombir squinted. "On what scale?"

"Zero if we're all dead," Rory said. "And ten if they're all dead."

Tugg said, "I lost six dvaergs. We didn't kill any of them."

Rory shrugged. "The two wounded I saw may yet die. Unless they have a healer. Burns are deadly. An infection may take a week to kill it, but it may be 'walking dead' and not know it. The one I cut up bled from a neck and leg wound. A lot. It'll bleed out unless bandaged or healed."

Hombir said, "A three then."

I nodded. "I was thinking two. We lost six, and they maybe didn't lose any. Yet we bloodied them. That, I think, is a first for them, so an extra point for that." I nodded at Tugg. "No offense. But I think the various trade wagons that have gone before were taken by surprise. Maybe an axe landed. There's been no sign of marauding until the Nikkel Bakken disaster."

Sett said, "There's been no survivors either."

"The point I'm trying to make is, let's not get overconfident." I searched their eyes. "And let's evaluate our tactics. What worked? What didn't? What could be done better?"

Hombir nodded. "The air shield wall spell worked."

I grimaced. "Yeah, but not long enough. The beast attacking the center had almost figured out that if it layered my wall with more ice, I couldn't hold it up. Your fireball was the distraction I needed."

"The fireball wounded one," Rory said.

Serafina, standing ahead of the group, her head turned eastward with a hand over her eyes, swept the horizon. "Except in a blizzard, we can't be certain we'll always see them beyond forty strides."

Mick said, "T-they can't s-see us either."

Rory hugged Serafina. "Your eyes worked and helped us get the drop on them."

"They be big." Tugg grinned, his beard lifting high. "We can spot them easily enough when it be not snowing."

"But then it can outrange you with its weapon," Hombir said. "But not our fireballs."

So far, the Jörmonruks hadn't shown an ability to see through the snow any better than we could. At least by day. Was that a function of the big round eye? Could it not see in the traditional sense? Did it sense in other ways?

I said, "We have four days of travel ahead of us. They know we're out here. They know we can punch back. Today we saw two. How many will we see next time?"

Mick crowed like a rooster. Then he stepped left and right and clucked like a chicken.

After a minute, Rory said, "That's enough. The gods! I don't understand why you do that."

"Grow a pair," Sett said.

Mick stopped squawking, but yanked at his hair.

"No need to be vulgar," Serafina said, glancing over her shoulder.

Sett spat off to one side.

Mick's shoulders arched up and then down. "I don't know why I do it either. It's an overwhelming sensation. I-I have to do it. It releases my fears."

Serafina turned around with a half grin. "Really? It unsettles me greatly and lights a fire under mine."

"Oh." Mick continued to yank at his tawny strands. "Sorry."

The half-alvae resumed her watch.

I touched the spot under my throat, where my snowflake lay beneath my red woolen cape, and cleared my throat. "Back to my original question. What parts of the battle plan do we keep, and what do we change?"

"Keep the fireballs," Rory said. "Use the wall shield, but shift to fire. Fire melts ice."

"If they work at it, their ice blast might snuff out the fire," Hombir said.

I agreed with the possibility. "But worth trying at least once."

Tugg grunted. "How wide can ye make the wall?"

"My wall of air covered twenty of your Avarkæsir in the first rank." I gritted my teeth. "It's as wide as I can make it and still have it fifteen feet high."

Hombir said, "Same here, except I covered twenty-five soldiers."

Tugg said, "Then instead of going seventy warriors wide like last time, we arrange the front line to no more than thirty soldiers. With a second line of shields, and a like number of crossbows behind them."

I brushed snow out of my eyes. "Hombir sets up the air shield and I go ahead of him and test the fire shield. If mine works, then Hombir can drop his wall and can blast them with fireballs. If it doesn't, then I'll drop mine and blast them with my fireball incantation."

Rory paced. "That's a thin front."

Mick said, "It strikes me that the beasts don't think laterally." He fiddled with his tawny hair. "I mean, Master Belkin's flanking attack worked well. Of course, there has to be someone to engage them, to distract them from the front."

Rory nodded. "I knew you were here for a purpose. You solved the marauders' trek across the Ice Plains and now you spotted a potential weakness. Though, I'm uncertain your assessment is accurate in total. They may not think laterally. But don't forget they can communicate silently. Perhaps that ability has a range, and it's why the second Jörmonruk bugled."

I said, "They have just one eye. Maybe they don't see well to the side. And now that I think about it, their ice rays aren't all that accurate. I mean, it strafed the ground, and the beast ran it forward to the shield wall spell. The second blast was more accurate, though."

Rory pointed a finger at me. "I was going to say the same thing."

"I be not following," Tugg said. "So what if they cannot aim well? The ice kills."

I half-turned, putting the wind at my back. "It means the best thing to do, if you're not behind a wall of air or fire, is to run to their side or rear. And to attack that way as well."

"Oi! That be a field commander's dream, to attack from the rear all the time." Tugg shook his head. "Not realistic."

"But with these monsters, I think it's not as hard as we've become accustomed to." I sighed. "Rory's attack worked because of his unique speed. The rest of us might manage it if we're disguised." I turned to Mick. "You still have that invisibility scroll?"

Mick patted his overcoat. "Aye. But I'm not running in with my dagger."

"No. I was thinking pitch and flaming arrows." I winked at him. "You soak them, and Tugg's crew lights them on fire."

Mick's eyes lit up. "Aye. That I can do."

Sett asked, "How will me folk know when and where to shoot flaming arrows?"

Tugg pointed a meaty hand. "A good question. The first be obvious: wherever ye see a beastie. But as far as Mick being invisible, I don't know."

Jonuku said, "I have some dye. We'll get all the vials of pitch a green or blue shade."

I said, "Alright. Rory and Mick can be in charge of distracting them. Tugg, you're in charge of making flaming arrows. Hombir and I will test our magic shield wall combinations."

Was that enough? "I'm thinking ahead. Let's say we discover the fire shield works well. With two fire shields, we can expand the front line into a sort of half bowl and shoot arrows from the sides. Removes the need for Mick and Rory to run around."

Rory said, "Arrows won't be effective at over twenty paces."

"They are if all we want is to light them on fire." Hombir said.

My husband frowned. "Not just one arrow. They used their hands to deflect the bolts. You'll need more than a handful at a time."

Tugg grunted. "Means we have to coordinate. Range of forty be shy of their ice ray, so that problem remains. We should prove the value of the fire shield first."

Sett smiled. "I like the idea of getting close. I wonder what a score of us can do with axe work. If we be right at their feet, chopping away, can they still do their spell?"

Hombir said, "I wouldn't think so. If the ice ray is cast magic, then any blow should disrupt their spell."

I crinkled my nose. "I think it's an innate ability. Don't count on the disruption. But again, it might be worth trying...if you get the chance."

Serafina spoke over her shoulder. "We need a third mage."

"Aye," Tugg said, "That would be of tremendous assistance."

Sett stared at the ground, the snow covering what had been a barren field of grass. "I be wrong."

We waited for him to go on.

"I apologize for me earlier behavior. And me words." He looked up, finding the half-alvae's emerald eyes. "Yer eyes give us a chance." He pointed at Rory. "Yer courage and yer feet, information." He choked on something as he eyed me. "Yer magic, and Hombir's too, the strength to best these beasties."

Serafina bowed her head an inch as her face darkened. She smiled. "Thank you."

I said, "And your troops provide us the opportunity to do all of that."

After a few moments of silence, I pointed at Mick. "You're in charge of the vials of pitch. Make at least a dozen. Work with Jonuku to get them full of dye."

Tugg said, "Aye. We'll make some of our own and give it to the soldiers without crossbows. We'll get some arrows wrapped in flammable cloths."

I smiled at the group. "That was an excellent discussion. Now we can walk to Kral Azza Rid with confidence."

Mick whooped, his fist pumping the air.

"Confidence," I said. "Not exuberance. And yes, there's a difference."

The group disbanded and made preparations to head east. Tugg and Sett elected to bury their dead instead of building a pyre, citing the proximity of the Jörmonruks. That proved an arduous task for the mining-oriented dvaergs. But in their true never-quit fashion, they got it done.

Chapter Twenty-Two

AMBUSHED

RORY

A day later, we crossed a narrow river that was half frozen over. While it slowed us down as we worked on getting the wagons across, it allowed us to refresh the horses and replenish our water supplies.

Tugg said, "This here river flows northwest and then turns to Is Vann. One of three such rivers feeding the Ice Lake during the spring and summer months."

A day after that, two days out from Kral Azza Rid, Serafina and I were riding point as a new snowstorm wailed around us. The wagons and dvaergs were a quarter of a mile behind us. The snowflakes were so fat and fluffy and the air so thick with them, we could see maybe a double crossbow shot.

Serafina said, "I can't believe it's snowing again."

"Usually, there's a three- or four-day break between blasts. But because the first one quit after two, and the second one had a half-day pause, Tugg is unsure how long this one will grip the plains. Plan on four days. Five if it's bad."

She pointed at the ground. "We're already riding in snow knee high to me."

After the second storm, the snow hadn't melted. "Until well after spring, it's going to pile higher. But don't fret. We're about to see the warm confines of—"

"There!" Serafina pointed to the northeast.

My head snapped, following the direction of her fingertip.

A giant shadow moved.

"Come on. Let's warn the others." I turned my mare around.

"Oh, no!" Serafina cried out.

I glanced back. The healer had turned her horse around but hadn't heeled the mare into motion yet. Instead, she was still watching over her right shoulder.

My gaze followed hers. "Well, Lokke's spawn."

I counted six dark orbs shuffling toward us.

Not waiting to see if there were more, I demanded, "Ride!"

I let Serafina surge ahead of me as rays of ice roiled the earth behind us. The rime crackled and blew snow high into the air, leaving a ridge of ice above the ground. The blasts dwindled off twenty strides behind me. They weren't yet within range. Serafina had seen them in time.

I spurred my mare into a gallop. Foot stomps thudded in rhythm behind us.

Great. Just great.

I shouted at Serafina's backside. "They're running after us!"

After several eye blinks of the horses galloping, I lost sight of the beasts. Other than tracking our hoofprints, they were running blind in the snowstorm. Based on my prior dashing about, I knew the horses could outpace them. That was the good news.

The bad news was, they were between us and Kral Azza Rid. And as the thumping behind us continued, they appeared serious about trading blows; they had retribution on their minds.

At a gallop, it took a couple of minutes to reach the dvaerg advance line. I waved my hands over my head. "Form up!"

I searched for Ingefær or Hombir. Spotting my wife, I yelled at her. "Shield wall!"

She ran over, her boots trudging on the already-trampled-down snow.

Serafina shifted south. "I'll get Hombir."

After Tugg brought the group to a halt, his dvaergs bustled into position.

I gritted my teeth. We had talked about a narrow front flank. But there were six of the beasts. Maybe more. I dismounted next to Ingefær and Mick, and waved Tugg over.

While he trudged through the snow, I secured O'erlevendeh in my saddlebag. He snapped at me a couple of times, not liking how tight I made his bed.

When Tugg arrived, I said, "There's six beasts coming. At least."

"Six?!" Mick shouted.

"Lokke's spawn." Ingefær raised a finger, telling me to wait. She went through the gyrations, blowing into a cupped hand and sprinkling dust that I presumed to be made from the bones of goblins. Words were uttered. Varanusian. A language that befuddled me. Might as well pull my tongue out and cut it at the base.

"Go on," she said.

Hombir shuffled through the snow with Jonuku and Serafina in his wake. He found a spot ten strides to our right, nodded at us, and faced east. We watched the dvaergs form up. The wagons were rolled backwards. All the preparations for getting into our designated positions took too long.

Serafina shouted. "Look!"

I scanned the horizon. With a lessening of the wind, I counted eight heads, a hundred strides out. They spread out, forming an arc like the riser of a longbow, with the curve centered on us.

Ray beams erupted, strafing the ground as they meandered toward the dvaergs. Still thirty strides off, the beams stopped...for the moment.

"Hurry, Hombir," Tugg said. He waved a hand at me. "I have to go." Tugg raced off to join his troops.

I glanced at the line. Sett had placed himself in the center of the first rank. Normally, the backside of dvaergs made it hard to discern who was who. But not with Sett. Though hunched, he still stood a head above everyone else.

Ingefær raised her voice at the d'oglemann mage. "Let's do it backward to what we planned. I've got the air shield wall already up."

Hombir nodded, pulled sawdust out of a pouch, and waggled his hands.

A fire shield bloomed into place, a wide rectangle glittering orange and red as flames snapped and popped some five strides before Ingefær's air wall. Hombir's fire shield wasn't as wide, leaving a couple of paces on each side where the air shield wall spell twinkled at the edges.

The downside to a fire shield was that no one could see through it.

I commanded four of Hombir's d'oglemenn. "You two, go left. Keep your heads down. You two, go right. Come back and tell us what you see. And spread out."

They looked at Hombir, who had Jonuku by his side. The mage nodded and said something in his native language. The foursome hopped off.

We waited. The Jörmonruks were studying us, plodding closer, step by step. Perhaps talking amongst themselves via their minds. The quiet filled me with dark thoughts. I preferred hearing the eerie, tinny crinkling of their ice rays.

Getting what I wished for, a ray beam struck the far-left of the wall of air. Ice accumulated. Ingefær grumbled.

Hombir shifted his fire shield to the right.

The ice ray disappeared from view. A hissing sound erupted in the air. It was as if a thousand pots of water boiled at once. Even at my distance, copious amounts of steam rose through the air.

"It's working," Mick said.

Serafina dug into her breeches.

I eyed her. "What are you doing?"

"Got my wand of summoning." She shrugged. "Might come in handy."

I nodded. But I was unsure. She had tried to use it once before. After summoning three raccoons, she hadn't tried again. Maybe some small animal could work as a distraction? Something a Jörmonruk would worry about stepping on.

I winked at her. "If you use it, try to summon a porcupine."

She grinned.

Mick slapped three vials into my hand. "The unmarked one is for healing. The two with red x's on them are filled with pitch and colored with blue dye."

"I need a torch."

"Tugg's folks can light them on fire." But he handed me two unlit ones. I tucked one into my belt, and he lit the second one with his tinder kit.

"Be careful," Ingefær said, her jaw muscles tight.

"Worry about holding the line." I moved behind her and kissed the nape of her neck. "We'll be alright."

We held our positions, neither side doing much, other than the beasts taking turns to blast at the fire shield. I knew that because of the steam and noise. The high pitch of the ice beams also came in bursts.

It had been a dozen moments since Hombir had shifted his spell and, so far, nothing penetrated.

They were feeling their way through. I said, "I'm going out and around."

Ingefær's lips stretched thin. "Is that such a good idea? You could throw the pitch from behind Tugg's line."

"Serafina, how many do you see?" I asked.

She frowned. "Not sure. Four?"

I shook my head. Where were the other ones? "I need to disrupt whatever they're planning."

My wife grunted.

I took that as approval, not that I needed it. *Do I go left or right?* I was thinking left, because that was north. And that was the direction they should come from...based on our prior encounters. Had they given flanking a thought?

"I'm going north." I winked at her. "Can't stand waiting around."

I didn't even get to take a step, as a Jörmonruk appeared on our left flank at max visibility. Where the Hel were the two d'oglemenn?

I cursed and glanced over my shoulder as shouts erupted behind me. Another beast showed up on our right flank. This one was already in range of the dvaergs on that side.

They had outflanked our shield walls.

"Fire!" Tugg yelled.

Most of the dvaergs aimed left, while a smattering aimed into or above the fire shield wall. Like pesky flies buzzing around a horse's hind end, the Jörmonruk swatted at the few that came close. I didn't see a single arrow score. The beast was out of their range.

From the front, the four Jörmonruks had spread out. Ice rays slammed into the left side of Ingefær's shield wall, while steam hissed against Hombir's fire shield. The d'oglemann mage shifted his wall to protect the dvaergs.

The Jörmonruk to the south stepped closer and raised his hand. An ice ray strafed along the ground and into the far right flank.

"Troll shit." I turned to Mick. "You still have that invisibility potion?"

He nodded.

The beast from the north approached as if on tender feet. Which gave us a few more breaths. "Use it. Take out the one on the left. I got right."

I tapped Ingefær on the shoulder. "Give a shout before you cast fireballs."

She nodded, sweat forming on her brow as she dealt with keeping her invocation up.

Tugg hollered. "Right flank. Reform the line! Fire at will!"

I sped off south at double human speed, taking an angle on the beast.

Tugg yelled. "I need a shield wall here!"

Where 'here' was, I didn't know.

Ingefær's voice strained against the whistling of the wind. "Yours, Hombir!"

I lost sight of my wife and the others as I sprinted southwest, angling forty paces from the beast encasing Tugg's soldiers in a mound of ice.

The huge, white-furred beast shifted his ray beam to me, the ice ray furrowing ruts in the snow. Roskva appeared, and I burst forward. The beast's deadly ice blast trailed behind me.

I continued past the creature, thankful that the beast chose to turn away from the pile of frozen dvaergs. Slowing, I turned and faced the beast. I waggled the lit torch high in the air. "Yah, yah. You can't catch me."

I doubted he could understand my words, but maybe he took the gesture as insulting.

It must have. The beast strode after me.

Good.

I ran at a quarter of Roskva-imbued speed south-eastward, causing the beast to change its angle.

After two hundred strides of my slow slog through the snow—slow by comparison to what I could do, but just fast enough to keep the Jörmonruk out of range—I'd gone as far south as I wanted and turned east. The ice beam strafed the ground as the Jörmonruk ran after me.

Time to lose the beast on my tail.

Roskva kept me from getting exhausted, as we sprinted ahead until we were lost in the snowstorm. To get close enough without getting struck asunder by an ice beam, I had to have the element of surprise. Which meant I needed to sneak up on them.

I hoped Mick was dealing with the beast attacking from the north.

Having lost my pursuer, I sprinted northeast at half Roskva's speed until I thought I was in the main Jörmonruk group's rear—the four Serafina had seen. Feet stomped off to my left, but the sound receded as the beast went past, still heading southeast.

I peered into the blizzard, moving northeast, then northwest. When I had first run southeast, my plan had been to flame the lone Jörmonruk. But as it was occupied—searching for me, I hoped—my plan changed. Now I wanted to take out the beasts assaulting the center. I had to trust that Ingefær's shield wall held, and that Hombir would adapt to wherever the next threat came from.

A sense of urgency filled me. Fears of Mick handling a beast by himself, invisible or not, grew inside my gut. At half my normal speed and using the gusting northern wind as a guide, I jogged toward what I thought, and hoped, was west.

Soon enough, I spotted four shapes, their backs to me. Slowing to a walk, I crept up behind them.

I arrived at the rear of the Jörmonruk line; three of beasts laced their cold rays into a fire shield, presumably Hombir's. The fourth one added to an already humongous wall of ice and frost. Each beast was about five paces from the other.

Would the beasts tire of casting their spells before Hombir's and Ingefær's spells waned?

Doubtful. Hombir and Ingefær had spell limitations: the spells' size, duration, and stamina. These ice creatures seemed to cast ice rays at will. And there were more of them than our two mages.

Now and again, I spotted arrows flying through the fire shield. Some were on fire. All fell short.

I threw the first vial of pitch to the center between beasts two and three. Before it landed, I threw the second vial to the right—Ingefær's left flank—between beasts three and four. The snow turned blue around the beast's clawed feet.

The noise spooked the one on Ingefær's end, and it ceased its beam and began to turn around.

Behind me, the heavy stomps of a Jörmonruk told me my rear was exposed.

I raced as fast as my magic and Roskva would let me. In that blink of an eye, with me still ten steps away, the other three Jörmonruks turned off their magic and turned.

I lit my second torch with the first and threw it at the closest pool of pitch. Not waiting, I dashed right and tossed the second torch just as a pair of beasts screamed out and a stream of rays blasted the ground behind me.

"Come on, Roskva." Not looking back, I sprinted northwest to get out of their range, drawing my sword as I went.

I soon lost the pounding of heavy feet to the wind's howling, though the screeching of burning beasts gave the whistling wind a haunting echo.

After half a minute, I stopped running to go over what I knew. Aye, there was at least one, maybe two, chasing after me. Three were on fire. The one beast that had come up behind me could be the first Jörmonruk from the south flank attack. Or it could be a seventh beast.

With both spells still up, I felt better that the line wasn't about to be breached. But then I remembered the Jörmonruk on the north flank, and the two missing d'oglemenn. And Mick.

"Shit!" I said to myself and turned west.

A few seconds into my sprint, Ingefær's voice pierced the air. "Fireball left!"

Mirror imaged...that was my flank! And Mick's.

Chapter Twenty-Three

DEATH, ON ICE

INGEFÆR

The weight of the wall strained against my shoulders and my mental grip on my incantation. Shifting it was difficult, and raising it, impossible. For some insane reason, the beasts continued to hurl their frost blasts at our walls.

I chanced a glance to my far right, where Rory had darted and dashed, toying—I hoped—with the Jörmonruk. There was a wall of ice a stride and a half high and six strides wide, encasing five Avarkæsir. Other dvaerg soldiers now hid behind the beast-made obstacle.

But for now, the south flank was clear.

Where Rory had run off to, I didn't know. Closing my eyes for a moment, I heaved hard, trying to expel an enormous sigh out of my chest.

Surveying the center flank, Tugg's warriors lobbed arrow salvos, some tipped with rags soaked in pitch. Whether the flaming arrows did anything to the beasts behind the wall of fire, I couldn't tell. For all I knew, the arrows fell short.

The last I counted, there were four beasts on the other side of the center flank, at least one of which attacked my air wall. But maybe it was two. The rest battled against Hombir's incantation.

Grunting at the physical weight of my invocation, I glanced left, where Mick hopped on a horse and rode wide of the Jörmonruk, bearing down from the north.

The front four were keeping us pinned down, while the other beasts struck at us from the sides.

The Jörmonruk ignored Mick and instead blasted our left flank, strafing ice across a half-dozen Avarkæsir, starting at their knees and working the beam up.

I couldn't move my shield, it was frozen in place. So I let it go. The mass of ice remained standing.

Tugg yelled. "Left flank. Aim left. Fire at will."

A salvo of bolts flew in a looping arc. At their range, and firing into the wind, the crossbow bolts fell well short of the target. It was like the creature knew the range of crossbows.

The dvaergs holding that side of the line were iced over. The Jörmonruk tried to get at the next rank, but its own ice wall blocked its incantation. That caused the beast to shuffle forward.

I hollered at Hombir, who stood off to my right. "I'm dropping my air wall. You take over."

As soon as Hombir widened his wall of fire, lowering the height from six strides to five, I released my spell. I dropped my arms and realized I couldn't feel my shoulders.

Serafina shouted. "Look! To the left. A second beast."

Another Jörmonruk advanced from due north. That couldn't be the one that chased after Rory. Could it?

I glanced right. A second beast came into view, where Rory had raced through minutes ago. Or maybe it was the first one that had chased after him.

Where the Hel was my husband?

"Troll shit." We were being surrounded. "Tugg. The right flank!"

Tugg got his troops moving. Nothing to be done but to rush the beast while firing crossbows.

I focused on the two on the north end of our messed-up formation. Mick appeared through the gale and flurries, galloping on his horse from the west. He threw a vial of pitch. It struck the beast on the shoulder, the fur turning blue. A second later, Mick threw his torch. The beast twitched an arm, and the torch was flung away, never coming into contact with the flammable stuff.

An explosion to my right, the center flank, shifted my gaze. Fire flamed beyond the fire shield, climbing a dozen feet higher than the top of Hombir's wall. Then a second explosion erupted.

A grim smile formed. *There* was my husband.

With my husband to the center left, I shouted. "Fireball left!"

I screamed into the wind and had to hope Mick heard me.

Tugg yelled. "Fire!"

Bolts flew at the beast on our right flank as Sett led the charge with a host of dvaergs with battle axes, while a dozen with crossbows shot looping arcs high in the air, using the wind to increase their distance.

With a host of warriors frosted over twenty strides in front of it, the Jörmonruk stopped its ice beam and flailed its gargantuan arms in front of its eyes, swatting bolts out of the air.

Aha! They have a weakness. I changed my spell.

Instead of a fireball, I lanced three fiery darts at the beast targeting Mick and his horse, aiming high at its round orb.

The beast wailed as its massive claws flew to its eye. With a 'whoop', the Jörmonruk fell backwards and bounced once. Then lay still.

The second beast on our north flank slid to a stop in the snow. It raised an arm and raced a frost beam at the galloping Mick. I breathed a sigh of relief as the deadly ice ray fell short.

I had but a moment and used it to shout at the others. "Fire at the eyes."

Hombir's arms were splayed wide as he held the wall. I couldn't hear the sound of any ice rays, and was about to tell Hombir to cease his spell. But then I saw a shadow move on the other side.

A ray of ice strafed over the top of the shortened fire wall. The beast's beam lanced the ground a couple of strides behind Hombir and Jonuku.

Hombir was quick to raise his fire wall, hiding the enemy anew.

Shifting my gaze south, dvaergs chopped at the beast's legs. The ice ray laced the ground before the Jörmonruk's feet, freezing the warrior's heads in one swipe after another.

I could sail a fiery bead at it, but then the other dvaergs would be killed. Instead, I strafed a set of fiery darts at the beast a hundred strides away, aiming at its eye.

The spell flew true, and with the white-furred beast preoccupied, the black, round orb was pierced thrice.

Another beast fell backwards.

An arm tugged at my sleeve. Serafina's voice rasped, her eyes bulging. "Jörmonruk coming fast."

I spun around and invoked another set of fiery darts.

Mick dashed in on his horse from behind the beast and threw a vial of pitch, followed by a torch.

The beast bellowed, its entire left side in flames.

"Behind you!" Serafina yelled at Mick.

I peered into the blowing snow. A shadow shifted. It was too far for my spell.

Mick, however, was in range of the beast's ice ray, which tore the ground as it raced for the young man.

Mick dismounted, swatted the mare on the ass, and unrolled a piece of parchment.

In the blink of an eye, Mick winked out of sight.

Smart. I hoped he was shrewd enough to run away from the beast.

The Jörmonruk bugled a 'wheoo, wheoo,' and lumbered toward us at a run. It continued its ice beam as it leaped and bounded through the snow. The earth trembled.

With what appeared to be a practiced slide, the beast skidded to a stop beside the first flaming Jörmonruk, lancing its blast of ice toward the dvaergs who had refilled the left flank.

I was about to let my fiery dart spell go when the beast turned sideways. It continued to fire its lethal frost incantation, finding warriors to encase in its ice.

I canceled the fiery darts, because the beast's position shielded half of its eye and it used its other massive paw to peek through, limiting what I could target.

"Get away, Mick!"

You're in my range now!

I waited for a breath. Dvaergs were dying before me. I lined a fiery bead at the Jörmonruk, setting the detonation zone four strides behind the beast.

The fireball exploded, burning the beast's entire back side. Its ray beam faltered, and it fell to the ground. And, as luck would have it, the smoldering beast fell atop the first one, getting a second dose of fire.

Serafina asked, "You alright, Miss Ingefær? That's four, by my count."

I nodded. "One more. Be ready."

I hollered. "Hombir! Fire darts to their eyes!"

Hombir's snout dipped and the fire shield wall dissipated, revealing two Jörmonruks. One was charred on his right side, and the other one—still white and fluffy—stood to the beast's left.

They were fifty paces away from Tugg's front line—in range with their infernal weapon.

Tugg yelled. "Steady! Aim for their eyes."

I hurried to get my fiery dart spell activated before the beasts rumbled into my range. "I got the charred one."

The half-burned Jörmonruk raised an arm and fired its blast of ice. It fell short of the dvaerg line, but it walked the weapon in. The other beast bounded twice and lifted an arm, ravaging with its destructive blast of ice.

Arrows flew. Beasts' arms flailed.

Hombir got off his salvo and took the unharmed beast down with three darts to the eye.

I fired at the half-burned brute. Three direct hits into its orb.

It died like the others, with a wail as it fell backwards.

Some distance away, a bugling sound filled the air. Three short blasts. The pounding feet thrummed through the ground ahead of us to the left.

Tugg said, "Watch the flank, lads!"

I cupped my hands around my mouth. "Rory! Don't be a hero!"

With the wind blowing and the snow flying, we gathered ourselves. I had Serafina restore my stamina, though I could have cast one more. Hombir had cast three as far as I knew. He waved off Jonuku's aid.

I searched for my husband. But there was no sign of him. Tugg got reports from his sergeants. We gathered together.

I asked Tugg, "How bad?"

"Beasties got in some good licks." He frowned. "Two score plus one. Be a grim day."

Hombir said, "I'm missing four from my group."

Serafina said, "What you need is longer-ranged weapons."

Tugg nodded. "Aye. But we don't have them." He sighed. "Something with range can't be carried on the back."

I said, "There's at least five dead Jörmonruks, I think."

Serafina pointed. "Six. There's a mound over there that isn't snow."

I said, "We can't stay here. Sorry, Tugg. We need to gather ourselves and keep marching."

Tugg chinned at Sett. "Gather the dead in a pile. We set a pyre and march. Twenty minutes."

Hombir flipped his snout at a pair of d'oglemenn. "You two, search for kin. Stay together, but far enough apart."

Sett organized a group of warriors and began chiseling away at ice statues. The pair of d'oglemenn ran off to the south.

I scanned the area. "Mick! Come on back."

"I'm right here," he said from behind me.

I about jumped out of my skin. Turning with a growl, I said, "That wasn't nice."

Mick, still invisible, said, "Sorry. I forgot you couldn't see me."

"Can you stop the spell?" Serafina asked.

"Not that I know of," Mick said, the voice emanating from empty air. Now I knew how Rory had felt when I was invisible during our escapade in Vanaby.

"Well, stay out of the way, then." I rotated my shoulders, which ached. I pointed at Mick's horse, which had run off to our west. "Don't go after your mare just yet. We'll do it together when we know it's safe."

Serafina and I, along with Hombir and Jonuku, kept watch on the horizon. While I looked for white-furred beasts, I kept an eye out for my husband.

Where are you?

When the dead were assembled in a pile atop some of our firewood, pitch was poured. We stood in a circle as Tugg, then Hombir, said a few words. Sett set the mound of dvaergs aflame.

Serafina scowled. "That's grisly."

Tugg nodded. "Aye. But it beats leaving them for scavengers—or worse, the Jörmonruks to strip them of their flesh."

Sett said, "We could have buried them. But with the hard ground—we be in a rocky basin—it would have taken all day. Time be not a luxury we have at the moment."

The half-alvae shuddered, whether from the implied threat or leaving the dead to burn, I didn't know.

Tugg put an arm around her. "I don't care for it none, either."

I got Serafina and a still-invisible Mick together, and we retrieved three of our horses, one of which was Rory's. With Hombir and Jonuku watching our flank, we spread out and searched to the west for Mick's mount.

We found her pawing at the snow, trying to get something worth eating.

Mick said, "I got her."

When I saw the stirrups shift and the reins hanging above the horse's head, I knew where Mick was.

"Now on to the hard task." I gritted my teeth. Had my husband succumbed? A gut punch roiled my insides. With a quivering jaw, I said, "Spread out, twenty paces on me. Keep an eye out for Rory."

You better not have gotten yourself killed.

We moved east, and I got Hombir, Jonuku, and the five surviving d'oglemenn to form a picket line. We hiked past the two smoldering beasts, then shifted direction to the four dead Jörmonruks in front of what had been our center flank.

We stood there, our gazes trying to penetrate the blowing snow. Tugg and what was left of his company trudged up to meet us, the wagons rolling behind him.

"Rory!" I scanned north, east, then south. "Rory!"

Tugg peered north, a meaty hand over his bushy brows. "Clouds still be as dark as iron. Another day of windblown snow for sure. Maybe two."

I shivered. "I-I can't leave my husband out here. Can we take an hour? With more folk searching, we could cover a lot of ground."

Tugg's beard scrunched. "There be a caravan to deliver."

Sett said, "I'll help. Permission to ask for volunteers?"

"There!" Serafina pointed northeast.

From out of the swirling white flakes, Rory strolled into view, cleaning his sword with a rag. He lifted his blade high in greeting.

I gnawed on my lips, waiting for him to reach us. I was both ecstatic and angry.

When he was near enough, I spoke, my words clipped. "I'm glad to see you're alright." What I wanted was to strangle him for his running around, endangering himself. Then smother him with hugs and kisses.

"And you as well." Rory's gaze took us all in. "How many did you get?"

"There's seven dead in total back there," Serafina said.

He grinned. "I got me an eighth. One got away. Hobbled him, though. There's a blood trail running north." He looked at me. "I decided not to chase after it."

I grunted. "Good call." Maybe my anger at his antics waned a little. Maybe.

Overall, the battle had gone well. Losing even one person meant it wasn't a complete success. But we had bested the enemy. Unless there were a hundred more of them, I felt confident we could take them.

After Rory mounted his steed, we rode east, the sun setting on the Ice Plains. I gazed into the darkening snowstorm. It worried me that one had gotten away. How would they adjust their tactics? Would we arrive at the dvaerg keep before they found us again?

Chapter Twenty-Four

KRAL AZZA RID

RORY

As we made for Kral Azza Rid, Hombir and Tugg sent messenger birds to update Kral Bar Aggen and Tyrrby about the beasts and their—mostly—unsuccessful ambush. I tried to force a smile, but there were too many dead we'd left behind.

I glanced at my wife. She glowered back. It's not that I did anything wrong, other than take too long to dispatch the ones I had chased. I would have told her about my dashing in and out, using the thick flurries to hide my approach and again to cover my escape. But that would earn me her ire. I didn't have fireballs like she did. So, I took care of the problem in the most advantageous way I knew—with Roskva's help.

My entire encounter had taken nigh on half an hour. I was being careful, tracking and trailing behind, letting the beasts think I'd run off before striking again.

"The good news is," I said, looking at my wife in profile, "I don't think there are any more of these things in our way. Can't guarantee it. But if there were more to the east, I think the two I chased—now one—would have gone that way."

Ingefær grunted.

Invisible Mick said, "You risked your life to learn that?"

A twinge of a smile formed on my wife's mouth.

"Well, that was a secondary learning. No, I was testing their ability to see in the storm and to coordinate amongst themselves. They didn't put up much of a defense to my marauding." I scrunched my shoulders. "I don't think they've experienced something like me before."

"Yes," Ingefær said. "I understand their confusion now."

At least a corner of her lip had turned up.

I turned to the quiet Serafina. "We have point. In case I'm wrong."

Another entity let me know they weren't happy: O'erlevendeh. The pup whined and yipped, still tied down inside a saddlebag. I spoke in soothing tones. "Soon, you'll have a feast." Tonight, of water and bread. But two nights later? My gut growled.

The snow came down thick and steady, flying almost sideways in the wind's gale. Between the moonless night and the copious snow, I could see, maybe, twenty strides ahead.

Serafina shook her head. "Shouldn't we stop? I can't see anything."

"Tugg said to march another hour. That way, we'll be certain to reach Kral Azza Rid by nightfall of the day after."

Ingefær added, "And we'll be two hours east of the ambush point."

At the appointed time, we stopped and pitched tents. Serafina, Mick, Vendeh, and I crawled in and wrapped ourselves in a blanket, and sat on another. Ingefær was busy casting warmth spells around the camp.

The lump of Mick's blankets revealed his lower half, with the rest of him remaining invisible. "The invisibility scroll saved my backside."

Not having seen Mick in action, I asked, "What do you mean?"

"I had it tucked in my belt, handy-like." Mick sniffed. "I rode the horse in from the side, got the vial of pitch to break, but the thing saw the torch and swatted it away."

"Maybe you should have turned yourself invisible before you started throwing stuff," Serafina said.

"I thought about that." Mick scooted down under his blanket. "But I worried that a lit torch would reveal me just the same. The way I did it, I kept the torch on the opposite side of my body, so it couldn't be keenly seen." He harrumphed. "Didn't matter. A second one showed up behind me. I never read so fast in my life."

"So, you can read?" I said, playing with my pup by letting it gnaw on my leather-gloved finger.

"*Can* and *like* are two different questions." By the sound, he yawned. "Gives me a headache."

Serafina asked, "Do you think the beasts see well in the dark?"

I nodded. "The blackness of their eye has to help them. But I also think their one eye gives them a disadvantage. They have to walk their lethal ice rays toward the target."

Serafina rolled over under her blanket. "That's useful information. Miss Ingefær says their eye is also a weak spot. One strike from a fiery dart and it kills them."

"I'm going to need a second crossbow." With my speed, I had a chance to dash in and fire before they saw me. But if there was more than one, they could also get lucky and freeze me to death.

Ingefær crawled into the tent. "I need a restoration spell, please."

"You about done?" I asked.

"Yes. I'm ready for a good long nap." Ingefær plopped herself beside Serafina. When the half-alvae finished the incantation, my wife laid her weary body down.

"Uh, what about us?" Mick's bodiless voice asked.

"In a minute." She stretched her shoulders.

After Ingefær cast a warmth spell, I tucked myself in. She rolled over onto an elbow. "You did good out there, Mick. If you hadn't flamed that beast, it would have broken our flank...and maybe Hombir or I wouldn't be alive."

"That would be a calamity," I said. "I'm of the opinion we're going to need more mages."

Mick said, "Aye. Two is not enough. A lot of dvaergs died."

Serafina grimaced. My wife grunted.

The lad hadn't seen much death in his brief life. Not till he joined up with us this past summer. I wasn't counting killing normal-sized humanoids and already dead things.

Raising my chin at Mick, I said, "I'm glad you're with us. Your wax tablet and your lateral thinking helped to turn the tide."

Serafina nodded. "You're a good teammate, Mick."

"Ah, you guys are making me blush."

I couldn't see if it was true.

"Don't feel left out, Serafina," I said. "Your healing and your eyes are obvious aids to the group. If not for you spotting the beasts earlier today, we'd have been ambushed for sure."

Ingefær sat up. "I almost forgot to tell you. They have a weakness."

I waited.

"Their eyes."

Mick giggled.

Serafina said, "I already told him."

My wife explained. "When Tugg's folks launched their crossbow salvo at close range, the Jörmonruks covered their eyes. I then fired a series of fiery darts at one, and it did the same thing, but it couldn't stop the magic."

I cleared my throat. "I'm getting a second crossbow."

"Don't get too cocky, Rory," Ingefær said. "But I agree your speed gives you an edge."

"I said this earlier." Mick went on. "We need a ballista. I've seen some drawings. They're big. But you can make them portable. Put them on a wagon. Against these brutes, each ballista would need to pivot fast, so the base needs to be a mount that can swivel."

I'd seen one atop Kral Bar Aggen's outer wall. And dvaergs were geniuses with mechanical designs. "Tugg's folks should know how to build one."

"I imagine the dvaergs at Kral Azza Rid should know too," Ingefær said. "We'll discuss it once we reach the keep."

Finished playing, I fed O'erlevendeh dried jerky and let him drink water. Ever since leaving Nikkel Bakken two weeks ago, the whelp had filled out and grown to stand halfway up my calf. His baby teeth had come in, too. Had we been out here that long?

He no longer fit comfortably inside my tunic. Nor did he care to travel in such a manner—so I carried him in a saddlebag when I rode—not that he cared for that either. I would have to let him walk beside me soon. Before I went to sleep, I finger-fought with him, keeping my gloves on. Which, more and more, didn't stop those growing fangs from penetrating.

"Ow!" I waggled my bleeding finger at him. "Not so hard, Vendeh." I tousled his fur and stuffed him under the top blanket of my bedroll. "Get some rest, pup."

***

Two mornings later, the gray clouds headed south, and by noon, we rode our horses under the bright sun. The air didn't warm up, though. In fact, it grew colder, aided by the blasted wind.

Serafina and I rode northeast of the main column, trying to cover two flanks at once. O'erlevendeh hopped through the snow for a while, but it was deeper than he was tall. Soon enough, he let me put him back into the saddlebag.

With the sun shining, the visibility was good. But as we neared Azza Rid, the land undulated, creating a series of rolling hills and corresponding valleys, with ranges dropping to a quarter of a league when in the vales.

The Dreki Mountains swung northeast. Then, as they bent back southwest, the sparkling white walls of Kral Azza Rid glistened in the late afternoon sun.

Tugg and his dvaergs took the lead and marched us toward the gates, meshed into the thirty-foot high walls. Watch towers shot up another dozen feet. A pair of dvaergs in each observed our progress.

We were expected, but entry was delayed until approval was received. With the portcullis raised, and the creaking of the main door as it swung wide, permission to enter was announced. The second half of the door swung in, letting the wagons roll through.

Tugg cupped his hands. "Could use some arms to help carry the supplies in."

That got the keep active.

Tugg gripped hands with another dvaerg, introduced as Regg. The dvaerg was stouter in the chest and in the gut, but not as tall. His gray beard flailed in the wind. Sett greeted the Avarkæsir leader of Kral Azza Rid.

"Oi!" Regg said, looking up, grinning. "Ye be a big one." He shifted his gaze to Tugg. "We be glad to see ye brother. Premier called for rationing two weeks ago." He patted his gut. "Though me Aimee had me cutting back already."

"Ye get our birds?" Tugg asked.

"Aye. Both." Regg shrugged. "Tall tales ye be telling."

Sett shook his head. "Not tales. The beasts be big."

As we moved through the outer keep, I scanned the area. The amount of space appeared half as big as in Kral Bar Aggen. It was a similar setup, though, with the crop fields and animal pens taking up most of the space.

The fields were covered in snow. But what struck me as odd was the lack of livestock. I saw no hogs, cows, or sheep. Just a dozen horses in two pens. Perhaps they were all in the barn. But if so, there couldn't be that many animals. Ten cows? Twenty hogs? For a keep with a purported number of two thousand dvaergs, that wouldn't feed them for long.

Outside the metal keep doors, we were introduced to the leadership group and led inside the mountain. Tugg's dvaergs and the five remaining d'oglemenn, not counting Hombir and Jonuku, set up camp inside the white walls.

Serafina became the focus of the Kral Azza Rid dvaergs. Their stares were hard, their jaws closed tight.

I broke the ice. "How long has it been since you've had an alvae or half-alvae beyond these doors?"

Regg looked at me without a hint of a smile on his bearded face. "Long? *Forever* long enough for ye?"

Mick grinned. "First time for everything."

Tugg said, "She be under my personal protection."

Whoa! I knew they were making eyes at each other, but such a proclamation spoke of something more. I hadn't been paying attention.

Serafina blushed, which meant her silver-green face became darker.

Sett said, "Her eyes saved us from being surprised on two occasions. Damn useful."

I smiled. We had a convert on our hands. He'd been gruff and downright insolent when we'd first met. But after each Jörmonruk encounter, he'd softened. Which proved the old saying true: battles forge unusual bonds.

I pulled O'erlevendeh out of my wulv overcoat. "I'd like to bring him inside. He needs some fresh meat."

Regg backed up a step, his eyes growing wide. "Be that a...?"

I nodded. "Yep. The sole survivor of a Jörmonruk attack. Those white-furred beasts killed an entire pack."

"As long as ye don't let it run loose." Regg motioned at the door. "If it bites someone, ye and it be spending yer time out of doors."

I kneeled beside the pup. "Behave." When I stood, I asked Regg, "If you have a thin rope or a strap of leather, I'll make sure he doesn't go off marauding."

Inside a squarish room with a bar on one end and an open kitchen on the other, the leadership group sat around two round tables. I got two straps and fashioned a collar and a lead. The whelp wasn't keen on either, but I got O'erlevendeh to heel. "Supper's coming."

Tugg started his report, telling Regg and a few other Kral Azza Rid dvaergs about our travails crossing the Ice Plains. He enumerated the attacks on Nikkel Bakken, the pile of d'oglemann bones a couple of days' hike east, and the pair of attacks as we hiked to Azza Rid, listing the names of the dead. He then described the Jörmonruk.

Hombir said, "We'll need to talk to your chief mage or the keeper of your legends."

"Aye," Tugg said. "We found a strange symbol carved into a pine tree." He raised his arm high. "Fifteen feet up."

Regg whispered to a compatriot and sent the dvaerg off. "Describe these beasties again."

Which Tugg did.

Heads shook.

I asked, "Have you seen them before?"

"Never," Regg replied. "A fable that died out a long time ago. But we have a few hunters missing...from this past winter."

That tracked, and Ingefær said so, asking Mick to show his wax tablet.

Regg's jaw dropped. "Seven attacks? Ye be sure?"

Heads bobbed in unison. I said, "Near as we can figure, they began their plundering right after Winter Solstice."

Food, water, and a dark ale were served. Tugg, Sett, and I enjoyed the ale. While it had a fruity flavor, one I couldn't place, it was malty and super smooth.

I grunted. "Hmm, tasty. I've not had this kind of brew before. What's the fruit?"

"Blueberry," Regg replied. "Also has a dash of nutmeg and chocolate to balance it out. Don't drink too much." He touched his head. "Kicks a bit. Not kind in the morning."

The pup couldn't stand it anymore, not with the aroma of cooked beef. He jumped onto my lap and shoved his big head between my arms. "Hey, careful. You almost spilled my ale."

I fed him small chunks of the meat. The pup was happy, chewing away. Dvaerg eyes watched me; Regg shook his head.

We ate in relative silence. About the time I wiped the last of the gravy with a hard piece of bread and fed it to the whelp, a threesome of dvaergs arrived.

The biggest one around the gut took the lead, his dark brown eyes buried in a mound of bushy eyebrows. He stepped before Regg, his hands on his hips. A gray beard dangled past his belt buckle. "What be this nonsense of fairy tales coming to life?"

Regg introduced us to Zakk. "He be the chief miner, and our stoutest mage. He—a"

"I be the keeper of legends, too." Zakk frowned, his beard dipping.

We described what we'd seen.

Hombir said, "My old tome says it's a Jörmonruk. They're fifteen feet tall, covered in white fur, and have one gigantic round eye."

Zakk scoffed. "No doubt ye all be suffering from an illusion."

I rose to my feet. "This is ridiculous. We know what we saw. I killed a couple." I waved an arm. "My compatriots killed more. Tugg has lost, what, two score of dvaergs?"

Tugg climbed to his feet. "In the last attack. More earlier. They didn't die from an illusion. They were blasted by ice rays."

Zakk harrumphed.

Hombir said, "There's more for your consideration." He motioned at Mick. "Show him your drawing."

Mick got his tablet out again. "This is a rendition of the symbol we found carved into a pine tree."

Zakk stepped back, his eyes wide. "The gods! What blasphemy is this? Ye dare hoist a symbol of the Father of Lies at me?"

Mick lowered the tablet. "S-sorry."

My wife said, "You're saying this snake symbol is a sigil of Lokke?"

Zakk's head darted left, then right. His gaze stopped on Regg. "These outsiders be not very keen." Then his eyes shifted to Serafina. "And they travel with the unclean ones."

Tugg stepped closer to Zakk. "Oi! Don't be insulting me friend. We be alive because of her talents."

I moved beside Tugg. "We're supposed to be working together."

Ingefær set her utensils down, one hand going to her waist. "Focus on the task at hand. Is the symbol Mick showed you one belonging to Lokke?"

Zakk's bushy white brows furrowed. "Aye."

Regg asked, "How far from here did you spot the sigil?"

I scratched at my beard. "Ten days, I think."

"Halfway between here and Bar Aggen?" Regg's dark brows grew tight.

I waggled my head. "Closer to their half. A day or two out of Nikkel Bakken."

"I'll have to inform the premier." Regg looked up at Zakk. "Anything else ye can tell us? The beasts they describe—be they Jörmonruks?"

Zakk shrugged, then nodded. "Aye, if that be what they saw. But they be dead for thousands of years. Can't see why they showed up all of a sudden."

"Nigh on a year ago," I said, "is when they first showed up. The first missing—presumed destroyed—caravan occurred a moon shy of a year ago. Right after Winter Solstice."

Zakk said, "I'll consult me records. None of this makes sense."

One of the dvaergs who had accompanied him in said, "How much ale have ye consumed?"

"Aye," said the second one. "This sounds like a lark. One not suitable for *guests.*"

Sett rose and towered over everyone. "It be no tale. Stop yer insults and engage yer brains. We be dealing with evil. And all it has to do to win is to have us come to blows over words."

I couldn't have said it better myself. I particularly liked the 'engage yer brains' bit.

Perhaps I grinned too wide, for Zakk huffed, turned, and stomped out. His two companions followed in his wake.

Tugg and I sat back down. Tugg asked, "What do ye think, Regg? Will we get aid, or not?"

Regg scowled. "What sort of help?"

"More warriors," Tugg said. "And we have an idea to build a portable ballista."

Regg sipped at his mug. "The latter be doable. We've plenty of timber and iron. The former...I ken not. The premier likes our isolation."

I chinned at him. "But we can ask for volunteers, right?"

Regg grunted. "I suppose."

A foursome of dvaergs, dressed in blue linen shirts and brown pants with suspenders, sauntered in.

Regg said, "The quartet will sing for ye. It be custom to tip them when they be done."

I nodded. "Not my first keep. Thank you. Tell us a little about Kral Azza Rid."

Regg drained his mug. "Well, it be about two thousand years old."

Mick said, "I thought you and your kin helped to quash the first Jörmonruk invasion?"

"We did," Regg said. "The war with the white beast be what caused us to spread out into three keeps. Azza Rid to the east and Fal Is to the west of Bar Aggen. We be outposts to protect the Realm from invaders." He leaned close. "And not just the Jörmonruks."

Serafina frowned. "Who else?"

I piped in. "He means the Jotunn."

"Aye." Regg's beard dipped at the corners. "Had no trouble from them. Then again, we haven't traded with them, either."

The dvaerg next to him chuckled. "They ain't got much besides snow and ice."

"Ice grizzly pelts," Ingefær said.

Scowls crossed the Azza Rid dvaergs' faces.

I said, "We've seen six of the blue-skinned giants. Got attacked by them, as well as a trio of ice grizzlies."

Regg let out a guffaw. "Ye be telling tales again."

Tugg shook his head. "No. I be there."

An appraising eye swept over us. "Ye get around."

It was my turn to laugh. "I try to mind my own business. But..."

"Misfortune befalls Master Belkin," Mick said.

The quartet finished up a nice harmony of lilting notes. They started on a syncopated song with the baritone and tenor taking turns providing the melody. Not understanding Dvaervish, the song meant nothing to me. But the singing was quite good.

I got a hold of O'erlevendeh and held him even with the table. "Any more meat? Doesn't have to be cooked."

Regg sent a dvaerg off. He then licked his lips. "What be yer plans? Do ye ride out tomorrow, or do ye stay till after Gods' Day—which be less than two weeks out—or do ye wait until Spring Equinox?"

Less than two weeks to Gods' Day? We'd spent more time on the Ice Plains than I had ever wanted.

Hombir said, "We cannot wait. The Jörmonruks know we know they're out here. They also know that we have mages and can kill. Every day we delay, they'll harden their position—wherever it is—and make it all the harder to wipe them out."

Mick hiccupped.

Serafina asked, "Is there no way to make peace?"

Tugg shook his head. "If the children's fables be true, no. All overtures—the sending of emissaries—resulted in dead kinfolk."

Sett added, "All the dvaergs of Bar Aggen worked together to eradicate the evil. Nothing has changed, as far as I can see."

Mick asked, "Where did they come from?"

Regg scratched at his beard. "That be a Zakk question. But if I remember the tales right, they be always here, north of the Dreki Bergs. It be our exploring back then that led us to them."

The dvaerg returned with a plate of uncooked pork, sliced into strips. I thanked him and took to feeding the pup. His hunger remained unsatiated.

Ingefær asked, "We agree about hunting the Jörmonruks, right?"

Her gaze swept the table.

Regg shrugged. "Like I said, ye'll have to petition the premier. I suspect ye'll have to ask for volunteers."

Tugg sighed. "That be not the task I be given." He looked over at Sett. "Our task be to deliver the goods here. If we found out what be doing the pillaging, then that be a bonus."

Sett nodded. "Aye. Like with Regg's folk, we'll ask for volunteers." His eyes narrowed, "Ye know I be coming to avenge me brother."

Tugg raised a finger. "Aye, me as well. We'll have to ask the others. The best time to strike be now. They be in the area and we know their weaknesses."

I said, "I'm for doing the hard job that's ahead of us. If not us, then who? If not now, then when? After the beasts fortify their position is too late. Who knows—right now they could have a hundred hungry mouths they're raising for future mayhem."

Mick crowed like a rooster.

I let him finish. "No. It's now or never."

Regg looked uncomfortable while the quartet switched to a new song. This one was soft, the counter tenor taking the lead. To me, it sounded like a love song.

Tugg slapped the table. "We request an audience with the premier."

I slapped Mick on the back. "And your aid. This young man has helped us to unravel a puzzle. He now has a wonderful idea to help us defeat them. Tell them, Mick."

Mick took a deep breath. "We need ballistae. Not just one like referenced earlier. Four would be better." He described his ballista on a wagon, with the ability to elevate and swivel.

"That be easy enough." Regg looked around. "Might take a couple of days to put together."

The dvaerg beside Regg waggled his head. "Aye. One. Four will take a lot longer. Unless the entire keep of carpenters and smithies be sortied."

Regg grunted. "Aye. That won't happen. And expect to pay premium pricing."

The dvaerg next to Regg said, "Mounting them be not the problem. It be rolling the wagon through three feet of snow."

Serafina said, "Right now it's at two feet."

"Give it a couple of days." Regg's beard dipped at the corners.

Mick added, "We need a thirty-degree arc, at a minimum."

That caused brows to furrow.

"How big ye be talking about?" Regg asked.

"The weapon has to have a range of at least a hundred strides," I said. "Their ice ray blasts are good to sixty or seventy paces in bad weather.

Might be eighty on a clear day. But I'm guessing. We've been fortunate that both encounters were in blizzards."

Ingefær said, "It needs to be big enough to take down a five-stride-tall hulk."

Tugg said, "The farther it can shoot and the larger the projectile, the bigger the ballistae has to be. The design must fit on a flatbed cart, where maybe two soldiers can cock it. We need to keep it light to have any chance of rolling through three feet of snow."

Ingefær nodded. "And, as Mick mentioned, we want four of them."

Regg's lips twisted. "I don't know what the craft builders will want, but it sounds to me like a couple hundred of silver per ballista."

Hombir said, "I will pay for the cost."

He hadn't haggled; he needed Nikkel Bakken to be repopulated.

Tugg raised a hand. "Kral Bar Aggen will split the cost with ye." He eyed Serafina, his brown eyes going soft. "Don't ye fret none. I'll get ye enough volunteers."

Serafina was going into harm's way.

As we broke up, I stood and cornered Regg. "I could use a gallon of milk. Better if it was in, say, four small containers?"

O'erlevendeh had devoured the plate of pork, and now lay nestled in my arms. The whelp yawned.

Regg jumped. "I cannot believe ye be caring for it."

I shrugged. "Can't see pups come to harm." I eyed my wife, who had stood with me. A serene look occupied her eyes. I didn't believe them.

Regg eyed me. "Ye be a touch daft, yah?"

Ingefær slapped my shoulder. "Oh, yeah."

I grinned.

The quartet broke up. The dvaerg who had sung bass came by with a cap he held upside down. We took turns tossing silvers into it. He nodded his thanks, and the foursome piled out of the dining hall.

Regg said, "I'll see ye get some milk. Don't let the beastie run around. Me folks won't agree with yer assessment. Or with me letting ye have it in here."

We moved to our rooms down the hall and deeper into the mountain. I think Serafina was the happiest of us all, to have a roof over her head. She bubbled with excitement as we walked through our new surroundings.

From looking askance at the ceiling to finding succor in it, she'd had quite the turn.

I looked forward to several days of rest...and not having to keep my eyes flitting about. We'd see plenty of conflict soon enough.

It was funny how we all agreed to go back out there with almost no debate. The symbol in the tree had us worried, and—based on Zakk's revelation—it was a devotion to Lokke. I realized we hadn't told the mage that the thing was magical.

Chapter Twenty-Five

CULTURAL ROADBLOCKS

INGEFÆR

The respite was nice. Kral Azza Rid was like the other dvaerg keeps, full of tunnels and filled with dvaergs. Dvaergs loved to mine and preferred staying indoors. They were competent at working with rocks, gemstones, and metals. With a fifth of their numbers dedicated Avarkæsir, honor warriors, they knew how to fight, too.

These dvaergs weren't as friendly as the ones in Kral Mik Mithal, the one keep on the south side of the Dreki Mountains. For that matter, the dvaergs of Kral Bar Aggen were friendlier as well. I gathered the difference here came from their isolation. They were the farthest keep north and east of any, so they didn't have many visitors. Perhaps it was their proximity to the alvaes, which controlled the lands south of the Dreki Mountains...though the city of Vanaby was three hundred leagues away.

Alvaes and Dvaergs hadn't gotten along ever since time began. Most of it came from their dedication to the different god factions: the Æsiere and Væniere. The gods of Allefar, Tordenvaer, Tyrrell, and Eirene of the Æsiere matched up against Furæyar, Haemdol, Fraedra, and Kvaesir. There was the Forgotten War, too, the settlement of which decreed alvaes would never expand north of the Dreki Mountains and the dvaergs wouldn't go east of the southern spur.

Oh, there were emissaries in one another's home region, but visitors were quite rare. Serafina's presence was the kakkerlak in the salad. I shuddered at the vision of the six-legged, black-carapaced insect crawling in my food.

Our news of an awakened vile legend was a sore point. Nobody liked to hear bad news. And the premier of Kral Azza Rid sounded like a curmudgeon, and I had yet to meet him. Perhaps the half-alvae's presence within their precious keep added an affront to misfortune.

We stayed in the outer sanctum, where there were rooms for two dozen visitors if some folks slept on the floor. At least we had access to a privy and a dining hall, which Regg kept staffed.

Outside, in the chilled wind and persistent snow, the Kral Azza Rid dvaergs provided the timber and worked under Tugg's supervision in constructing the mounted ballistae. The sound of hammers pounding and dvaerg chatter was a constant. As was the grousing of dvaerg crafts folk working out of doors. The soldiers and hunters were used to going out for brief spells—a couple of days at most. A good bet the rest had never ventured beyond the keep's doorway.

During a break for lunch on the second day since our arrival, Hombir, Rory, and I were outside, and we cornered Regg.

I asked, "I'm wondering when master Zakk will return with some information about the Jörmonruks?"

Regg groused. "I know, I know. He promised to tell ye what he knows. He spent all of yesterday prattling incessantly to the premier about increasing the keep's defenses. So perhaps he'll get to it today."

"An attack against your keep doesn't concern you?" Rory asked.

"Of course it does." Regg waved an arm. "These here walls, while not as tall as Bar Aggen's, be magically imbued against frost and ice. They cannot get in."

"There is the portcullis and massive wooden door," I said.

Regg shrugged. "Bah. They'll have to bend over to come in, one or two at a time. We'll blast them."

I wasn't as confident as Regg sounded, but I was happy to hear they had extra protection against the beasts.

Hombir emerged through the keep's metal doors. Behind him came a ruffled-looking Zakk. He wore a heavy wulv coat, and his head was wrapped in a gray wool scarf, covering all but an inch of his eyes.

Hombir said, "Zakk has some information, but I convinced him to come and tell everyone."

Zakk harrumphed. "Mighty strange what be happening around here."

I waved Serafina and Mick over, while Rory hailed Tugg.

When we were gathered in a loose circle, I said, "Thank you for coming. What can you tell us about Jörmonruks?"

"Bah." Zakk waved a gloved hand. "Not much. If ye read the children's tales, then ye know everything I do."

Hombir pressed him. "What about their magic abilities? So far, they just used their ice rays."

Zakk nodded. "Aye. The books say all Jörmonruks have the ability. But whether they be born with it or it comes during puberty, like our mages, I ken not."

"Do they know any other type of magic?" I asked.

Zakk shrugged. "Aye. They have mages like we do. Can't tell ye what planes they harvest the best. I would assume air and water based on the ice blast incantation."

Rory asked, "Any weaknesses besides their eyes?"

Zakk's head snapped toward my husband. "Their eyes be flawed?"

Serafina said, "One shot with a fiery dart or an arrow and it kills them."

Zakk grunted. "Hmph. That be new information. At least to me. Are ye sure?"

I nodded. "Absolutely. But the trick is to get close enough without getting struck with their spell."

Zakk said, "Their eyes see well in the dark, so aim for daylight encounters."

Rory said, "They see about as well as we do in a snowstorm."

"Sure, sure." Zakk tugged at his beard. "But they see body heat, just not far, so the books say. So be careful of that."

Mick frowned. "I don't know. When I turned myself invisible, it was like they couldn't see me."

Zakk peered through his wrap at the young lad. "Ye be a mage?"

Mick shook his head. "No. I read a scroll."

Zakk stroked his bearded chin. "Hmm. A simple invisibility incantation wouldn't hide yer body heat. I mean, unless the spell be designed to do so. Perhaps it be a function of the scroll's incantation?"

Mick swallowed. "You're saying...I got lucky."

Zakk shrugged and glanced toward the sun. "Blasted thing be bright. Any more questions?"

I asked, "What can you tell us about their lives? Why do they do what they do? I mean, do they have homes, do they like to farm, craft things, that sort of thing?"

Zakk scoffed. "That be daft. They like to pillage and plunder and eat anything that isn't one of their own. The books I've read don't mention any sort of trade or interest beyond taking from others, then stripping the flesh off their victim's bones."

Rory asked, "And their ties to Lokke?"

Zakk's chest heaved. "Ah. Therein lies the Realm's vexations. The Father of Lies be crafty, underhanded. I can see why the beasts would worship him. But other than the evil they wrought—same as him—I know of no connection."

"But where did they come from?" I asked. "It's been over two thousand years since they've been seen."

Zakk studied his feet. Then he looked up. "I ken not. That be the mighty puzzling thing. Perhaps this Vidarr Allefar, as I've heard him called, did something when he brought the drekis and magic back."

Rory stepped forward, but I put a hand on his shoulder and said, "Let me." Turning to Zakk, I continued. "I'm not saying that's not possible, but I think the way you framed it is wrong. You've all heard about what he did, banishing the gods to Asagard?"

Zakk's eyes narrowed through the scarf as he eyed me. "Aye. I heard. Blasphemy. One of us best a god?" Zakk laughed. Then he said, "But I appreciate the return of magic. That be helpful with mining, and with keeping the walls and ceilings where they belong." He waved an arm toward the keep's metal doors. "We have four new mages. That will help with our efforts. The premier has grand plans."

"Speaking of mages," I said, "Are there any worth their weight? Any who might want to join up with us? We could use a third mage."

Serafina said, "Even a fourth."

Zakk smiled, but his eyes narrowed again. "No. No mages are available."

Regg said, "He's been petitioning the premier to prevent any from going. Even volunteers."

"Why?" Rory asked.

Zakk's jaw tightened. "Because the defense of the keep be our primary responsibility."

"Balderdash," Tugg spouted. "Attacking be the best defense. Wiping these beasts out be our chief charge."

Regg nodded. "Aye. We didn't win the last war by staying in the keep. The legends state war parties went out."

Zakk smiled, his brown eyes cold. "Good luck convincing the premier."

I turned to Regg. "Can we solicit warriors to volunteer for the campaign?"

Regg nodded. "Aye. Zakk's counsel doesn't prevent it."

So, we could have more warriors, but no more mages. "What about healers?"

Regg said, "Ye can ask."

Zakk shook his head. "The order be coming down today: no healers may volunteer. We may need every single one of them...here."

I growled loud enough for the others to hear. Zakk's words vexed me.

Mick said, "Is there a prohibition on your mages, even yourself, from teaching our mages new spells?"

Zakk's eyes narrowed anew. "No."

Mick's words sparked an idea, as I knew how the dvaergs liked to mine with magic. "Hombir and I would like to learn how to blast through rock."

Hombir tapped Regg on the shoulder. "Can you put the word out that we'd like to talk to them? We will pay for any lessons."

Zakk agreed. "I'll ask." He raised a hand chest high. "If there be an opportunity to earn coins, I see no problem. As long as they stay behind the walls."

The dvaerg mage turned and left.

We circled around Regg.

Rory asked, "Can we ask for volunteers?"

Regg sighed. "Aye. I'll put the word out. But don't expect too many. The premier's declarations about mages and healers will squash enthusiasm."

"And you?" I asked, "Can you come with us?"

Regg shook his head. "No. I be ordered to stay behind."

He hadn't told us that before, and it irked me. I was never a fan of politics, and we were thick in the muck of it.

Mick said, "Well, at least they're helping with the ballistae."

A cry—a sort of half cheer—sounded behind us.

We turned to look.

Muggs, a doughy-looking dvaerg with an almost fully gray beard, shouted from a cart. "The first one be done!"

I raised my chin. "Time to test fire it?"

Muggs raised a fist high. "Aye. We'll set a target up outside the gates."

A dvaerg ran off to get some horses. When the cart was hooked up, we trudged outside the keep's walls.

A pair of dvaergs hiked out onto the snow-covered plateau and placed an empty barrel forty strides out.

Rory said, "We need it to shoot farther."

Muggs nodded from atop the cart. "Aye. We be sighting it in."

The dvaergs near the barrel ran back in, and another pair of dvaergs cranked the ballista rope against a coiled spring.

Muggs loaded a six-foot long wooden pole, about four inches thick, into the crook of the weapon. "All clear?"

A couple of dvaergs to the side shouted, "Clear!"

Muggs aimed and fired. The giant bolt sailed over the heads of the horses—who shied at the sudden noise—whistled through the air, and struck the ground several paces to the left and a half-dozen strides past the barrel.

Different dvaergs mounted the wagon and toyed with levers and ratchets.

Regg waved at us. "Come on in. This may take a while. At least we know it works."

Rory grinned. "Aye. Now to build some more."

That afternoon, work began on a second ballista.

In the evening, the leadership group returned to the dining hall and gathered at a round table. Rory and I sat together. Mick ate between Rory and Serafina. On the other side of the half-alvae were Tugg, then Hombir, and Jonuku.

I said, "I like the idea of having long-range weapons. What worries me is the snow."

Mick nodded as he stuffed roast pork into his mouth. "Will the ballistae be light enough for the horses to pull through two feet of snow—or three?"

"Don't talk with your mouth full," I said.

Rory pointed a fork at me. "When we made for Is Vann two years ago, we left the wagons behind. They were loaded down with supplies. These carts have but one thing on them."

"When was that?" Mick asked. "I mean within the moon's span."

"Right about this time," I said. "We experienced Gods' Day a week after we left the wagons."

Rory frowned. "We have that to look forward to."

"What's wrong with Gods' Day?" Serafina asked.

I said, "Nothing itself. In fact, when the fog rolls in out here, it warms everything up. But when we were here two years ago, is when Vidarr heard the gods talking."

Serafina's eyes darted around the group. "You told us the gods have been banished. You weren't fibbing?"

Tugg shook his head. Hombir's gaze dropped to his plate, a heavy sigh rumbling past his lips.

Jonuku said, "No. It's true."

Rory nodded. "In Slangeh Buktah, where we were last year at this time, it felt like mist had rolled in from the ocean. No one saw a god."

Serafina said, "I was a prisoner then. Another prisoner reported seeing Haemdol. But they were questioned by the guards, and their story fell apart."

Mick chuckled. "Aye. Matt, a guy I used to run with, claimed he saw one last year. But when he described the god he saw, we all knew he was trying to fry our eggs."

I nodded. "The gods are locked away now."

Mick rolled his eyes. "I know you've been saying that...and I believe you."

"But...?" Rory asked.

"How can you lock away the gods?"

"Vidarr did it," I said. "With the Valknut and the Rod of the Dreki combined."

Serafina stuck a fork into a cooked pear. "Zakk doesn't believe it."

I retold of our efforts to save the Realm from Ragnarök. I finished with, "They were ready to destroy the Realm in order to free themselves."

Rory added, "They don't care one whit for you or me."

Tugg grumbled. "Aye. Not a one."

Hombir swallowed. "It was a perilous time."

We ate in silence for a while.

A dvaerg marched in; the look on his face would kill rats.

Tugg stood. "What do ye want?"

The dvaerg jabbed a finger at Serafina. "She should not be here."

Rory asked, "And who are you?"

The dvaerg's beard ruffled. "I be Dikk."

Tugg put his hands on his hips. "And where should she be?"

"*Begone* be where she should be." Dikk raised a fist. "Alvae be vile. Deceitful."

Tugg slugged him. They sprawled to the ground, with Tugg on top.

Bending over Dikk, Tugg growled, "Do not insult me friends. She be the reason more of mine be not dead."

Hombir called out. "Stop! The both of you. We're on the same side!"

Tugg grunted and stood up. He helped Dikk to his feet. "I be sorry for slugging ye."

Dikk's brown eyes darted around the table. "Yeah. Ye be sorry, alright. Alvae lover."

Tugg raised a fist.

Dikk waved a hand. "Bah. Ye ain't worth it."

He stomped off.

Jonuku shook her snout. "I think he's more concerned with the message we brought than with the half-alvae's presence."

"He just takes it out on her," I said.

Serafina said, "There's always one dick in a crowd."

Mick added, "Two when Dikk's around."

I thanked Tugg for standing up for Serafina.

He waved a paw at me. "Bah. Dikk be a dunderhead. I know her worth."

We finished eating and went to our rooms.

The following day, we emerged to a snowstorm. Dvaergs whistled as they worked, happy the sun was a dim object behind the clouds.

I found Regg and told him about Dikk's behavior.

Regg scowled. "I be sorry about that. Know that most of us be not like that."

Rory cocked his head. "Really?"

"Well, a half-alvae be new for all of us." Regg smiled through his beard. "But folks don't insult others. Not unless they do something first to earn it."

Despite his words, Rory and I watched Serafina's back. Not as much as Tugg did. The pair traveled around together, watching the construction of the ballista.

A couple of hours after the noon meal, a dvaerg dressed in robes—instead of armor or a work tunic—came out of the keep entrance and walked over to Regg. The dvaerg stood half a head shorter than Regg, and its shorter beard started lower on the jawline. The gap between the beard and the ears indicated the dvaerg was female.

The two dvaergs spoke for a moment, then Regg pointed. "This be Muan. She be a fledgling mage. A year and a half of expertise...such as that goes."

Muan bowed.

I followed suit. "Hombir, come here."

When the d'oglemann mage arrived, Muan introduced herself. "I be told ye want to learn some mining magic?"

I nodded.

Muan smiled through her thin beard. "A thousand silver."

Hombir and I raised our brows almost in unison.

Hombir chuckled as he wagged his snout. "I don't believe it. The Ice Plains be threatened, and everyone wants to make coin."

Muan darkened, her brows pinching. "Ye want the help or not?"

I put a hand to my chin and tried to look studious. "Tell us about your areas of expertise."

"I have access to the plane of air. I be using me spells to dig ever since the last Spring Equinox. Whites be me primary color. The other mages use earth. One of them, Jenn, draws on the elemental plane of the Aether. Next to Zakk, she be the eldest. Jenn be in charge of me training, which be difficult with her relying on earth and me air."

I nodded. "Air is good. Hombir and I both channel the plane."

Hombir's snout dipped. "Helpful. But before we agree to your fee, describe your mining spell. Does it explode rock? Or bore a hole? How does it work?"

Muan's short-bearded chin bobbed. "I guess I can tell ye that. But the words, motion, and material will cost ye."

Hombir and I nodded.

Muan went on. "I use the air spell after Jenn has moved rock. She creates a fissure, a kind of narrow slit, a half-foot deep. I force a ray of air inside, then pack in more and more air. The rock explodes from the pressure." She smiled. "Together, we mine."

Hombir sighed. "I hope a letter of credit will suffice as payment?"

Muan's mouth puckered.

"I don't have that much coin on me," Hombir said.

I called Rory over, and together we counted out fifty gold pieces.

Muan's eyes went wide. "Not much gold around here."

"It's all we have." I smiled at her. "Should make you popular."

I turned to Hombir. "Either you or Vidarr can reimburse us."

Now that she'd been paid, Muan put cupped hands to her lips. She blew harshly. "*Pakke luften sammen.*"

I understood the words to mean, 'compress the air.'

She blew again and repeated the phrase. She then flailed her hands outward, mimicking an explosion.

To my right, a flash crackled the air, ruffling my hair.

"Ye want to be looking at where ye want the air to go. Also, the more ye repeat the spell, the bigger the explosion."

Hombir said, "The material you use is your own breath. The words I understood, and the motions appear simple enough. Is that all we need to know?"

Muan nodded.

"What's the range?" I asked. "You wouldn't want to be too close to the explosion."

"Sixty paces be recommended," Muan replied. "Tis the extent of me range."

Off the top of my head, I couldn't think of a practical application of her incantation, outside of mining. "What else do you know?"

Muan said, "I can shoot a ray of air. It shoves the dirt away. But I haven't gotten strong enough to make more than a scratch in the rock. I have managed to close a door with it."

Hombir raised a taloned hand. "When you shoot this ray of air, how far does it go with meaningful force?"

"Meaningful?"

"How far away are you from the rock you're trying to make a hole in?" I asked.

"Ah, thirty paces." Muan smiled. "Jenn be at sixty."

Sixty paces? That might be helpful. I huddled with Hombir. "That might be useful to scratch at their eye. Might even pierce the soft flesh of the orb."

He grunted. "A fiery dart will do the same and has a longer range."

I turned back to Muan and said, "Since we paid a thousand, we'd like to have the spell components, material, and incantation sequence for your air blast."

Muan went through the motions and uttered the Varanusian. Once more, she used her breath.

Hombir and I practiced our new spells. When we were sure we had it, we thanked Muan, and she left. I heard her singing as she strolled away.

I smiled at Hombir. "She's just using her breath. I use goblin bone dust for my air shield wall. What would happen with the incantations if we substituted the bone dust for air?"

Hombir smiled. "Ah. That's good thinking. I feared we'd gotten robbed."

I had other ideas, like adding sawdust to the incantation. Might need a different set of words and hand motions, but I envisioned a ray of fire coming out of my finger.

As Hombir and I turned our attention to the construction of the second ballista, Rory called out. "Time to eat. The light will be gone in a minute or two."

The second ballista wasn't quite done. But it had the shape. At this rate, we would be finished with our four ballistae in two more days.

Chapter Twenty-Six

SEEKING TO KILL

RORY

Six days after arriving, we had four completed ballistae and nine volunteers anchored by Muggs. Most of the Kral Azza Rid warriors were grizzled and growing round about the waist. Their reason for coming? There wasn't much left to their lives, and an adventure seemed a fine note to end on. One way or the other.

"No valor, no renown," was Muggs' stated reason for coming. He'd also said Dikk's mouth had run like mead on Summer Solstice, and that was a chief reason we didn't have more warriors.

Since arriving, we'd received no word from Tyrrby. Perhaps the birds hadn't survived the weather. It was also possible that Vidarr and the Foremost were somewhere else in the Realm.

A bird from Kral Bar Aggen had shown up yesterday. Premier Mina authorized a well-armed scouting action. Tugg no longer needed to ask for volunteers.

We had Ingefær and Hombir for mages, neither of which thought their new spells would amount to much. Muggs and the others brought the soldier count to a smidge over two hundred.

I feared we would need their entire strength. My gut told me that the number of Jörmonruks still out there would dwarf the amount we had killed.

We rode out in the middle of a snowstorm for a couple of reasons. First, I figured that in two days, the storm would blow over and we'd be close to where the last attack had taken place. Perhaps we would find some clues. Yeah, I was being optimistic. The other reason was that Tugg reckoned the depth of the snow would get worse the longer we waited.

I was dismayed that the Kral Azza Rid premier had refused to augment our strength, and I said so as we stomped through the snow.

Tugg grunted. "I agree."

He summoned a messenger bird, tucked a note into a pouch designed for it, and tied it around the bird's legs. As we watched the bird fly off, he said, "I wrote a message for the premier last night. I told her the premier here has a hollow head. We need strength in numbers. Not to sit behind the walls."

Mick said, "Their walls protect them against the beast's ice rays."

"Bah." Tugg swatted at the comment. "When trade routes stop, how will they fare way out here? Oh, they grow some crops and have a bit of livestock." He found my face. "But you didn't see any in the other pen, did ye?"

Mick said, "Ah. The Jörmonruk can besiege and starve them out."

"Right ye be, lad."

Hombir and Jonuku marched amid five surviving soldiers from Kobber Unter Smuss. The d'oglemenn had taken a tremendous hit to their numbers, if I counted the enclave of Nikkel Bakken.

I rode behind a group of dvaergs, who were assigned the duty of stomping the snow flat. They rotated every half hour. Behind me were the rest of Tugg's soldiers, and behind them were four carts, none of which had canopies. Instead, each one had a ballista mounted on their deck.

The arc cover of the weapon was but fifteen degrees to one side, or thirty in total. We had tried to go wider, but ran into stability problems with the interlocking wooden rings, which made the things accurate.

Metal would have fared better in terms of arc coverage and durability. But that would have taken yet more time, and the smithies from Kral Azza Rid didn't want to come outside.

Behind the carts were six wagons, four of which were empty. The fifth one carried our supplies and our tents. The last one was half full, loaded with timber and coal. At least Tugg and Muggs had 'borrowed' enough mounts for our needs.

Taking the rear flank was a handful of Tugg's Avarkæsir, plus Muggs and his nine. Muggs smiled a lot. He and his companions joked half the time, then grumbled about the freakish winds. They would be a joy to be around when the sun poked through the clouds.

After stopping near noon, I rode at a trot to the front, letting O'erlevendeh run along. It was too soon for him, given the depth of the snow. But he needed to grow up faster than normal, and this would build his muscles the best way I knew how.

I let him work up an appetite, then gave him chunks of uncooked hog. The whelp had benefited from the rest stop. He had access to milk and got plenty of table scraps to boot. His teeth had shot in, and now I wore gauntlets whenever I played with him.

He'd doubled in size since I picked him up in that cavern weeks ago. Both in height and now weight. He was going to get grumpy with me once my rations ran out and he went back to dried pemmican.

I let Ingefær and Serafina catch up. Dismounting, I scooped up O'erlevendeh and put him into my rucksack, letting his head stick out so he could see. He growled at first, then whined. But I didn't let him out.

My wife asked. "Are we ready for this?"

"Ballistae, fireballs, crossbows, and my fast feet." I inhaled the cold air. "We better be."

Serafina said, "Don't forget Mick's vials of oil."

"How many did he make?"

My beautiful bride smiled. "Thirty. He kept six and handed out the rest to the dvaergs and d'oglemenn."

I nodded. "Have you tried your new spells?"

She sighed. "I've been able to get a thirty-stride blast of air to poke a hole in a pine log. It isn't much. Hombir says with practice, I might double my distance or bore twice as deep. I tried using the goblin bone dust, but so far, my gestures or my words aren't quite right. Battle conditions are a terrible time to practice."

"How precise is the blast at that range?"

Her lips pressed together for a moment. "Very accurate at thirty. The logs I strafed showed a gouge, as wide as it was deep—about half an inch. After that, the precision wavers, with me missing by an inch or two for every stride beyond."

"If you hit me at thirty strides, it sounds painful." I looked into her blue eyes.

She nodded. "Human skin? Sure. Armor or the Jörmonruk's fury hides? I don't know. Their eyes? I'm betting it will hurt. Fiery darts are more effective because of their range."

"What happens at forty strides?"

"Nothing," Ingefær replied. "It's like the blast evaporates. Hombir says the compressed air dissipates, and might feel like you were punched by a child."

"And what of the mining spell?" I pressed.

She shook her head. "I got it to work. In soft soil, I dug a hole knee-deep in less than a minute, using two spells. But I can't see much use for it."

We rode on. I pulled my hood tight as the chilled wind blasted ice pellets. O'erlevendeh hunkered down.

At our next rest stop, I hiked over to Tugg, with the rest of Injustices Righted in tow. "This storm started yesterday. How long will it last?"

Tugg scratched under his beard. "Four days. Maybe five. Ye feel the bitterness?"

Ingefær grunted. "I do."

"The sting is something fierce," I said. "I can't keep my eyes open."

Tugg grinned, touching his salt and pepper brows. "That be what these be for."

Serafina smiled, her emerald eyes twinkling as she looked at him. "Makes you look distinguished. I like that."

Mick cleared his throat.

A ruddy-faced Tugg said, "The more moisture, the longer the storm lasts."

We rode on for the rest of the day, heading due west. The following day, we turned north-westward based on my report of the escaped Jörmonruk running north.

The direction was treacherous any time of year, but doubly so in a snowstorm. Any time sightlines to the Dreki Mountains disappeared, the chance of dying on the Ice Plains increased. In a blizzard, it increased tenfold.

The day after, Serafina and I moved out front to scout ahead, the horses slogging through the piled-high snow. O'erlevendeh complained about being in the rucksack, but I couldn't chance him being in the snow when an attack came. To my mare's distress, I set him atop the saddlebags behind me, and tied two pieces of rope to the collar I had fashioned in Kral Azza Rid.

"Stay," I said.

He jumped a couple of times before he figured out he wasn't going anywhere. His claws dug into the blanket he sat on. When they grew longer, they would pierce through and into the horse's hide.

I patted the top of the saddlebag straps. "Lie down." But the pup remained upright, his head turning left and right. Maybe he was a natural born scout.

At a rest break approaching dusk on the fifth day since leaving Kral Azza Rid, we were all getting restless. We should have run into the beasts by now.

I said, "They must have come east quite a way to get between us and Kral Azza Rid."

That observation earned me nothing but silence.

Tugg looked around. "Too open here. Go look for a suitable spot to hunker down."

I laughed. "It all looks the same to me."

He grumbled. "Go check one more ridge over and let me know."

That was the thing with the Ice Plains. It was like it had been rolled out by a baker with a divot in his rolling pin. Most of it was flat, but every so often, there was a crest. I knew, based on looking at maps years ago, that the whole thing sloped toward Is Vann. North of the Ice Lake, I suspected the ground rose. But I was guessing.

Serafina and I rode west. It was as if we rode up a gentle slope, which itself was odd. A couple of minutes later, we reached a definitive crest; the slope was steep: six or seven strides high over ten times the distance.

I looked at the half-alvae. "We need to see what's up there."

We climbed the ridge, reaching a flat plateau. "That doesn't make any sense."

Serafina pointed. "It's nothing but snow as far as I can see."

I pressed my horse forward.

We reached the edge. The slope went down, at about the same angle as what we had climbed.

From our little perch, all I saw was flat land before us. Every inch was covered in two-foot-plus deep snow.

Serafina's green lips puckered. "This terrain confuses me."

I rode down the ridge with Serafina following. We walked the horses for maybe forty paces when I stopped. "Whoa."

Before us was an iced-over body of water running from left to right. Reaching behind me, I patted O'erlevendeh's head. "Fresh water."

Serafina snorted. "How thick is the ice, or is it solid?"

"No, not yet." I pointed north. "Follow it long enough and you'll find Is Vann."

A tingling sensation ran up my back.

Serafina pointed. "Shadow."

The whelp growled.

"I'm an idiot," I said. "Of course, the beasts would be near water."

A frosty ray zapped the earth thirty paces to our right, on our side of the river. The monster appeared in the mass of white flakes flying about and stepped toward us, closing the distance.

"Ride, Serafina. Warn the others."

Run or reconnaissance? If this was one roving sentry, I could dispatch him. I dismounted, pointed my mare back east, and slapped her on the ass.

O'erlevendeh yipped in distress.

Sorry, pup.

Roskva flashed into view and waved her frond arm over her head, back up the slope.

Using my magicked feet, I ran south along the frozen river, getting distance from the Jörmonruk.

The beast shifted direction to chase me. Good. I slowed so I wouldn't outrun it, then shifted direction again. I crossed the river by heading west, slipping and sliding on hard ice.

Ten strides behind me, the ray beam rippled the air and gouged the ground, ice forming on top of the already-frozen river as the ghastly weapon followed me in a looping arc.

On the other side of the frozen riverbank, Roskva skidded to a stop before me and cowered. Which meant that I should, too.

Plowing snow into the air with my feet, I slid and fell on my ass, softened by a mound of snow.

Fate smiles upon idiots at times. Today, I was exhibit number one. I climbed to my feet as a ray blast from a second creature created a block of ice in front of my feet. Had I kept going, I'd be a chunk of frozen flesh.

One beast I could take. Two would be trouble. And with water nearby, frozen though it was, I had the sense I was close to their lair. Which meant there were a lot more than two in the area.

Time to go.

Using Roskva speed, I dashed south once more, away from the beast behind me, and widening the gap between myself and the second one.

I changed vectors, moving east, losing the Jörmonruks in the snowstorm. I slid more than I ran across the frozen river. If not for the rivulets of blown snow, I would have fallen hard.

When I reached the ridge, I patted my back. My crossbow was tied to my mare.

Idiot two times.

Up on the ridge, I slowed to a run as Roskva winked out. Using the wind as a guide, I angled northeast, searching for the tracks of my mare and Serafina's horse. Running in this stuff without Roskva was going to tax my stamina.

A minute later, to my right, I heard a series of bright barks. O'erlevendeh. Though I couldn't see the others, I said, "You saved me!"

But what I could hear, maybe the Jörmonruks could too.

I changed direction and ran down the slope.

Reaching the bottom, I jogged for a second minute and found the dvaergs forming a thirty-stride-wide arc. The ballistae carts were behind them: two in the center and one on either side. The two on the ends pointed off to the side to increase the overall coverage of the ballistae.

Reaching Serafina, I gathered my mare's reins, climbed aboard, and ruffled O'erlevendeh's furry head. Then I huffed air.

Ingefær heeled her horse and trotted in my direction with Tugg, Hombir, and the others hiking after.

She was shaking her head when she reached me. "I thought we agreed no heroics?"

I smiled big into her scowl, trying to bluster through her anger. "No. I don't remember agreeing to that." I made what I thought was a cogent plea. "Every encounter dictates tactics despite the overall strategy." Not that we had an overall strategy, but I didn't say that. "I did what I had to do to help us win—to keep you and the others safe."

Her brows narrowed; jaw muscles tightened. Her frosty glare said plenty. No point in adding to my woes by telling her about my close call.

"Yeah, alright," I said, still smiling. "No more heroics. But don't forget, my skills are well-suited to harass their rear flanks."

Tight-lipped, she nodded.

Mick weighed a vial in his hand. "How many?"

"Two, so far." I glanced at my wife. "But we're close to their camp."

CHAPTER TWENTY-SEVEN

DEATH, ON ICE, REPRISE

INGEFÆR

I chewed on my cheek; Rory's escapades wore my patience out. How could he be so cavalier with his life? I wasn't clueless. I knew we were all at risk of being killed. But I took calculated risks…to make the enemy overextend their capabilities, not to overextend ours.

Once more, Rory had rushed into battle alone. Like the first time, he sent Serafina off for her safety. The man over-relied on his fast feet. But in a snowstorm like this, he could run up on one of those bug-eyed monsters, and that would be it.

Hombir broke the icy silence. "They coming this way?"

Rory shrugged. "I ran south, leaving them near the river. Not sure they're following me."

Tugg asked, "How far be the river?"

Serafina replied, "Not far. The ridge is maybe eighty paces wide. It's on the other side, another fifty strides beyond."

Mick hiccupped. "They know-*hic*-we're here. They know-*hic*-we're hunting them."

"Based on their actions, they think they're the hunters," Rory said.

Not a gram of self-awareness could be heard in my husband's voice. I growled at him. "They'll kill you if you insist on going it alone."

"It's all about who sees who first," Rory retorted. "And with Roskva..." he patted his legs, "...and my feet, I'll never be surprised."

"Well, with you gallivanting about, our element of surprise is lost." I was still vexed at his heroics. Diverting my wrath, I turned to the group. "What's our best alternative?"

Tugg said, "Staying here at the bottom cedes the high ground to them."

Muggs had come forward. "And the longer we wait, the bigger the chance they will take it."

We were encroaching on their territory. Nothing like fighting one-eyed cornered rats the size of Jotunn. I asked for details about what Rory had seen.

He repeated Serafina's description of the ridge. "It's not all that high. Seven strides on this side and eight on the other. Of course, the ground slopes toward the river."

"Alright, we take the high ground here." I nodded up the slope. "Get the troops, carts, and wagons rolling."

The western edge should have a grand view of the river valley. Well, not in the snowstorm.

I grumbled under my breath as the next logical action was to do the opposite of what was safe...for my husband. "Take Serafina and scout ahead. Don't go down to the river."

He mock-saluted me and wagged his head at the healer.

"Don't leave him alone up there," I said. "Conk him on the head if he tries to run off."

That earned me an eye roll from both of them. But while Rory might risk his life to satisfy some internal whim, he wouldn't endanger hers—not without cause.

"No horses," Hombir said. "And crawl the last dozen strides so you don't expose your heads."

My husband and Serafina stomped up the snow-covered ridge. O'erlevendeh yipped and yanked at the leads Rory had set up. That was altogether too much noise; no point in drawing the beasts to us. I marched over and untied the ropes, taking the pup into my arms.

He nipped me and jumped away, working hard to run after Rory in the deep snow.

Mick made a move to chase after it, but I called him back. "Let him go. He's Rory's pest, er, pet."

After waiting a minute to give Rory and Serafina a lead, Tugg's dvaergs trudged up the hillside in a line forty dvaergs wide and three deep, with the Avarkæsir wielding crossbows in the front. Another two score of his soldiers urged the horses to pull the carts and then the wagons up the incline. The balance of his troops took up flanking positions to the north and south. Muggs and his nine operated two of the ballistae.

The soldiers to the north and south acted as scouts. If the Jörmonruks attacked from the flanks like last time, dvaergs would die before Hombir or I could set up a shield wall.

I looked at my booted feet. The trampled snow came to my calves. Where it wasn't stomped down, it crested above my knees. Squinting into the gale of snow, I estimated the visibility at seventy strides. That was a neutral factor. If the wind slowed, it would be to our benefit. If the flurries thickened, theirs.

After climbing the ridge, I tied my horse to the right of the two center ballistae carts, then climbed aboard. Muggs grinned at me from atop the left center cart. I don't know what he was happy about.

Standing behind the bench seat, I peered westward as we rolled across the top of the flat crest. I couldn't see Rory and Serafina in the flying snow. Given the ridge's width, I should be able to see him. Where the Hel was he?

Steadily, soldiers and carts advanced westward. Every head swiveled, searching.

Just as the last canopied wagon carrying our supplies rolled to a stop behind me, a shout came from the right—from the north.

A pair of ice ray blasts ripped through the snow-covered ground, and seconds later the ice obliterated the wheel of the rightmost ballistae cart. The second lethal beam struck higher at the weapon.

Dvaergs jumped off the cart. The horses bucked and yanked at their leads. But with the amount of snow and a missing wheel, they weren't going anywhere.

As I pinched sawdust and made the motions to cast my spell, the Jörmonruks shifted their ice rays and strafed across the ground, striking several retreating dvaergs. Rime caught their legs, then their torsos, before encasing their heads.

I ripped off a fireball to the north, set to explode just past the beasts. After the bead flew off, I worried about Rory and Serafina being behind them.

Mick turned his steed east and took off back down the ridge. What was he thinking?

My fireball exploded, illuminating and incinerating the pair of Jörmonruks. They dropped to the ground and rolled. That put the fire out, but I saw their charred flesh, front and back.

As they wobbled to their feet, I ripped a second bead at them. The snow obliterated the sight lines of the tiny fiery bead, but the second blast flashed bright and dropped them for good, leaving a pile of smoldering flames.

I scanned for Hombir.

He had moved to the front of the dvaerg host, standing in the middle of the ones wielding crossbows, perhaps two dozen strides west of me and ten more to my left. The dvaerg host had stopped at the crest's edge, overlooking the valley with the river I had yet to see.

Tugg hollered something in Dvaervish at Sett, pointing at the ice-encased ballista and dvaergs, and the panicked horses.

Where in Hel were Rory and Serafina?

I shouted at Sett as he ran past my position. "The ballista should be operable."

He waved an axe at me and shouted orders as he moved to the frozen wagon. It wouldn't move without repairs being made. I didn't have time to feel bad for the dead.

Shifting my gaze to the front lines, Hombir pointed northwest.

I searched in that direction.

Rory!

Serafina hiked by his side and O'erlevendeh leaped in Rory's footsteps to keep up.

An explosion of ice struck the ballista cart to my far left. Two white-furred brutes showed up on the ridge south of us and struck the exposed Avarkæsir flank.

The dvaergs ratcheted the weapon as far left as it would go, while a pair of dvaergs cranked the cocking mechanism.

Too slow!

Ice struck the horses, stopping their panic.

As I was about to shout at them to get away, Hombir erected a wall of fire fifteen feet high, forming an arc on the left side that covered half of the ridge. The screeching of ice rays against flame lasted for several long seconds, then stopped. From my higher vantage point, I watched the heads of the two Jörmonruks back up and disappear into the storm.

I glanced back at the farthest cart to my left; the ballista hadn't fired. They couldn't get enough of an angle and were busy repositioning the cart by lifting the rear by hand.

I jumped off the center-right wagon and scrambled forward...just in case the beasts showed up from Rory's direction. With Hombir occupied, Tugg's front flank was exposed. In a way, the troops there acted as bait.

Rory, Serafina, and O'erlevendeh climbed the ridge and pushed through.

When we met up, he shook his head at me. "We've awakened the hive. Serafina saw at least a dozen shadows."

I nodded. "Two pairs took turns attacking from the right and then the left." My arms crossed my chest. "Why were you out that far?"

"We stopped at the edge to wait for you. But the pup either sees them or senses them. O'erlevendeh ran out there. He wouldn't come when I called, so I had to chase after him."

"Had to?" The gods! That pup was going to be the death of him some day.

I hope not today.

Serafina nodded. "I went with him to make sure he returned."

Rory's head swung from left to right. "Where's Mick?"

I pointed east. "He went down the backside of the ridge. Last I saw him, he was moving north."

"Lokke's spawn!" Rory growled. He stepped past me. "I'm going to find him."

I was about to chastise him again when he spun around. "You know what? They've become unpredictable. We should too."

"Your plan?"

"At random intervals and in random directions—but not northeast, not where I'm about to go—shoot a fireball. At max range."

It sounded crazy. But...

Rory grabbed his crossbow in one hand, scooped up the whelp in the other, and raced for the backside of the ridge.

I nudged Serafina. "Go tell Hombir what I'm doing. See if he can shift the wall of fire back toward the center left." Reshaping a wall that far took concentration...and time. "Tell him he's got the center; I'll cover the flanks."

As she ran off, I considered how I would enact Rory's suggestion.

Sending a bead beyond what I could see was not how I trained. I had to take into account that after some twenty strides—for I stood that far from the western edge of the ridge—the ground dropped.

I re-climbed the ballista cart, still farther behind the line, for the added height improved my angles. As I waved my right hand, I pinched sawdust and pointed my finger, aiming slightly down and right-of-center, where Rory had come from.

The fiery bead flew for a distance before I lost sight of it. At my max range, a hundred twenty strides off, fire flashed bright enough to be seen in the snowstorm. And for a moment, in the reddish haze that filtered through the blowing snow, I saw a pair of Jörmonruks, their arms and legs flailing as they rolled in the snow.

"Rory, you're a genius." I had two spells left before I got woozy, and three before I swooned. So instead of engaging in more random attacks, I conserved my stamina until Serafina returned. I searched the battlefield as far as I could see.

Hombir re-formed his wall of fire, covering the front flank. I screamed at Muggs, who was on my left. "Turn the wagon to face more south!"

I got the dvaergs driving the ballista cart I was on to angle northward, yet keeping the field of fire to the front covered. The gods! We were making it up as we went along.

The dvaergs at the far-left cart had shifted it to face south by south-west. They clambered aboard, and another pair cocked the ballista. A second later, a duo of beasts lanced two dvaergs who were adjusting the weapon's elevation.

The ballista fired, bucking the cart. The six-foot-long shaft of pointed pine flew off, missing a beast by the width of a human hand.

The shooters scrambled, but the Jörmonruks each caught one in their deadly rime.

I shot a fiery bead at them. The explosion took them. But after they dropped, they rolled south, out of sight.

"Hope you don't have healers." Was I evil to wish them pain and suffering? No. They killed indiscriminately. There was but one way to deal with such creatures. Death to them all.

The damned Jörmonruks were taking out our ballistae. The wagon-mounted weapon on the far left was operable, but not maneuverable.

"Muggs, get some dvaergs to take over!"

Muggs' beard dipped, and he shouted orders in his native tongue.

I shouted orders in mine. "Get the draft horses from the covered wagons!"

Arm gestures were followed by a pair of dvaergs running off to do my bidding.

My head snapped to the north ballistae. Sett and six more dvaergs were engaged in grisly work. They chopped their dead frozen friends loose so they could get to the iced-over ballista.

The cart pointed too far west to be of much use. It would have to be repositioned as well. The ballistae plan sure had sounded good in theory.

Serafina came back. "Tugg has lost troops. The beasts have engaged up front and are strafing to the sides of the fire shield wall."

"Troll shit," I exclaimed through gritted teeth. I'd been so busy with the flanks, I hadn't seen their attacks.

"They lost a healer." Serafina waved a hand. "Jonuku has healed some of their wounded. I don't understand their language, but the dvaerg chatter didn't sound happy."

Knowing what I knew about Avarkæsir, they weren't talking about running. They were ready to charge. But was that wise?

I glanced westward. Tugg was in the middle of them, his arms gesturing.

"I need a stamina restore." Taking a deep breath, I swallowed my fears. "After this fireball." I let one go. On a hunch, I sent it straight north, following the ridgeline just past the smoldering hunks lying in the snow.

In the flash of red light, a pair of creeping Jörmonruks caught fire. "Got ya." With the wind blowing south, the smell of fresh burning fur blew at me. I found it...pleasant, even if my knees wobbled.

Serafina healed me.

To the northeast, on the backside of the ridge we were on, a beast erupted in flame. Mick must have used a vial of pitch. In the light of crackling flame, I spotted Rory. He fired his crossbow just as the blinding snow obliterated my sightline.

"Mick, you're a genius, too."

Serafina said, "I have a vial of healing if you should need it."

I nodded. Though if I cast enough fireballs and she cast enough healing spells, she would be the one to need it first.

I let a ball of fire go left of center, racing out past Tugg and his dvaergs, once more angling down. It flashed, illuminating nothing but the seared-away snow.

Hombir's fire shield went down; it had been up all of ten minutes. His spell hadn't lasted as long as in the past—the act of moving the fire wall such a long distance was the cause. His hands moved. Another one took its place.

With Jonuku behind him, he could hold the line for a couple of hours.

"Does Jonuku have a vial of healing?" I asked.

"Aye," Serafina said. "All the healers and Hombir, too."

What if the monsters waited us out? What if we spent all our spells and our healing potions as they used their hit-and-run tactics?

Do we retreat or stand our ground? Or do we go on the attack?

The decision proved easy. At least to me. We came here to make the Ice Plains safe.

I nudged Serafina. "Tell the others we can't wait here. We have to attack."

Besides, the Avarkæsir would prefer it.

Serafina's eyes bulged. "But we don't know where they are."

Experience guided my next words. "Sure we do. The beasts are to the west. Whether just on the other side of the river, or half a league, I don't know. But for you and Rory to spot so many, and for so many to be sniping at us, we have to be close to their camp."

She nodded and ran to tell the others.

Feeling rascally, I sent a fiery bead due south. Just as it exploded, a foursome of Jörmonruks charged from the north.

How had I not seen them? I hadn't been looking. I needed more eyes.

Sett and a handful of dvaergs were busy hacking ice. They charged, axes held high.

Two beasts stopped and strafed the advancing dvaergs. They never had a chance. Sett died holding an axe high over his head.

The two other Jörmonruks lanced the wagon. The weight of the ice caused the wagon beams to fail, and it crashed to the ground, though the ballista didn't fall over because it was encased in a rigid block of ice.

I blinked myself free out of a few moments' stare. Anger at the deaths of so many shook me. I shot a fiery bead at the foursome. As the bead raced north, two beasts turned to the east. The other two lumbered toward me.

The bead exploded, catching the rear duo. The icy rays from the front pair lanced the ground as icy death raced toward me.

The dvaergs on the cart with me jumped to the ground. I backed up, waving my hands like a maniac. Words gushed from my mouth.

But I wasn't fast enough.

Their frost beams found me.

I cowered, covering my face with my arms, interrupting my spell.

And lived.

What?

The ice rays crackled and shimmered in the dim light of the blizzard. It was like the sun shining through a waterfall. How beautiful.

Instead of turning me into an icicle, their beams tickled. Cold air whipped through my clothes. I felt chilled and had goosebumps all over. Well, except for one spot. Right underneath my throat. Right where the snowflake with the fiery opal was attached to a choker chain.

I had forgotten I had protection from cold magic.

All around me, ice built up on the ballista and the cart's right-side wheels. Ice formed a wall around me in a half circle, rising higher and higher.

From my right, Rory let loose a bolt, striking a beast in the eye. It fell like a rock thrown off a cliff, sending a plume of snow high into the air.

Rory dropped his weapon in the snow and pulled a second crossbow off his shoulder. That had to be Mick's.

A second beast died and hit the ground.

The two beasts farther north rose to their feet, charred all over and smoldering. Rory scooped up something white and raced northeast.

The pair gave chase.

One of them stopped to look to its right. As it raised a hand, a vial of pitch crashed into its upper torso, its fur stained blue, followed by a torch. Mick's face reflected fire, and a grim satisfaction.

The fourth monster turned. Mick ran south, but he was in range. And if I could see him, the beast could too.

From behind the Jörmonruk, Rory stabbed it in the back of its knee. The gods! He was so fast.

The beast careened backwards. Rory jumped out of the way and slashed at its head. O'erlevendeh pounced, sinking his baby teeth into the beast's neck. I doubted they would penetrate the fur. But the killing instinct was there.

A noise to my left caused me to turn. Dvaergs were on the march.

The six dvaergs who had jumped now remounted the cart. Their eyes were wide and their jaws hung low. I smiled and patted my necklace.

"Break the ice off the ballista." It was covered in a solid wall of ice. I checked to see if the horses had been killed. They hadn't. I got the driver's attention. "Get this ballista to the western edge of the ridge."

The ballista wouldn't be firing for a while. It seemed the Jörmonruks recognized the danger of the weapon and focused on taking it out. Was it sheer luck of their random raids, or did they have prior knowledge?

I untied my horse from the back of the cart and jumped off just as Serafina returned, huffing. I motioned for her to join me. "Come on."

She looked pale, but climbed aboard her mare. "What do you have in mind?"

I didn't know. "To the other cart." The last one that was operable. The one manned by Muggs.

The ballista shifted forward, rolling to keep pace with Hombir, the Avarkæsir to the front, and the mage's fire wall ahead of them.

Serafina and I trotted after them. Catching up, I tied off my horse and helped Serafina climb aboard. In front of us, Hombir reached the western ledge.

I urged the dvaergs driving. "Get right up to Hombir's backside. The d'oglemann mage."

Muggs grinned as he aimed the weapon over the heads of the line before us. The ballista was cocked and loaded.

Mick arrived, huffing for air, and squeezing O'erlevendeh tight. "Don't fire northwest for a minute or so."

My heart shivered. Rory was going out alone. Again.

"You take over messenger duties for Serafina." I swallowed anguish and fear. "Have your vials ready, and don't let the pup loose."

Serafina said, "You stay on the south side of the cart, I'll take the north." Her plan was designed to minimize loss of life in the event of another surprise beast attack.

Our cart stopped moving. Hombir stood at the edge of the ridge. What was going on?

I shifted my gaze and spotted Tugg's Avarkæsir and Hombir's firewall in front of them, though it was held several feet off the ground to protect the troops still on the slope.

Peering westward, I discovered why the entire formation had stopped where it did. Sixty paces ahead of the firewall, a foursome of Jörmonruks blasted their ice beams against the flaming shield.

Dvaergs looped crossbow bolts high into the air. But they fell short of the enemy.

Soldiers down the ridge on my left cried out. Four more Jörmonruks—two of them now black instead of white—strafed their deadly ice into Tugg's kin.

From atop the cart where I now stood, I fired a bead west-southwest and down.

The fireball exploded, illuminating the area. But the blast fell shy of the four Jörmonruks. It was like they knew my range. Or perhaps, I was just too far back and too far north from the dvaergs' left front flank.

The fireball had lit enough to reveal yet four more Jörmonruks crawling toward Tugg's troops along the sloped ridge.

I glanced at the ballista to the far left. The dvaergs saw the beasts, but the slope of the ridge took away the angle they needed.

Everyone had thought the ballistae were a grand idea. We had gotten off a single shot.

I sent a second salvo. The area ignited in red flames, revealing the beasts' backsides as they retreated. It had to be because I had spotted them.

I employed Rory's suggestion of being unpredictable. It had been over a minute, so I let a fiery bead go northwest. No beasts.

Serafina asked, "How many is that?"

"Four or five." The next one would wear me out.

Mick squawked. "This is terrible. Next time, remind me to tell your friend Vidarr to keep his damn coins."

It wasn't about the money anymore. I think he knew that—he was venting his fears and frustrations.

I let a fireball go straight west at maximum range, leaning against the ballista for support. When the bead exploded, I caught a foursome blasting their death rays at the fire shield, and two more who were racing forward.

The gods! How many of them were there?

The buggers were smart. They poked and prodded at our flanks without a pattern.

Be unpredictable, Rory had said. He had it right.

As the firelight dimmed, I caught sight of more beasts pulling the fallen out of my range.

"Heal me. Hurry."

Chapter Twenty-Eight

THE SIGN OF EVIL

RORY

After gashing the throat of the last Jörmonruk with my blade, I doubled back to find Mick. Handing him the pup, I said, "You two help Ingefær. Hurry."

"Where will you be?"

"Tell her not to fire northwest for a couple of minutes. I'm going around." Hefting the young man's crossbow, I said, "I'm going to hold on to this."

Mick scrambled up the ridge, taking a slanted approach. In mere moments, I lost him in the blowing snow.

I looked at Roskva. She stood there with her frond hands on her squarish hips. Her blockhead revealed no emotion, but the stance conveyed irritation. My tactics had forced her to aid me. Again.

I cocked both crossbows, loaded them, and raced north past a pile of smoldering beasts. The immediate area flickered—a creepy red cast over the snow.

After a couple of hundred strides, I turned west and traversed the snow-covered ground. I sped down the ridge and raced toward the river.

A fireball illuminated the flurry of flakes well off to my left. There was a momentary flash of silhouettes. A lot of them.

Great. Just great.

A dvaerg's cry defied the wail of the wind. What was Tugg up to?

I ran west at a normal sprint for another minute, then slowed further as I turned south.

Roskva's creamy orange stick-like frame stayed with me. She caught my glance and shook her head at me. Inside my head, I heard her sigh.

I lifted both crossbows up and stomped through the snow. Sweat poured down my backside, and my thighs screamed. Running through snow, even with my fylgjæ, showed me how out of shape I was.

Images loomed to the southwest.

I kneeled, knowing that the beasts would have to look into the driving sleet. They stepped closer, their eyes on the ground at their feet. They weren't expecting me.

I aimed high at an eye and fired. I dropped the crossbow and fired the second bolt at the second beast's eye a moment after the first bolt hit.

A bugle sounded behind the two now-dead brutes. But unlike the sound I had heard a week ago, this one comprised one long and two quick notes. A long breath later, the bugling repeated.

A fireball erupted a hundred strides ahead of me and half that distance to my left, lighting the sky for a moment. The flames revealed more shadows.

My jaw dropped. There had to be twenty of them. Eight stood in a row, firing their cold beams as they retreated. That revealed the outer edges of a fire shield. The dvaergs were attacking, using Hombir's incantation to cover their advance.

Four beasts peeled off and came at me, their arms raised in firing positions. The red light dimmed, and snow filled my vision. But they could fire blind.

Do the unexpected.

I raced west. Cold rays crackled the air and furrowed the ground behind me.

A minute later, I sprinted southward again. Roskva's sparkling figure paced me. It was like she ran atop the snow. Ingefær often complained that she couldn't see my fylgjæ. That was a good thing with these beasts. Though I wondered if my sparkling spirit could be taken by an errant blow.

The wind wailed its violent fury, slashing the wet flakes sideways. Fortunately, the storm smacked into the back of my wulv pelt cloak and hood. I had gone north first on purpose.

As I traipsed southward, the snow crunching beneath my feet. To my right was a strange-looking mound of snow. Or more like a long, narrow hillock covered in the white stuff. It seemed out of place, almost unnatural. A hundred strides later, I made out an odd glowing orb at the southern end. Between eye blinks, sometimes it radiated green, other times a soft orange, and then a mesh of blues and yellows.

I stutter-stepped my way closer.

Another fireball flamed the skies well off to my left. It caught me off guard, and I couldn't see if any beasts were caught in it. The light dimmed before I got to a count of twelve.

At thirty paces, I could see the glowing thing was not an orb. It was something that formed three circular shapes, one laid outside of another. The outer two rings, each about two feet wide, were woven in a sort of symmetrical design, radiating in alternating yellow and blue hues. The third inner ring was a foot wide, but it was the most brightly lit—it pulsed orange, its glow coming from bizarre letters or symbols, seemingly suspended in midair.

Were they sigils?

"Well, troll shit." That was the most unnatural thing I've seen out on the Ice Plains. Ever.

However, what concerned me the most were the double *S* shaped snake heads, one high and to the right, and one low and to the left. They were—no doubt—unconnected to any mechanism that would keep the ward floating there. The heads were dark jade, while the bodies shone as if made from luminescent emeralds. The snakes were mirror images of the glyph we found in that pine tree grove. But ten times bigger and brighter.

Great. Just great.

I was tired of saying that.

After ensuring Roskva was still at my side and that no Jörmonruk was coming at my rear or side flanks, I crept closer. How the Hel was the contraption standing up on end—like a dinner platter on edge?

What had Zakk said about the snake heads back at Kral Azza Rid? *A sign of evil. A glyph belonging to Lokke.*

As I studied the circular sigil, yet another fireball blast lit the sky. The ward blocked some of my view, but I was sure two Jörmonruk had caught fire.

A bugle sounded—three sharp beats—out of sight in the snow, but close to the other side of the monstrous ward.

I crept to the end of the odd-place mount and saw that the giant sigil stood upright because it was ensconced in icicles and frost—all along the bottom edge and up the curved sides.

Another bugle. The same three sharp notes.

Roskva tugged at my sleeve.

I ignored her and, while crouching, shifted forward to see better.

Two Jörmonruks peered southeast, half their backs and half their left sides to me.

One of them bugled again. The same shrill three-beat blast.

The one not bugling turned around. It bent its massive head and walked into the circular sigil and...disappeared.

What the Hel?

I reloaded the crossbows. And watched. A fireball went off to the southwest. Giant bodies caught on fire—perhaps three? They dropped and rolled. With the flames out, I lost sight of them in the snow.

In twos and threes, the Jörmonruks came running, turned, and stepped one at a time into what had to be a portal, disappearing with a flash of orange.

I slid half-way down the mound on the back side of the circular glyph. Lying flat on the mound's slope with a raised head to see, I had to be almost invisible to anyone looking.

I counted heads, smiling whenever one was charred over. Fourteen beasts had moved into the portal before the Jörmonruk who had bugled followed them to...wherever. Where were the others? Dead, perhaps?

I stood and stretched. Taking my time, I moved closer until I was within ten paces of the monstrous sigil.

An invisible force grabbed me. My feet stopped moving. I couldn't raise my arms.

A voice resonated inside my head. *Who are you?*

Huh?

My vision clouded over. I lost sight for a moment as a pressure right behind my eyes popped my ears. I tried to yell, but whimpered instead. The invisible force held me upright, otherwise I would have fallen to my hands and knees. My head hurt, my stomach raised the stakes, and bile rose up my throat.

Where's my sword?

What sword? That was an unconscious reply, one I hadn't thought to say.

The power pulled me closer. I dug my feet in. But my efforts were clumsy, my feet not responding with any sense of urgency. The snow didn't help.

"Roskva!" I shouted in my head.

I slid forward, a fresh pain erupting behind my eyes. The pressure pushed at my eyeballs so hard, they wanted to pop out of my head. I spewed what was left of my breakfast over my cloak.

"I want my sword!"

When sparring with Vidar, he once mentioned that going limp when an opponent had you, if done right, could force the grip loose as the sudden weight was borne by the assailant.

I didn't so much as fling myself to the ground as I raised my feet up. Which allowed me to fall on my ass. In an eye blink, I rolled over onto my stomach. Though blinded by a searing agony, I used my hands and knees to scamper away from the round object until the pain behind my eyes subsided and my vision returned.

The voice in my head had been a man's. But the image that flashed in my head was that of a sword. My memories followed up. The sword was identical to the one I had once worn. The sword that had once controlled me. *Laehvateinn.*

Laehvateinn was Lokke's sword?

"Shit."

I looked around me. Roskva had gone. The wind abruptly slowed to what felt like a brisk ocean breeze. For the first time in a day, snow fell straight down instead of sideways.

Off to the southeast, Dvaervish chanting filled the air, and the fire shield radiated a dark red.

I clambered up and over the mound, keeping my distance from the gigantic sigil.

"Over here!" I shouted.

Holding a crossbow in each hand, I raced east and slid down the mound. Keeping wide of the circular artifact, I moved southward. Several breaths later, I held up my hands as dvaergs on the north flank spotted me and leveled crossbows in my direction.

I shouted. "All clear. The Jörmonruks have left the field."

A moment afterward, the fire shield went down, and I looked at a horde of Avarkæsir, anchored by Tugg. Their jaws were set and their beards were full of frost and—by the looks in their eyes—fury.

The mass moved toward me, the rear flanks holding their axes and shields high. When the front line, wielding crossbows, reached me, Tugg called a halt. I waded through the ranks.

Tugg raised his bearded chin. "They be all dead?"

I shook my head. "No. They ran off. Used a magical device." I pointed. "You'll see it soon enough."

He started up his troops, and we reached the spot with the round sigil. From the front, it was eighteen feet across.

Mouths hung agape. Ingefær, Hombir, Serafina, and Mick, holding my pup, joined us on foot.

I pointed at the massive ward. "They pledge fealty to Lokke. Not that it's news."

I shook my head at the memory of being controlled by the artifact. How was Lokke speaking? The vile god was locked away in Asagard. Wasn't he?

Ingefær came up to me and slapped me on the shoulder. Hard. "Nice to see you, husband."

I was in no mood for her questioning my tactics. So I grabbed her around the hips and pulled her tight to me. I kissed her. It took her a moment before she kissed me back.

Someone cleared a throat.

I let my wife go. "We have bigger problems than the Jörmonruk."

Silence greeted my words.

"The Jörmonruk, this sigil portal...artifact...thingy." I struggled for words. "Well, I don't know where it goes, but I can tell you that Lokke is behind it."

Tugg *pshaw'd* me.

Hombir said, "But that's not possible."

Ingefær put her hands on her hips. "Explain yourself."

Taking my pup into my hands, I took a deep breath. "I cannot get within ten paces of it. Otherwise, some...force tries to take a hold of me.

Not just my body, but my mind. There's a being behind the power, and it wants its sword back. It wants Laehvateinn."

Ingefær gasped.

Tugg shook his head. "Impossible. The sword be stored in our vault. Protected by glyphs."

I jabbed a gloved finger. "I'll bet they're not as powerful as this one here. Go on. Look. But one at a time. And maybe have a friend tie a rope around you, 'cause whatever it is, it tried to suck me in."

While many of the Avarkæsir thought I was frying their eggs, Tugg knew me. "Do as he says, lads. Volunteers only. One at a time."

One by one, dvaergs took turns—with a rope around their chests—moving closer to the circular sigil. Then they came back and shrugged.

After the third one, everyone was back in front of me, looking at me like I was a purveyor of mangled children's fables.

Tugg said, "No one reports any strange feelings. No one be talked to."

I locked eyes with Ingefær. "I know what I felt and heard."

She had a go in approaching the massive ward with a rope tied around her waist. I watched her get within a foot of it.

I frowned and scratched at my beard. "What the Hel?"

Ingefær came back and searched my eyes. "Not concussed. Are you positive?"

I nodded. "I know the feeling of a foreign force in my head. It was a man's voice. It asked for his sword. And an image of Laehvateinn flashed. I'll go to my deathbed with my testimony."

She was trying to believe me. She got Tugg to tie two ropes around my chest, then told me, "Go slow."

Yeah. Right at the giant glyph.

"And you accuse of me of being careless." I sighed and stepped closer.

At ten paces, the tugging returned. My eyes itched, and the surroundings dimmed so much, I swore the snow turned gray.

I was pulled. No, yanked. It took the dvaergs holding the lines by surprise.

In the few seconds I was within range, my mind was raked over coals. My brain was on fire. My jaw clenched so hard I couldn't scream. Instead, my teeth ached.

"I want my sword."

I ended up on my back, a dozen strides away from the portal glyph. If not for the wulv cloak and my leather armor, I'd have serious rope burns on my chest.

Groaning with a pounding headache, I got to my feet. "See!"

The two dvaergs holding the rope nodded in unison. One said, "Aye. Something jerked him."

The other said, "It didn't want to let go."

Chapter Twenty-Nine

A SECOND CONCLAVE

RORY

Thirty paces south of the massive sigil, Ingefær, Serafina, Mick, Hombir, Jonuku, Tugg, Muggs, and I circled around in the gale snowstorm. I hugged O'erlevendeh for warmth.

Lokke's words—if it was him—echoed in my mind. My relationship with Laehvateinn rushed back in full force. She was like sweet ale. A couple of sips tasted good. But quaff four steins inside an hour, and things went dark. Upon waking, the body hurt, and the mind screamed in agony with no recollection of what had transpired. If only that was the worst of it.

Tugg asked, "Where did they go?"

"No idea." I had Mick get some milk from my rucksack. "They walked into that...thing...and disappeared."

Ingefær said, "No one is going through that ward." Her eyes locked onto mine. "You, especially."

I shuddered, spilling some milk as I held a bowl for the whelp to drink. "No. I'm the last person to go near that contraption." I had no desire to speak to Lokke, nor to be controlled by him. Laehvateinn's behavior had warned me off for life. She was all about vengeance and blood. And I'd spilled plenty trying to quench her thirst.

Muggs growled. "The cowards. They run off after getting a bit bloodied."

Tugg said, "How many survivors ye got?"

Muggs scowled, his bearded face all hair and lines. "Six still standing. Three be icicles. Ye?"

Tugg sighed. "Lost another sixty-five today. Me second-in-command included."

Great gods, that was horrible. It left Tugg with less than a hundred and forty warriors.

Hombir said, "There's six of us left, counting me and my wife."

He'd lost a warrior as well.

Tugg pointed at Muggs. "We be four or five days from Azza Rid. Send four, either on foot or take a wagon. Report our findings. Ask for a company, but make sure a healer and a mage come along."

Muggs pursed his lips. "I don't know. Me premier be pretty set in his thinking. I doubt Zakk agrees to come. The other mages, well, they be not worth much." He scratched at the back of his neck. "But I'll send a group for ye. No harm in asking."

"Why not a bird?" Mick asked.

"Unreliable in this weather," Tugg replied.

Would a report of finding the beast's lair jar the premier from his defensive thinking? Or would he think his warriors had been enthralled?

As if she read my mind, Ingefær said, "What's more important is to let the Realm know what's going on. If nothing else, have them send birds when the storm clears."

Something we could do...if we were still alive to do so.

Muggs spat at the snow-covered ground. "Aye. Me warriors have seen the beasts with their own eyes. They'll do some convincing to at least get yer birds sent."

"Which leaves us with...what the Hel are we going to do?" I let the whelp finish licking the bowl, then had Mick repack it.

Serafina said, "We should scout around. Maybe there's a clue out there...somewhere."

Her suggestion tickled a memory. "Oh! Behind the sigil is a long and narrow mound. It doesn't appear to be natural."

"What do you think it is?" Mick asked, then hiccupped.

Scratching the whelp under his chin, I said, "It may be a mound of dirt. Like when you dig a foundation for a home, you scrape earth and level it out, which gives you a nice flat surface in one spot, but a pile of dirt in another."

Hombir nodded. "Aye. We've dug dens in our enclave and took the extra dirt to the farming fields."

"You think they're underground?" Ingefær asked.

"Don't know." O'erlevendeh nipped me. "Ow. You'll get fed when we have time."

Muggs said, "If they be underground, under the mound...why not have a normal opening? Like a cave."

Serafina asked, "Don't they need air to breathe?"

Air holes and bolt doors. I smiled. The recollection of the Vala's tomb floated back to me.

I nodded. "They've got some kind of access to air, or they teleported somewhere else entirely. Perhaps the mound was made for a different reason."

I tucked the pup into my backpack and got bitten for my efforts. "We work in teams. I say we start at the sigil end and work our way up the mound. We look for air passages...or a bolt hole."

Ingefær nodded. "Two teams. One on either side with a mage and healer."

Tugg asked, "How many warriors you want?"

My wife looked at me.

"I don't know. No more than six doing the looking and prodding. Otherwise, they'll step all over themselves. But the rest need to shadow our movements, just in case."

Ingefær said, "Hombir will take the east, I'll take the west. Rory and Mick and another six warriors will search the center of the mound as we work our way north. Tugg, if you agree, split your forces into two groups and have them shadow our movements from ten paces. Fire on sight."

Muggs said, "Me and the rest of me folk will work with Rory. Give me a moment while I send off the group to Azza Rid."

"Split the vials of pitch and the torches between the groups," I said. "Let's see what this mound is hiding."

I didn't know, but I had a feeling. The mound was long, and it started and stopped for no apparent reason, except for the circular monstrous ward at one end.

Folks got moving, sorting themselves out into teams. Muggs didn't get any volunteers, so he ended up ordering four of his warriors to get going.

Tugg got a dozen dvaergs to make camp, another dozen to work on the frozen-over ballistae, and a third to build a pyre for the dead. The rest of his soldiers split up and took up flanking positions.

Mick pointed at the sigil. "Who made it?"

Ingefær replied, "The Jörmonruks."

He shook his head, his tawny hair flinging out of his hood. "No. That can't be. They hurl ice rays with abandon. But other than that, what else have they done? Have they shown an affinity for complex magic?"

They hadn't. At least, not yet. The sensation of my bowels flowing inside of me made a rather unpleasant noise. I didn't lose control, but it was a close call. Mick's observation implied that we hadn't yet met the brains of their operations...just their brawn.

Folks looked away at my distress. I would have preferred for Mick to crow like a rooster.

Serafina said, "Where did they come from? These beasts were last seen in the first epoch. Where have they been? There's a score dead. All full-grown adults. I can't believe they've survived out here for their entire lives and never once has someone come into conflict with them."

Tugg scratched at his beard. "Hmm. Ye be saying ye don't think the beasties are under this mound?"

She shook her head. "No, that's not it. They might be or might not be. Where have these giant beasts been all this time?"

I pointed at the circular glyph construct. "Maybe they teleported here."

"From *where*, is what I'm asking," the half-alvae retorted.

Plane travel was limited to a very select few...like Vidarr. Even Ilmarien couldn't do it. Vidarr had traveled to the Void and the Aether. The gods be damned. We needed the Haví of the Aether.

Ingefær said, "Hombir, get your tomes. Before we search, see if you can decipher any of the orange letters or symbols."

While the d'oglemann mage ran off to get his rucksack, we approached the ward. I stayed back a dozen paces. Snow whipped at us, and the wind cried out in fury. But we were determined to make sense of the sigil and maybe the Jörmonruks.

Jonuku said, "Remember. They're evil. And Master Belkin believes Lokke is involved. The Father of Lies." She shuddered.

Tugg growled. "The gods be banished."

Muggs retorted. "Oi. That be blasphemy."

"Has your premier not told you what happened almost two years ago?" I asked.

Muggs' eyes narrowed. "No."

I turned to Tugg.

"Birds were sent out about eighteen moons ago. Me premier sent one to yers. Of that I be sure. I be there, Muggs. I be at the battle to save the Realm. Vidarr Allefar says so, and I believe him."

"Who be this Vidarr with a god's name?" Muggs hands went to his waist, his chin lifted high.

I sighed. "Now is not the time for that debate. Hold your questions, and if you would, please take our counsel for the spirit of it, even if the details bother you."

Muggs stared at me, but nodded. "We be talking about the Father of Lies. Be great if he be banished."

The gods had been banished to the plane of Asagard. Or it was more accurate to say that the rainbow bridges between the planes had been destroyed, preventing travel from Asagard to the Void, which acted as a hub between the other planes.

We had Vidarr's word for it. But as we'd almost died in the skirmish, we believed him. Vidarr had wielded the Rod of the Dreki and another artifact known as The Valknut.

Serafina's question remained. Where had the Jörmonruks come from?

Hombir returned and flipped pages in his book.

Serafina said, "It's pretty in its own way. The intricate weave in the outer two circles has a pattern to it. I like the blue and yellow hues. Soothing."

Mick hiccupped. "Not to me."

Ingefær pointed. "A few of those sigils seem familiar."

"Aye." Hombir approached and pointed at the fish-looking one to the upper left.

Then at the arrow symbol to the lower left.

Then he jabbed a talon at the backward P:

"These three I find in this tome. They are ancient Varanusian."

He looked down into his book. "They're together here. The arrow is for honor. The fish, for nobility. And the backward P signifies the opposite of joy, so terror, or perhaps danger or death. The context talks about nobility requires honor in the face of danger. But there's a sidebar comment about the arrow one, stating it may mean war, which fits with the 'danger' rune. So, what it means on this here large circle, with the three symbols separated by five to seven other runes, I cannot say."

I cupped my hands as I spoke into the wind. "You know what we haven't done? You haven't detected for magic. I mean, I know it's magical. I saw it in action. But the reveal magic you showed us earlier may provide a clue."

Hombir grinned, revealing a row of sharp teeth. "Ah. Brilliant."

Ingefær said, "But I will search for magic first. It reveals wards."

Mick chuckled. "It's one gigantic ward."

I didn't think he was wrong. It had to be a portal and sigil artifact.

My wife shushed him and had the others step back and to the side.

I encouraged her. "Vidarr didn't release the Draugar until he tried to *dispel* a ward. You should be fine detecting one."

She glanced back at me and shook her head as she sighed. She cast her find magic.

The gods! The artifact glowed such a bright orange, it hurt my eyes.

As it began its slow fade, Ingefær inspected every surface she could see. She went behind it and peered up and down, then over. After several long minutes, the glow disappeared.

She came around to the front. “Nothing. No wards.”

Which seemed strange. Then again, many of the runes would be glyphs, and any attempt to wipe one out would be met with mayhem, both beastly and magical.

Hombir stepped up and cast his show magic. Instead of orange, there were hues of brown and black, each laced with looped strands of gray, or perhaps silver.

“I know what black means,” I said. “The plane of Hel.”

Mick stomped left, then right. His head bobbed. But he didn’t crow. And I had thought he was getting better.

“The brown is the plane of earth.” Ingefær frowned. “Why?”

Serafina pointed. “The heads moved!”

Mick crowed as he stomped his way over to me. Back to the old Mick.

The half-alvae was right. The snake heads had reversed position. What did it mean?

Tugg asked, “I don’t suppose anyone wants to touch it?”

Lots of shaking heads.

Muggs said, “Bah. I’ll do it. Stand back.”

My wife tried to talk him out of it. “We can’t help you if you disappear. You may wind up in a room full of the beasts.”

Muggs pulled his double-headed axe off his shoulder. “Alright.”

I said to his back, “Just touch it. Don’t walk through like the Jörmonruk did.”

He nodded. Folks cleared the area.

Muggs approached and, with a meaty finger, touched the outer circle, just above where the ice was caked over it.

His head snapped left, then right. “Nothing.”

He found a spot to touch the second circle. After waiting a moment, his finger alighted on the honor symbol—the arrow—as it was within reach.

The inner circle, composed of runes and letters, blurred for a moment. At least to my eyes.

Muggs turned around. “It moves. The inner circle moves. Do I turn it?”

I shouted. “Not yet. Let Mick make a notation of it. So we can reorient it back to where it was.”

Mick looked at me, licking his lips. “Volunteering me?”

I splayed my hands. “You have the wax table and stylus.” Before he could come over to surrender them to me, I added, “And the artistic talent.”

A quick smile flickered. Mick nodded and took to drawing. When he was done, he moved away.

Muggs took a breath. “Here goes nothing.”

He spun the inner circle with care, letting the nobility symbol come into reach. Despite not being attached to anything visible, the snake heads stayed anchored in the middle. So far, the heads hadn’t moved again.

Muggs played with the wheel until it had made a complete revolution. “Nothing.”

My wife said, “We’re no nearer to a solution. Perhaps this is a waste of our time. And I don’t want to play with this construct. We need Vidarr.”

I agreed. I got the sense we were missing something. But the feeling didn’t give me an idea of what to do. Besides, I was tired of watching...and waiting. I hated waiting. “Let’s search for air holes or a bolt door.”

Muggs said, “I can walk through.”

Ingefær said, “No. That’s folly. We go through when we know what it does or where it goes, not before. And we go in force. Not alone.”

Muggs nodded. "Aye. That makes sense."

Serafina said, "That was brave of you to offer."

Muggs nodded. "I see ye riding out front. That be brave, too."

Tugg harrumphed.

I think he was blushing. But I was far enough away, and there were plenty of snowflakes flitting about, so I couldn't be sure.

Mick pointed. "The inner circle isn't quite right. The funny-looking

should be on top."

Muggs eyed the structure and shifted it. "Happy?"

Mick shrugged.

We organized ourselves into three teams. I went the long way around to meet Mick, Muggs, and three more dvaergs.

"Spread out." I took a lit torch from Mick and passed it down.

The six of us stood a couple of strides apart, covering the not-quite-flat mound that spanned ten paces. Off to my left, to the west, was Ingefær, Serafina, a d'oglemann, and three more dvaergs. To my right, Hombir, Jonuku, Tugg, and three dvaergs scouted the mound from the side.

I let my team track back toward the circular contraption. They found nothing, which we had expected. I stepped north into the blizzard, snow pellets slashing at my face.

Chapter Thirty

ESCAPE HATCH

RORY

Through the blowing snow, with a crossbow in hand and a whiny pup on my back, I searched the ground before me. "Stay in line. Those on the ends, keep pace with the group on your side. We stay together."

Other than the howling of the wind and an occasional whimper from O'erlevendeh when he expressed his displeasure, the Ice Plains were spookily quiet.

We'd traversed perhaps half of the length of the odd-placed mound when Roskva popped up beside me. She pointed north.

"Jörmonruks!" I pointed left and right. "Tell the others."

Two breaths later, two ice rays strafed the ground and serpentined their way toward us.

"Back!" I hollered as I dropped my torch.

With magicked feet, I raced northwest. My plan? Divert their attention.

The good news was I could see maybe eighty strides. The bad news was, the beast's range doubled that of my crossbow. Well, tripled, if I wanted to take out an eye shooting into the wind.

But my speed...that was the battle changer.

At Roskva's maximum speed, I sprinted until the sounds of freezing, crackling, and popping ceased. Double checking, I made sure I was out of sight. Shifting angles, I moved at Roskva's half-speed—twice that of my maximum—into the wind for a couple of breaths, then jogged east at a normal human pace, my head swiveling about.

A white-furred beast stood atop the mound, leaning southeastward with its head, peering into the wind-driven snow. The fact that it was there meant it had past knowledge of my attack style. The ginormous head snapped toward me. An arm came up.

Engaging Roskva speed for two quick blinks, I slid to a stop a stride before it. As the ice beam shrieked its frigid blast above my head, I fired my crossbow at a steep angle, aiming at the eye.

I didn't hear the squelch, but I had to scamper out of the path of the falling Jörmonruk. As the monster thudded, a plume of snow was thrown high into the air.

I dashed south, searching for beast number two.

I hoped Ingefær or Hombir didn't cast a fireball. While I could outrun the bead, I had to see it coming before it exploded.

Going at full speed, for Roskva remained by my side, I raced back toward my group, using the long and narrow mound to guide me.

I need not have worried, for soon I saw the burning body of the second beast.

Mick spotted me and warned the others.

Seeing the others safe, Roskva winked out, and I took a deep breath. "How did you fare here?"

Tugg said, "Two casualties."

Serafina said, "Then Miss Ingefær got a wall of air up, and while the beast fired at it, Mick got some pitch on it."

Hombir finished up. "I hit it with a fiery dart spell."

Mick shrugged. "I was a distraction."

Ingefær said, "You got pitch on it. It helped."

"Good teamwork." I pointed behind me. "There has to be a bolt hole. Let's go find it." I scanned the group. "As I remember, the mound is two hundred strides long. We've searched half."

With a fresh torch in hand, I followed the vanishing tracks of the Jörmonruk. They disappeared because of the blowing wind and snow, not anything magical.

A minute later, we passed by the beast I'd killed with an arrow. A minute after that, we reached the end of the mound. I scratched at my beard. "Those two came from somewhere."

Serafina said, "Perhaps they were late in returning and were making for the circular ward?"

"Maybe." I scanned the area as I moved back to the mound. I studied the almost-blown-away tracks of the beast. "Move off." I waved at everyone, circling the last traces of a print. "I need more light."

My wife cleared her throat. "You want someone to come by you with a torch?"

"Yeah. Hurry." I waved a hand to my rear. "Come behind me."

What was odd was the complete lack of tracks after this one. The two prints south of it were about as faint. There should be more prints to the north, but there weren't.

I kneeled with the torch above my head.

Mick stood behind me, a second torch lighting the snow-covered ground.

The wind made a mash of things. I got my dirk out of my boot and used it and my arm to swat the snow away.

I swiped again.

"Aha!" I pointed at the ground. "There's a seam here. Help me clear the area of snow. Use the torch to melt it."

We got more hands as the seam proved to be a massive circle, some two paces wide.

Mick asked, "What is it...I mean besides a bolt hole?"

Ingefær had crept up to see. "It's a formed chunk of ice."

I spotted a small indentation dead in the center of the circular block of ice. Without waiting for Ingefær to cast one of her spells, I dug a finger into it.

I punched at a hole in the snow as big as my thumb. "Now what do you suppose that's for? It's too small to be an airhole for such a large cavern."

Mick said, "It's the way to open the access hole. You have an iron bar tied to a piece of rope. You shove it through lengthwise. On the underside, it swings flat to the ground."

I looked up at him. "You're a genius. Now go find something like that on the beast I killed."

"Wait," Ingefær said, "Hombir and I can destroy it with our mining spells."

"I prefer Mick's method." I looked into her blue eyes. "Save your spells for the monsters."

She kissed the top of my head, which was the hood to my wulv cloak. "Go, Mick."

"Ah, alright." Mick sniffed. "Can a couple of you come with me?"

Muggs chuckled. "No worries, lad. I got yer back."

We waited for a couple of minutes.

When Mick and Muggs returned, they came empty-handed.

"We thought about going to the other one, but he'd burned up pretty good." He shrugged. "I can go look if you still want."

Ingefær blew into her hand. "No. Hombir and I got this."

Hombir nodded. "It already has a hole. Just shove the air into it."

At my wife's nudging, we stepped back.

Tugg said, "Will it make a lot of noise?"

Hombir said, "A lot? No. But some."

"That ruins the element of surprise," Tugg said.

I sighed. “I know. But time is a factor as well. Who knows what they’re doing? If they’re even below us.”

My wife packed the air, gesturing with her hands. She then made the explosion motion. Instead of any burst of noise, what I heard was more of a crackling and tinkling.

I edged my way over, torch held high. “You cracked it.”

Tugg kneeled beside it and swung an axe. The entire contraption plummeted.

Peering into the hole, I said, “Seven or eight strides down. There’re rungs cut into the dirt.”

Except they were over a stride long. Still. We had a way in.

Muggs asked, “How much noise did that make?”

“Enough for any sentries near the hole.” I called for Serafina. “Tell me if you see anything.”

She peered into the depths and shrugged. “Nothing.”

With the three teams gathered around the hole, I asked, “What’s the plan for going in?”

Tugg got some rope from one of his soldiers. “Use the ladder, but with a rope around ye.”

“As wide as it is, we could do two at a time,” I said. “But once folks are down there, they’re going to need a wall of air, or fire.”

Tugg called out. “I need a volunteer to go first. Make sure it be safe for the mages.”

“No, I’ll go down first.” I hated the idea of being more important—more worthy of protection—than someone else. I understood it was because of my skills, but I still hated it.

My wife blew out air. “I’m not thrilled about any of us going into their lair.”

Mick said, “They may not be in there. The two that came at us may have been stragglers like Serafina said, or scouts sent out hours or days ago.”

While the logic permitted it, I said no. "It's too coincidental. And the tracks say they came from below."

Muggs said, "The longer we delay, the odds increase that someone will come looking for the two we killed earlier."

Tugg got a rope around Muggs. They put a rope around me. More ropes were put around my wife and Hombir.

Tugg said, "We do this quick. First pair goes down, the second pair be right behind them. Healers, get ready, yer next."

Hombir said to Ingefær, "Shape the wall of air as you go down. Then, once you're at the bottom...well, you'll have to angle it to get it past the others, and shape it to fill the shaft."

I turned to Serafina. "Can you tell if it opens into a room or a tunnel?"

Serafina got on her knees and stuck her head into the hole. She got up. "Looks to be a tunnel heading south."

"No torches," I said. "We need what is left of the element of surprise."

Ingefær held out her hand. "Mick, give Rory your light."

Ingefær pinched goblin bone dust. Hombir dug into a pouch and pulled out a splinter of wood.

"Ready?" Tugg asked.

No, but there were few options.

Muggs and I were lowered into a very dark and very deep hole.

Chapter Thirty-One

GOING DOWN

INGEFÆR

When I reached the bottom of the hole, the first thing I noticed, besides the pitch black, was the stench. My nose curled at the odor of offal, spoiled meat, burned hair, and something else I couldn't place. Not a single scent did I like. The good news was, Rory and Muggs stood before me with no Jörmonruks in sight.

I resized the wall of air to take up the cavernous darkness angling down and to the south. With a four- or five-degree slope, it had to be six strides high and four wide. Big enough for two Jörmonruks at a time, and four of us.

Muggs, Rory, Hombir and I scooted forward to the edge of the landing, inches before the massive shaft went down. I was reminded of our trek into the tunnels beneath Hexerei Mansion. Not pleasant memories.

I whispered, "No loud noises."

Rory brought his head to mine. "The good news is that based on the layout, the hatch cover crashing down may not have alerted anyone. But the lack of a sentry bothers me. Do they think they're safe down here?"

I turned to Muggs as dangling feet hovered above and behind us. "Wouldn't you set a guard at the bolt hole?"

Muggs nodded as Serafina and Jonuku reached the ground.

There was space for two more, and we waited for Tugg and Mick. Tugg raised his voice as he spoke to the shadows above. "Hold up, lads. We be discussing things by the looks of it."

I updated the group.

Tugg peered into the darkness. "Aye, mighty strange, no one be here to stop us."

Muggs nodded. "They be overconfident."

Rory said, "Maybe they're not aware of tracking skills and felt safe with the round block of ice covering their bolt hole."

"It's too dark down here for me to see," I said. "Rory, light the stick on my command. Hombir, ready a bolt of lightning, just in case. And have fiery darts ready. I have to shift the wall of air to cast my incantation."

When he was ready, I told Rory to bring the magical beacon to life. The shaft ambled downward, but appeared to level out as a bend in the ceiling caused the light to shine farther on the lower parts of the tunnel. Several whooshes of air filled the air. Some folks tugged at their capes. Others gnawed on lips.

"No beasts." I studied the walls and the ground at my feet and up the sides.

Mick pointed. "There could be a sigil guarding the passage." His finger angled up. "Could be up there, too."

I fumbled with my mage pouch to get at the flaxseed. I cast a find magic on a three-stride-wide loop, a circle, that went from the ground, up the sides, and across the ceiling. "You're a genius, Mick."

He shrugged. But I saw him darken a shade.

A foot-thick line of orange glowed on the ground, reaching from one wall to the other. Within it was a large white shape.

I growled. A ward.

Hombir said, "I'll dispel it. You've used several spells since our group meeting."

Serafina said, "It looks to be a simple shape."

Mick said, "There was a similar rune on the inner ring of the circular construct."

"Good catch." My thoughts shifted at the idea of the ease of dispelling wards—or the apparent ease. The tunnels beneath Hexerei Mansion had simple-looking sigils, too. But I mangled clearing them somehow. Well, at least one, perhaps two.

The glow of orange and white was fading when Hombir moved his hands, wiping the air in the sigil's shape. In the blink of an eye, the orange light winked out.

Muggs said, "This shaft be wide enough for three, easy. I got middle."

"Hombir and I will take the sides." I shifted the wall of air to cover our advance. "Ready?"

Rory shook his head. "And what am I supposed to do?"

"Be patient," I said. "You've done plenty already."

He grunted. "Best to douse the light."

He did so, and we shuffled down the shaft for several strides in near-pitch black.

Tugg hissed up the bolt hole. "Need Avarkæsir with crossbows down here."

Mick said, "Doesn't seem much point in bringing us all down. We can't do anything but stand in a line."

"Rory's rubbing off on you," I said. "Healers behind the mages. Tugg, Rory, Mick, you can fight for the next positions amongst yourselves."

"Ha, ha," Mick said. "I'll be in the third row."

Other dvaergs ambled down, each bearing a crossbow. Three by three, we ambled down the shaft until the slope leveled out.

Tugg commented on it. "The entrance tunnel be a wee bit steep by our standards, but nothing untoward for footing."

I said, "We'll scout out the tunnel until we meet with resistance. The smell tells me someone has lived down here for a while. Whether they're still here, I don't know."

Mick said, "We're coming through their back door. What if they leave through the front door? You know, the big circular scary-looking thing?"

I stopped the procession. "Well, crap."

Serafina said, "Don't break up the team."

Rory patted her on the shoulder. "Ah, the training is paying off. That is the correct first response. But in this case, I think Mick has the right of it."

Tugg said, "I got this. I'll take a score of warriors busy with other tasks. We'll create a line from the bolt hole to the sparkling contraption. If we see a beast, we'll shout up the line."

"Wait," Rory said. "But what's going to stop them from running for it, or worse, killing your messengers...and you?"

I turned to Rory. "Go with him. That way, with your speedy feet, communication would be certain."

He frowned. "I don't like leaving you in harm's way."

I gave him a look without rolling my eyes. "You don't? What was all that gallivanting about?"

Serafina shushed us. "Not so loud. Please."

I touched my snowflake pendant. "I'm protected."

He grunted.

I said, "Take Mick with you." I held my hand out. "The light stick, please."

Mick said, "You's making it up as you're going along."

I flashed a smile. "Never faced off against these beasts before. 'Always be learning,' my da used to say."

Rory said, "You don't think there're any contrived traps? Mick is good with those."

I shook my head. "No. The beasts' giant claws couldn't have made anything intricate or small. If there's a gadget or snare, it will be big enough for us to see."

I hoped there weren't any. Or if there were, I hoped we would spot it in time.

Facing Mick, I said, "Your mind has blossomed, of all places, on the Ice Plains. I'm not sure what we'll find, but your suggestions have aided everyone. I'm quite glad you'll be with my husband. Keep him safe."

Rory winked at me. "I'll watch his back." He leaned in close. "Be careful."

I winked back. "That's my middle name."

He leaned in and we kissed. While short, it was deep and full of desire and longing. His teeth pulled my lips as we parted.

He and Mick followed Tugg back to the ladder made of ice. Dvaergs with crossbows filled the gaps.

Still whispering, I said, "Muggs, get the Avarkæsir to load their crossbows."

I faced the group behind me, keeping the wall of air aloft, protecting my rear. "Alright. For the d'oglemenn of Nikkel Bakken and Kobber Unter Smuss. For the dvaergs of Kral Bar Aggen and Kral Azza Rid, and for the inhabitants of the Realm. We scout their tunnel or tunnels. We kill any still here and breathing. I'm going to keep the wall of air down to a height of twelve feet. So, if you see one and have an angle, shoot first, ask questions later. Holler if you're using pitch and torches."

The height of twelve feet was shoulder high on the Jörmonruk. I hoped the arrows took their eyes before they figured out they could raise a beastly arm and lance us with their lethal ice.

My eyes adjusted to the darkness. I couldn't make out details, but I could see outlines of people. Where things turned coal black, there were walls, ceiling, and floor.

Step by step, with Muggs to my left and Hombir on the other side, we hiked down the unlit shaft. Ten strides in, I stopped. I chinned at Serafina and, with a soft voice, said, "Get your wand of summoning out. I have an idea."

Serafina got the summoning rod out of her breeches. "What do you want me to do with this?"

"You summoned raccoons earlier. They're great at seeing in the dark. See if you can get a pair to show up. Send them ahead to be our eyes."

Serafina scowled. "But...they'll be killed."

I nodded. Good odds. "Sorry. The Jörmonruk eye appears well designed for seeing in the dark. I don't see another way for us to see farther than they can."

She took a deep breath and nodded. Serafina used the wand and—without the need of material or motion, just words—she got three raccoons to wink in at her feet.

She pointed down the tunnel. I shifted the wall to let them scoot under. For a few strides, their furry rears and tails provided an outline in the darkness. Then they disappeared into the inky black.

I stood there, my eyes trying to penetrate the tunnel air, my ears straining for any sound.

Serafina kept us updated. "Thirty strides ahead. I think. Nothing."

"Keep them going," Muggs said. "Best idea I've seen yet."

Jonuku asked, "How is it you can communicate with them?"

Serafina scratched at her hair. "The summoning spell creates a link, sort of like a befriend incantation. My will becomes theirs. The first trick is thinking like them, so they understand. Then I have to decipher the images they send back. But I feel their wants and fears, so that helps."

We shuffled forward with a bit more confidence, knowing we'd get a warning.

Serafina whispered. "Wait. The tunnel splits. And there's some sort of, um, den, in between."

We stopped.

"Den?" I asked.

Serafina said, "No, that's not right. A room for storage. I think. They're thinking they should go investigate. Might be something tasty in there."

"Not yet," I said. "Focus on spotting monsters."

Hombir said, "Two tunnels. Going east and west?"

Serafina said, "Based on the images, no. They angle off. Southwest and southeast." Then, "Wait."

We heard the shrill of an ice ray.

The half-alvae whimpered. "They're dead."

Muggs said, "Raccoons be not a part of this landscape. They have to know we be coming."

"How far ahead?" Jonuku asked.

"Forty, fifty paces." Serafina's sleeve-covered arm moved across her face.

"Do we send a fireball?" I asked.

Hombir shrugged. "Might be too late. And who knows how far the beast was when it killed the coons?"

"Alright then." I looked at Hombir. "If nothing comes this way in the next minute, we go forward. If the raccoons made it that far, we know there're no traps."

He nodded, his hand going to his waist, where he kept his mage materials.

While we waited, I nudged Serafina. "We need more eyes, Serafina. Something smaller, less noticeable."

She worked the wand and sent six rats, each about a foot long, down the tunnel. I choked back a squeal, for I hated rats.

I peered down the shaft as far as I could see, half happy when the rodents' shadows disappeared into the muck.

When the minute was up, still no Jörmonruks had investigated. Were they luring us in?

We shuffled forward. "Try to see what killed the coons," I said.

Rory got those heebie-jeebie feelings when things tracked him. Now my sixth sense went off. I didn't want to go farther.

I turned to Muggs. "How long to make a tunnel this size?"

"Without magic? A crew of ten would need years to dig a tunnel this wide and this long." Muggs scratched under his beard. "But with magic, maybe a moon or two."

"A moon?" That didn't sound too long.

"Depends on the rock." He scratched at the wall, then licked it. "Compressed sediment; high limestone mixture. It be said that long ago, this place used to be under water." He shrugged. "I don't know, lass, maybe a hundred strides in a moon."

I glanced around me. In my mind, I considered the possibility of suffocating them or burying them so deep, they died of hunger and thirst. It was the first time in my life I felt so much hatred for a species. I didn't like the emotion. At all. But with all the dead d'oglemenn and dvaergs, and the Lokke sigils, I knew they were evil. We had to do everything in our power to wipe them off the face of the Realm.

"Does anyone want to collapse this tunnel?" I heaved a heavy breath. "You know, suffocate them? Starve them?"

Muggs said, "No. I think they will dig their way out before they starve. Well before they die from a lack of air. They dug these with magic, they'll do it again."

Hombir said, "We have them hemmed in. We finish it."

"Even if the lot of us dies?" I asked.

Hombir's jaw clenched. His scale-covered snout bobbed.

I said, "Rory counted fifteen heads going through the artifact. None of us know how many were inside beforehand."

Touching my throat, I felt the magical snowflake with its fiery opal at the center. "I have to go in. Alone."

"The Hel, you say," Muggs said.

"Don't be daft, Miss Ingefær," Serafina said, her hand grabbing a hold of my cloak and not letting go. "Mister Belkin won't let me live if you go in by yourself and something bad happens."

"I have protection," I said.

"Maybe from their spells," Hombir said. "But not if they rush you."

"I am, or used to be, an Ære Warrior."

"They be five strides tall." Muggs chuckled. "I thought I be the foolish one."

"Don't mock me," I said, glaring at him.

Muggs shrugged. "Don't say foolish things."

Rory would have said something similar.

Before I could retort, a dvaerg from behind us raised his voice. "Oi! Ye cannot go down alone. Aye, ye might have a magical trinket. But ye well ken that magic be not the only way to take a life."

Serafina got close, almost nose to nose. "Perhaps they have a crossbow or two. They've seen ours. The last two encounters, they used our battle tactics."

I didn't think they'd built a crossbow. How would their taloned claws permit it? Maybe not arrows, but spears. I nodded to myself. That would be a problem in the hands of a near giant. For me.

Jonuku said, "We cannot set up camp and wait them out. We would need to stay out here for a week if not an entire moon," I said.

The mention of moons and months brought another thought to my mind. "Gods' Day is tomorrow."

"The rats," Serafina said, "Are at the tunnel split."

She shrieked. "They're coming!"

The counterattack began.

CHAPTER THIRTY-TWO

CORNERED ANIMALS

INGEFÆR

The shrill of at least two ice rays echoed off the tunnel walls.

Serafina clawed at her eyes. "Ah! They're all dead."

"They're just rats," Muggs said.

"Don't be cruel," the half-alvae said.

"Shush," I said. "Hombir. Fireball. Thirty-five strides. Now."

It was a calculated risk that the shaft we were in would gobble up the volume of fire Hombir's invocation created.

"Everyone down, low to the ground." I lowered the wall of air to four feet and let the d'oglemann mage know.

As soon as his fiery bead left his finger, I raised the wall.

And just in time, too.

By the dim illumination of the flitting fiery flame, ice rays crept down the hallway toward us, raising icicles and sending up plumes of dirt and rock.

The icy rays found my wall just as the fireball exploded. A blast of air shoved at my magical shield, and I grunted with the effort to stay upright. Then the heat and red flames flashed at us.

In the aftermath, husks of two fallen Jörmonruks, their bodies burning, lit the far end of the tunnel. We were about thirty paces from the split of the tunnel and an opening into a room full of burning crates.

Muggs said, “Great call. Come on.”

I pushed the wall ahead of us and we hiked down the shaft toward the burning bodies, which, together with the burning crates, put off a growing plume of smoke. The tunnel ahead of us filled with it. I lowered my wall of air to let it stream above our head and up the shaft toward the bolt hole.

Ten strides later, unable to see because of the smoke, I stopped our advance and turned to Serafina. “We need another advance scout. Something that can show you the position of the Jörmonruks. Send them into the two offshoots.”

I was about to say, ‘and the storage shaft,’ but knew that nothing living would want to go where there was a fire.

Her lips trembled, but she nodded. She used the wand of summoning. The air shimmered and a score of kakkerlaks popped into existence at her feet.

Serafina pointed down the hall, then used her hands to form a split. “Raise the wall a bit. I told them to investigate.”

We waited for the six-legged insects with black carapaces to scramble forward.

That gave the fire and smoke time to dwindle some. Despite the plume shooting above and past us, enough of the smoke swirled beyond my air wall to turn noses at the stench and foul our breathing.

The half-alvae grimaced in the dying fire-red glow of the dead. “I can’t understand what they see. With one pair of eyes, the images make sense. With three? I could make sense of it if all of them looked in the same direction.” She shook her head. “But with all the kakkerlaks? It gives me a headache.”

“Then what good does it do?” Jonuku asked.

"Well," Serafina sniffed. "I'll know if something kills them."

Muggs called down the line. "Aim high, lads and lassies. Their eyeballs be fourteen feet off the ground. Be ready to fire on me command."

There was no need to stay quiet anymore. The fireball had announced our presence.

Thirty paces ahead of us, the dead bodies moved, dragged off to the rightward tunnel. The thinning trail of smoke continued to flow above and past my wall.

"I need to know what the kakkerlaks see," I said. The insect made me want to vomit. Like the time when I found them on food. But we needed them now.

Serafina scowled. "Fine." She closed her eyes, then opened them.

"What did you do?" Hombir asked.

"Killed all but two." She sniffed again. "One in each shaft. There aren't any beasts in the left tunnel. There're four upright beasts on the right. They're moving off. I'll have the kakkerlak follow. What do you want me to do with the one on the left?"

I said, "Have it go down the left tunnel until it comes to any sort of doorway or split. Then keep it there. It's going to guard our rear flank."

The closer we got to the smoldering crates, the more the dregs of the smoke affected us. Our view of the tunnels was blocked at the split. I hacked into the crook of my elbow. The fumes roiled over the top of my air wall, and backfilled. In moments, we were all coughing and rubbing at our eyes.

My voice came out like a wheel grinding on a rocky road. "Serafina, what are the beasts doing?"

Serafina said, "They dragged the two dead into a side opening. Hold on. I'm sending the kakkerlak there."

At the storeroom, the contents of a dozen crates lining both sides smoldered. We shifted over to the western shaft to get out of the smoke. I wiped at the edges of my eyes. The others blinked often and hacked.

"Look out!" Serafina shouted.

I ducked on instinct, but kept the air wall shield upright.

A moment later, three raucous thunks, in quick succession, struck my shield. By the remnants of the firelight, two iron bars clanked to the ground, the noise echoing off the tunnel walls. The third iron bar quivered as it struck the magicked wall and stuck there. I would have thought it impossible.

"What the Hel?" I said.

Muggs' voice was full of approval. "That be hurled with a mighty arm."

Or magic.

The rod hung there. Despite being twelve feet long and a couple of inches wide, the weight was tolerable.

"They're smart," I said. "They've developed missile weapons. Or perhaps they had the knowledge, but are using it for the first time."

"Aye," Muggs grunted. "Iron bars. Must be from the plunder. Part of a wagon."

"Incoming!" Serafina shouted. "Three sets of feet!"

At least they didn't see the kakkerlak, so we had warning.

Yet again, two bars clanked to the ground, but this time, the tips were on fire. The third, burning at the sharpened tip, stuck in the wall right in front of me. The flame went out as the iron continued to quiver.

Hombir said, "Now they're using fire."

"They can see us, but we can't see them." I asked, "How far out is your kakkerlak?"

"I don't know, but I can send it deeper."

I nodded at the half-alvae. "Do it. Describe any offshoots, if you can. And stop it if they see feet."

She shook her head. "The last they can do. The first is difficult. They see motion and I sense that. To them, all walls look alike. Whether a foot tall or a hundred. So far, neither one has sensed anything worth eating. That's what they keep telling me. I have to tell them to focus."

Everything always has a limitation.

"Hombir, fireball at sixty paces. Let me know when you're ready."

His hand motions clued me in; several long seconds later, he nodded.

I lowered my shield to waist high in front of him. "Go." One of the quivering iron bars fell to the ground.

Hombir's fiery bead flew down the tunnel.

I raised the air wall to full height. "Everyone, down."

"Feet!" Serafina yelled.

Three more iron bars crashed into my wall. Two bounced off, but the third punched through.

It ripped between Muggs and Hombir, past Jonuku and a dvaerg, and struck a dvaerg behind them, skewering him and another warrior at his rear.

Muggs cursed. "Nasty brutes. That one be strong."

I said, "I think it's embellishing the throw with magic."

Shifting my gaze down the tunnel where three dead Jörmonruks lay on the ground, their white fur turning black as the flames ate at them. After the roar of the explosion, I never heard a sound coming from the beasts or anywhere else.

With the area lit ahead of us, I spotted a series of openings to the right. "I think those are rooms."

Serafina said, "At least ten beasts left, if Mister Belkin has his count right."

"We move forward and stop before the first opening, just before the bodies." I led the way with the wall of air before me, trying to see into and past the smoldering smoke.

Two steps into our approach, the spell withered. "Not now! Wait." I hurried to invoke a fresh wall of air incantation.

That's when I heard what sound like a cry. A high-pitched sob. "What is that?"

Jonuku said, "Sounds like an infant."

Hombir said, "Wait on the wall shield."

I looked at him and saw that his arms were gyrating.

My hands trembled. I took a breath to steady myself. "After this, Serafina, I need your aid."

Hombir ripped off a fiery bead. We could see it as it passed through the smoke coming off the three dead Jörmonruks. It sailed on toward something green that shimmered at the far end of the shaft.

The fire ball exploded, lighting everything in a burst of red and orange, and blinding me for a moment.

From the side opening at the far end came a bugling. "Whoo-hah, whoo-hah." It repeated several times before the sound dwindled in volume, then ceased.

What did it mean?

My wall of air came into being, and with haste, I reshaped it to take up the entire shaft.

Serafina restored my stamina.

I considered lighting Mick's artifact, but Hombir's fireball had caught something on fire in the last opening on the right, and it illuminated the tunnel beyond the bodies burning in it.

"Forward." Into the smoke. Eight steps later. "Stop."

"Serafina, get your kakkerlak to scout the opening."

"Oh, oh." Serafina pointed behind us. "There are three flashes of white coming behind us."

Hombir said, "I'll put up a fire shield. Muggs, get your shields up and crossbows ready. Fire at will."

Hombir turned around and invoked his wall of fire. He then wobbled. Jonuku healed him as I studied the area before me. The smell of the three dead bodies on fire ahead of me wafted past the edges of my air shield.

But the smoke collected there, blocking my sight. The wall of air didn't fill the irregular tunnel completely, and the smoke pushed through. In mere seconds, smoke curled around us, making the shaft unlivable.

The unmistakable sound of an ice ray echoed off the walls behind me.

"Fire!" Muggs yelled.

Arrows flew despite the lack of target.

An iron spear punched through the wall of fire and took two dvaergs through the throat.

"Fire!" Muggs hollered. "Aim high!"

Keeping a focus on maintaining my shield spell, I pinched sawdust and made my motions, hurling fiery darts at twenty, thirty, and forty paces. I envisioned all my shots to strike thirteen feet above the ground, left, center, and right. I was guessing.

The shrieking sound of the ice ray against the fire wall ceased. But a second iron bar sailed through and found its mark in yet another Avarkæsir.

"We're shooting blind." I hollered, "Muggs! Get your team ready to fire. Hombir. On three, drop your fire shield."

I was making it up as I went, all the while glancing down the hallway, checking for the white-furred monsters.

Jonuku counted off.

The fire shield went down. Crossbow bolts flew. As did an iron javelin.

The bar found Jonuku, piercing her chest. She keeled over, her eyes already dead.

Arrows flew, and several found the eye of the third Jörmonruk to our rear. It teetered and crashed to the ground.

Dead beasts to the front of us and now dead ones to our rear. Worst of all, dead soldiers and a dead Jonuku.

Hombir's jowls quivered as he crouched by his wife. His watery eyes searched Serafina. "Can you save her?"

Serafina crouched and put her ear to Jonuku's mouth. From experience, I knew she also looked for a rise and fall to the chest.

The healer shook her head. "I'm sorry. She's gone."

Hombir let out a wail of torment that sent a shiver up my spine. He pulled out the iron bar by pulling it through. Ten of the twelve feet had traveled through her scaled torso. Another two and Serafina would have been hurt. Maybe killed.

Motion to the front caught my eye. Gray smoke swirled around white splotches and disappeared.

Which way did they go?

"Keep contact with the kakkerlak. They may be going around."

These beasts fought like cornered animals.

Hombir climbed to his feet. "I'll kill them all." He pocketed a vial that had to have been on his wife's body.

"Yeah," I said. "I'm with you."

Taking Rory's earlier advice, I became unpredictable. I shifted the wall of air to the right and sent a fireball halfway down the remaining shaft's length, splitting the distance between Hombir's blast and the three smoldering Jörmonruks.

It exploded. Much of the flame went sideways, into an opening. Sound emanated through the hallway.

It was a shriek, similar in tone to Hombir's at seeing his dead wife. The surrounding rock and limestone quaked. Then the sound ceased, and the rocks quieted.

"What was that?" I asked.

Hombir said, "Go. I'll watch our rear."

"Serafina, I need a report on what's in this next room?" I pinched fresh sawdust.

She closed her eyes and stifled a cough. "No sign of movement. Just rock and wood."

We crept forward, with me curving the wall of air to take on the extra area covering the opening.

The rock and wood the kakkerlak had seen appeared as a coffin—four flat sides. I skulked while keeping the air shield filling the tunnel.

The interior of the rectangular shape was sunk down. Inside each one, furry arms and legs sprawled and waved. Their grayish lips wiggled and their mouths puckered. But they didn't make a sound. At least, not one I could hear.

"Why, those are cribs," I said. "These are baby Jörmonruks."

Hombir showed up at my elbow. "Six of them." He wiped at his snout. "Everyone out."

"Who's covering the rear?" I asked.

"You." Hombir pulled a blade from his hip.

I couldn't cover two flanks by myself. "Everyone, in here."

We left Jonuku and the dead dvaergs out in the hall. The rest of us clambered inside and I put the wall of air up to cover the entrance. We were trapped inside, the same as their offspring.

Serafina whispered into my ear. "You're going to let him kill the babies?"

I chewed on my lower lip. "Hombir, is what you're about to do necessary?"

Serafina asked, "Or is it vengeance for your wife?"

Hombir chuckled. "Both. We can't let them grow up."

"We haven't tried to make peace." Serafina's lips trembled. "It's murder."

"The babies?" Hombir nodded. "We don't know how to speak to them. Not the babies, or the grownups. They haven't tried to surrender, or to parlay. I'm not willing to risk any more lives."

I searched Serafina's emerald eyes. "You?"

The half-alvae snarled. "No. It's still wrong, though."

I nodded, knowing I wasn't ready for the guilt, though I knew it would come soon enough. "Hombir's right. They killed an entire village. You saw the sigil of Lokke."

Serafina nodded, her spine straightening. "Aye. I did."

Hombir wiped his bloodied knife and put it back into its sheath. "It's done."

That was quick. And never a whimper or a whine.

"How old, you think?" I asked.

Hombir's beady black eyes found mine. "Don't know. Don't care."

I looked at the bodies. Less than four feet long. I did math in my head. If a woman had a baby a foot and a half in length and the baby grew to six feet, then a newborn Jörmonruk—all else equal—would be less than four feet at birth, assuming fifteen feet represented a full-grown beast.

Yeah. These were newborns. Less than a moon was my guess.

Once more, there was a high-pitched wailing, and the rocks trembled. From above, a few small rocks fell on us.

I took a huge breath. "The next opening. There are some still alive."

CHAPTER THIRTY-THREE

DEATH'S KNELL

INGEFÆR

I wiped the sweat off my brow. We'd been down here for a long while now and I'd been holding a wall of air—a second wall of air—ever since descent. Most combats are a couple of spells, maybe as much as a dozen, but all within a couple of minutes. This one dragged on because the enemy was here and knew we were as well.

Nodding at Serafina, I said, "Send the kakkerlak down to the next opening. If it's like this one, it's a room as well."

After a long minute, she said, "There's movement in the next room. That's all I know. The kakkerlak scampered to a corner."

Muggs asked, "And the kakkerlak to our rear?"

"No sign of moment." Serafina rubbed her temples. "I'm getting a headache from having to think like the insect."

"Think?" Muggs' bushy brows created a deep furrow.

"Well, it's sending an image, and when it spots movement, a pulse of fear." She flashed a smile while tapping her head. "With two of them, it's a mighty mess."

"Huh!" Muggs picked at a tooth. "Who would have thought the insects had feelings?"

A wail, like that of a mother whose baby had died, jarred my spine.

We ambled out of one room, turned down the shaft—filled with the remnants of smoke—and crept forward until I spotted the break in the wall.

Muggs pointed. "There be a gap to me left. Five paces ahead."

Hombir said, "I'll cover you."

I didn't ask how, but I trusted him.

I snuck a peek into the next room. It was dark, except for the flickers of flame coming from the dead Jörmonruks ten strides ahead of us. I guess I'd gotten used to the stink, for it no longer bothered me.

What could bother me after letting babies be skewered? There was no time for it now, but I knew I'd be bawling later.

In the middle of the room stood four beasts, each armed with iron bars. A fifth lay on the ground, half charred. It looked big in the belly. The prone one's arm pointed.

Iron javelins flew. Two stuck into my air shield and two bounced off. Followed by ice rays that, in the blink of an eye, caked onto my wall.

I grunted with the effort of holding it up. "The room's twenty by twenty, and eight paces high. Will a fireball be too much?"

Hombir glared at me. "No. The wall of air will hold it back."

Maybe. There were seams along the edges.

The gods! The weight was becoming cumbersome. "That, ugh, requires too much timing. *Ugh*. The ice blasts are coming steady."

"Open a seam on the right side." Hombir grabbed Muggs by an arm. "You and a friend lift me up."

"In a minute, I'm going to let it all go." Sweat poured into my eyes. I waited till Hombir was lifted off the ground, standing on Muggs' and another soldier's shoulders.

The ice was building up, head high and down. The beasts aimed at our heads. Now I understood why Hombir wanted elevation.

"Hurry!"

Hombir's arms moved. I eased up on the wall's right side, pulling it back a half foot from his waist and up. The concentration taxed me to the edges of consciousness. The spell was designed for gross movements, not miniscule ones.

"Agh! I'm about spent."

Just as Hombir neared completion, the prone beast waved both clawed hands, and a wave of dirt was dug out of the ground and hurled against my shield wall.

Hombir's fiery bead slammed into dirt and dropped at our feet. The d'oglemann mage stomped it out as he snarled at the enemy mage. "You gigantic pile of troll shit!"

I shoved us back while leaving my wall up against the piled-high dirt. In moments, the entire doorless doorway was covered in ice and dirt.

"That's the mage on the floor. She's pregnant." I let my wall of air go.

Serafina gasped. "They entombed themselves."

My shoulders and arms screamed as I stretched them. "The way the beast moved the earth, they can get out any time they want."

Muggs nodded. "Aye. That one, and perhaps others like it, dug this tunnel system out in days, not weeks."

I turned to Hombir. "We learned mining spells."

He licked his lips. "What's the plan?"

"I use the spell for digging, and create a hole big enough for one of your fiery beads to fly through."

"You think that will work?" Serafina asked.

"Won't know until we try." I pointed up and down the shaft. "Serafina, keep an eye out."

She frowned. "One kakkerlak is in the rearward tunnel. The other is inside the room."

"Oh?" I smiled. "What are the beasts doing?"

The healer shrugged. "There's some movement, but what they're doing is unclear."

I put my ear to the wall of ice-covered earth. Feet shuffled, or a body was being moved.

I growled. "Muggs, you got sentry duty. Let us know if anything comes at us from the south. Watch the side tunnel and whatever is down by the greenish glow."

With the smoke dissipating, the far end of the tunnel shone in a lime-green hue. The sightlines weren't clear, so I wasn't sure where the light came from.

Muggs nodded. "Aye. Gents. To the front. Ye four, cover the rear." He glanced at Serafina. "Let us know if anything be coming."

Moving to the far left side of the opening, I invoked the spell I had learned days ago, aiming for a spot knee high. Hombir lay down on the ground behind me, eyeing my progress.

Which was slow. I used the stone dig spell to take chunks of dirt out. But my chunks were never deep. After four such spells, I quaffed a vial of healing.

After another four incantations, I had a six-inch deep hole. I sighed, "I'm exhausted."

Hombir took my place and dug some dirt, getting deeper than I did. He looked up at me. "Time for the air expansion variant. You cast the fireball."

From my knees, I checked with Serafina. "All clear?"

"Very quiet."

Muggs said, "Aye. Nothing be moving."

From the north end came the sound of a rock skidding along the ground.

Everyone moved to face the fresh threat.

"What was that?" I asked.

The healer shook her head. "Didn't come from the east shaft."

"Oi!" came Tugg's voice. "Anyone here?"

Muggs hollered, "Ye scared the troll shit out of us. We be alright. Got some beasties trapped down here."

Tugg sauntered into view. "Aye. That be grand. We be wondering what be taking ye so long. Be coming to brag about killing four of them, but I see ye've got yer share."

Muggs grinned. "Aye. Double ye for the moment." He pointed toward the earth-covered entryway. "Going to triple ye soon enough."

I asked, "Where did the beasts come from?"

"I'll tell ye about it later. Rory wants me back quick-like to report. Any reason to keep an eye on the artifact?"

Hombir shrugged. "Maybe. But I doubt it."

I said, "Aye. Just in case. We haven't explored everything yet. Found us a Jörmonruk who knows magic. I shouldn't be surprised, but I am. Tell Rory I love him."

"Bah," Tugg waved a hand at me, then winked. "Tell him yerself."

Which was his way of saying, *be careful*. He turned on a heel and left.

I breathed a sigh of relief. At least Rory was alright. I nodded at Hombir. "Air expansion time. I'm ready."

The dvaergs reassembled themselves to either side of the entrance.

"Serafina," I asked. "Any movement?"

She closed her eyes, grimacing. "Um, I think there's a beast pacing in there."

Which revealed nothing bad or good.

Hombir invoked the air expansion spell. By his mannerisms, I knew he shoved air into the hole we'd made. He grunted with the effort of packing the air.

Hombir nodded. "Ready?"

I lay prone on the ground a stride behind him. Pinching sawdust, I went through the motions while bobbing my chin at Hombir.

I don't know how much air went into the dirt wall, but the explosion sent plenty of it at the both of us. And while Hombir's spell didn't punch a hole to shoot a bead through, the spell robbed the wall structure of support. It all cascaded down in waves, covering Hombir's shoulders and head.

I shoved myself backward and jumped high in the air, letting the fiery bead fly through the opening. "Duck!"

I covered my head, so I didn't see what happened. But I felt and heard the explosion, my ears ringing. Heat flashed at my back. The back of my cloak caught fire.

I flopped onto the ground and rolled around. Serafina threw her cloak over my head.

When I was certain I wasn't on fire, I climbed to my feet and lost my outer garment. Three dvaergs were scorched from the neck up, their beards half-singed away, their brows gone. If not for their helmets, they'd be bald. As it was, they tottered on their feet.

Muggs shifted back from the north tunnel. "They need healing."

I looked past the mound of dirt. Bodies in the room smoldered and burned. There was some wooden furniture inside, and it crackled with flame. Fresh smoke poured out through the half opening.

"Heal them," I said.

Serafina summoned what I knew to be air, water, and earth to cleanse and heal the burned area of the closest dvaerg to her. She stopped and dug out a vial of healing, quaffed it, and healed the other two.

While she did that, I pulled Hombir out by his feet. He sputtered as he climbed to his knees and spat dirt out of his mouth. Rising to his feet, he wiped his elongated snout.

While the bodies crackled and the smoke rose high and out toward the bolt hole, Muggs and another dvaerg bashed through what was left of the ice and earth half-wall.

We stepped through dirt, then the ash of broken pots and clothes. Approaching the closest beast, I used the tip of my sword and brushed away strips of charred fur and skin. If it was still alive, it should have elicited a response.

We moved through the other three sentries, for it appeared the dead beasts had stood in a line.

Serafina pointed at the largest beast lying on its back. "That's a female. She's pregnant."

The prone Jörmonruk I'd seen half-charred before was nothing but cracked black skin. What fur remained on her body was as dark as coal and as short and sparse as the stubble on a human male going on sixteen. But the bulbous belly rose from below her round, flattened breasts.

Her legs were splayed wide and blackened, crusted blood had once pooled there. She'd been in childbirth. The equivalent of for the beasts. Their mage had been indisposed at the worst of times...for them. I wondered how the battle would have gone if she hadn't been incapacitated so.

The belly fluttered.

"Shit," Muggs said. "There be a baby inside."

I looked at Hombir.

He smiled, showing his pointy teeth. "Your turn."

My stomach roiled, and I threw up. Wiping bile from my lips, I said, "I can't do it."

Hombir shrugged. "It'll die a slower, longer death. Suffocate in an hour?"

The gods! A second round of nausea took me.

Muggs ripped the sword from my weak grip. "I'll do it."

Before I could object, he ran my sword through the beast's gut, stabbing not once, not twice, but three times.

"I don't feel so good." I rolled to the side, away from my vomit, my backside swooshing up dirt and ash. Stars filled my eyes.

Serafina's emerald eyes hovered above me. "You need me to heal you?"

I shook my head. "Water."

When she brought the skin, I had her and Hombir help me sit up. I took a long draught. After making sure my mouth was clean, I turned to Muggs. "That was unnecessary."

He wiped my sword against the beast's leg, then he used a cloth to polish the blade. "Well, I don't like to see suffering. And as Hombir here said, the baby would die in an hour."

Had we eradicated an entire species? The water I'd drank tried to come back up. But I held it down and got to my feet. Retaking my sword, I said, "Thanks for doing the dirty work."

Muggs grinned, his ragged, yellow-stained teeth visible through his bushy brown beard. "I've seen a lot of death in me days. Killing be not pleasurable, but it be a necessity."

I wobbled forward. "Let's search this room and get going."

We found a pair of gold bands on the female's wrists. They'd resisted the fire.

I said, "I'll bet they're magicked."

Muggs' eyes shone. "I'd like to claim one of those as me plunder."

Hombir said, "There will be time for that later. We have more tunnels and rooms to search."

Serafina heaved a heavy breath. "I think this is the lot. It's been quiet since we attacked this room. No one else has come. While you were puking, I sent the kakkerlak down the eastern tunnel. No sign of anyone moving about."

I nodded. "Alright. We ensure the place is clear, then we look at that green glowing thing I spotted at the end of the tunnel."

Hombir erected an air shield wall, and we investigated the side opening to our left. It connected with the central opening, which had contained the crates at the north tunnel split. The area was dark as night on a cloudy day inside a cavern. I couldn't see anything. But I smelled and tasted smoke.

I lit Mick's light stick.

Crates. Lots of them. Glancing north, up the central extra-wide tunnel, or storage area, the fire hadn't gone past the first fifteen strides. Looking right, another forty strides of crates lined both sides.

"All the plunder over the past year," I said. "We'll check it later."

We moved through the shaft cut and into the eastern tunnel. It was a mirror image, with three grand rooms decked out with stone beds, block-shaped tables and chairs, wooden shelving, and piles of clothes as dirty and ratted as year-old wash cloths.

Where the west side had the baby room, the east side contained organized piles of loot.

"Well, look at that," Muggs said, his big grin returning.

There were three heaps of silver, each about two feet high and four feet around at the base. Two smaller mounds contained gold and jewelry, respectively.

The room also had a furnace. Logs and planks—most likely from the wagons—were lined up against a wall near it. And three huge piles of coal fronted the forge.

Serafina put her hand close to the massive furnace, which was four feet on a side, encased in inch-thick metal. "Cold."

Muggs rubbed his fingertips across the metal plates. "Hmm. Not steel. Something tougher."

He hit it with the handle of his double-headed axe. The room rang out in a hollow tone. My ears ached.

"Pretty notes." Muggs got busy inspecting how the furnace was assembled. "I don't see any joints or bolts. How did they put it together?"

Hombir said, "With magic."

Muggs frowned. "Well, spit. I'd like to take some of that home with me. Show it around the keep."

He got down low and pried the head of his axe beneath a corner. He grunted as he heaved...and heaved...and blew out a gut full of air. "Won't budge. Too heavy."

"Come on," I said, "I want to see what makes that green glow. But first, we need to make sure this place is empty."

It was my Order of Gixus training, ensuring the place was as secure as it looked.

We circled back to the bolt hole. There, we split up. Hombir and I took the outer shafts with a foursome of dvaerg soldiers, while Muggs, Serafina, and the rest of the remaining Avarkæsir went back down the middle.

"Double check that each room is empty of beasts." I pointed down the western hallway. "Let's go."

My team finished first, arriving at the source of the greenish glow. We'd had the shortest distance and the least amount of things to look at.

Muggs' team came in last. "Couldn't help it. I opened a few of them crates. One had silver fox pelts. Very valuable."

Serafina said, "There were spoiled apples in another."

I jabbed a thumb over my shoulder. "What does that look like to you?"

I turned around, and together we examined the duplicate of the circular sigil. The blue and yellow two outer circles glowed just enough to cast a green tint. The inner circle, shining orange in the immediate area, was dwarfed by the bright green glow of the twin snakes.

Serafina pointed. "Same runes. At least the funny *Z* is on top."

I checked for the nobility, honor, and danger symbols, pointing them out to Hombir.

The d'oglemann mage nodded. "Aye. Do we check for wards and the type of magic?"

I shook my head. "No. Let's reconnect with the others and discuss our next steps. I'm exhausted."

Muggs nodded. "Agreed. Tugg mentioned them killing a few beasties. Let's compare stories."

Chapter Thirty-Four

THE PRICE OF VICTORY

RORY

After Tugg returned and reported all was well, we got busy and made preparations to leave. The wagons remaining, along with the two ballistae carts still operable, were pointed east. Tents were built near the frozen river, several hundred strides away from the sigil monstrosity. Finally, the dead were prepared for a pyre.

And still the others hadn't shown up.

I grumbled to Mick. "What's taking them so long?"

The lad shrugged. "You can always go check."

I looked at him. "You trying to get me in trouble?"

Mick chuckled. "Maybe. I know Miss Ingefær doesn't like it when you look over her shoulder."

"Sometimes, Mick. Sometimes."

There were moments when she liked me to take the lead and put forth effort in protecting her. But we'd split up, and Tugg had said the area was clear. So why was it taking so long?

The snow had lightened in intensity, even if the wind continued its shrilling. I jogged north, along the western side of the mound...just to look around.

Peering into the thinning snow, I didn't see any movement. Running back, I spotted Ingefær's red hair—she no longer wore her red wulv cloak—and raced off to the west using my magicked feet.

I did a half loop and then strolled back into the main group from the south. "Oh, hi. Glad to see you're all safe."

Muggs said, "Not all of us." He pointed with a gloved hand. "Brought back the dead."

Tugg motioned with his head. "The pyre is over there. We'll have a ceremony after the dinner meal."

I looked at the sky. The sun, cloud covered though it was, was brightest on the western horizon. Wow! We'd been at this for an entire day. My stomach grumbled.

From out of my pack, O'erlevendeh growled. I laughed. "I fed you already. You had some very tough Jörmonruk thigh."

He'd chewed and swallowed like it was his last meal. Fur and all. I hoped it wouldn't constipate him.

I stepped over to my wife, and we hugged, then kissed. "I worried about you."

Ingefær looked at me with those ice-blue eyes. "I worried about me too. It was grisly down there." She surveyed the area. "How many did we lose up here?"

Tugg chewed on his beard around his mouth. "Nigh on a hundred souls be lost today, counting the ones ye brought out."

"What happened down there?" I asked.

She told their tale. The air wall, the iron javelins, fireballs, baby Jörmonruks, and a beast who knew magic. She finished up. "There's a copy of the circular sigil inside."

I said, "We killed four. They came out one at a time, but all of them within a minute."

Mick said, "I stood on the mound and threw vials of pitch as they came out."

Tugg said, "The thingy glows bright a moment before a beast pops out."

"Yeah." I smiled, knowing that we'd survived. The price of victory had been great, though. "Tugg and another warrior threw torches, and the rest of the soldiers formed two half rings and shot bolts at their eyes. One beast got by the first line and fired his ice ray. That's what killed four more." I scratched at my beard, now five weeks old. "Using my speed, I hamstrung the beast, then someone shot it in the eye."

Ingefær said, "I saw a streak of white running out of the room farthest to the south. We were busy, so I couldn't go check. Hmm. They must have got cold feet and tried to run off."

I bent low next to her ear. "Could you have used me down there?"

My wife looked at me, and she frowned. Her words were soft, so only I could hear. "No. Not to battle. But to hold me when the babies had to be killed. One beast was still pregnant."

She shuddered into my arms, and I hugged her tight as she let her tears go.

While we both fought for justice, she preferred not to kill. While I—well, sometimes I enjoyed it. That had something to do with Laehvateinn and her need for vengeance.

When she had settled, I pulled back to bring in everyone and raised my voice. "Tonight we eat, then there's a ceremony for the dead. Tomorrow, Gods' Day, we will destroy the sigils. We cannot leave until their magic is expunged."

There was a nodding of heads, but also grumbling. Another day spent on the Ice Plains. Though in reality, Gods' Day out here would be rather pleasant.

Ingefær announced, "After that, there are the spoils to sort out. We'll need at least two good wagons."

She grabbed me by the arm and pulled me to Hombir, who had taken a seat on the ground. He was rocking, holding another d'oglemann in his lap. It was at that moment I realized—the body was that of his wife.

"Oh, Hombir, I'm so sorry."

"My condolences," my wife said.

Hombir sighed, and his voice trembled. "Thank you. The task is done. The cost was high for too many."

Dinner was a somber affair. War excitement waned, and the horrific cost in lives came to the forefront. My wife ate little. Vendeh made up for it.

After the meal, Tugg got everyone gathered around a massive pile of timber, all laden with bodies. He'd used the broken-down carts to build the base. The dead dvaergs lay there with their weapons across their chests. The d'oglemenn, along with Jonuku, were stacked in the middle.

"What a horrid sight," Ingefær said. "I never want to come back to the Ice Plains."

"Me neither." I cleared my throat. "You know, there's the one pine tree southwest of here with those snake etchings." I stayed quiet for a while. "They moved. The snakes. Someone has to deal with that."

"Not us," my wife said.

I nodded. "I have this feeling there's more than one pine tree sigil out there."

"Vidarr's problem," Ingefær said, her arms folding across her chest.

Tugg shushed us. "Oi! Me lads and lassies. We be gathered here to honor the dead. They sacrificed so that we may live. Have no doubts about that. It could have been ye in that first cart to be destroyed. Or maybe ye." Tugg didn't point, which I thought was smart. "The dead had the unlucky position of manning the left flank, or the outer perimeter, or the rear guard. Such is the way of the gods. They call us though we be not ready. Remember that they died for ye. Don't waste yer life. Live it to the fullest. Make it mean something. Aye?"

Tugg nodded at Muggs, who lit the pyre. The two of them watched the wood catch, and the flames spread higher and higher. When it was going full bore, the entire area was lit in red hues.

"Now, if ye want, we'll say personal goodbyes. Find an empty spot and speak to yer kin." Tugg took a knee close to the ring of flames.

It had to be hot, for I was double the strides behind him and my face felt flush. Though it snowed and the wind howled, sweat trickled down my hairline.

One by one, then two by two, dvaergs circled the pyre. They spoke to the dead for moments to minutes, then got up and returned to their place. Ingefær and I moved forward until I couldn't bear it anymore.

Taking a knee, I spoke of the dvaergs I knew. Most of all, I spoke of Jonuku. "You are—were—a no-nonsense healer. You always kept Hombir pointed straight. Because of you, he focused on his clan and on the mission. I know he will miss you. As will I. Go to Valhalla in peace if that is your path."

I got up and moved back. Though the sentiment was quite common for the first three eons, at least as history noted it, Vidarr had said the way to Asagard was permanently blocked. Vidarr believed it to be so because when he'd closed the way—by destroying the nine rainbow bridges to it—he'd lost contact with one of his three fylgjæ. I don't remember her name, but Vidarr said she could see his fate, his future, and she'd always arrived in time.

In a way, like my Roskva.

We gathered up with Mick and Serafina. I said, "Get a good night's sleep. Tomorrow could be long. And dangerous."

Mick hiccupped. "But the beasts—they're all dead."

"Yes. But we tackle the circular sigil in the morning," Ingefær said. She stretched. "I need a back rub."

"I'll do your bidding," I said.

My wife chinned at Mick. "Why don't you and Serafina find your own tents? There are, alas, plenty of extras."

Mick eyed us. "You two speaking in code?"

Serafina chuckled. "Duh. Come on."

Morning came, and with it the heavy fog of Gods' Day. Thick split pea soup was how my da used to describe it. Along with the meshing of two planes—well, that overstated it—cold areas warmed and warm areas cooled. The big thing about Gods' Day two years ago and before that was that folks would venture out of their doors to see if they could spot a dreki god.

Back then, the gods showed up as massive drekis: giant scaled beasts that breathed fire. But ten times the size of the drekis that had returned almost two years ago. There were variations, like the color of their scales on their bodies and wings. Allefar, the Father of All, had one purple eye with the other one missing—fortunately, I didn't know that from personal experience.

The reality of it, and Tugg knew it, was that the gods were frauds. They were bigger than the Jotunn by a head, light blue skin where it showed, and incredibly powerful. It was the first Ragnarök that had banished them to their plane, and they couldn't cross. But they had ways of communication, using vassals, who communicated to those who could venture to the Aether.

They had wanted Vidarr to stop the second Ragnarök—which we could all appreciate—but not to save the Realm. They wanted to use the power of the conflagration to free themselves from their prison.

But Vidarr had sniffed out their deception. He had used the Valknut and the Rod of the Dreki to close off the plane of Asagard, so the gods couldn't even show themselves through the mist to others. Their vassals no longer could penetrate the Aether.

Which is why I was dumbstruck at hearing a voice in my head when I got close to the Jörmonruk's ward. Based on the voice, a man's voice, and his desire to reacquaint himself with Laehvateinn, it had to be Lokke.

But it made no sense.

So it was with trepidation that I scampered to within fifteen strides of the sigil to watch Hombir and my wife deal with it. The glyph that may have been put there by the Father of Lies.

We could have left the task to Vidarr. But as we were here, and it was Gods' Day, there didn't seem to be a better opportunity.

Why was Gods' Day a good time?

My inkling, and one Ingefær and I discussed at length last night, was that since the attacks from the Jörmonruks had begun after the previous Gods' Day, the sigil had been placed here exactly one year ago. If we didn't deal with it today, something evil may yet come out.

I called to Mick. "Make sure it's still set on the odd-looking *Z* rune."

Mick consulted his wax tablet. "All good, Master Belkin."

"The gods, Mick. Call me Rory. Everyone else does."

Chapter Thirty-Five

A LAST HURRAH

INGEFÆR

Peering through the mist and haze, I studied the huge artifact. Hombir was beside me, and Mick, Rory—with O'erlevendeh—and Serafina were off to one side. The half-alvae would do double duty in restoring our stamina. We each had a vial of healing in our pockets, just in case something bad happened. Like Draugars appearing because we fumbled in removing a glyph.

Several squads of crossbowmen encircled us and the circular contraption with Lokke's sigil in the center. Tugg and Muggs had gone down the bolt hole with twenty warriors to sort through the plunder. The rest of the group was spread out to the east, fronting the camp and the river beyond.

I eyed Hombir. "We checked for a ward yesterday. Do we try to fireball it? Or hurl lightning bolts?"

Hombir's mouth twitched. "I want to, but..."

Yeah. "Something so intricate and beautiful has to have some sort of protection." I turned to Mick. "What do you think?"

Mick studied it, his hand to his chin. "You know, there's a part of it we don't see. The base and sides are covered in ice."

It was, for the first time since leaving Kral Bar Aggen, not freezing. I removed my wulv cloak. "That's an interesting observation."

I called for a pair of torches. When they were brought forth, Hombir and I each took one. I went to the west side of the structure, and he the east. We held the torches to the base.

After a score of minutes, my back ached. "This is going to take too long. More timber!"

We built two separate fires near the front of the structure. Mick pointed out that the back was encased as well.

I rolled my eyes, but not at him. "Right you are."

A second set of fires was built to the rear.

We waited. Off to my right, Rory paced, O'erlevendeh trailing in his tracks. After a while, the icicles showed signs of melting.

A dvaerg watching from the backside of the contraption said, "Ye know, we could break it off with a couple of swings."

I nodded, scratching at my hidden necklace. "Aye. But might it release a sigil?"

He shrugged.

After a half hour of the fires burning, much of the ice around the base, front and back, had melted clear.

Hombir, Mick, and I circled the artifact.

Mick scowled.

"What?"

"How's it staying upright?" He pointed. "We've removed the support. How is the enormous circle still standing?"

I sighed. "I'm extremely glad we brought you along. You don't think the inch-wide metal it's made of would stay up by itself?"

He shook his head. "It's eighteen feet tall, and just as wide. It would need a foot, if not two feet of width, to even have a chance of staying vertical in these winds."

The two outer rings were wide enough to catch air. "Aye." I sniffed at the mist, not quite cold, billowing about. Then it came to me. "We dig."

Hombir asked, "Why?"

"Mick's right. Something is supporting this. And it's hidden beneath the contraption."

"The dig spell?" Hombir asked.

I shook my head. "No. Let's try shovels."

Dvaergs were called from camp, and soon they had spades scooping dirt. Fresh mounds sprouted around the structure.

I said, "Try not to contact the circular shape. We've touched it before and nothing happened. But..."

Several pairs of brown eyes glared at me. But after some sighs, they went back to it.

A dvaerg named Gegg, standing two feet inside a hole, tapped the shovel against a side. The spade pealed. "Aye. It be supported by buried metal."

"How deep?" Hombir asked.

"Deeper than the hole I be in," Gegg replied.

"Keep at it." I swallowed my fears. "Get past the last of the metal."

Rory shouted at us. "This is going on too long."

"Go play with your pup," I yelled back.

An hour later, we had the depth of the supporting metal plate. It spanned nine feet and went down for five.

A rather harsh gale blew through the area. The circular structure didn't sway or waver.

I turned to Hombir. "There has to be magic holding it upright."

"Find magic time," Hombir said.

I did my thing. The circular artifact glowed brilliantly in orange.

And there, three feet into the hole, was a white sigil:

Mick shouted from behind the construct. "You have a ward back here."

I moved around the circular construct. “Huh. I’ve not seen something like that before.”

Hombir poked his head around. “It’s an awkward ***H.***”

Hombir got his rucksack and conferred with his tome.

As he searched, I asked Mick and Serafina, who had joined us at the backside of the construct. “Any ideas?”

Mick’s lips curled like he’d eaten a lemon. “Don’t know much about runes.”

Serafina shook her head. “It’s not Alvaesh or Realm’s Tongue.”

We had a dvaerg come and look. He shook his head. “Never seen anything like it.”

Hombir stabbed a taloned finger at a page in his tome. “The arrowhead pointing west on the front side means pain, or death.”

Mick squawked.

Serafina cuffed him. “Settle down.”

He hiccupped instead.

Hombir darted a glance at Mick, then to me. “The ***H*** with the slanted cross brace means either destruction or chaos.”

“Not m-*hic*-much of a dif-*hic*-difference, is there?“ Mick said.

“Do you dispel them one at a time, or both together?” Serafina asked.

“Hmm.” Hombir rubbed his snout. “Never tried both at the same time. I think that makes sense.”

I puzzled over it for a moment. “No. We do the slanted ***H*** first.”

“Why?” Mick asked.

“Destruction and chaos comes before pain and death.” I shrugged. “At least in my mind.”

Serafina cocked her hooded head at me. “You’re just guessing.”

"A little," I admitted. "Going with logic. Breaking bones and destroying buildings leads to pain, both physical and emotional. Wars are chaotic and lead to the death of soldiers."

I didn't mention when, once, chaos followed death. When King Maerek had been killed, what followed was the Great Departure. The disappearance of the drakes and drekis had led to a decline in magic and much confusion and disruption for the next thousand years.

"But first," I said, chinning at Hombir, "do your show magic."

By this time, the two sigils had faded. From the backside of the contraption, Hombir cast his incantation. Blacks and browns showed up.

Mick's hiccup stopped. "The black hues swirl about the orange circle of runes and the two snakes. The brown tints eddy about the two outer rings and the base."

"That makes sense," Serafina said. "The Jörmonruk mage controlled the plane of earth."

I nodded. "Perhaps she set this thing up." Then I scowled. "But then, where did she come from?"

"Does it matter?" Mick asked. "Remove the wards and I'll be happy to take a hammer to it myself."

"Bold of you," I said, winking at him.

I spun in a circle. "Alright. We're going to remove a ward. Be ready for anything."

Mick got a fresh torch and a vial of pitch. Hombir took the front of the structure while I moved to the back. Serafina stood at the east end.

Rory crept closer from the west, the whelp in his arms. Well, he crept as close as he dared. "Tired of waiting," he said.

"Get your feet and blade ready," I said.

The dvaergs who had helped dig cocked their crossbows, forming two loose half-circles behind me. They leveled their weapons at the ground.

I cast a find magic so we could see the sigils one more time. In betwixt the orange glow, I memorized the simple ward, an ***H*** with a slanted cross brace.

I whooshed air. "Here goes."

Uttering the dispel magic incantation, I wiped the air with lemon peels soaked in vinegar for material. Two deft strokes up and down, and then angling the third stroke from left to right.

The circular artifact rattled in the wind, metal creaking.

"It's going to fall over," Mick said.

But it didn't. It leaned a bit, and the sides and top wobbled as the air gusts billowed past and through it.

The good news, in my mind, was that nothing untoward happened. No beasts materialized, no noxious vapors filled the surrounding air.

"Go, Hombir," I said as I backed off to one side, getting an angle to cover the rear and the front, as I grabbed a tuft of woolen carpet with the fingers of my left hand. A lightning bolt was deadlier than fiery darts and would do less harm to friends than a fireball.

"Wait!" Serafina shouted. "The snake heads moved."

I stepped back and peered at the green snakes. They had moved. Both heads were in the middle. Which made for an odd-looking snake. Then the black eyes blinked.

A sensation of weight surrounded my head, as if a Jörmonruk grasped my skull between its massive claws. Pressure. Ugh. My hands flew to my head. "Argh!"

Rory shouted from behind me. "Hurry the Hel up, Hombir. Something's got my wife."

My eyes clouded over, and a buzzing filled my ears. A gruff voice screamed inside my head, reverberating around like my head was in a cave. "Get me my sword!"

I wanted to say no, but the thought wouldn't come. My jaw clenched hard, rattling my teeth.

"You will get me Laehvateinn or you will die."

More pressure. A sharp pain stabbed my skull just above my right ear. It was too much to bear, and I....

When I woke, there were a half-dozen eyes peering over me. Each pair was held up by blurred figures. I blinked. The green pair belonged to Serafina. Though nestled under furrowed brows, the dark brown pair was full of warmth.

"Shh," Rory said. "You're alright now."

I worked my jaw to release the pressure inside my head. My vision cleared further. "Uhm. That was...painful." My hands went to my head. "I have a headache."

Serafina said, "I can heal you, if you wish."

"Are you sure you're alright?" Rory cupped my face in his hands, his eyes searching mine. "What happened?"

"Just felt like my head was in a vise." I reached up to touch the spot above my ear. "Someone or something tried to crack my head open right about here."

Serafina nodded and healed me. The headache cleared up quick. The spot above my ear itched for all of a moment. "Thank you."

Rory helped me to my feet. O'erlevendeh jumped at my ankles.

"He wants you to pick him up," Rory said.

I frowned at the puppy. What happened to him wasn't his fault. I squatted and he jumped into my arms.

That's when I noticed the construct had fallen over. I found Hombir. "You got the sigil?"

His snout bobbed. "Aye. The wind did the rest."

"It's how we got whatever was controlling you to stop." Rory dipped his chin and kissed me on my forehead.

Mick had found a hammer while I'd been...indisposed...and he and several dvaergs whacked at the metal construct. The clanging brought the headache back.

I said to Rory, "It was Lokke. And he wanted Laehvateinn."

I pondered the why. Why would a god need a sword? Something to mull over when we talked with Vidarr. And he was going to get talked to.

"He didn't enter your head, did he?" Rory asked, fresh crinkles forming around his eyes.

I shook my head and regretted it. "No. Just his voice."

Chapter Thirty-Six

PLUNDER AND SPOILS

INGEFÆR

Heaving a heavy sigh, I said, "Now we go to the circular sigil inside their burrow."

Rory scowled. "You should wait and rest."

"No." I stood straighter. "I've been healed. Hombir, Serafina, Mick, and anyone else who wants to go inside, come on."

I gave the pup to Rory, and we hiked to the bolt hole in the dense fog. The cool moisture felt good on my skin, refreshing me. We climbed down the rungs made of ice. Rory followed.

"Don't go near it," I said.

He grunted, stroking his pet's ears.

We went down the west tunnel, bypassing the burned dead. A smell of decay filled my nostrils, but I kept my breakfast down.

"The stench is thick," Mick said. "Smells like—"

I cut him off. "Nobody wants to hear that."

O'erlevendeh sniffed the air and growled.

"See," Mick said, "he agrees with me."

We arrived at the inner sigil. And found it fallen over.

"Well," Serafina said, "That's nice to see."

To be safe, I cast a find magic, followed by a show magic. "Just the tiniest bit of faded orange."

Rory approached. "Double checking. If I act weird, well, push me away."

He didn't.

Mick frowned. "I didn't bring my hammer."

Tugg said, "Ye know, it be a pretty piece of artwork. Well, not the snakes. But the rest of it."

"You can't drag it out of here," I said. "The bolt hole is too small."

Tugg nodded. "Yer right. Let's chop it to pieces. But carefully. The metal be made of something I've not seen before."

By the time Tugg and Muggs got everything worth salvaging out of the tunnel system—scraps of blue and yellow ornamented metal, and orange runes included—and the wagons loaded, it was nearing dark. We agreed to camp here one more night.

Tugg said, "Tomorrow, winter begins in earnest. It shouldn't snow, but the cold will be all the fiercer with no cloud cover."

In the morning, under a bright but cold sun, we worked to collapse our tents and pack up the last of our gear. We had just enough hay for the horses for the return trip to Kral Azza Rid. I spotted Rory with O'erlevendeh on the back of his mare, an extra leather pad for the whelp to grip onto. The pup had doubled in size since Rory had pulled him out of the cave. Behind the pup was a white-furred leg.

"What are you doing with that?" I asked after riding over.

"Food for the pup." Rory smiled at me. "He's got his teeth in. And as cold as it is, the meat will keep."

"That's yucky," I said.

"Hmm. Agreed." Rory took my hand. "But it's what he eats. If you take a turn feeding him, cut the fur off first. Or else, you know..."

I shook my head.

"It will show up in his poop." He chuckled. "I thought it might cleave to his innards, but no, it just makes for a gnarly pile of scat."

"You can be disgusting sometimes."

He shrugged. "That's nature for you."

Rory, Serafina, Mick, and I rode point. Gods' Day had melted some of the accumulation and now the snow was right at two feet high. Still, the horses worked hard. We alternated with a score of dvaergs who tramped down the snow for us and for the carts and wagons behind.

That evening, I broached a subject I knew to be dangerous. "So, anyone see a god yesterday?"

Serafina's golden brows narrowed. "No. But I'm so old that if I haven't seen one now, I never will."

"Ye be not that old?" Tugg showed off his dimples.

The half-alvae healer blushed. "Well, no. But, I mean, it's typical for alvaes to see a god before their thirtieth birthday. And for humans, I'm told, it's by their eighteenth."

Mick sighed. "Aye. That's true. And here I am, eighteen and nothing."

Rory stroked his pup. "You might have seen one two years ago. But after that, Vidarr shut off the plane to Asagard."

Mick guffawed. "He left a gaping hole then."

"Yeah," I said. "Something's not right. But my point is, the gods aren't good. They're not worthy of your prayers, pleas, and sacrifices."

Dvaergs around the campfire grumbled. Someone raised their voice. "Blasphemer!"

Tugg stood. "She speaks true." He raised a meaty arm and swung it about the camp. "Anyone see a god yesterday?"

There was more grumbling, followed by shakes of heads.

Muggs chuckled. "Most of us be too old to see one now, so the fact no one has seen one be not proof positive of yer claim."

I stood. "Agreed. We're not looking for immediate converts. All I'm asking is that you keep an open mind. Give it a couple of years, and, when you're in your keeps, ask the young ones."

Four days later, we woke to a howling blizzard. The snow had made a vengeful return. Temperatures were bitter. Hombir, Serafina, and I, and one surviving dvaerg healer, kept the tents warm that evening.

On the fifth day since leaving, we arrived at the outer keep of Kral Azza Rid past the noon meal. Upon seeing us, the dvaergs on the ramparts cheered our return.

When we rolled into the compound and dvaergs began unloading crates, there was a noticeable uptick in the frolicking. Muggs went around describing our exploits. I knew that by his hand gestures and the wide-eyed looks of his listeners. Dvaervish was another language I wanted to learn.

Regg, the keep's Avarkæsir leader, made the rounds. With me, Rory, Mick, Serafina, and Tugg huddled around three crates of silver and a smaller one of gold and jewels, Regg said, "Good to have ye back. Ye had quite the success, I see."

Muggs appeared. "We need to discuss the sharing of the plunder."

"Piracy Recovery Law applies," Rory said. "We have it on the authority of Tyrrby."

I smiled. "We're going to divvy up the coins and jewelry on a per person basis of all those who came with us. Even the dead. Their share will be given to their respective leaders to hand over to their immediate kin."

Tugg provided estimates of the recovered coins and jewelry. "There be a little over a hundred thirty-five thousand silver, and shy of seven thousand gold. The jewelry will need to be appraised. Don't fret, Muggs, ye'll get yer share."

I shifted the conversation. "Any birds from Tyrrby?"

Regg nodded. "Aye, arrived yesterday. An Ilmarien and a Vidarr Allefar will arrive in a week or so. Message asked that ye wait here."

Tugg asked, "And from me keep?"

"Oh, aye." Regg cleared his throat. "Yer premier asked that we let ye and yer kin stay as long as ye want, and we're to grant ye access to the inner sanctum. Me premier agreed."

Regg scowled and chinned at Serafina. "Alas, the half-alvae must stay in the visitors' area."

Tugg shook his head. "That be daft. We would be all dead if not for her."

Regg sighed. "I counseled against, but be overridden. Sorry."

Tugg turned to the half-alvae. "In that case, we won't stay long. And all me warriors will make do with the outer keep."

Regg's dark olive skin darkened under his beard. "I be sorry ye feel that way."

Tugg eyed him. "I know ye tried yer best. But it be not good enough." He sniffed. "I won't make an issue of it with yer premier, but I'll remember his slight."

Regg grumbled. "Well, no need for that." He turned to Serafina. "I be sorry. But it be out of me hands. Don't ye worry none, Dikk be not permitted beyond the inner sanctum doors."

Serafina studied him. "Aye. Just some harsh words. I'm no worse for the toil."

Tugg nodded at Regg. "Let's go eat and drink some ale."

"And tell some tales," Muggs said. He pointed a finger at me. "This one here be worth watching. Nerves of steel."

With the beasts? Yes. With killing unborn babies? The thought brought bile to my mouth. What had we done? I suppose it was necessary, but I didn't like it. My stomach heaved at the memory.

Rory held up O'erlevendeh. "Some milk and raw meat, please."

We kept to the outer visitors' area for four days. During that time, we told our story many times as we listened to a variety of musicians each night. The food was good, the warmth of the fire better. The whelp kept close to Rory.

Tugg and Serafina huddled near the fireplace more often than not. At times, she would giggle and he would chuckle, but much of their conversation was quiet.

Mick enjoyed talking to various dvaergs about their craft of mechanics, trading his stories of defusing traps.

Rory and I got some quiet time alone, and that helped to soothe my spirits. I now wore the moniker of baby killer. My hand hadn't done the deed, but I hadn't stopped the others. Why some sentient beings couldn't make peace was beyond me. And the knowledge of what we'd done would haunt me for the rest of my life.

We kept Hombir company. Losing Jonuku had hit him hard, and he was morose for a while. All we could do was be with him.

Past dinner on the fourth day, he said, "I need to be busy. Rory, you had asked to have your sword magicked, and I agreed to do it if we succeeded. I will fulfill my promise to you. What is it you would like me to do?"

Rory grinned. "Thank you, Hombir. I want to imbue the sword with a sharpness that never fades, and for the blade to flame on command."

That endeavor took the fifth day—and required Serafina to heal Rory's hand.

Chapter Thirty-Seven

GOODBYES

RORY

Over breakfast of the sixth day since returning to Kral Azza Rid, I put my arms around our two charges—I couldn't say *younger* charges because Serafina was as old as me and Ingefær combined. "You two have brought renown to the team. Mick, with your smarts and out-of-the-iron-box way of thinking; and Serafina, your healing and sight are irreplaceable. Both of you contributed to saving lives."

"Does that mean I get a raise?" Mick asked.

Ingefær said, "You're already getting equal shares of the spoils."

He winked. "I know. Just having a bit of fun."

Tugg came into the dining hall, wearing his wulv cloak. "We be packed up and ready to go. It be two weeks or more to reach Kral Bar Aggen. The storm will end tomorrow, and that gives us the best chance to make for home."

He held out a hand and asked Serafina to step toward him. Tugg dipped his head to hers. "Yer eyes be like emeralds, yer skin like silver. Yer hair be gold. Ye be beautiful. I have enjoyed sharing me time with ye."

Serafina blushed. "Thank you. You are kind and honorable. And handsome to boot."

She swallowed with difficulty as Tugg gripped both her hands. "Lass, I wish to court ye proper. But I have duties back home. Mayhap I can call upon ye, this summer?"

She smiled. "That would be lovely. I look forward to it."

Mick cupped his hands. "Kiss her, already."

Tugg waved a meaty hand at the lad, but took Mick up on his suggestion.

Tugg let go of Serafina and turned to us. "We'll stop by that nasty pine tree ye found. Ye be sure it be not warded?"

My wife nodded. "Very sure. And as it is a living tree, there shouldn't be any buried sigils."

"Aye. We'll chop it down. The word has gone out to search for more of them. We'll keep Tyrrby informed."

We took our turns hugging Tugg. Serafina smooched him for a long moment, and Tugg left. The whelp barked, then whined as the dvaerg leader shuffled out of the dining hall entryway. I scooped him up and rubbed his ears. As it was swirling ice pellets outside, we didn't go out to wave Tugg off.

Ingefær faced the half-alvae. "I believe you're still blushing."

Serafina's green eyes sparkled. "It's a warm, fuzzy feeling."

"What? Tugg's beard?" Mick asked.

She slapped his shoulder. "No, silly." She patted her chest.

The next day, Vidarr and Ilmarien arrived. We gave them our report. Nearing the end, Ilmarien chinned at O'erlevendeh. "You going to keep him?"

Nodding, I said, "Yes. He's quite smart."

Ilmarien's brown eyes drifted to my wife, his brows arching.

She shrugged. "He's a puppy. But he's getting himself under control."

I shifted the conversation back to our report. "What concerns me is the ward on the pine tree and the possibility that there are more of them."

Mick pulled at his tawny hair. "Can you find them all?"

Vidarr held up the Rod of the Dreki, a two-foot-long silver rod with a golden orb at the end. The handle was slightly curved and made of iron imbued with specks of blue and red.

"With this, I have...hmm...influence over the Realm." Vidarr licked his lips. "I can do a lot, but not everything. For example, I cannot stop it snowing for more than a day, and where I've blocked the snow in one place, it sprouts in another. With it, now that I have your description of the glyph in the tree, I should be able to isolate their locations...if there is more than one."

He shrugged. "If there are more, felling them may involve my friend here," he nodded at Ilmarien, "or perhaps it would be best for the dvaergs and d'oglemenn take them down. I'll let you know if we need your aid."

Serafina shook her head. "I don't want to come back to this place."

Ingefær chewed on her lower lip. "Get their help first. But the tree sigil doesn't bother me as much as the pair of gigantic circular ones. They were a portal of some kind."

"Mick, show him your drawing," I said.

Vidarr studied it. "May I take this back to Tyrrby with me? There are some books I need to consult."

"Isn't that where we're going?" I asked, looking at Ilmarien.

The dark-haired man nodded.

Ingefær said, "The crux of the problem, as I see it, is how did the circular contraption get built? Because I'm of the opinion that the Jörmonruks arrived afterward."

"Right," I said. "Zakk, a mage here, tells us the beast hasn't existed for over two thousand years."

Vidarr nodded. "Two thousand five hundred eleven Gods' Days, to be exact. I received your bird and have studied up on the white-furred beast. I didn't get your bird about Lokke's snake glyph. Perhaps that bird perished in the storm. But the Jörmonruks were aligned with the Father of Lies. The dvaerg war against them cost more than a thousand lives and a half dozen mages who knew their craft."

He fussed with a bowl of water, swirling a taloned finger in it. "How it was built, I can only speculate."

Reflecting on Mick's earlier observation, I asked, "You closed off Asagard, right?"

"Yes. Of that I'm sure." Vidarr's golden slits studied me, then the others. "But there was a war raging then. And now that I think about it, I didn't—well, couldn't—determine where each of the gods were when I severed the bridges connecting the plane to Asagard."

My mouth dropped. "You're saying—"

My wife jumped in. "You're saying that maybe Lokke and some other gods are *not* in Asagard?"

"Then where are they?" Serafina asked.

Mick hiccupped.

"I'm only guessing." Vidarr licked his lips anew. "The Void is where I saw Lokke last, along with a few others."

"The-*hic*-the *others* being?"

"Helene had attacked me," Vidarr said. "So had Tordenvaer and Allefar. There may be others, but they were elsewhere, guarding the rainbow bridges to our plane."

I stood. "How many gods are out there?"

Vidarr motioned for me to sit. "Don't yell. I don't know. One seems likely, now."

"That would be Lokke," Ingefær said.

"And he's in the Void?" Serafina asked.

Vidarr shrugged. "Seems so."

"But-but," Mick stuttered.

"So, on Gods' Day," Vidarr continued, "when our plane sort of touches the edges of Asagard, the Void and the Aether do funny things too. I don't know how to describe it. I've been to both planes on Gods' Day and it doesn't feel any different. But, I'm hypothesizing here, perhaps Lokke, who is a crafty mage, could command enough sorcerous power to construct the rune gateway. And he somehow transported the beasts from the plane of Hel. Or maybe Helene helped."

"The gods!" I half-shouted. "Helene is out there, too?"

Another shrug. "Don't know."

"How come Lokke didn't come through the portal?" I asked.

Vidarr sighed. "Can't be certain, but I think the gods have to cross via a rainbow bridge. Or perhaps the Realm, along with the Rod of the Dreki, have a sufficient shield to stop him, but not the beasts."

Ingefær asked, "Where's the Valknut?"

Vidarr's eyes glossed over as he expelled a vast sigh. "Disappeared, along with the trunk it was stored in, last Summer Solstice. My tomes say it travels the planes every ninety-nine years. Could be in Asagard now, or perhaps the Void or Hel."

Mick squawked, but Serafina was quick to smack him, and he quieted down.

"Lokke doesn't have the Valknut, does he?" I asked.

"If he did, we'd have bigger problems." Vidarr forced a smile. "So, I don't think so."

Ingefær shook her head. "All this time, I thought we were safe from them."

Vidarr's snout dipped. "To a degree, we are. The Valknut's true powers only come into play when the forces of Ragnarök are raised. And that won't happen for another eon. Sure, it has plenty of its own powers. Which I think would affect our plane, our Realm, but only on Gods' Day."

Mick got a hold of his hiccups. "I would have preferred that you fry my eggs. But you're serious?"

Vidarr nodded.

I turned to Ilmarien. "You're awfully quiet."

He drank some of his water. "Vidarr knows a lot more than I do. His supposition comes from a discussion with all the Havís and the Foremost. I was there and am still struggling with the possibilities."

Ilmarien put a hand on Vidarr's. "When do you want to leave?"

"Tomorrow." The d'oglemann Haví looked at me, then the others. "Don't eat or drink tonight. We leave at first light." His golden slits studied the whelp. "Think he can travel via teleportation?"

"Uh...well, I guess we'll find out." I stroked the pup. "Nothing to eat for you tonight."

"Great. Just great," Ingefær said. "He'll chew on the blankets."

As we packed our gear that evening, I reflected.

It had been a tough assignment. Less mystery and more pure violence. Yet we had survived, and our reputation increased, as well as our purse. But the price we had paid had been steep. Not with our blood, but with the blood of our friends.

Ingefær hadn't quite come to grips with the baby killing. I wondered if she ever would.

And there was more work to do in our future. I was sure of that. Lokke was on the loose.

Having heard the deep gravelly voice asking for Laehvateinn told me we weren't done dancing.

THE END

After word and Also by Rene Vecka

AFTERWORD

Hey, thanks for reading *Death, On Ice.* I hope you had a thrill reading it, cause I had a blast writing it. Would you be so kind as to leave an honest review on https://www.amazon.com/or https://www.goodreads.com? Reviews are the lifeblood of an author. It also lets other readers know if the novel is a good fit for them. Thank you.

I want to offer you a deleted chapter (bonus really) from *Death, On Ice.* The chapter, *The Making of a Sword,* got shrunk to a paragraph or two in the final version. It's a window into my magic system and there's some humor at Rory's expense.

The bonus chapter is available on my website (Treats tab). You'll need a password to get in. Here's your clue: The name of the dvaerg leader from Kral Azza Rid, who goes on the final expedition with Rory and the others. Website: https://renevecka.wordpress.com/

ALSO BY Rene Vecka

The following books have been published by the Author as of July 2025.

Mid Dreki Realm series

In Search of Justice https://books2read.com/u/3koB78

In Search of Kin https://books2read.com/u/4jNrYo

In Search of Gods https://books2read.com/u/49dnrw

In Search of the Rod https://books2read.com/u/b5w9BG

At Searches' End https://books2read.com/u/m2nZYr

Madcap Adventures (standalone novels)

Not for the Faint of Heart https://books2read.com/u/31o8jW

Deadly Dungeon https://books2read.com/u/3JAePX

Death, On Ice https://books2read.com/u/4E172z

Short Story Collection

The First Viking, and Other Grim Dark Short Stories https://books2read.com/u/bQAN9P

Acknowledgements

A novel comes together through the hard work and support of many individuals.

First, there's my wife who supports me all day, every day. I am a blessed man. There're the folks at Apex Writers who chip in with weekly writerly advice. Then there're the Superstars Writers Conference folks, where I learned things about the business of becoming an author. And there's Colin, who helped me with my website and provided moral support. Thank you all.

Regarding this novel, Tom and Sam read the first draft and provided immeasurable aid. There's my book coach, Nicole, who helped me get deeper into the characters' heads and heightened the suspense throughout.

Mandy provided copy editing services. Any mistakes remaining are my own.

Thank you!

René

About the author

Rene Vecka is (mostly) retired from financial services and spends much of his time imagining new characters in new worlds. He's a reader of mystery, science fiction, and fantasy. He writes what he reads. Mr. Vecka has published five novels in the Mid Dreki Realm series, and a short story collection titled *The First Viking and other Grim Dark Short Stories. Death, On Ice* is the third novel of the Madcap Adventure series. He's also written a modern day murder mystery and thriller titled *Queen Sacrifice*, which is being solicited to agents. Mr. Vecka also has two sci-fi novels drafted in near time and near space, preliminarily titled *Blade Foxxe.*

The Author lives in the foothills between Denver and Colorado Springs. He lives with his wife, two dogs, and two cats. Occasionally, his three children stop by. He's a chess player, reader, and writer, and most of all, a Christian.

You can contact him:

https://www.renevecka.com

https://www.facebook.com/czechveck

https://www.instagram.com/czechveck

https://www.bookbub.com/authors/rene-vecka

email: rene@renevecka.com

www.ingramcontent.com/pod-product-compliance
Lightning Source LLC
LaVergne TN
LVHW041111080826
845145LV00007B/1768

9781958049204